"Do you remember those stones you once kept for me?" Bainbrose undid the weighted end of his purple sash-of-office, reached into it, and dropped the pebbles into her palm. Once again the glassy beads made her skin burn and tingle.

"Never cared for them, either," Rifkind said, handing them back as soon as she recognized them.

"They're Flame-stones. These are old and worthless—that's how I come to have them—but the legends about the stones would indicate that you could replace your ruby from them, if you ever found the source of the Well and the Black Flame."

As Rifkind knelt, staring at the black pebbles, she felt a light but icy cold touch on her shoulder, almost as if the Goddess were leaning over her shoulder to study the stones Herself. The Bright One was present!

"Tell me more about this Black Flame," Rifkind sighed. "I think I may find these stones more interesting than I had first thought."

RIFKIND: PRIESTESS, WARRIOR, HEALER, SETS OUT ON A NEW MISSION FOR HER GODDESS:

THE BLACK FLAME

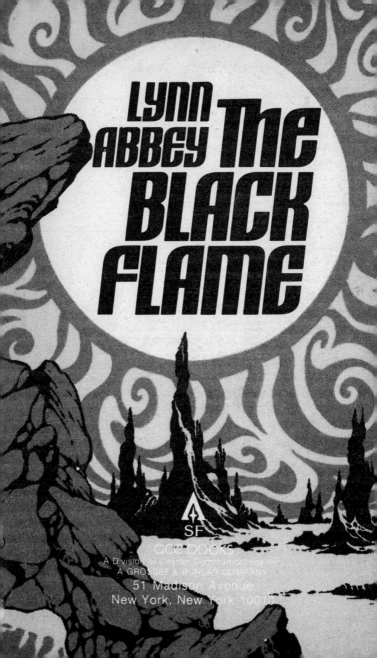

LYNN ABBEY

THE BLACK FLAME

SF
ace books
A Division of Charter Communications Inc.
A GROSSET & DUNLAP COMPANY
51 Madison Avenue
New York, New York 10010

THE BLACK FLAME

Copyright © 1980 by Lynn Abbey

Illustrations copyright © 1980 by Steve Fabian

An ACE Book

First Ace printing: May 1980
First Mass Market Edition: January 1981

Published simultaneously in Canada

2 4 6 8 0 9 7 5 3
Manufactured in the United States of America

THE BLACK FLAME

Dedication

To my grandparents
Robert and Lillian Abbey
A. Draper and Helen Dewees

PROLOGUE

Firelight flickered on the walls as Rifkind, desert-bred, stood close by her hearth, braiding her long black hair into thick plaits, listening to the murmuring crowd-noise below. Shivering, she tried to force her fingers to increase their pace. Though the mighty walls of Chatelgard had withstood the worst the Imperials could bring against them, they were not proof against even these first drafty hints of the winter that would soon isolate Glascardy from the world.

She had another reason to hurry: drifting up from below came the heady scents of roasting meats. Rifkind herself had supervised the installation of two extra spits in the massive kitchen hearth—that was but one of many tasks and duties she had taken on when she had assumed the role of Lady of Chatelgard, a role most strange to a warrior and healer, but one that she would fill as well as she was able ... in all ways but one.

She had already decided that if she was to stay at Chatelgard through the Winter it must be as its Lady; pride forbade her any lesser role. And anyway, Ejord had already made it clear that the benefits to Chatelgard of the

1

healings of an Asheeran witch would be outweighed by the superstitious dread engendered in the commoners.

The great brass bell that had summoned the defenders of Chatelgard in the recent dark times now sounded in a happier cause, and Rifkind gathered her dark green skirts in a movement that had become as practiced as her sword swing. After a week of trail rations a feast, even if it meant playing lady of the manor, was worth hurrying to. As she ran down the cramped stairway that led to the Great Hall, the hilts of her knives, strapped against her thighs, glinted in the torchlight, as did her many ornaments of gold and silver. In many ways Rifkind was still a thorough barbarian—such as in her desire to be adorned always by wealth and by weapons.

"Rifkind! . . . I mean Milady Rifkind, have you heard?" An officer with more grey than black in his beard hailed her as she entered the Hall.

"Heard what, Greybeard?"

"Amnesty, that's what! There's to be no more forays against the stragglers still in the mountains, and the prisoners already in the keep are to be escorted to the borders. Ejord's declared it so. What do you think of that? *Amnesty*, by the gods!"

"As for the prisoners, it's obvious we must kill them or let them go," she said, not adding that she would have killed them, as would any self-respecting Asheeran. "But I wonder if we dare be so gentle with men still in arms. Better we hunt down every one of them lurking still in Glascardy."

Greybeard attempted to shrug in sympathetic agreement, but the glancing blow that had taken part of his ear had paralyzed the muscles of one shoulder as well. "Some ways he's the image of his father—and one of them is he runs his own show his own way. But though the men might not like it, if Ejord wants an amnesty, for him we'll enforce it!" He hoisted his goblet, slopping a healthy quantity of its contents on Rifkind in the process.

After a wet pause she said, "There's no doubt of that." She proceeded to work her way deeper into the crowded hall, more grateful for the information than the second helping of cider.

The veterans who had first rallied to Ejord's side at the onset of the civil war that had pitted Ejord and Glascardy against Ejord's father Humphrey and the Empire had come to accept her as a leader second only to Ejord himself. It had been harder for her to accept them. But now, war over, she drank from the many proffered goblets and wished that she had brought one of her own so that she could share in turn. But as she finally made her way to where Ejord sat alone on the dais, her thoughts took a darker turning.

"They tell me you've decreed an amnesty for all your father's men still at large in Glascardy," she said, as soon as she was near enough to speak discreetly.

Ejord, after a glance of recognition, looked away. "They pose no real danger now that Father has left to winter in Lowenrat."

"You'll win no gratitude for this from either side—only festering wounds."

Ejord nodded. "But Glascardy has been in war as well as at war. The cider we drink is from last year's pressing; there'll be no more feasts, or cider either. The wounds may fester with my amnesty, but the men will be at home. They'll see to their families and plant their crops instead of ruining somebody else's fields in my name." He paused. "This isn't the Asheera. Raiding and warfare destroy us."

Before Rifkind could reply, the grizzled officer who had first accosted her made his way across the room and clapped Ejord in a one-armed embrace. He handed

Rifkind his cider, but did not offer to embrace her.

"You're not drinking, Milord!" As Lord, Ejord could not drink from another's vessel—though as a special compliment he might himself offer his own to a liegeman.

"You're right, Greybeard," Ejord answered. Suddenly there was no trace of the fatigue and sadness he had allowed Rifkind to see. "Here I've ordered all this cider brought up from the cellars, and no one's fetched *me* a drop!"

"Disgraceful! Even today, when there's no servants nor masters, exceptions can be made ... I'll correct your condition myself, as I'm in need of a refill anyway." Seizing Ejord's goblet, Graybeard made his way back into the crowd.

"There's a snow-ring around your Bright Moon, Rifkind," Ejord said, once they were alone again. "Have you seen it?" He paused for a long moment, staring at the table as if it held a secret. Then: "When next it is full the passes will have become closed till Spring."

"Your cider, milord! Enough for a start, anyway," said Greybeard, who had returned with brimming goblets.

But even the potent cider and the old officer's joviality could not dispel the silence that was growing between them.

"It will be different now," Ejord said at last.

"I know."

"I need a wife." Greybeard chose his time for an atypically discreet withdrawal.

"I know that too," Rifkind said without looking at him. The subject had come up before. "There are things I can do. I'll stay with your army, if you don't totally disband it. I'll discipline your servants. I'll keep food on the tables if I have to hunt it down myself. These things I can do of my own will, but I cannot be your wife without ... without Her approval."

"Yet still I need a wife."

"You must look elsewhere."

"I have. She is en route from the lowlands. I have said nothing definite as to the purpose of the invitation, but I will now."

Time froze around Rifkind while she absorbed Ejord's words. She wasn't surprised, not truly. She knew the realities of a Dro Darian aristocrat's life as well as she had known those of an Asheeran hetman's daughter. And in the depths of her heart she had known that Ejord would not deny his inherited obligations as she had hers.

"You knew I would refuse you?" She said, angry with herself for the quaver in her voice.

He nodded. "Chatelgard—all of Glascardy—belongs in part to you. No one may dispute your right to live here as you wish and as long as you wish unless he dares to take issue with my rights as well. But ... I have many duties."

"You'll announce your coming marriage tonight?"

"Yes, after the feast."

If the assemblage noticed the silence at the head table, they did not respect it. They called upon Ejord to make several speeches before and during the long meal. As it wore on Rifkind felt the tiredness of the past weeks more keenly than she had expected, and the small amount of cider she'd drunk affected her far more than it should have. The roomful of cheerful people became a receding blur unless she forced her concentration to part the sea of babble. And though the food was uniformly delicious, once initial hunger was assuaged her appetite was no match for her weariness. Finally she gave in to her fatigue.

"I'm tired, Ejord, too tired, really. I need sleep more than food. I'll fall asleep during your announcements." She stood up from the table.

"Rifkind?" Ejord said softly to her.

She turned.

"If you had said 'yes,' if you said 'yes' right now ..."

There was something in his eyes that said far more than words could. For a heartbeat Rifkind held her breath, waiting for the momentous revelation of the Bright One bestowing Her blessing. But there was only the raucous, indistinguishable laughter of the men and the painful openness of Ejord's face. She turned and fled.

She had ascended the first of several staircases to her quarters before came such tears as had not blinded her since childhood. Still, she had run the corridors without thinking so many times that her feet continued the journey to her rooms without the aid of vision. Fortunately even ever-solicitous Jenny, Ejord's close half-sister and now Rifkind's maid, was absent. Rifkind bolted the door behind her, determined that no one witness her mortification.

When the tears were finally staunched, she turned her attention to the silver-disk manifestation of the Bright Moon, circled by five, not one, snow-rings.

Why?

All the tortured permutations of her questions and her bitterness as well resolved into that one word. It radiated from her with a force that roused Turin in his distant stable, but did not perturb the impassive Goddess. Lord Humphry had first given her this suite of rooms because they afforded Chatelgard's best view of the rising moon. Now all three of the rooms were illuminated by Her light, and Rifkind could not summon the energy to shutter the windows against Her. She sat, knees drawn up to her chin, in the wide casement of the largest window, studying the light patterns through the grisaille glass.

I could cast the stones again, she thought, but they will do nothing to bring me peace. The Bright Mother will not reveal Her favor. I would have to take Ejord to my heart and bed before I could know Her judgment—and then it would be too late.

But I cannot stay here now: No matter what else I imagine of my future, if I remain I see an unknown wife's spiteful unease, or my Goddess with Her gaze averted from me.

Though her face and hands betrayed no tension, Rifkind's mind darted from one rejected pathway to the next, seeking escape from the untenable position in which she found herself.

Suddenly her thoughts were interrupted.

"Rifkind, may I come in?"

"No."

"Rifkind, it might help if you talked to someone."

She got up from the casement seat and quietly approached the door.

"Rifkind, I'm your friend. You can talk to me."

Although she might argue that she had no friends, had no need of them: only allies for longer or shorter times, that she got all the companionship she needed from Turin and her Goddess, Rifkind nevertheless did at last recognize Ejord's old tutor Bainbrose, and she opened the door to her cold, dark room.

The old man walked with a cane; his days of captivity had been less than comfortable. He never spoke of them but Rifkind, with her healer's instincts, knew that his body had been broken and that though he had managed to return to Chatelgard, he would live there for only a few years before death came for him. He propped his cane against the stone mantle and pottered about at her neglected hearth.

"Well," he began with his back still toward her, "there's no good to come from holding back your anger, and you must be angry with someone, if only me for forcing myself on you. Greybeard spoke to me before the feast."

"I'm not angry. Healer's don't get angry with their fate."

"Fighters do."

"I'm not angry. Here, let me do that." She offered him a hand up, then knelt by the hearth. "Everything is moving in perfectly understandable patterns. There is nothing to be angry with. I'm tired, that's all, as I told Ejord."

"Has anyone ever told you that you Asheerans are incapable of anger because you lack the philosophical sense of revenge of civilized folk?"

Despite herself Rifkind smiled as she stepped away from the hearth. Bainbrose knew well that revenge among the clans sometimes took two or three generations to reach its climax.

"That's better. A little warmth, a little light. Chatelgard's a dismal place at night without a fire. No offense to your Friend out there, but moonlight can't disguise the fact that Chatelgard's just a mountain fortress with window-glass."

"Chatelgard is dismal at any time of day or season."

"Even better: now you're arguing." The old man settled into the one comfortable chair, leaving Rifkind to perch on Jenny's mending stool. "Now, tell me all the reasons it's so dismal."

"It needs no reasons," she replied, her voice flattening.

"Not better. Rifkind, my child—my friend—the only other friend you have is going to bring a sixteen-year-old bride into this admittedly always-dismal place in a fortnight, making it very awkward for you to remain here, true? And the only reason he's doing so is because that flat disk you venerate has disobligingly failed to provide you with the wink that would let you send the brat packing back to her family!"

"What else was I supposed to do?" Rifkind demanded, arising as she spoke.

"A vast improvement. You are *supposed* to do what you want. You're a very talented, not to mention powerful, young woman. *You,* if no one else in this dismal fortress, are supposed to do what *you* want to do!"

"I'm not a wife. I cannot do wifely things. Even with Her permission I'm not sure I could! Doesn't he understand that? What more does he want from me?"

"That's anger, my friend. I know Ejord as well as anyone—I'll try to answer your question. There is nothing Ejord loves more than this land of his. He'll do anything, well, hopefully not anything—that's more his father—to be the sort of lord his people need. Everything is subordinate to that; therefore he will have a wife and an heir.

"What Ejord loves simply becomes a part of Glascardy for him. But when he loves someone as much as I suspect he loves you, and he can't make that person a part of Glascardy, then he'll push you away from him for your own good."

"As he sees it," Rifkind amended, paying no heed to the rest of what Bainbrose had said.

"Ah! Precisely! But is there any other way for him to see it?"

"You talk nonsense."

"Then, Rifkind, what is your purpose? Why can't you be the Lady Overnmont both Ejord and Glascardy need?"

"The Goddess. I'm a healer. A healer may take lovers, but not a love. *She* must be ever-supreme in my life. That is the price of Her gifts."

"Close the shutters and go downstairs. Stop his announcement, there's still time. You've served that uncaring bitch-goddess far better than any ten other healers could."

Rifkind nodded, but did not move towards the door. "I want to be a healer! I just want to be what I already am!" she exclaimed as a new onset of tears and sobs demanded immediate release.

Bainbrose held her hand tightly as she fell to her knees beside him and hid her face in his long scholar's robes. It was some moments before she raised her head and blotted her eyes on the sleeve of her dress.

"I don't know what's the matter with me. I never act this way."

"Absurd. You *are* acting this way, and I think it's vastly preferable to staring out the window, or whatever you were doing before I got up here." The old man gingerly flexed the hand she had just released.

"I was thinking about home—about the Asheera. It was never the place I remember it to be, but sometimes, now, I wish I were back there." She thought of things Bainbrose could not have understood and shook her head as if to clear them from her mind. "No, there's nothing left there. I'd be alone, more outsider than I am here. I think I'd like to go somewhere far from Glascardy or the Asheera, someplace where there would be nothing to haunt me."

"Some would say it is a deficiency of character to change one's surroundings in time of crisis—running away they'd call it. But I've made my life out of wandering, and I've no regrets. I've drunk the wines of every vineyard in Dro Daria. In your case, though, I recommend a sojourn to the Felmargue—and take Jenny with you."

"I've never heard of the Felmargue, and I certainly won't travel with a domestic."

"You underestimate Jenny. The Felmargue is far away and different enough for your needs. If you can imagine all of Dro Daria as a big circle," he gestured roundly, "and Glascardy is here," his right hand grabbed a point on the edge of the circle, "then, the Felmargue is ... here!" He stretched his left hand out as far as he could.

"Across the death-wastes again? Thank you—I think I prefer winter in Glascardy."

"One of the reasons Dro Daria is so big, and the Felmargue so far away, Rifkind, is that *we* do not travel directly from one side to the other. All of your Asheeran relatives are waiting for us if we do. We go around the edges."

"No. Going away's not a good idea—a deficiency of character, or whatever you called it. I don't want to run anymore. I have nothing to do there, any more than I do here. Someplace has to be my home. I've chosen Chatel-gard, no matter what."

"Ah, child, you *must* leave, and I think you know it. Even Jenny knows she must depart this place to find what she wants. Reasons arrive for you *after* you need them, not before. But, since you need a purpose—go find the Well of Knowledge and the Font of the Black Flame."

"Flames are not black and water, not knowledge, comes from wells."

"Yes, if they exist at all, that particular well and its water are most definitely peculiar. Most say they don't exist, or maybe they did a long time ago, but not anymore. Do you remember those stones you once kept for me?"

He undid the weighted end of his purple sash-of-office, reached into it and dropped the pebbles into her palm. Once again the glassy beads made her skin burn and tingle.

"Never cared for them, either," Rifkind said, handing them back to him as soon as she recognized them.

"They're Flame-stones. These are old and worthless— that's how I come to have them—but the legends about the stones would indicate that you could replace your ruby from them if you ever found the source of the Well."

As Rifkind knelt, staring at the black pebbles, she felt a

light but icy cold touch on her shoulder, almost as if the
Goddess was leaning over her shoulder to study the stones
Herself. Rifkind's Goddess, the Bright One, she who had
maintained unrelenting silence throughout Her priestess's
period of personal anguish over Ejord, did not wait for
Her disciple to formulate an entreaty for guidance.
Rifkind watched with bitter irony as Bainbrose lifted each
stone into the beams of moonlight.

"Tell me more about this Felmargue." She sighed. "I
think I may find these stones more interesting than I had
first thought."

"It's a swamp. A vast swamp, at least as large as all of
Glascardy, unexplored, cursed, inhabited by savages.
Very warm and very wet."

"I've changed my mind. I don't think I want to know
about swamps." But it was already too late, and she knew
that too.

CHAPTER 1

Rifkind pressed her face against the coarse red-brown hair of Turin's mane. The pungent horse-smell blocked the foully oppressive odor that had kept her awake. None of the raft dwellers seemed to sense the change that had come over the always heavy air of the Felmargue. They all slept peacefully on the straw mats that cluttered the raft, disturbed only by the everpresent clouds of tiny insects. Rifkind couldn't define the—perhaps it wasn't a smell at all—the *difference* between this night and the others, even to herself, and in frustration had left her mats and pots of insect repellent and gone to Turin and linked with him.

You feel it too? she thought—not to him, but herself; their empathic bond did not allow so precise a communication. It's too active to be a curse. It hangs heavily over us, yet no one else seems to notice.

The Bright One was out there behind the clouds, but Her power was diluted by the opaque night air. The raft —actually a collection of a dozen or more small rafts— drifted along without guidance. They occupied the trailing raftlet, though its position was a matter of purest

chance; it might just as easily have been leading the misshapen assemblage. Rifkind scratched Turin's forehead
between his arm-long horns and watched as another on
the raft stood up and stared into the darkness then walked
toward her.

"Rifkind?" Jenny whispered from the raftlet where the
goats and chickens were confined.

"It's me," Rifkind confirmed, stepping around Turin.

"Is something wrong?" Jenny, whose tendency to fret
had been aggravated by their winter's trek through Dro
Daria, had come to regard Rifkind's nocturnal wanderings as a portent of impending emergencies.

"Probably nothing more than that there's no breeze at
all and the air just clings to us."

Jenny nodded into the darkness. "I don't know how
they stand it. How they can just curl up and sleep when
the air is foul and dead like this is beyond my comprehension."

"Get used to it or never sleep. Simple. I can understand
that; I've slept in some pretty uncomfortable places myself. What I don't understand is how they can be so
blissful in their ignorance. We drift along with the current
all day, and if we don't get snared by the weeds and roots,
we drift along all night. They can't possibly know where
we are going! I'd feel better if they measured the sun or
the stars, but when I spoke to Chandro of Zamdurac and
the Followers he looked at me as if I were slow-witted.
Brel's tits, even the Wet-landers know Zamdurac's location in the sky and how to tell direction by it and the
Followers. But these Quais! They just nod and smile then
shake their heads at me."

"But they've been nodding and smiling since we left
Belfelis three weeks ago. Why aren't you sleeping tonight?"

"It's Full Moon, perhaps that's it. I don't know, Jenny.

Tonight the swamp just seems more menacing. I'm a fool for being here and a criminal fool for having dragged you along. It's nothing—go back to bed and try to sleep. If the wind doesn't pick up we'll all be poling tomorrow."

"You're right about that last, but I'm here because I chose to be."

Jenny threaded her way back through the collection of rafts to the one where she and Rifkind kept their belongings stored in big oil-and-wax-sealed baskets. Rifkind remained sitting cross-legged at Turin's side, letting his chestnut tail improve on the work of the insect-repellent smudge pots while she rubbed a polishing cloth along the blade of her sword. The cloth removed minute nicks along the blade's edge and the movements performed a similar service for her nerves.

She had been at her task for some time when suddenly the raft lashings creaked as if caught by a brisk wind, though the air remained deathly calm. Rifkind sprang to her feet, sword poised. The creaking stopped as suddenly as it had begun, yet the water beneath the rafts seemed to ripple faster than before. Now there was a new odor in the air, one that hadn't been there before yet was somehow the palpable epitome of all that had disturbed her. The raft shuddered and spun sharply. Turin screamed uncomprehending protest as the heaving movements threw him off balance.

The Quais were awake now. "Ornaq!" The single word was raised in dissonant chorus. Rifkind recognized the name of the Quais' boogeyman, the nightmare monster with which they chastised their children and which she had dismissed as unreal. The dark waters around the raft boiled. One animal's scream rose above the chorus as a ghostly phosphorescence outlined one of the goats as it was lofted quickly out of sight by a waist-thick tentacle. Even brave Turin reeked of fear, but Rifkind had no comfort for him as her eyes adjusted to the eerie glow of a forest of tentacles swaying in a circle beyond the raft.

"Dear Bright One, Goddess of the Moon, Mother of the Gentle Night, let me not die in this forsaken, stinking, cursed place!" Rifkind prayed softly so that none but her Goddess, hidden behind the dense clouds, might hear her desperation.

She hurried to the raftlet where her other weapons were stored. The Ornaq made a liquid, sighing sound as its tentacles wove over their heads, seeking the soft flesh of those who had entered its lair. A pair of grasping man-dibles clacked at the tip of each appendage; coated with poison if the legends were true. The Ornaq's skin, the Quais had said, was tough as cured leather. Rifkind had scant time to wrench a long knife from the baskets and assume a defensive stance before one of the tentacles swooped down on her.

She slashed at the thick thing with a life-or-death stroke, careful, despite her desperation, that the thing would re-coil from its injury with an arc that would not pass over her head; the Quais had also claimed that the Ornaq's blood was corrosive. Already the raft resounded with moaning confirmations.

There were fifteen men on the raft, assorted women-folk and children, and Jenny and Rifkind. Only the men and Rifkind fought the creature and only Rifkind had a metal weapon, one capable of more than annoying it.

A shriek pierced the air and was cut off abruptly. Now there were fourteen frightened men waving their clubs and crude spears at the overwhelming foe. In the darkness Rifkind could not see who had been plucked to his death. The Ornaq paused in its attack to feed; there was a chance it had loosened the suckers which had held the raft fast in the deadly lagoon.

"Quickly! The rudder, the poles!" a man shouted.

The women scuttled forward to thrust long flexible poles below the water's surface, pushing with all their strength, seemingly indifferent to the dangers to which they were exposing themselves. The band of Quais would count themselves victorious if even a few survived the encounter. Phosphorescence arose from the roiled water to illuminate the trapped rafts. Rifkind could see Jenny struggling with the poles along with the others. The castle-bred woman could not fight in Rifkind's manner, but her courage was above reproach.

"It has us still!" A woman called back from the leading edge, even as the monster whipped out a fang-tipped arm to silence her forever.

The poles had rammed into the obscenely huge body of the Ornaq. The women crashed into each other trying to reach safety behind the men. Jenny was almost to the center of the rafts when a tentacle wrapped itself around a leg and she was slowly dragged backwards toward the water, screaming.

She slid slowly toward the edge of the raft, clawing at the mats with one hand, using the muddy pole as a club with the other. None of the men broke their line of defense to help her.

Swearing loudly in all the names of her Goddess, Rifkind surged across the intervening distance, and contracted with a final scream that lent extra power to her sword as it slashed down across the entrapping tentacle, severing it. Jenny's screams reached new intensity as the thing's blood touched her leg, but were lost in the Ornaq's scream as its small mind registered knowledge of its first real injury. A numbing roar bubbled up from beneath the raft. The forest of tentacles focused over Rifkind.

"Bright Mother of us all, I shall not be killed by a demon-spawned curse such as this!"

Rifkind's voice challenged the Goddess, invoking the

Bright Moon's power to flow within her. She let go of the sword and knife to raise both arms above her head. Dwarfed by the waving, clacking weaponry of the Ornaq, she longed for the lost ruby that would have enabled her to summon power from the air itself without begging for it. Her mind left that thought to die a swift, unnoticed death and directed its energies to an entreaty to the latent power of all living things. If the Goddess were willing, and the life forces themselves were willing, the healer could become a conduit and reservoir of vitality and strength. Risking total vulnerability Rifkind ascended into the tal-spirit state of ritual magick, calling throughout the Felmargue for living allies in her battle against the curse.

Knowledge of the ancientness of her enemy flooded into Rifkind as her allies rushed to her. The parameters of reality changed as she absorbed the life spirits of the swamp. An aura of shimmering color clung to all those small creatures whose kind lent her the power of their natural creation with which to fight the abomination. The Ornaq itself was a sickly orange blob that smeared itself across the water and into the air, a cursed leech sucking true life into its perverted form. Its lust was a vacuum hungering both for the bright tal-spots of the humans and the lesser glows of the animals.

In Rifkind focused the hatred of all the small creatures of the swamp that had lived in terror of the ever-hungry abomination. She picked up her sword again and countered the first assault of the Ornaq. More tentacles than she could count swerved and hissed down upon her. The sword moved with uncanny swiftness to defend her, but inflicted no telling damage upon the enemy.

"It is not enough!"

Knowledge of certain defeat flowed through her, weakening her more than the venomous bile that slobbered onto the mats at her feet. Life forces alone could not defeat this ravenous enemy who thrived on their agony. Rifkind's thoughts rose in a demand that would wring strength and power from unliving objects, if the Goddess would allow it now that the ruby was gone.

Air above, water and stones below, give me your strength!

She felt no response to her plea and parried the next sinuous attack with her own dwindling strength. Panting, she leaned on the sword and remembered that faith and invocation alone had never been sufficient for the great works of magick, else every true believer would be a sorceror. Without the ruby talisman Rifkind felt as impotent as any other wishful worshipper. She made herself ready to die in the next onslaught.

Then a swirling wind surrounded the raft, breaking through the cloud cover. The Goddess's serene face looked down upon the beleaguered raft.

"For Your honor and glory! For the life of Your priestess!"

Suddenly Rifkind's sword was charged with a light that only she could see. Screaming her battle cry, she called the Ornaq to its death. It answered, flailing slime-dripping tentacles, as the unspeakable hulk of its body hove into the silver light of the Bright Moon.

Now the Ornaq radiated the foul odor of everything that had ever died in its part of the vast Felmargue. Despite the shield of her power Rifkind gagged from the stench while the unprotected people beside her fell into helpless retching.

Knowing that she might kill the creature yet still not save the Quais and Jenny from its death throes, Rifkind stepped off the raft. The water shuddered as tiny, mindless life coagulated beneath her feet to support her weight. Her balance was precarious at first; she had never needed to stand on the surface of water before. The

Ornaq's sounds became tinged with fear and frantic before the unprecedented strength of life within its lair. Rifkind called upon the life within the water to carry her forward and guard her retreat.

Lacking true life the Ornaq was invulnerable to true death, but the relentless cutting of her sword destroyed each fang-tipped appendage thrust at her. Vitality oozed away from its gouged surface, fouling the water but lost to the creature forever. Rifkind continued hacking at it until there were only foul lumps in the water beneath her feet.

"For Your honor and glory—thanksgiving for the life of Your priestess!"

Still supported by the water, Rifkind knelt. Her breathing became slower. Her heart no longer pounded and her tal made the shift from divine warrior to priestess, exchanging the powers of aggression for those of peace and healing. She thrust one hand below the surface and extended the other to the Goddess. Her mind shifted into the language of the Old Ones, unused by men except in ritual.

The Ornaq stench was carried up in a spiraling wind, drawn from the violated waters by her chant and the healing powers the Bright Goddess had given her. When the waters ran clear again, Rifkind staggered blindly back to the raft.

"Use the poles, get us away from this accursed place!" she demanded in a parched voice.

She crawled, unaided, to the small raft that harbored her possessions. The sword bounced when she dropped it to the mats, a measure of her exhaustion. The Quais were as openly awed by their deliverance as they had been terrified by their danger. Only Jenny dared approach the priestess with a mug of watered beer.

"Are you hurt?" she asked, offering the mug.

"No, only tired to the death. I must rest." She set aside

the mug untouched. "It has been a long time since such powers flowed through me."

The mooncast shadow of the Quais-man Jevan fell over them.

"You have slain the Ornaq," Jevan began, his tone stiffly formal. "For generations the Quais have lived in terror of the beasts that were born in the destruction of our lands. Not even the memories of the Fathers could help us. You have brought metals back into our world. You have destroyed our enemies.

"I doubted you, Rifkind, as did the others. We had planned to take you deep within the Felmargue and leave you on a tree-island in punishment for breaking our taboos. None would believe that our savior could be . . . a woman—until it was shown." The unthinkable finally made real through speech, Jevan relaxed, showing even, white teeth in a generous smile. "Our Fathers told us that one would come from the outside and lift the curse the gods placed on our land. Once there were many false saviors, and the Fathers grew cautious. It was better to doubt the legend of the Leveller, who would end our punishment, than to anger the gods still further. Only the Leveller could break the conditions of our damnation by carrying metal within the swamp; you are the one."

Rifkind was too tired to do more than smile at this sudden change of heart. Even the news that her months-long quest had almost ended in an isolated death failed to rouse her ritually numbed emotions. She extended a fatigue-trembling hand to him.

"Only some of us believe—the others still have their doubts. You must be even more cautious until a balance is reached. The raft is too crowded. Chandro stands on the other side. No harm shall come to you from me or mine, but we are outnumbered still."

Jevan smiled again, released her hand and retreated.

The ebbing of the ritual power had not proceeded so far that Rifkind was beyond its influence. She saw the burning sincerity of the young man and in a rare burst of precognitive vision saw chaos rampant on the rafts with Jevan and Chandro in a bloody confrontation. The images were important but in her exhaustion Rifkind could not hold them in her thoughts. They faded before she truly recognized their power and immediacy. She slipped deeper into exhaustion until restorative trance surrounded her, to purge the ravages of ritual magick from her body.

CHAPTER 2

Rifkind was roused from her purging reverie by mind-filling anxiety.

Turin?

Her eyes opened. She snapped upright, sitting alone at one corner of an isolated segment of the raft while the Quais were gathered around a head-tossing, half-rearing war-horse at the opposite end. Rifkind loosened the catch-straps on her throwing knives and daggers and began a stealthy stalk toward the Quais' gathering.

How long? she wondered absently, picking her way over barrels and baskets with little sound. Not long enough. I'm still tired and hungry—But Turin's so aroused I can make no sense of the images he gives me, only that he feels ringed by danger and threats.

The Quais' raft-home was, in actuality, a series of rickety rafts loosely lashed together. The chief Quais occupation, other than hunting, trading and talking, seemed to be unending repair and replacement of the reed-and-log platforms which supported their culture in the absence of hard dry land in most parts of the Felmargue.

The Quais children leaped from one pod to the next,

seemingly unmindful of the brown-green water beneath them. It was not an ability that came easily to a water-wary Asheeran such as Rifkind. Her progress along the raft-pods was further impeded by the moss-like vines that trailed down from the innumerable overhanging tree-limbs to attach themselves to the unwary. In three weeks of travel under them she had failed to overcome the shrinking distaste she felt every time one touched her.

"Rifkind."

An urgent whispering voice she recognized as Jenny's called from the shadows. She hoped the Overnmont woman would be more coherent than the war-horse.

"Jenny? Where are you? What's going on? You're crouched somewhere in the dark, and Turin woke me out of a sound sleep."

"Down here, behind the barrels."

"He's gone mad!" Jenny exclaimed once she had Rifkind's hand in hers. "After you came back on the raft, his spirit left him and has not come back. Jevan tried to reason with him, then to restrain him, but..."

Jenny's whispered narrative was interrupted by a wailing, keening sound that rose from the pod where Turin and the Quais goats were kept.

"When the ancient gods punished the sorcerors of the Black Flame who had misled and betrayed our Fathers," the high-pitched male voice shouted, "they punished our Fathers for their mistakes and created the Felmargue to remind us of our sins until such time as we were worthy of forgiveness. We were forbidden to worship our old gods and forbidden to arm ourselves with metal lest we forget our punishment.

"Now this woman, with swords and knives, and loudly worshipping a Goddess who had no power in our Fathers' Felmargue, asks, no, demands to be taken to the Hold, the one reminder of what we once were, the symbol of Their promise that They will forgive us in time. Because of her *metal* and her *unknown* goddess she overpowered *one* Ornaq, and now there are persons on this raft calling her the Leveller, saying this *foreigner*, this blasphemous *woman*, who knows nothing about us, is our promised savior, the one who can erase the difference between Hold and Fel!"

"He's quite eloquent," Rifkind said, staring at the disheveled, screaming man in whom she could barely recognize the quiet gentleman who had first allowed them on the raft.

"Our savior will not flout the taboos we have lived under for generations. Our savior will not be a metal-fouled female. This creatures Rifkind is a false savior, a servant of the old sorcerors, as all the others have been. Show her the Hold and the gods will never forgive us. We'll live in this swamp all our days and all our children's days!"

"What started him going like this?" Rifkind asked, crouching down again beside Jenny as the man continued his tirade.

"I'm not completely certain myself. You had just fallen asleep when he started. At first he was here, and shouting at me, but you didn't wake up. I rather hoped you would and set him straight, but I guess you were too exhausted. Eventually I guess he figured he'd frightened me enough and started screaming at Jevan and his friends.

"I don't think he's actually tried to get very close to Turin, but the noise and the torches bother him, and Turin is very good at frightening others. Except when Jevan tried to drag him into the lean-to, and Chandro hit him, I don't think he's actually hurt anyone."

"Turin is not some mindless Darian beast who shies at light or voices. And you're not one to go hiding behind barrels. There is something more."

" . . . And Jevan has succumbed to this temptress. He

calls her Leveller and offers that we will show her the way
to the Hold. Jevan, without consulting the rest of us, without consulting the Fathers, has decided that we, the
Felmarquais of raft-Chandro will betray all the generations of obedience."

"He says the same things over and over again," Jenny
explained, seeing that Rifkind was still straining to hear
the chief. "Over and over that Jevan should not have wel-
comed you back aboard what he now calls 'raft-Chandro'
after you killed the Ornaq. He thinks that he, Chandro,
should have made that decision, and if that decision had
been turned over to him, as it should have been, then he
would have left you out there standing in the water. He
thinks the ancient ones, whatever they are, move on the
raft now that the Ornaq's dead. I don't understand about
the Fathers at all, but at least we've heard of them before."

"The Ornaq's not dead," Rifkind said absently, then,
noting the look of panic in Jenny's torchlit eyes, added, "It
never was alive—it's the product of a very old and powerful curse, an unholy collection of life essences that had
been sucked down there into the mud. The pieces will
start to grow again at once, including the main body."

"Will it return? We haven't moved very far with all this
yelling."

"It won't be a threat again for a long time: generations,
as the Quais are so fond of saying."

Again Chandro's shrill voice broke through the conversation and Jenny gripped Rifkind's arm.

"The Felmargue is our home, *our* home. We will not
see it destroyed by outsiders, adventurers who seek the
treasures left on the Hold. We will not be enslaved again!"

"Whatever he is saying now," Rifkind whispered more
to herself than to Jenny who still held on to her, "the anger
has been in his heart much longer than we have been on
his raft in this forsaken swamp."

She squinted, looking for the pulsing spot of Chandro's tal. She found it, glowing like a small coal, on his chest.

"Men can become mad quite suddenly if something disturbs their tal-spirit, but Chandro's shows no sign of recent change. And there are no ancient ones or 'Fathers' in this part of the swamp."

"But Chandro is mad," Jenny protested. "He called me a 'whore for the gods' and said he was 'entitled' . . . "

Jenny did not complete her thought, and Rifkind finally understood the sense of panic in the woman's eyes and voice. As much as the Overnmont woman wished to find a husband and settled life during the course of her journey with Rifkind, Chandro's threat would scare her more than any threat of murder.

"Perhaps it will be best if we travel through the Felmargue alone after this," Rifkind mused.

"We have no way of knowing where to go. Jevan only just offered to take us to the Hold where you've said we've wanted to go from the beginning. I had no idea they were planning to strand us. I'm afraid."

"Perhaps when we leave, we will have company. I was not surprised by their treachery, but if Jevan's group gets thrown off the raft, I think we'll be safe enough with him, now. Chandro was not the one who offered to show us the way, and we do seem to have brought long-standing anger out into the open."

"Enslave them! Sell them to the Belfais!" one of the Quais shouted from the crowd that surrounded Chandro.

"Leave them for the Ornaq to find!" another yelled.

"She slew one Ornaq—best we kill them ourselves," came the response to that suggestion.

Filled with mob-courage, none of the speakers had apparently considered the implications of assaulting an Ornaq-slayer. But Chandro had succeeded in rousing and dividing his people. Turin's images of panic raged and battered against Rifkind's consciousness. The reassurances she had attempted to convey to him were insufficient to fully counteract the swirling emotions of the crowd. Rifkind cautioned Jenny to remain inconspicuous in her hiding place while she moved closer to Turin.

" . . . and the others with them!" Chandro exhorted his following as Rifkind hunkered down behind a bale of hay and used her healer's skills to calm the goats while she wondered just how many "others" were involved.

As she expected, Chandro radiated far less madness than his enrapt listeners who believed what he merely preached. A closer study of the crowd revealed that despite her first impressions, all the Quais were not in attendance. The children and several of the adults, including Jevan, and Chandro's eldest son, were missing. The absence of the children was easily explained. Roused once from their sleep already by the confrontation with the Ornaq, they would have been given a swallow of one of the potent herbal broths distilled on the raft and would sleep until well past sunrise. But the missing adults were the youngest and strongest of the small yet crowded group—and the ones most likely to chafe under the strong, but aging and increasingly intemperate, Chandro. She scanned the torch-lit crowd a second time to be certain.

Rifkind was certain now that she and Jenny were minor players in a long-standing struggle for control between Chandro and Jevan. Quite probably neither man much cared what happened to the two strange women in their midst. The battleground had simply become the legends and traditions, the victor would keep the raft and the supplies, the loser would share the fate of the women. She remembered the flickering precognitive visions of her trance—the future had come to pass.

Crouched in the flickering shadows, Rifkind reached out with her mind both to calm Turin and to share his

vision of things. Sensing her presence nearby he quit his
frantic head-tossing and pawing. His Rider wanted to see
what he saw and required a steady vantage point to make
sense of it. His nostrils flared, his eyes bulged and the
horns pointed at Chandro, but he held still.

So, it's murder as well as rape that Turin feels in
Chandro's mind, Rifkind thought as she withdrew from
Turin to gaze at the Quais herself. Rape is no surprise in
a culture like this—we would keep the women of the
caravans after we killed the men. I had not expected
murder—that makes no sense. Turin must be confused,
likely Chandro wants to murder Jevan, not us.

Chandro's now familiar harangue goaded his fellow
Quais to do something he himself would not bloody his
hands to do. Rifkind, from the experiences of her nomadic
childhood, gauged the fiber of the men and women gathered on the raftlet better than Chandro did. They were
riled to action, and, unless Chandro allowed them their
rampage, they would turn and devour him. It would be a
mindless murdering, either way, but Rifkind had no in-
tention of witnessing it. She crept back to the raftlet where
Jenny hid.

"We have lost our choice, Jenny," she said slowly, leading the way back to the raftlet where their belongings
were stored in the tightly woven oiled baskets. "We're
going to have to get off the raft and find our own way—we
can't wait until the dust clears, they mean to make us part
of the dust."

Jenny grumbled a hesitant agreement as they lashed
the baskets together with ropes hastily ripped out of the
deck of the raftlet.

"Can't we untie this raftlet from the others and take it
too?" Jenny asked after dipping her hand experimentally
in the live water.

"Yes!" Rifkind agreed. "Yes!" repeating herself several

times with increasing enthusiasm for Jenny's idea. "And, be quiet, stay here with the raftlet. I've got to get Turin, somehow. They'll never notice one of the pods is missing in the fight they're about to have."

Rifkind drew her dagger and freed the raftlet from its fellows. It continued to move with the others in the slow current, and the two women had to grab on to the water weeds and shrubs to halt their progress until the larger parent-raft was drifting around a tangled, floating island. Chandro's voice had been drowned out by calls to abandon, or preferably kill, Jevan, his followers, and the two women. Torches could be seen fanning out over the collection of raftlets as Rifkind eased herself into the thick water that came above her waist.

"There, I've wedged you in against the roots here. I'll be able to find my way back, so don't you move. Now, I'm off to get Turin."

"Be careful," Jenny added needlessly.

Things brushed by Rifkind as she pressed on through the swamp to the large raft. She wore heavy quilts that became water-laden and threatened to drag her into the soft, yielding mud bottom, but they also protected her from knowing if a particular bump was a submerged branch or one of the eely sucker-mouths that throve on the ever-abundant decay of the swamp. Her hunger had completely disappeared. The Ornaq would make no distinction between the harmless song-birds and the great cold-blooded prowlers. It had always been hungry and anything alive and moving had been food. If they were, as Jenny said, still in the Ornaq's water there would be few predators, but a submerged branch was enough to make her uneasy.

Once she lost her footing and slid down an oozing embankment to fill her nose and ears with foul swampwater. She spat violently and righted herself, scrambling awkwardly in the sodden, crawling quilts until the water around her was only waist-deep again. A startled bird rushed up in front of her, shrieking alarm as its nest-area was disturbed, but the commotion on the raft was already far enough advanced that no one noticed the bird, or Rifkind's dark, wet torso gliding along the edge of the raft. Her mind touched Turin's and compelled him to silence as she clambered onto his now-dark raftlet.

Fights raged around the several lean-to's at the center of the raft collection as Chandro's loyalists ferreted out Jevan and his friends. Children squalled as they were rudely roused from their drugged sleep by a second waking nightmare.

Rifkind waited motionless until she was certain none of them had time to notice activity on the raftlet where the animals were. She used the dagger to rasp the ropes free and then to fashion a crude looped harness for herself. If Turin ever got off the raft into the mud and deep water, there would be no way of getting him on it again. The suckermouth fish would have a feast. Of course, with Turin she would also get the goats, stupid bleating creatures that stared at her while their mouths worked endlessly rechewing their dinners.

"Jump!" she hissed at them, waving her arms to frighten them into leaping over onto the larger, noisy raft.

But she had touched them with her tal-spirit earlier; the goats continued their chewing as if she weren't there. She picked up the largest of them and threw it across the gap. It bleated its injured dignity and surprise. Rifkind looked across the water to see Chandro clutching a shortened mud-pole, ready to throw it at her.

They stared, unmoving, at each other. Rifkind felt heartbeats of danger as she clawed, unseen, at her wrist to drop the wetly recalcitrant handle of a concealed knife into her hand. The goats, seeing their leader scrambling around Chandro, leaped over the water of their own accord until Rifkind and Turin were alone on the slowly drifting pod. She was not Chandro's enemy. He did not fear the legends he had inflamed the other Quais with, and she had no grudge with him that demanded blood. Still, they saw each other.

Rifkind bent down, never moving her gaze from Chandro's silhouette, and draped the loop of the rope harness over her shoulder. He did not move to stop her. She slid slowly into the oozing water, her boots squishing as they reached the mud. Turin moved about on the raftlet to watch Chandro now that she could no longer see below his shoulders.

The mud offered little purchase for her feet. The slow current seemed suddenly an irresistible force against the weight she must pull. Rifkind closed her eyes and put her full strength into the harness; sank to her knees in mud, almost inhaling the live water as it rose above her. But the raftlet began to move and when she rose for air, Chandro had turned away.

CHAPTER 3

It's getting light. I should have found her by now, Rifkind thought.

The effort of pulling the raftlet had blinded her to the first signs of dawn, and the rosy light had all but given way to the full light of the sun. Only a few stars remained visible. The Bright One had slipped below the horizon long before and the dull coppery disk of the Dark Moon now dominated the brightening sky a few handspans above the soon-to-rise sun.

She wouldn't have tried to go off on her own. No. Jenny's headstrong, but she's not foolish, and she's afraid of the swamp. She wouldn't have moved unless her life depended on it. She would have left the raft anyway. Even an Ornaq would not have eaten the raft.

Rifkind's shoulders ached from where the rope had cut into them. Her feet were sore from the boots and the now wet and lumpy foot-bindings. She held the coarse rope taut at arm's length in front of her to ease the pressure on her raw shoulders. The current, barely perceptible from atop the rafts, was an unyielding, tireless foe.

The birds had begun their early morning chorus, and,

of course, their diet of insect life as on the wing they
swooped down to investigate the warm, salty life-form
emergent from the swamp-waters. Rifkind waved the
cloud of them away for an all too brief moment of peace.

She hauled herself up onto Turin's raft with fatigued,
trembling arms and sat dripping misery and exhaustion
in the pale light of dawn.

I'm lost. Jenny's lost. We're both lost, and lost to each
other. Neither one of us will ever get out of this damned
swamp! she muttered and Turin nuzzled the side of her
face as she sat staring at the floating island.

Though Rifkind's protests had been loud and sincere
when Bainbrose and Ejord, not to mention Jenny herself,
had insisted that she would need a companion on her
journey, she had to admit, to herself if no one else, that
through three long months of travelling, Jenny had
proved herself time and time again. The red-haired, blue
eyed woman had spent all her life in one castle or another
until the civil war brought her to the camp-kitchens of the
army. Out of politeness no one mentioned her mother,
but her father was Lord Humphry and the lord had seen
to it that the least of his children received a proper educa-
tion. She was intelligent and attractive, with a pragmatic
stubbornness and a sweet voice that had talked them out
of more than one tight corner during their journey.

Almost as soon as they were out of sight of the fortress
the two women had had a day-long argument. Jenny never again referred to Rifkind as "milady," admitted her
hopeless and proscribed passions for her half-brothers,
including Ejord, and her determination to do something
other than wait on better-born women, even if it meant
starving. For her part Rifkind had conceded that a lifetime
of skirts, dances and poetry as well as the despised
"domestics" did not have to leave a woman devoid of spirit or vigor. Rifkind even acknowledged without criticism

her friend's determination to find herself a "proper man."

The current made streamers of the trailing roots and leaves from the island's tangled mat of vegetation. Rifkind's eyes followed their slow curves long moments before her mind focused on them.

It spins, she thought dully, without enjoyment of this new iota of information. If I stayed here long enough, this spot, with its three purple flowers arranged just so on that vine, would come back in front of me. And Jenny . . . ?

Rifkind tried to envision the island, spinning slowly, carried along by the current, but gave up after a few futile and static images. Her notions of water were still limited to brief rain-squalls and kettles boiling over a fire. The few times Ejord's army had camped by a lake or forded a river her mind had been occupied.

Turin shared the defeated, lost-feeling of her mind. Flaring his nostrils against the wind he sought the scent of the red-haired one who fed him tender young shoots pulled off the passing foliage. Rifkind, in turn, shared his sense of failure. But there were other means of finding Jenny now that she had stopped fighting the raftlet, the current and her own exhaustion long enough to think.

Tal-mind was, in fact, easier to generate in her dreamy exhausted state. She centered easily in her mind and waited. The landscape changed; became more alive. It seethed with the milling stomach-spirit tals of the myriad birds and insects. A red nimbus shone around and in everything. There was too much life to see Jenny. Rifkind relaxed and the tal-nimbus faded back to simple-vision reality. There was still another way, but Rifkind hesitated to try it until the Dark Moon's presence was fully overcome by sunlight.

There had been a time, before her self-exile from the Asheera, that the sun-spirit would have been the greater danger—she would have preferred to work her rituals in the light of the Dark Moon rather than risk the insanity-bearing lightstorms spawned in the full day. Now her greatest dread was of the Dark Moon, despite knowing that its power was tied to that of her benevolent Bright One.

She let the sunlight fall on her face before chanting the ritual. Her tal rose from the pit of her heart, past her eyes and then above her to the separate ethereal realm accessible only to those to whom the greater ones, the gods of all Dro Daria, had shown their faces and powers.

The red nimbus of mobile life obscured the vibrant green of the plants. Turin's tal, ebbing back and forth from heart-spirit to stomach-spirit, loomed next to an odd emptiness that would reveal, to anyone else possibly able to see it, that Rifkind had left her body.

A largish concentration of more intense red glimmered to one side, just within her perception; the Quais raft still headed for the salt marshes and the trapping ranges. Another pulsing mass quivered in the lee of a different floating island. There were several tal-spirits within the mass, several damaged by injury. It would demand investigation, but it was not Jenny.

Jenny was, as nearly as Rifkind from her rarefied position could determine, still on her raft, and still wedged tightly into the undergrowth of the island; in her exhaustion Rifkind had simply passed by unseeing. Rifkind narrowed her attention to the one tal-spirit and, because she understood Jenny's being, examined the ethereal signal more closely. Like a small beacon Jenny's tal radiated her most intensely felt emotions.

Bright One—she's been attacked!

With that heartfelt thought Rifkind's ethereality dove back within her. She opened her eyes, breathing hard and pulse pounding, as if the unknown had been about to attack her own body.

She was attacked—not injured, only attacked, Rifkind reminded herself, slowing her breathing. She is safe.

Belatedly, in the light, Rifkind noticed a stripped sapling lying on the rush matting of the raftlet. Poling would be a great improvement over hauling the raft through the water. Nonetheless, Rifkind had taken her share of duties with the Quais men rather than the women. Poling through the mud was a new and initially mystifying process for her, and it took nearly an hour to backtrack to where Jenny was waiting.

Jenny had surrounded herself with their baskets. A branch hacked from the overhanging tree-limbs, with both ends sharpened to crude points, lay across her pulled up knees. The knife Rifkind had given her shortly after they had left Chatelgard was clenched loosely in one hand as she slept. Rifkind halted her own raft before waking the other woman.

Two—no, three months before Jenny had been a demure lady-in-waiting in the Overnmont retinue with a future of children, embroidery and candle-lit madrigals stretching before her. The Jenny sleeping lightly in front of Rifkind on the raftlet reminded her enough of herself that she judged it prudent to be quiet and careful in rousing her.

Had the baskets not shielded Jenny's face from the sun, Rifkind would have interposed herself to block out the light and cast patterns of shadow on her closed eyes until they opened and consciousness returned. Instead she called, and thought, Jenny's name, much as she would reach out to alert Turin. The war-horse, though, was uniquely attuned to her mind and felt her calls as a sameness, not the otherness shock that showed on Jenny's face as her eyes flashed open and her grip tightened on both the knife and the stick.

"It's you!" she exclaimed, exhaling her panic.

"You've learned well!" Rifkind responded with unconcealed admiration.

"Things started moving toward me after you left. *Eyes!* It was dark and all I could see were these eyes staring at me. Then it was on the raft here with me. I hit at it with your knife, and it made noises like I'd never heard before. But I kept on hitting it until it fell off the raft. That was even worse because it attracted more, different *things* that didn't really make noise, just splashing sounds—but I could hear their teeth working."

Jenny paused, looked down and recoiled from the red-brown stains on the rush mats. A leathery-skinned arm a quarter the size of her own lay severed at her feet. Its talons were stained with blood from three short gashes on Jenny's arm. Biting her lip Jenny kicked the remains into the water between their rafts, where almost at once ripples and bubbles appeared on its surface.

"I hope it was dead before those other things got to it," Jenny said, her deeper, softer, nature already resurfacing.

She stood up slowly as she spoke, shook her hair loose from its combs and began to rebraid it. Rifkind watched in bemused silence until Jenny had fixed her thick hair into a perfect coif and retied her apron. Jenny was now ready to face the morning.

"We should start to think about food and water. What sort of things do you think we can eat out here?" Jenny asked.

"Well, for a start, I think you just pushed our breakfast over the edge," Rifkind said drily, and they both laughed. "We should be able to snare fish and birds as the Quais did, once we get organized. Hopefully we can eat anything that wants to eat us."

They began lashing the two raftlets together as the Quais had taught them to do.

"When I was looking for you, I saw others not far from

here. I think I could locate them again later on. There's too much sunlight now to be able to see tal-spirits clearly. But I thought they might be Jevan and the others Chandro wanted to kill or throw off the big raft."

Jenny wrinkled her nose before answering. "Do you think that's wise? They might see us as the cause of their trouble. Shouldn't we just try to retrace our way back to Belfelis?"

"No, we'll go forward. The Quais go out to the salt marshes by drifting along with the swamp itself. We've seen that. We're further into the Felmargue now than any of the Belfais ever were with their oared boats. Perhaps the Hold is visible from the salt-marshes, if not perhaps we'll find the current the Quais use to get back inland—I don't think they pole the whole distance."

"The Felmargue is so big we'll never find the Hold. We should try to go back."

"It is easier and safer to go on ahead. They told us that the Hold was a legend, now we know that that's not true. Who is to say how many other 'legends' are fact and how much the Quais have said to confuse outsiders? They are a lot like my own people in that respect. Besides, I don't think we could possibly backtrack. This island floats around in circles—there aren't many landmarks, and if we do find one, chances are it will have moved.

"Besides, I suspect we will find help when we find those I saw earlier."

"They might not be Jevan—maybe it's Chandro, or Quais we've never seen before!"

"Even so I've seen that some of them are hurt, and I can turn that into safe passage for us without offending the Goddess. First we might as well rest. I couldn't heal anything right now."

"I'll sit guard then."

The sun was already high in the heavens and drawing

water out of the swamp in hazy clouds, Rifkind reclined
in the narrow shadows of the baskets, but the sleep she
had craved since her battle with the Ornaq still eluded
her. Even the whisking sounds of Turin's tail lashing at
the small horde of insects hovering around them irritated
her thoughts. Something broke the water with a splash
and she sat bolt-upright.

"Fish," Jenny explained and pointed to the faint ripples.

"Can't rest. Maybe I'm too hungry. Might as well get us
some dinner."

Unhampered by the Quais taboo against metals, a pro-
hibition in some way connected to the punishment the
Quais frequently alluded to, a punishment that was supposed to have created the Felmargue swamp itself from
once-rich farmlands, Rifkind split Jenny's sharpened
stake at one end and lashed a throwing knife into the cleft.
Then they waited, silent and drifting, as Jenny had un-
wedged the lashed rafts. Shedding the damp, sticky quilts,
Rifkind faced the afternoon sun in a bare-armed linen
tunic. Winter in the Felmargue was at worst chilly and
damp, and on most afternoons when the sun shone it was
as warm as a summer's day in Glascardy. The swamp
sun had already darkened her skin to a Quais-like brown.

"Until now, I'd never seriously considered the possibility that we might never get back to Chatelgard," Jenny
said almost wistfully.

"You can't say I didn't point out the dangers before we
left. You could have stayed with Ejord. His new wife was
coming up from the valleys, and she would have been a
gentle lady to wait upon, from what was said of her."

"She was going to bring all her own ladies with her,
and Ejord would not have forced me upon her. Even if
. . . I don't think I could get used to waiting on his wife

like that. He wanted her to be happy, protected—since he couldn't have you."

There had been few secrets in the Overnmont household. Even someone like Rifkind who strove to keep herself apart from the gossip of the servants knew more than she wanted to about everyone—and knew as well that her own life was common knowledge in the servant's quarters.

"Still that was no reason for you to come with me. You were well liked. There was no need to settle for being someone's lady-in-waiting. Ejord would have dowered you."

"I know."

There was no bitterness left in their conversation; they had shared too much since leaving the grey mountain fortress to want to hurt each other. Rifkind still mulled over the failure of the Bright One to bless Ejord's proposal and Jenny divided her thoughts between her questionable birth and her hopeless love for her half-brothers.

Twice Rifkind threw the spear at a movement in the water, only to pole their ungainly craft over to the floating, bare-bladed, spear and begin the waiting again. They had drifted until the island was lost in the hazy distance behind them. Turin suddenly became agitated, fretting despite Rifkind's sub-vocalized reassurances.

"I smell something," Jenny said, in the midst of Rifkind's futile efforts.

"Fire," Rifkind commented after a moment.

She stood up and faced into the wind as the war-horse was doing. The barely perceptible breeze that ran counter to the current in this part of the Felmargue carried the tinge of burning green twigs and the even fainter aroma of fish, opened, spitted and roasting.

"Food! We haven't eaten all day!" Jenny exclaimed, forgetting that it was not their food they smelled.

"We've drifted towards them, they must have anchored in some way. They've gotten food and started a fire, but they've still got one, maybe more, who are too badly injured to move."

Rifkind broke down the crudely unsuccessful spear to hide the taboo-breaking metal, and grabbed a pole to direct the raft toward the now-visible smoke.

"Will they feed both of us? Only you can heal their wounded."

"Getting them to accept both of us won't be the problem. The Quais are like the Asheerans—nomads. At the best of times they've got barely enough for themselves. In bad times it's much worse. I can remember the Gathering making a blood-line in a very bad dry season. They excluded three clans. The members of those clans had a choice, they could divide up the clan possessions among the individuals and try to join the clans inside the blood-line or they could wait and die. The Gathering had barred them from wells that they had thought were theirs.

"We were powerful in those days. My father took in many of their warriors and all their full-blooded women and horses. Some of the others found homes. No one wanted the old or the children—they wandered around the camps until they finally died." For a moment Rifkind's mind was that of a nine-year-old watching her distant cousins grow thinner and weaker. "But those we did take in became our blood. We shared with them and suffered equally from then on."

"Are you saying that they are going to leave us out here to die?" Jenny asked.

Rifkind nodded. "They might, if they're so desperate they can't risk healing their injured. But I'm hoping they will be like my father—hopeful enough of the future to take risks."

"I don't feel very hopeful."

"We've got some things in our favor. It was one thing for them to plan to abandon us deep in the swamps when we were ignorant of their customs and they had no debt to us. Their own customs will go hard with them if they acknowledge that we have shared danger with them. I can't force them to accept us, if we fall outside their blood-line, but if they are undecided I can place pressures on them through my healing. I have learned things I did not know before about binding life forces. I could keep animals from their traps and fish from their lines. They would welcome us to remove the curse."

Jenny nodded, though Rifkind was aware that she had not convinced the woman who had grown up in a well-organized society and in a stone castle. The Quais knew, as the Asheerans knew, that they did not dominate their world but were merely tolerated by it. Rifkind hoped she would not have to use the Quais' taboos and customs against them.

CHAPTER 4

The easiest approach to the Quais was guided by the slow, strong current of the swamp, and as the rafts were ungainly to steer and their intent was peaceful, Rifkind chose to follow the easiest route. By nature and practice she and Jenny were quiet, and Turin had been trained to a stolid patience years before. This was in direct contrast to the Quais who, with their children, animals, quarrels and songs, normally cut a noisy swath through the air. Even without children or animals the raft was too preoccupied and talkative to notice their upwind approach.

"Hello, the raft!" Rifkind shouted across the water.

Waving her hands so they would be sure to see her, Rifkind repeated her hail. Faces could be seen turning toward them and a flurry of activity ensued around the small fire. Rifkind thrust their sapling-pole deep into the mud to initiate the maneuvering of the raft against the current.

"Rifkind!" Jenny shouted, her voice cracking. "Spears!"

Rifkind glanced up to see the Quais loose three of their stone-tipped spears. She grabbed Jenny's shoulder and pulled both of them down to the rush mats. The Quais

were indifferent weaponeers, with less than indifferent
equipment—but not so poor as to justify standing full-face
to a flight of spears. The spears went wide and were
slowed to ineffectiveness by the time they struck the water
in front of them.

"C'mon, we've got to get this thing farther out of range."

Rifkind crawled to the sapling. It was slow, painful
work to ease out of range of what Rifkind guessed their
greatest lucky throw might be. The Quais, however,
seemed content to have driven the intruders off with one
flight and were not about to waste anymore of what
would have to be a limited supply of weapons.

"So, what do we do now?" Jenny asked, rubbing her
elbows from where they had chafed on the rushes while
they belly-poled the raft out of range. "Can you use your
bow on them?"

"I could, they'd be in range for me. But there's no sense
to that. I don't want to kill them. What point? I want to
heal their wounded and get us a decent meal in the process."

"I told you they would blame us."

"I suspect they're frightened rather than angry. There
isn't any reason for them to blame us. Without us they'd
be part of the Ornaq by now."

"They don't remember that. We don't need them anyway."

Rifkind surprised herself by not agreeing. She could
hear herself saying what Jenny said, but was aware that
now there was a part of her that had passed beyond the
untrusting self-sufficiency that Jenny for the first time in
her life aspired to. Her eyes followed the wary movements
of the Quais, while her mind sought after the incidents
that had changed her own opinions. Introspection had
never suited her, however, and she quickly abandoned it
in favor of watching the Quais.

"We have to convince them that we mean no harm. They're jumpy. We should assume their leader is one of the injured," she said after a long silence.

"We should just drift by them. We'll learn how to catch our own fish, sooner or later."

"Umm." Rifkind nodded, but without truly hearing what Jenny had said. "We'll just convince them from outside their throwing range."

She hailed them as before, calling until her throat tore from the strain of shouting.

"Go away."

"You have injured men with you. I can help them!"

"We don't need your help."

"You have injured people who will die if I don't help them. Ask them, if you can, before you say you don't need me."

It was a gamble. The tal signals she had seen earlier were unfamiliar. She had known they displayed distortions and had guessed the distortion meant injury and that if she could perceive injury in an unfamiliar person, the physical damage must be extensive. Perhaps so extensive that they had died in the long, steamy afternoon? The Quais huddled together and chose a new spokesman, a woman.

"What assurance do we have that you mean us no harm?"

"I got rid of the Ornaq."

They conferred among themselves again.

"Why do you want to help us?"

"Chandro didn't want us on his raft any more than he wanted you." Another wild guess, she didn't know who had finally won the battle, but the numbers had been in favor of Chandro and the group they now faced was small. "We are not Quais. We do not know the Felmargue as you do. We're hungry and tired, but we can heal your injured."

"Come forward slowly."

"Is there any other way?" Rifkind asked under her breath as they shoved the sapling into the mud again. "If we get nothing else from them, we get another pole for this thing. One for each side."

The Quais tossed them a stiff rope which made the final approach easier. The small fire burned on the floating island; Chandro had cast them off without one of the stone-pit raftlets and they could not afford to weaken the rafts they did have by cooking on them. The three who had thrown spears at them each had bruises and cuts to show they had been in a brawl, a fourth stood uncomfortably in the last days of her pregnancy and three more lay unconscious and moaning on a separate raft. One of the injured they recognized as Jevan by his woven leather armbands.

"Do you have clear water?" Rifkind asked as soon as she stepped onto the Quais raft collection.

"Not yet," the woman who had directed their approach responded.

"I can work without it then. I will need a fire though, Elyssa. Can you start another one over there?"

"It could be no larger than this one . . ."

"That will be enough."

Now that they had successfully joined the Quais, Rifkind left the social pleasantries to Jenny, who had always gotten along better with them than had Rifkind.

Instead she knelt by the three victims of Chandro's oratory. The woman had been hit hard on the head, and an ominous blue stain had already spread across the side of her face. A young man, face contorted by pain and swelling, had large splinters from a raft-pole still protrud-

ing from a gaping wound in his groin. Grimly Rifkind
considered her rash promise to help these people. Jevan,
however, presented her with the most difficult problem.
His wounds were not so serious. He seemed more asleep
than unconscious, but he was closed to her gentle investigations. She pressed the back of her hand against his
cheek and confirmed her fears.

Like Ejord, she thought, his life-forces run invisibly.
Nothing could touch him, not the most potent sorcery. No
god can threaten him, and no healer heal him. No wonder he was so willing to show us to the Hold—the legends
have no power over him.

Rifkind walked to the baskets on their own raftlets, now
being lashed with the others. Her mind had already
begun planning the rituals she would need for the two she
might be able to work with. Though Jevan had said no
more than a handful of words to her since she met him,
she felt her impotence to help him deeply.

Jenny brought her pieces of roasted fish, and root-
tubers, all of which she gulped down without tasting.

"What's wrong?" Jenny asked while handing Rifkind
handfuls of herbs from their baskets.

"Jevan."

"He doesn't look as badly hurt as the others. Is it something deep within him?"

"No, or yes. I can't see anything. He's like Ejord—un-
reachable by ritual magick."

Rifkind had become so accustomed to confiding in Jenny that she did not recall that no one other than she and
Ejord knew of his hitherto unique abilities. An array of
emotions swept across Jenny's face until her features settled in an uncharacteristic dullness. Rifkind realized that
she had started something within the other woman's
mind that would have far-reaching effects. Her concepts
of friendship and loyalty were advanced enough to feel an

obligation to pursue the effects of her gaffe; at that exact moment, however the water and herb mixture boiled up noisily and friendship was a distant second to the duties the Bright One had set before her.

"May I help you during the healing?" Jenny asked, and Rifkind noticed that her eyes were wide with hope and excitement.

"Get me more water."

Jenny moved away quickly, but not before Rifkind saw the disappointment in her face.

I'm not ready for another pupil, she thought to herself. She remembered her disastrous experiences with Linette, who now, if rumor was correct, shared Lord Humphry's bed. I have too many conflicts within myself. It is barely a year since the Goddess had turned her face from me and I could not heal at all. Jenny would make a fine healer, if Muroa were here to teach her. Can't she see that I have enough trouble guiding myself on the proper paths, without undertaking showing someone else the way?

The essences of the boiling herbs scalded her nostrils as she bent low over the steam. The aroma triggered the dormant knowledge of the ritual language of the Old Ones within her. For a brief moment she heard the harsh, unfamiliar sounds as they issued from her mouth, then they were comprehensible and the Quais who gathered around her in curiosity spoke gibberish. She gestured to drive them back from the injured. Glowing streams of life-energy circled the two injured who were open to her healing powers. Jevan lay enclosed by a translucent glow that hid his features and gave no map of his injuries.

The blue stain under the woman's skin showed as a sickly turquoise that grew in rhythm with her pounding heart. Rifkind rested her hand on the woman's chest and slowed her heart until the stain's growth was stilled. Her fingers moved through the life-force cloud above the stain, learning that it was the woman's own weight and movement as she fell which had done the damage. With her fingertips Rifkind probed the extent of the rampant pressures and damage, then slowly worked her way beneath the turquoise smear.

It lifted with an oozing sound. Even through the excitement of the ritual Rifkind could hear gasps and retching from those who watched. Steamed herbs exchanged with the stain, replacing death-lust with life. The turquoise contracted in the air above her fingers and was gone. Rifkind drew lines in the air to guide the woman's life-force back to the afflicted area. She removed the exhausted herbs and laid them in a soggy heap near the fire.

Ravages of illness or personal accident could be removed with the sensitive fingers of a healer. Violence was often more stubborn, and the violence of foreign matter left within the body the most intractable of all. She turned to the seriously injured man without much hope of similarly spectacular success. She laid more herbs on the injured man's temples and neck to relax the pain-contracted muscles and pulled the ruined teeth from his mouth as she closed his cuts and lifted out his many bruises. It was all palliative corrections, but necessary before beginning the major task of removing the raft-pole fragments. He should have been dead long before she attended to him, and might be soon. Healers were far from infallible and could not keep a man from his final, appointed death.

Rifkind returned to her brazier and filled it again with water. She willed Jenny to watch it until it boiled and then to bring it to her. Images of Rifkind's desire boomed into Jenny's head, and she did as the healer wished, though the words she had actually heard sounded like curses.

The water would fill the life-force channels in the

ritual-transformation, if she could remove the splinters and fibers of the pole and leach out the rampant pestilence which had spread throughout the man's body. Such pestilence was the inevitable result of a neglected injury.

Her fingers wove through the air above the wound, learning its nature until she could hear its name. Any injury so violent in nature would have its own ritualized name and be subject to calling. His body writhed as the wood shifted in response to her summons, but the fragments would not come free. Rifkind lifted her hands before more damage was done. Withdrawing a long knife from a hip-sheath she repeated the process, holding the knife lengthwise between her palms. The splinters moved more freely but still they twisted and tore. The man would surely die if they were so rudely ripped from him.

She drew blood from her own wrist and coated the edges of the knife with it. The knife shone with her essence. Again she called the names, only this time the knife was not a magnet to draw the injury out. Her own life-forces streamed down from the knife, hissing as they chased after the splinters and fragments. A darker stream then arose from the wound and congealed on the knife before Rifkind placed it next to the pile of wet leaves.

Careful not to spill a drop despite the ruddy heat of the metal, Jenny set the brazier down beside Rifkind, who dripped fingerful upon fingerful into the cavity, completing and mending the life-force channels where she could and laying her hands on the half-hidden organs until they vibrated in proper rhythm again. The life-force flowed sluggishly within him and pockets of virulence remained beyond her reach, but there was nothing more she could do for him until his body adapted to the healings she had already performed.

Feeling more fatigued than she could remember,

Rifkind turned to Jevan. Her own determination demanded that she at least attempt a healing. Ejord and Jevan were mortal, and all mortals needed and responded to healing. They bled and grew, even if some difference in them concealed their essential structure from the Bright Moon's priestess.

The silvery home of the Bright One had risen, although it was still obscured by the more brilliant sun. Rifkind instinctively located her Goddess and placed herself so that Jevan's body lay between them. Still, nothing became clear within the translucence. Sighing, she took the now-cooling water from the brazier and patted it blindly on his skin, hoping that the body beneath her hands could absorb it.

She sat back on her heels, the glow before her faded, replaced by Jevan's sleeping form. Rifkind's hands shook so that she could barely pick up the knife to clean it or commend the spent herbs to the dying fire. She checked each patient again. Though Muroa's teachings had mainly been arcane and ritual medicine, Rifkind had learned common-sense care as well from the old woman. She arranged them into the most comfortable positions for their wounds, coating those exposed portions of their bodies with loose cloth and setting small, smoking pots of insect repellent beside each of them. Neither the Quais nor Jenny could tell that she had completed the ritual part of her healing.

Jevan opened his eyes when she lit the pot of repellent next to him.

"We found you?" he asked, clear-minded enough to recognize her.

"I could not refuse your offer," she said simply, laying her hands on his eyes to bring sleep to them again.

"Will they be all right?"

"How did you heal them?"

"Why did Affa cry out so when you touched her?"
Questions sprang from everyone.

"I don't know, I hope everyone will recover. Only time will show. I will have to help some of them again, but now I must rest. Jenny will know if I should be awakened."

She didn't remember finding the baskets, or putting the brazier away, nor the somewhat cold fish fillet she gulped down without tasting or chewing. The hard lumpy surface of the raft beneath the rush mats was real for a brief second, then there was only blessed rest and sleep.

CHAPTER 5

"It is good to smell the salt-marshes again after so many months in the interior," Jevan exclaimed, standing up from a breakfast of day-old fish.

Rifkind remained quiet. The Quais were insistent that the salt-marshes could be smelled in the air of the mild breeze that had sprung up after three days of humid doldrums. To her the air simply, and overwhelmingly, smelled of swamp; salt, bracken or fresh water were moot distinctions.

She was appreciative, however, of Jevan's evident health. He was an attractive, lively man, tall and well-built. His smile was disarming, but while he was friendly, he also knew how to keep his distance from others, a trait not common on the easy-going crowded rafts. His eyes were as black as Rifkind's, but his features carried the regular Darian stamp rather than the exotic structure of the Asheerans. Like the others on the raft, his dark hair showed reddish highlights from the sun and salt. He had been up and about for over a day and complained of nothing more serious than a stiffness in his neck and shoulders. The woman, Affa, had joined them for breakfast, rising from the mats after three days of rest. Only a faint discoloration under her mahogany skin gave indications of her brush with death.

"We hit salt water before sundown. We had best fill what few casks that dog left us!" Drocour, of the sharp features and perpetual sneer, had already begun filling the small hardwood casks by tossing them over the side on leader-lines.

He gave Rifkind wide berth on the raftlets, and stopped just short of insubordination in expressing his displeasure over their Hold-bound course. His brother was Drogan, who still lay fevered and motionless on the mats where Rifkind had found him.

Three times in as many days Rifkind had pushed herself to her limits and beyond to save that young man. She openly doubted he would survive to need a fourth immersion in the arcane. The Quais were filled with awe at her healings of Jevan and Affa, and claimed they would harbor no ill-will even if Drogan died. Even Drocour professed to share this uniform sentiment—but Rifkind sensed a confused defensiveness in the man which she did not want to disturb.

"We'll get all the fresh water we need at the Hold," Jevan responded to Drocour's outburst.

"And no trapping at all!"

"No more arguments!"

Elyssa's sharp tongue silenced the resentful Drocour. She had been the one to permit Rifkind and Jenny to approach the raft. Only Jevan's infrequently expressed opinions outweighed hers. Elyssa seemed to possess far more common-sense and initiative than the others, male and female alike, and kept the raft moving and the Quais eating. While Quais women as a whole were ignored, exceptional individuals such as Elyssa commanded a certain grudging respect from the men.

"Is it true, though, what he says about the trapping? You have all taught Jenny and me well these past few days. We could head out on our own with directions, if delivering us to the Hold will take you far from your usual sources of food." Rifkind was aware of the hardship; Chandro had not been generous.

"Pay Drocour no mind. He would complain if we were still with Chandro! So long as Drogan's alive we'd be headed for the Hold anyway," Elyssa explained.

"Many's the time Old Pig-Belly threw someone over to get out of the trip to the Hold," Affa interrupted. "The rafts that follow tradition are few in number, and seldom range far from the Hold."

"Will we be trespassing on their territory?" Rifkind remembered the blood feuds in the Asheera.

"We Quais have no territory at all. Unless we each own the entire Felmargue. It is forbidden: we may not own things, nor hold grudges," Jevan explained.

"Not even if we meet with Chandro?" Rifkind inquired.

"Well," he hesitated, "we will not set foot on the old rafts—and even Chandro would not interfere with us now. The parting was not as violent as some I've heard told of back in Belfelis. The raft was crowded. We could not have enlarged it again and still passed into the hunting marshes. It was inevitable." Jevan was not very much bothered by the memory of the brawl.

"Then why didn't you simply leave earlier and save yourselves this?" Jenny asked, gesturing towards Drogan.

"Because until that night I was certain it would be Chandro and his pack who'd be set off half-provisioned!" Jevan's laughter turned the grim statement into a joke.

Rifkind left the group to attend Drogan. Except for some time spent fishing, she stayed with the injured man. He would not be the first who had died while under her care, but she viewed his impending death as a special failure because of her promise to Elyssa.

"He'll go soon," Drocour said, kneeling beside her.

She had not seen nor heard him approach.

"There's still hope," she replied automatically, not believing it herself.

"Once we reach the salt the Felmargue goes tidal. Once he feels the mud rise up under the raft he'll find his time. They always do, especially the ones like him who were born over the salt."

"Perhaps he'll survive until we get him to the Hold. Your legends speak of a descendant of the old sorcerors who still helps the injured and dying."

"I don't know. There might not be a Descendant anymore. We leave him men and supplies. They disappear, that's for sure: both the people and the supplies. I've never heard tell of someone who's actually returned to the rafts after being left on the Hold though. Oh, there're plenty of stories: 'The raft we passed last se'ennight passed a raft where someone said a distant cousin was on a raft where someone had returned . . . ' It's all the same."

It was the most Drocour had said in three days, and in all the time on Chandro's raft as well. His tone, though flat, was not particularly hostile, nor did Rifkind feel as uncomfortable as she usually did in his presence. Hopefully the salt-water had settled his own acceptance of his brother's fate.

"Then the Hold itself, is that legend or fact?" she asked.

"Both. Climb the ropes to the top of the Hold and you can see the ruins of something. Even I've seen that. There's birds and the like, plus some things that make the Ornaq seem tame, but never any sign of our injured, and no sign of the Descendant. Maybe he was there once, but died. It's been a long time since the Felmargue dropped."

"Isn't that just another legend?"

Drocour looked around them, then pointed to a grey

spire sticking out of the calm water at some distance from
the raft. Rifkind recognized it as one of the infrequent
fixed obects that Jevan sometimes used as channel
markers to set their course now that they were no longer
in the tangled interior swamp.

"Not a legend—that's the proof. Maybe a temple once,
or a castle. The water and mud have destroyed almost
everything now. The Felmargue was once a rich land like
Lowenrat to the east. Our parents many times removed
were free farmers, not wanderers like us. They lived in
peace and comfort with dry homes. The magicians stayed
in the Hold and didn't bother them.

"Then the magicians got arrogant. They challenged the
gods themselves. But it was the farmers, our Fathers, who
suffered. The magicians stayed in their fortress and the
gods couldn't do anything against them. The farmland
was pounded down until the sea rushed in. What the
Hold is, all the Felmargue used to be, and now we live like
animals.

"The Quais were forced out of their homes and flooded
farms. Metals lost their virtue, became rust in their hands.
So they built rafts and started living the way we do now.
They started the legend of the Leveller as a revenge to the
magicians who did this to them, I think. The Leveller—
that's the best of our stories. In their time the gods will see
that the sufferings of the Quais have cleansed them of
their sins and will call forth the Leveller to their midst to
remove the marks of their suffering. The Leveller shall not
be like other men, but the land will tremble and be restored, and between Hold and Fel there shall be no more
line."

Though she had more questions about the tales
Drocour told in language so unlike the normal Quais conversation that they seemed recited she held her silence

while Drocour glared into the distance and strode away from her.

Every part of Dro Daria had its legends dating back to the times of the Old One and the Lost Gods. Glascardy possessed Hanju, the somewhat maddened relic of those days and those gods. But the Felmargue stories were from a more recent time. The gods they described were those still worshipped in Dro Daria. The grey stone markers might well be the remains of a drowned society.

Jenny, Affa, Elyssa and pregnant Celical dangled hinged toggles of wood and twine off the side of the raft. When the previous day's quest for fish had gone well, as it had, they snagged bits of ripe fish through the toggles; otherwise they stabbed insects and worms and used the wriggling creatures as bait. It was a job requiring infinite patience and, Rifkind admitted, skill. She could see the shadow of a big fish as she tossed her own line into the water, but the hoped-for meal ignored her line as if it weren't there.

The Quais explained that the best eyes could not see accurately underwater and that she must wait until she felt the hard tug on the baited line before snapping it taut. Finally the fish mouthed a freshly caught caterpillar. She held her breath and snapped the line.

Strike!

The toggle did not kill the fish, making it necessary to haul the enraged, flapping thing through the water without letting it free until someone could snare it. If getting the fish to react to the bait-covered toggle was difficult, landing the fish was not noticeably easier. But Affa leaned far out over the water and the struggling prize was brought on deck.

Rifkind's reflexes were far better than average and

made up for her lack of skill and patience with the chore. She would have preferred using her bow on the huge flocks of ducks that now wheeled overhead, but the men were too openly envious of her curved bow and some of those arrows were tipped with stone and therefore not affected by the taboos. Even the affable Jevan had gone so far as to assert that he, as raft-leader, should take care of the bow.

After he had lost three chipped-stone arrows for her, and complained that the bow was obviously defective, she had put three arrows into as many birds, conducting her demonstration in silence and not admitting that she had never before done so well. Turin now guarded the archery equipment and the rest of their belongings.

The morning's breeze died early after steel-grey clouds rolled in, warning everyone on the raft that there would be a storm before day's end. Salt-water or not, the face of the swamp was changing. The heavy moss-hung trees so typical of the interior swamp were far fewer now. The floating islands were giving way to great stands of yellow-green grass crisscrossed by waist-deep avenues of clear water. The bottom was hard beneath a thin coating of silt.

Low rumbles of thunder could be heard in the distance. The breeze picked up and became a strong wind. Rifkind hacked a handful of the grass with her knife as they brushed by it, cutting her palm slightly on the serrated edges.

Dry as Asheeran bones, she thought. She bent the grass blades quickly and heard them snap. A wind-driven storm, if there's not enough rain to go with the lightning, could ride across this swamp as easily as it rides across the Asheera.

Drogan's fever was rising. Beads of sweat bulged out on his forehead. He had not been lucid since the brawl, but now with the leaden air pressing around them, he moaned half-intelligible words. Rifkind wet a bit of cloth and wiped his face. She touched her wet hands to her tongue—salt water. Drocour was proving right about his brother's time.

"It will not be long for Drogan. There is nothing more I can do for him," she informed Drocour. "He is speaking now, probably nonsense, but you might wish to be with him at the last."

Drocour nodded and left. Rifkind sat down heavily in his place.

Jevan spoke: "You did all you could, no one doubts that. We Quais don't expect miracles. There's no need for you to take this on yourself."

"I gave my word when we boarded this raft that I would save your wounded. I have failed," she replied, still caught in the depression of the failed healing and the warm humid wind.

"You have done your best. We have no knowledge of these things. Without you the three of us would have died —as it is, two of us live, and I am one of them." He laughed, as he always did when nervous.

"The storm will break soon. If we don't have a shelter for Drogan, I'm certain the storm will kill him."

Jevan shrugged. "That may be. You will be busy elsewhere, then. The rain will rile the swamp. The small ones will seek our raft for shelter, the large ones seek the small ones as food. Sometimes they find us instead." His nervous laughter erupted again.

"Does this mean we have entered the waters of another Ornaq?"

"An Ornaq in the tidal waters?" He shook his head, grinning at the thought.

Rifkind tensed. Laughter or disdain directed at her ignorance always infuriated her. To his credit, Jevan sensed her change in mood and sobered instantly.

"I know you would rather stay with Drogan, but it is a real danger—mire-dragons. Ugly cold-blooded beasts with short tempers and big stomachs. We will need your sword."

Aye, you'll need my sword, she thought bitterly, smiling all the while. It is a greater weapon than the snares and clubs you use, you can see that despite your taboos. You Quais are quarrelsome, not fierce. You prefer snarling to fighting. And beasts like the Ornaq or the mire-dragon follow you, waiting for your mistakes. Jenny has learned more about fighting and battle in the months she's been with me than you've learned in all your generations. And yet you dare sneer at someone not intimate with your foul swamp.

Yet, Rifkind liked Jevan and the other Quais. She would defend them. She removed her sword from its scabbard and began rubbing a fine coating of oil along its surface —a practice she'd begun after her first encounter with the effects of water on steel.

"Are you expecting trouble?" Jenny asked, watching her.

"Jevan tells me to expect mire-dragons during or after the storm. I worry more about the storm itself, with these dry grasses around us, but it would be unwise to ignore a direct warning."

"Will my knife be useful?" Jenny asked, carefully withdrawing the shining blade from her belt-sheath.

"To protect yourself, perhaps. But I'm hoping these mire-dragons will retreat from an aggressive stance; the Quais have never been more than nuisances to the meat-eaters of the Felmargue. That Ornaq, for example, never expected to be hurt while preying on a raft."

She handed the oil cloth to Jenny who proudly used it on the already blemish-free knife. A few huge, almost explosive, raindrops fell; the storm had arrived. The

Quais, typically, had never quite gotten around to erecting the shelters.

Gusts of winds blew embers from the fire, but they were quickly quenched by the raindrops. Drocour remained by his brother while the others rushed around lashing the lighter baskets to the raftlets. Rifkind tried to set up some sort of covering for the dying man, but retreated before Drocour's icy stare.

The swamp was quiet except for the advancing sheets of rain. While the others looked for shelter, of which there was none, Rifkind leaned against one of the tall baskets, sword sheathed across her lap, patiently awaiting whatever danger might come. She flinched as the first bolts of lightning sizzled into the matted vegetation around them. She went to Turin, pressing her palms against his shoulder until he lay down. The Quais rightly feared the shelter of the few isolated trees, but in the raft's openness Rifkind suspected that Turin's horns would bring lightning too.

When the rain had soaked everyone to equal discomfort without giving any sign of abating, a change overtook the Quais. Celical was the first to shed her clothing and stand naked in the rain. The others hesitated, smiling and giggling, then they too shed their clothes. The rain made tracks through the caked oil, dirt and sweat on their skins. For all the water of the Felmargue the raft-dwellers were very infrequent bathers. Their washings, such as they were, came only in the long rainstorms.

They splashed each other, enjoying the rain like overgrown affectionate children until prolonged close contact made it apparent they were not. Drocour gave no thought to his dying brother, unprotected in the rain, when he grabbed the willing Affa and wrestled her to the rain-slicked mats.

Jenny, in the properly demure attire of a mountain-bred lady on a difficult journey, crouched miserably

beside Turin, her face blushingly averted from the im-
promptu orgy. The high-necked, long-sleeved gown with
its apron and tightly drawn laces clung heavily to her
arms, legs, hips and breasts. Jevan tried to lure her into
their fun, was spectacularly unsuccessful and sat, just out
of her reach, watching the red-haired woman with rapt
concentration.

Rifkind chuckled under her breath. The setting was
new, the rituals unfamiliar, but the magic was the same
whether in the Asheera, Glascardy or the Felmargue.
Jevan was smitten, and though Jenny's heritage forbade
that she so much as glance over her shoulder at the naked
man, her interest had plainly been aroused. Rifkind suspected it might be in part due to the similarities between
Jevan and Ejord.

An arhythmic splash in the water drew Rifkind's attention away from the motionless not-quite-pair and the other, more active couples and trios. No mire-dragons appeared in their wake but, reminded, she watched more
closely in consideration of the obvious incapacity of her
companions. Before the storm Jevan had made regular
checks against the angle of the sun and the occasional
grey or green stone markers. During the storm he was
apparently content to let the raft drift as it would.

There's nothing he could do anyway, she observed to
herself as the raft spun once again, now headed backwards (insofar as the narrower end of the motley collection usually preceded the rest) down a channel surrounded by man-high saw-grass. Perhaps it makes as
much sense as anything else to spend his time flirting
with Jenny. She is more flattered by it than she dares admit, though I don't think Jevan would know from the way
she's cowering there next to Turin.

Lightning struck painfully close to the raft, ending the
games of the Quais. The concussive noise battered them

to a motionless silence. Rifkind reached inside a basket
for a piece of cloth to bind over her ears. The now-driving
rain obliterated the wakes, but it was unlikely anything
under the water would rise to its surface until the storm
had passed. Still, she kept her watch, as none of the others
did.

The storm passed. Insects rose from the brush, and the
birds after them. Fish broached the water in the distance
and a V-shaped wake cut across in front of the raft. A
greenish-brown snout lifted up, rows of ivory-brown teeth
visible within it, then teeth and snout sank below the surface.

It's deeper here than I thought, she noted. She stabbed
a nearby pole into the rain-roiled waters. But I've seen the
mire-dragons now. I know what to watch for.

If anyone else on the raft had seen the mire-dragon,
they concealed the knowledge better than Rifkind did.
The Quais were busy collecting the rainwater that had
fallen haphazardly into basket-lids and mat-gulleys. Only
Affa had thought to set out the cisterns themselves.
Rifkind watched and shook her head in silence.

"I think he's dead now," Jenny said as she approached.
"Drowned, no doubt."

She left her perch and approached the body. Drocour
and Jenny followed close behind her. Drogan's skin was
cooled and stiffened by the rainwater. Small puddles lay
over his open eyes and mouth, but he hadn't drowned.
The temperature shock from the wind and rain had killed
him.

Rifkind closed his eyes, but did not know what else to
do. Her own people buried their dead far from the wells.
Throughout much of Dro Daria similar customs were observed, although those of great honor must be interred
above ground in stone sepulchers. But, having seen the
Quais manner of caring for their sick, Rifkind doubted

they had honorable burial customs. The power of the Goddess had entered the dead man. She had allowed Her priestess to use Her name in an attempt to save the man. She would be displeased if the dead man were disposed of impiously.

Yet, it was not right to interfere with them, or to impose new customs upon them. The Asheeran cult of the Bright One never proselytized. The captives and slaves buried their own dead—there had never been a problem. Mortals nursed their sick and honored their dead, or so the old healers and priestesses had taught. It was not the place of a free-roaming healer to establish customs in a land far from that of her birth.

The Quais stripped the body of their brother and comrade then rolled him into the water without even the most minor of propitiary prayers while Rifkind watched outraged. Drocour wound his soggy hair around a polished horn ornament, his brother's most prized possession, and life on the raft proceeded without noticeable interruption.

Only Celical, who probably carried the dead man's child in her bulging abdomen, waited at the back of the raft as it passed over the body. Rifkind joined her in silence.

Be gentle with them, Mother, she prayed silently. They are innocent of Your ways and the ways of all gods.

They waited for the V-shaped wakes to appear.

CHAPTER 6

Rifkind's thoughts rose towards the Bright One, whose strength had entered Drogan's body and whose silvery image was now visible in the heavens: *The sinking of the land of their fathers has left them without any proper sense of place or reverence. They need help not punishment. They need someone much stronger, more dedicated and kind than I.*

The water was opaque brown from the rain runoff. They had passed over Drogan's body, she was certain of that, though there was no sign of it in the channel behind them. Except . . . except for the two hard black dots just breaking the surface and the V-shaped water-wake behind them.

The blood-red palate and its rings of teeth lifted for a short moment then dove beneath the surface in a flurry of lashing tail and short, clawed feet. Despite the muddy water a blood-stain spread. A gouged thigh broke the surface. Rifkind closed her eyes and fought down an unfamiliar wave of nausea. She had no entreaties left to put before the Bright One.

Bellowings echoed around the raft. The mire-dragons

were alerted by the fast passage of the blood through the water. More of the hideous beasts could be heard splashing into channels hidden by the stands of sawgrass. Rifkind opened her eyes to see the grass to one side of the raft wave and snap as the behemoth lumbered toward the carnage, stopping briefly to investigate the Quais craft.

Such creatures could not be subject to Her call, she thought, gazing at the body carapaces, long, toothrimmed snouts and spiked tails. She would not touch the minds of such creatures as these—they must be left over from the curse the gods laid upon the land to punish it. But, isn't the Bright One a goddess—one who might have joined with the others to quash the arrogance of the magicians Drocour spoke of?

The mire-dragon's belly hit the water with a resounding smack as it moved to join the others of its kind. Rifkind returned quickly to her own raft to unsheath the oiled sword.

"They're horrible. As horrible as the Ornaq!" Jenny said, moving to Rifkind's side for protection.

"And we've attracted them by heaving Drogan over the side like that. We've brought our doom upon us ourselves this time. I should have stopped them. They'll follow the raft, Drogan will not satisfy them."

"The Quais are little more than animals themselves! You saw them!" Jenny exclaimed, disturbed by Rifkind's willingness to blame herself.

"But I healed them. I brought Her presence to this raft, then I let them dishonor it, though I knew they knew no better."

Rifkind held the sword poised for attack, but in her heart she expected nothing short of disaster when she struck at the mire-dragons. She would fight to protect herself, Jenny and the innocent Quais, the same as she

had done against the Ornaq, but this time there would be
no beneficent Goddess watching, ready to offer aid.

Jevan and the others readily stepped aside to let Rifkind
stand at the back of the raft. Celical stared at her with a
dark, unreadable, gaze. Rifkind felt her grip on the sword
weaken as her palms sweated as they had never done
before.

Without wavering, or backward glance, Celical stepped
calmly off the raft. She staggered, losing her balance to the
uneven ooze of the channel, righted herself and began a
slow steady walk toward the feeding mire-dragons.

"Celical!" Rifkind shouted after her.

She turned to lay down the sword; Jenny caught her
arm.

"Let them go!" the red-haired woman demanded, using her greater height and weight to keep Rifkind from
following the doomed girl.

"Abomination!" Rifkind snarled, twisting suddenly to
throw Jenny off balance.

Jenny fell hard to one knee, her face mirroring the sudden pain she felt. The collection of rafts rocked back and
forth from the force of her collapse—but she kept her grip
on Rifkind's arm.

"I must go!"

"They don't deserve you!" Jenny cried through her
tears. "Let them make their own sacrifices!"

"No."

"I need you more! You'll do her no good! Don't leave
me here alone!"

Self-revulsion stifled Rifkind's words, but she relaxed
and no longer fought Jenny's weight nor strove to follow
Celical. It was too late, anyway. The Quais-woman was
lost in the tangle of mire-dragons and the spreading
blood-stain. Clouds covered the sun and the Bright Moon.
As always, in her own mind Rifkind had failed the One to

whom her life was dedicated. Jenny let go of her arm, but remained crumpled over her knee, crying with quiet, wracked sobs. The Quais, who had watched Celical follow her lover to death and the confrontation with Jenny, turned back to each other as if nothing had happened.

"I've hurt you—I'm sorry. I shouldn't have." Rifkind laid a hand on Jenny's shoulder and helped her to her feet.

"And I . . . I said I'd never say that. I promised when we left Chatelgard that I'd never interfere with what you had to do."

"You did what you thought was right. Can you walk?"

"If I'm careful. Nothing's broken or torn."

They walked slowly along the sequence of rafts. Turin nickered with concern as they approached. In the blindness of her determination to atone for imagined offenses, Rifkind had forgotten him, too. Her mind had been closed to him while her turmoil had been at its greatest. He felt no sense of betrayal or abandonment, only immense, flooding concern for both of them.

Rifkind burrowed into their baskets until she found a small flask of fiery liqueur made from twice-distilled wine. After offering the flask to Jenny, who took a hearty swallow, she had some herself.

"I am ashamed. We should have done something, at least, to comfort Celical and keep her from joining him. We have forgotten how to do such things. I am a poor raft-leader." Jevan stood before them. Rifkind turned away.

"You will have to learn . . . it's too late to go back to Chandro, and he wasn't much better," Jenny said in a maternal, scolding tone. "You have to help each other. Drogan should not have been left out like that in the storm. Rifkind tried to tell you this, but you were too busy with yourselves to hear her.

"And when he died—there are things which should be

done if someone has shared your life with you. Perhaps it is true that you cannot bury your dead; the same is true of sailors, who wrap their fellows in shrouds and commit them to the water. Even when there is no priest to offer a final blessing the man's friends step forward with words of commendation for the spirit. It is proper to rejoice at a birth or wedding, but death is a time for grief and quiet thought. It might have been you who was left out there to die in the rain. Can you say you've finished everything that you've begun?"

"I've never thought about it," Jevan said after a long moment, and followed his statement with a weak laugh.

In the growing twilight Rifkind stood still and listened to Jenny say things she had once heard Muroa and the other healer-priestesses say at the annual Gatherings, but had never, herself, thought to say. Yet Jenny did not recite the creeds of the mountain cults of Glascardy, nor of Mohandru, the nominal Lord God of all the Empire's lands, nor was her teaching exactly that of the Bright One, though the silver disk was once again visible in the sky.

Contemplation was not the mark of Asheerans, nor of their worship. It was likely, Rifkind concluded, Jenny spoke from her own well-thought convictions and that same sense of certainty that marked both her half-brother Ejord and their father. Rifkind could heal, defend and intercede with the gods—but Jenny's soft words would change the Quais.

" . . . and do you expect the Leveller to pound the Hold down to your level or to raise you up out of this mud?"

Jenny regained Rifkind's close attention by mentioning the Leveller legends.

"I had not thought about that either." Jevan's voice had shrunk to a whisper and he made no pretense of laughing.

"But you're bringing the Leveller to the Hold. Don't you

think you should think about what you're doing?"

She's found the knot! Rifkind thought. I hear the up-turn in her voice. But she doesn't back away from her own victories. And the more surprising that she doesn't realize she has special power over him through his love.

If she knew that, she might hesitate to draw tight the knot and change him. No, change all of us. Perhaps she does know . . . certainly she is . . . changed.

Jevan shuffled off to the other Quais. The mood on the raft had changed and for the better—though too large a portion of it was, for the present at least, shame. Drogan and Celical were past sight and held only in memory. Rifkind could remember laying rough hands on Jenny, who was a far truer student than Linette had been, or even than she herself had been to Muroa.

And Jenny? Rifkind was no longer sure she knew the stubborn lady's maid of Chatelgard. To be sure she had risen in the eyes of that most un-subtle of observers, Turin. The war-horse no longer labelled her Fire-head-that-is-gentle, but simply *Rider:* one who deserves the loyalty, strength and protection of such as himself.

He felt her presence in his mind, answered her probing thoughts by displaying the identity-image of Jenny, then, of his own will, thrusting forward his image of Rifkind, who was not only Rider, but ever-right and ever-free.

Suddenly Rifkind was aware that Turin had changed too. A war-horse, but stallion of the herd, as well, his instinctive need to renew his blood for the Riders had been intensified by the sudden presence of a Rider who had none of Turin's kind to love and protect her. Soon he would strive to fulfill his need at any cost.

The Bright One had drawn a veil over Her face. The others on the raft were quiet or asleep. Rifkind was alone. Inspiration and desperation led her to open the baskets and remove the suede pouch which contained her crystal moon-stones. She brushed away imagined dirt from an island of moonlight on the reed-mats and drew invisible signs across it. The stones were no longer attuned to her, so long had they lain unused in the baskets and away from her tal. She warmed them with her breath then held them against her closed eyes until they captured and held the warmth.

I feel Your movements through us, Mother-of-us-all, Rifkind thought to the stones, using the most intimate name of the Goddess. The identity and name of Leveller hangs over me. I believe you mean for me to play a role here—though I've served you poorly in the past.

Let me help Jenny. Her thoughts are pure, for all that she does not look upon Your face. Give me your counsels that I may pass them on to her.

Rifkind cast the stones into the light. They did not fall into one of the four hundred described patterns or their innumerable variants. It was unthinkable. Muroa had taught her all the patterns of the stones, that she might recognize and interpret the wisdom of the Bright One. Perturbed, and fearful, Rifkind released her tal from her body. It settled within the incomprehensible pattern on the damp rushes.

The crystals broke the world into colors she had never seen before, and a brightness that seemed impossible within the gentle reflected light of the Bright Moon. She extended herself to find reference and stability.

The past. Magicians and scholars pursued their craft, unmindful of the responsibility they bore to the life around them. They moved over the verdant land imprisoning its power. Their cloistered school atop the Hold was strong enough to challenge the living gods of Dro Daria: the pantheon.

She saw the gods—but with their attributes so veiled

that she could not tell which of them met the challenge nor who cast the mortifying blows against the land.

The Felmargue. Not merely a cauldron for life, but an anvil of punishment where the gods had spent their fury on a people largely ignorant of the arrogant rituals performed in their name. They came forward from the past and huddled beside her on the raft and in widely scattered dots throughout the expanse of this cursed, sunken land. Chandro and his people somewhere among them, as blindly punished as the rest.

The Leveller: a promise—or a curse? A giant figure veiled as the gods had been, striding across the swamp trailing a destruction not even the gods at their strongest had achieved. The strider brought a conflagration to the center of the Felmargue, where the Well of Knowledge and the Black Flame burned with such intensity that Rifkind could no longer tell what was bright or dark and drew her tal back to resist the fathomless lure of its depths.

The Hold: a serene plateau at the center of the Felmargue. A pure golden light was captured by the crystals and drawn to her. The Descendant, still innocent for all his years and all that he had been taught by the long-departed sorcerors of the school. A warmth grew within her as Rifkind felt the personality within the golden light.

He is a man both very young and very old. His spirit is complex and ever-changing, but gentle. She drew back and felt unfamiliar emotions stirring within her. Without having seen him or heard his name a longing had opened within her. *I could love him.* The thought was reassuring, not anxious or uncomfortable. He has pieces of me within him that I had never thought to find. Had I felt this way about Ejord? No, but then . . .

Her thoughts rose upward to the Bright One. The face

that was like no other face was smiling. Rifkind let the
golden light of the Descendant surround her again. But
before she could relax in its warmth a stealthy greenness
settled down between them, alien and malevolent. The
invader sought to bind her, to draw them both into some
blackness as evil as the one at the center of An-Soren's
ruby. Rifkind was older now, more powerful if not wiser.
She could not be captured once she had set her mind
against it. The otherness withdrew defeated, but the
golden one had been frightened. She found his name and
whispered it.

"Domhnall."

He resisted, but curiosity was stronger and he moved
toward her.

"Domhnall."

He approached, called by ethereal winds weaving with
his name. Rifkind felt his growing warmth and excitement. The same feeling swelled within her. She rose up to
greet the golden one, Domhnall. The warmth was broken,
exploded by the malevolence of the one Rifkind had
thought defeated. Domhnall fled back to the Hold where
Rifkind felt him turn in upon himself and disappear.

Rifkind was a healer and priestess of a gentle goddess
sworn to the service of life. But though her spirit sought
perfection in the service of the Goddess, she had been
forged a fighter and survivor long before the Bright One
had set Her mark in the bones of Rifkind's face. The
fighter surged forward and not even the perfection of the
crystals could contain it. Rifkind's tal separated from the
crystals as pure ice and fury.

Who endangers Domhnall? Who challenges me?

She pounced on the lingering anger and drew a name
from it before it could lie or withdraw. She moved
through the ethereal plane, in her mind envisioning the
ger-cat, lone predator of the steppes looking for one who

had dared approached its freshly blooded kill. This intruder, this cold green one, had hurt Domhnall. The ether responded to her emotions and projected the ger-cat's snarl far beyond the ends of the Felmargue. The anger's source was distant, beyond the swamps, but not so far from her as An-Soren had been when he'd first found her in the Death-wastes—when she had been as innocent as Domhnall, quivering in shock within the Hold, was now, Rifkind created a void in front of her and charged it with the quest of the intruder's true name. The void was gone, and in its place: Krowlowja.

You. Krowlowja. Face me!

The face grew, unwillingly and distorted. A woman's face, older and experienced, but dumbfounded by the strength of Rifkind where she had expected only Domhnall, Descendant and Keeper of the Black Flame. Rifkind called again and saw the entire figure, garbed as a priestess of the Baleric Oracle, whose prestige had never been sullied and whose home was far from both the Felmargue and the point where the void had found her name. So Rifkind called a third time and saw not a steam-filled grotto of the oracle, but a campfire before a military tent, and there, at the fringes of the vision, a face she had never expected to see on this journey—Lord, now Emperor, Humphry.

While Rifkind was lost in amazement, Krowlowja wrested herself from Rifkind's grip. Clearly this seeress had powers not common within an oracular order; if she described her visions, Humphry would recognize Rifkind at once.

Crosscurrents of thought fought for dominance in her mind as she gathered up the stones and centered herself within her body. Lord Humphry with a seeress of aroused power in a military camp outside the Felmargue. Domhnall, of the Black Flame, who had filled her with a warm excitement missing in her friendship with Ejord. Krowlowja's distorted fury at the disrupting influence of some unsuspected rival. And, running under them all, unseen, unvoiced, barely thought, the Leveller, striding across the lives and land of the Felmargue.

CHAPTER 7

"It's falling!"

"Watch below!"

"Damn ropes!"

The three Quais men shouted a warning to the others on the rafts that the system of pulleys and ropes was giving way, again. It was the third and last attempt of this their first day at the base. The Hold's green-glass sides rose more than four times again the height of the men who sought to scale them.

By tradition, each party left its scaling ropes in place for the next, but the corrosive salt breezes of the tidal Felmargue made short work of this technique.

Rifkind ducked, covering her head and catching an arm-length piece of the heavy, twisted reed-fiber rope as it struck her. Other pieces scattered over the raft and nearby water. In the distance a sluggish mire-dragon gave a warning snort at the disturbance of his afternoon sleep.

"Another waste of effort," Jevan said, approaching Rifkind and tossing the piece of rope she had been holding far into the saw-grass.

"Is it unusual for so many to be rotted through like this?"

"So many? Only three. There are landings like this all around the Hold. We'll find others."

"But what if they're all rotted through?"

Jevan stooped to examine the coils of rope they had all labored on in the days since the deaths of Drogan and Celical. All of them, Rifkind included, still had cuts and blisters on their hands from flexing and twisting the saw-grass to separate the internal fibers.

"All of them? Then I do not know what we would do. There are ways—I do know that. In our Father's time it was done otherwise. I do not know these other ways, however. It will be difficult if we must learn them."

"If you don't already know them," Rifkind snarled, "learning them will be more than difficult."

The constant warm winds had done nothing pleasant to anyone's disposition.

"It will take time, that is what will be difficult."

"We haven't seen another raft since Chandro set us adrift—will you have us wait until we *do?*"

"Let us hope we find good ropes tomorrow."

He forced a jovial smile, as if hope could be the solution to their problems. Then he walked away, leaving Rifkind to stare blankly after him.

They know, she thought, absently stroking Turin. *It's like it was with the mire-dragons: they were dumb-helpless until Jenny started asking if there wasn't something we could do to defend ourselves. They said "no" and smiled just like that until Chakri stood up and said he "remembered" that mire-dragons feared fire. Chakri of all people, the youngest one of the lot of them. He even "knew" how to bind the grasses together and where to look for natural pitch to make torches. These people cannot be as ignorant as they claim to be . . . yet why live in* fear the way they do, if Chakri always knows?

Rifkind was forced to believe that the Quais had knowledge squirreled away among them which could have brought their lives closer to the level of their forefathers. The Asheerans, had they known an easier way to get water, would not have clung to their meager wells. Turin's ears flicked at her as she pondered patterns too convoluted to be meaningful to him. He thrust his muzzle against her arm to guide her thoughts to a more useful pattern, such as scratching behind his ears or the broad expanse of forehead between his horns. She obliged.

"It's beautiful, in its own way."

Rifkind turned to face Jenny, an expression of puzzlement on her face until she realized that Jenny spoke of the glassy cliffs.

"I feel a residue of violence in it still," Rifkind answered. "It's as if the gods, when they found that they could not lay hands on the magicians, burned away the land. I no longer doubt the old legends of this place."

"I'm just as glad I can't feel that. I try not to think about the 'why' of the Felmargue, or the Hold. It doesn't seem fair that the gods punished the land and the farmers like this. It was only the magicians who deserved punishment."

Rifkind laughed out loud at the thought of divine justice actually applying to the gods.

"The motives of the gods are best left hidden from us," she explained more soberly. "And, we've never heard the magicians' side of the story."

"If the gods expect us to obey their rules, they can obey the rules themselves."

The true spirit of the Overnmonts. Humphry probably felt the same once, Rifkind thought as she stepped aside so that Jenny could scratch Turin's ears. After a while Humphry had decided that if the gods did as they saw fit, then

he could too. The farmers and peasants get scorched all
the same. Still, I don't see Humphry, even at his worst,
getting all our quarreling gods together as they did for
this. The Well and Flame combination must be some utterly unnatural and ancient power.

"How will we get Turin up there?" she asked absently
as she scratched.

"I don't know," Rifkind answered, dumbfounded at her
neglect. "I haven't thought about it."

"Do you think these ropes are strong enough to lift
him?"

"Even if they were, I don't think he would tolerate it.
Turin's done a lot of things for me that he didn't think
very kindly of, but nothing like being hauled off his feet
and . . ." She stared up at the point where the original,
now rotten, rope had disappeared over the top edge of the
plateau. "I'm not sure we could get him over the top, even
if he would let us haul him up there."

Turin, who knew he was the subject of conversation,
demanded more of their intentions. He pushed at the
fringes of Rifkind's thoughts until he found the image of
himself, legs dangling, imposed against the glassy rocks
beside them. Shaking his head and snorting emphatically,
he pulled back from both of them.

"No, I don't think that he'll be at all agreeable to it,"
Rifkind said as she blanked the image from her mind and
tried to calm him.

"What will we do with him?"

Turin then raised his head and sent a piercing whistle across the saw-grass. Normally quiet, his sudden outburst caused all save Rifkind to stare at him in wonder.
His Rider, however, joined him in listening to the wind.
She could just make out a faint answering call.

"Does he understand what I've said?" Jenny asked.

"Not directly. He's seen me thinking about the problem, and that I have no acceptable answer. He seems to have his own solution."

"How is that?"

"Apparently there are horses on the Felmargue for him to run with. He was foaled seven summers ago. If I'd stayed in the Asheera, I would have been obligated to share him with the herds for at least one breeding season. At Chatelgard . . . it never seemed necessary, and he never demanded it."

There were a few grey hairs visible on the smooth muzzle that she had not noticed before, a slight hollowness around his eyes, a different carriage in his neck that had not been there when they had ridden through the steppes. A chill thought ran through her that she could not conceal from him. Turin was mortal in the way of war-horses. He would have been retired to run with the herds by now, if there had still been a clan and gathering for her. She would have trained the second war-horse of her adulthood and be awaiting the first colt of his siring.

Turin stamped and pawed at the raft for her attention. Her thoughts could affect him only momentarily. He had no empathy for his own death. He was Turin. He had a Rider who guided his strength and who was his god as much as the Bright Moon was hers. There were other things, at certain times of the year; he could remember that. But the beasts of the wet-lands of Dro Daria had not been of his kind. They held metal in their mouths and responded to his empathy no better than unweaned foals. The urges had not been strong then. The one who answered his call now was not quite the same as he, but metal was unknown to this one also. He called into the wind a second time.

"I'll let him go this time," Rifkind said more to herself than to Jenny.

"Will he come back? What if he's too far away to hear you when we leave here?"

"Then I would know that he was dead."

There was a coldness in her voice as she imagined the world without him beside her. Again she shut out the thought, but knew that when Turin left her it would leave a scar deeper than the massacre of her none-too-beloved clan had done. In time she would be alone, perhaps later rather than sooner, but inevitably she would be alone.

"Are you all right, Rifkind?"

"Umm. We should see to the torches—it's gathering night."

They left Turin as the answering call was again carried to the raft. It seemed to Rifkind that it was both louder and closer.

Torches were lit along the perimeter of the raft to discourage the night-chorus from venturing too close to the Quais. The mire-dragons had not yet added their percussive bellows to the sound, but the lesser predators began their wanderings as soon as the light was no longer direct. The challenged stallion's cry cut the air with an unfamiliar note in the chorus, but no one inquired after it, and Rifkind offered no explanation.

"You are right," Jevan explained to them once Rifkind had left Turin's side. "Three times we have tried to lift our ropes up to the Hold. We would do no better tomorrow. The storms that weakened these ropes would have done the same to all the landings near here. We would have to find the landing of Quais who came after the storm, but before us. That is not likely either.

"It will be difficult, but we will seek after the knowledge of our Fathers. Both Drocour and Chakri have tried on their own, and found no answer. Now we shall all try together."

He motioned Rifkind to a circle of the Quais. Jevan was

about to reveal the mysterious way in which the Quais acquired their fragmented knowledge. She had the sense not to ask him any questions and took the further precaution of purging all curiosity and skepticism from her mind as she took her place.

A fist-sized chunk of glassy-black rock sitting more-or-less at the center of the group seemed almost incidental to the gathering. No one watched it or made gestures to it. Though Rifkind had not seen its like before, she discounted it as the focus of their efforts until she was awash in a tingling sensation.

Bainbrose's stones! This is the same feeling I got on the palms of my hands when I handled his stones, but much stronger—now I feel it all over! That is a Black Flame-stone!

But having discerned its nature did not tell her how to use it. Bainbrose had said his own trinkets were old and worthless, and the stone in front of her, though much larger, seemed similarly inert: it did not glow from the effects of her concentration, nor rise from the mats, nor change in any other observable way. She waited, occupying her mind with other thoughts.

Muroa had taught her patience above all else. Nighttimes of sitting motionless in the light of the Bright One waiting for something to happen, often not knowing what she waited for, and more often thinking that the lesson was the waiting itself. Muroa was as surprised as she those times she did hear the Goddess's voice—perhaps even more surprised than her radiantly happy student had been.

—You were lucky, Ger-cat—

Muroa had always called Rifkind by her childhood name.

—Only lucky. Others must display patience and wisdom to see the things that were revealed to you. You move through the rituals like a man in a dust storm, yet you never get lost. That is luck.—

I keep my mind and eyes open, but often I'm blind. It is not my fault, Rifkind protested to the voice of her teacher in her head.

—Pah!—

The old woman, her steely grey hair tightly braided and wound around her head, had eyes as sharp and bright as ever despite the deep wrinkles in her brow and cheeks. She tilted her head quickly to one side, then the other: an Asheeran gesture of derision, wordlessly chiding her pupil for the additional stupidity of not knowing she was both lazy and lucky. Rifkind cringed from the displeasure until she realized she was shrinking back from an image of Muroa contained within the Black Flame-stone. The image flickered and disappeared the instant Rifkind thought of the Black Flame itself and returned only when she again thought of Muroa.

So this is how the Quais learn from their fathers and grandfathers!

—Of course. They have no priests, no healers, no rituals. They'd be animals but for the stones they brought with them.—

But was it not these self-same stones that brought them to this condition?

The image of the old woman smiled but would not answer.

Suddenly Rifkind understood: neither dead nor alive would Muroa know anything about the Quais, nor the Black Flame!

The old woman smiled again.

—The Quais ask only what their Fathers knew, nothing more. They can't imagine knowledge that their Father's did not possess. You, Rifkind, can imagine much more than they, so naturally I can as well . . .

The image smiled and winked. A measure of pride in her student glowed on her face. Rifkind had almost gotten around the restraints the Black Flame placed on her revelations.

Yes, whatever you are, wherever you are, you are the true Muroa. Not even the Bright One herself could conjure you so completely.

They nodded to each other. Rifkind let the image fade. She created a wall of reality between herself and the stone. She was curious about its power, and wise enough to know that she could bring forth answers to questions that were best left unasked. Bainbrose had, no doubt, imagined that his stones were worthless, and the stones had obliged him. The uses the magicians of the Hold had put the stones to were best left unimagined.

The annoying tingling was not noticeable while she was enrapt by the stone and could be held at bay now that she had a better understanding of why she felt it. Moving only her eyes she glanced at the others in the circle. The Quais gave indications of sharing an experience through the stone. It was unnerving to watch the five of them pantomiming similar, meaningless gestures. But, try as she might, she was unable to lock into their visions. Jenny, also, seemed to be having a distinct experience through the stone.

Jenny mouthed words Rifkind could not hear and cocked her head attentively when she was not "speaking." Rifkind contrived to match the movements of Jenny's lips with her own, but before this or other mimetic behavior accomplished anything, the Quais completed their revelations and deactivated the stone. Jenny sat bolt upright, a startled expression on her face.

"We have found the answer," Chakri began before Jenny had recovered. "In the times after the Felmargue was created, our people ascended to the Hold to present their grievances to the magicians. It is not important what they found atop the Hold, only how they got there. The Fels was not completely flooded in those days and they still had metal that they drove into the surface of these cliffs. As the land filled with water, and metal became scarce, corroded and forbidden, they established the tradition of leaving the ropes in place after they departed."

He paused, looking up to meet the glances of both Elyssa and Jevan, who both nodded approvingly. He continued.

"There are storms within the nature of the Felmargue that can attack the ropes, as well as the metals, causing them to fall apart when a second ascent to the Hold is attempted. We ourselves have seen this. It has been our custom, then, to continue through the channels until a second landing was found where the ropes would still be intact. Only this one time have we tried three landings without being able to ascend to the Hold."

Again he looked up, the others nodded. Rifkind suspected that Chakri was repeating the images they had all seen within the stone, turning them into a consensus-memory, though why the job should fall to the youngest member of the company was unexplained.

"This has, however, happened before to our Fathers and others. Sometimes they would continue around the Hold. They say there are one hundred and thirty landings, but we suspect this is not true, as landings are lost with every storm and season. Still, they say there have been times when all the ropes at all the landings were rotted and the Quais had to search for a landing where the spikes of our most distant Fathers were still within the rocks, or, worst of all, return to the outposts of Lowenrat for the forbidden metal."

He looked up, they nodded and Rifkind had images of a futile journey.

"However, we remember that we saw these metal spikes in the rock at our first landing. We did not know what they were for, then. Now, we do. We should return there and attempt to scale the cliffs as we've seen our Fathers do, before we head back to Lowenrat."

Meaningful glances were exchanged by the Quais. Chakri picked up the Black Flame-stone, wrapping it in an old piece of cloth before returning it to a small basket that was quickly lost amid the jumble of the Quais community property.

"Have you seen this also?" Elyssa asked Rifkind.

"Yes," she nodded, lying, rather than confuse the situation and hoping that Jenny would have the sense to do the same, but they did not ask her.

The bull-bellow roar of a mire-dragon followed closely by the maddened whistle of the wild stallion cut through the air. Jevan glanced at each of the torches, and assured of their protection, ignored the noises of the night. The others followed his example, except for Rifkind who rushed to Turin even as the other stallion emerged onto moonlit high-ground. Turin emitted a harsh, deep challenge; a more instinctive and animal sound than any Rifkind had ever heard him make.

His front hooves lifted momentarily off the raft, throwing it and all the others attached to it into violent rocking motions that in turn frightened him. Rifkind reached out with her hand and mind to calm him. Only to feel a stranger beside her instead of the Turin she knew. The moonlit stallion, a hornless, scarred grey animal as powerful and noble as Turin in his own way, splashed through a channel to take a new position on a nearer islet of high-ground.

Go, Turin. You're free now. I've delayed your return too long already.

The horned war-horse turned, challenged, and made to

step off the raft into the channel, then hesitated, pulled back by some invisible rein which bound him, however gently, to his Rider. He wickered, low and pleading, staring at her from the raft's edge, waiting. Rifkind's hands remained helplessly at her sides. She had wished him free to follow his instincts, but there was a ritual, not a healer's ritual but a warrior's ritual, to undo the empathic bond between Rider and war-horse. A ritual that she had not learned before the massacre of her clan and her self-exile from the Asheera. The tension would destroy Turin. Rifkind could sense the despair and conflict within him and knew she had only moments to find the releasing ritual.

—Fool! Child!—

The ghostly voice of Muroa burst into the place between Rifkind's ears.

—He doesn't understand your thoughts of freedom and instinct. Give him the *image!*—

Rifkind laid her hands on the cheek-hollows beneath his horns. She saw him free, vanquishing the grey and splashing across the salty channels. His labored breathing steadied. He shook free of her and plunged off the raft, no longer a war-horse bound to a Rider. The grey spun about toward the still hidden herd of mares. Turin followed, his mind lost to Rifkind who watched and listened until the night was still again.

CHAPTER 8

The loss, if only temporary, of her companion of seven years left Rifkind dulled and dreamy. She neither slept nor was particularly awake from the moment Turin disappeared into the moonlight, through the early morning relocation of the raft and the slow assault on the green-glass cliffs of the Hold until the stiff reed-fiber ropes thudded down onto the raft and Drocour and Chakri shimmied down them from the plateau top.

"The ropes are ready for you—it is time."

Elyssa approached Rifkind with the same cold tone she had used when with Jenny she had first approached the Quais raft after the battle with the Ornaq and Chandro. The acceptance of the strangers that had culminated in the shared experience with the Black Flame-stone was gone and each woman faced the other without regard or sympathy for her future.

"I'll go up first, then the baskets. Jenny will watch the loading from down here, then Jenny will come up here herself."

Elyssa nodded without making any effort to deny Rifkind's implied distrust of the Quais once she was no

longer present to protect her belongings. The other Quais
ignored the departure of those with whom they had
shared so much. Only Jevan seemed affected by the impending separation, and that because of an affection for
Jenny that he was coming to understand only now that
she was leaving him. When understanding came to her in
turn, Jenny's artless face showed delight and consternation equally. Rifkind left them to find their own promises
and partings while she essayed the climb to the Hold.

The frayed reed fibers of the rope broke easily, embed-
ding themselves in her hands despite the horn-like
calluses—results of years of sword and ritual practice—
that covered her palms and fingers. She set her mind
against the discomfort and locked her feet, soles and
ankles against the rope. The breeze and her exertions set
the rope to swaying before she was halfway to the top,
and she made the mistake of looking down. The whole
raft was watching her, especially Jenny whose face was
pasty and her hands clenched white around Jevan's arms.

It is not at all like rising out of my body during tal-
trance, Rifkind thought, closing her eyes then opening
them at once. The vertigo increased when her mind
grasped only the swaying rope and breeze for reference.
I do not like this, but falling would be worse.

She straightened her back to continue her inchworm
crawl to the top. The ropes lay flat against the cliff-
overhang; there was no such thing as a pulley-arm at any
of the landings. Letting go, unwillingly, with one hand she
groped through the grass for the anchor-ring or anything
else reasonably solid with which to haul herself to safety.

Long weeks of relative inactivity had taken their toll of
her stamina. Before she had gotten to her feet and recovered her breath she had decided on an intensive re-
training campaign. She paused to remove the worst of the
rope splinters from her hands before tossing a second coil

of rope over the edge. Five times she lowered the ropes to haul up baskets of food, weapons and ritual implements.

When she and Jenny had left Chatelgard they had considered themselves lightly provisioned with two saddle-horses and one pack-animal. Jenny's mount and the pack-animal had been sold in Belfelis, and Turin now roamed out of sight on the salt-marshes. The pile of bundles and baskets seemed more formidable without him. Rifkind did not know how they would manage it. It was, however, a problem that would not have to be faced until they got Jenny to the top of the Hold.

Jevan demonstrated the basic rope-climbing technique, shinnying expertly to within an arm's reach of the top, but his virtuosity only convinced the anxious girl that rope-climbing was far beyond her. Rifkind could sense the growing impatience of the other Quais. She threw the second rope over the edge again, telling Jenny to loop it about her waist for extra safety. She didn't mention that the rope was not long enough to be anchored in the heavy metal ring, was only as secure as Rifkind's cramped grip upon it.

Jenny's feet tangled in her skirts. Ludicrously, given her obvious fear, she seemed more obsessed with maintaining her modesty against the breezes that playfully flirted with her skirts than in maintaining a steady clasp on the rope with her feet. Rifkind called encouragements down to her, Jevan shouted from below. But when Jenny glanced down to her recently revealed admirer, she froze. A whimpering scream escaped her lips. Rifkind twirled the slack second rope around her waist, and braced herself.

"Rifkind! Where are you?"

The girl's voice came faintly up the cliff and Rifkind edged forward reluctantly to smile and wave unenthusiastically.

"Don't let go of me!"

"I won't. Just keep on coming up. You're halfway here now. It's as easy to come the rest of the way as it would be to get back down to the raft."

"To go down I could just let go."

Rifkind blanched despite her dark complexion as Jenny released the rope with her hands, but the Overnmont woman caught it again a few handspans higher than before. She grimaced, clung tight and slid her feet up. Rifkind took in the new slack on the second rope. Moments later she lay on her stomach to get a grip on Jenny's arm as she crept into reach.

They almost lost hold of each other; then Jenny's fingers locked with shocking strength into Rifkind's shoulders. The vertical journey was over and Jenny clung to the shorter Rifkind, crying in relief.

By the time they released each other and returned to the edge of the cliff, the raft was already easing down the channels away from them. Jevan called back a farewell that brought new tears to Jenny's eyes, but they both stepped backwards rather than actually watch the raft disappear into the mists. The height of the Hold gave them a good overview of the Felmargue, with its innumerable pockets of mist rising to obscure the horizon, and only the faintest hint of the over-grown interior swam in the distance. Except for the retreating raft, nothing moved. Rifkind sought the trail of a herd of horses as desperately as Jenny had waved to Jevan.

"Just you and me again," Jenny said with a weak smile, brushing away her tears and wincing, as the gesture reminded her of the mess the climb had made of her hands.

"Let me see your hands," Jenny demanded.

The cuts and blisters were not severe enough to warrant healing. Indeed, such minor aberrations did not affect the life-forces which flowed through a person and could only rarely be remedied by ritual. Rifkind offered Jenny a small hook-tipped knife from her ritual stores to remove what splinters she could, and they shared a few drops of sweet oil for the scrapes and blisters.

"Which way?" Jenny asked.

"If I'm right the entire Hold is circular and where we want to go is at the center of it."

"Are you frightened?"

"Of what?" Rifkind countered while hauling both sets of ropes back up the cliff.

"Oh, the Hold . . . this place, everything."

"I don't know about you, but it feels so good to have solid ground under my feet again that I don't feel anything else at all."

They loosened the longer rope from the pulley-rings and began improvising a sling on which to carry the bulk of their bundles.

"Aren't you nervous about what we will find in the ruins of the magician's cloisters themselves?"

Rifkind shrugged, remembering but not wanting to mention the golden aura'd individual she had discovered within the cloisters.

"I'm beginning to believe the stories Bainbrose was telling us before we left Chatelgard about the powers of this place," Jenny continued, determined to have a decisive answer from her companion.

"I had thought that for him, they were stories; he had no idea of the true power of the Black Flame, or their source, the Well of Knowledge."

"But, last night . . . you didn't actually join with the Quais, see them climbing up these cliffs . . . did you?"

Rifkind let the half-knotted ropes fall from her hands. "No. My old teacher, Muroa, gave me a lecture on the Quais and the uses of the Black Flame."

"Ah! So that *was* a piece of the Black Flame. I wasn't

sure. I thought so, but I wasn't sure what it really was. I was expecting a fire or something, not a rock."

"You were seeing things too, weren't you? I watched your lips move. You were talking to someone."

Jenny shook her head as if to remove a lingering image. "Ugh! A woman, very pale, with *very* green eyes and unpleasant things to say. I was afraid at first. She said she could imprison my spirit—but I think that was just a threat. She kept on repeating how she could do it, so I guessed she was a lot like my Father. If he could do something, he did; when he couldn't, he threatened. Finally I told her what I thought of her and her threats."

Rifkind had the queasy sensation that Jenny had locked empathies with Krowlowja, whose features generally matched the description given. That, plus the unexpected comparison with her father, Lord Humphry, seemed to confirm that the Baleric seeress had been about in the ether the previous evening.

"What exactly did you say to this woman when you told her what you thought of her?" Rifkind contrived to keep her face and tone from conveying her fears.

"I told her that she wasn't real, her or her powers, any more than ghosts that steal babies or demons that poison milk. Then I said . . . I said you could make her disappear." Jenny's expression asked belated permission for her boldness.

"Did you tell this woman my name?"

"No, I don't think so."

"It's very important. Are you sure you didn't tell her my name? Sometimes ghosts *do* steal babies—if they were murdered in their lives and unavenged. And demons can spoil *anything*—if it pleases them to do so. And I don't really know if I could make that woman disappear—if she knew my name or where we were. Jenny, she was real."

Biting her lip Jenny focused inward a moment before answering.

"No," she said slowly. "Now that I think about it, I'm sure I didn't. I was going to. I had you right in my mind, but then, well . . . you changed. You became an old woman. That is, I think it was still you. You still had the healer's mark on your cheek and your eyes—pardon me for mentioning that, but I've never seen anyone with eyes like yours before. But once you changed I couldn't remember your name at all. How did you do that?"

Rifkind smiled and went back to her knot-tying. "I couldn't. That was Muroa."

"Now I'm even more confused."

"Try reminding yourself, as often as necessary until you believe it—there is much in the world that we cannot understand, only adapt to."

Rifkind felt Jenny's unabated confusion but said nothing more. The timeless, place-less spirit of Muroa had interceded in Jenny's vision before harm could be done. It was not a thing to understand. Rifkind was no longer herself certain if Muroa had actually passed beyond the reality of her cave in the Asheera or might not now be waking after a night of dreams and memories of her student and a world overflowing with water.

She'll blame it on her stomach, or the spices, Rifkind thought. She was always putting too much spice on the meat and then getting indigestion.

The completed sling was ill-balanced, awkward. But it was the best they could do. With the cliff-edge to their backs they headed into the interior of the plateau. The violence of the gods' punishment to the rest of the land was made more apparent in the Hold because here it seemed absent. The swamp swiftly became an unreal

memory as they walked through a land that might have
been Glascardy.

Song birds nested in green-leaf trees and protected their
nests from small furred predators. Fresh streams crossed
their path, at one of which Rifkind spotted the spoor of a
larger animal. Rock walls wound across the contoured
land, showing the boundaries of long-abandoned farms.

"The largest trees are all the same size," Jenny commented, noticing that Rifkind seemed to be spending
most of her time staring at them. "Oak and the like—hard
woods like the forests back home around Chatelgard, but
these are new forests, just the same."

"New? These trees look well grown. I couldn't span
them with both my arms."

"These are small compared to the great trees. Ten men
holding hands couldn't ring those. Think how much older
they must be! These have all grown up since the
Felmargue was turned into a swamp—I'm sure of that.
Those magicians might have been able to protect the land
around them from the gods, but it doesn't seem that any
of the peasants or farmers stayed to work on it."

"From what Drocour said, the Quais leave their injured
and aged here. You would think some of them survived
and would maintain the land. Or maybe the Hold is
much bigger than I thought and they only need a little of
the land at the very center of it."

Jenny spoke the words too lightly. *Was* there something
specific in the Overnmont blood that made them somewhat immune to the ritual and magickal aspects of the
world? How else explain the way they would comment
on divine curses as if such could have no effect on the lives
of mortals? Rifkind, at any rate, had felt eyes probing
them since they'd left the windswept cliffs and entered
this tranquil world. Drocour had mentioned things worse
than Ornaqs.

"It could be cursed," she said after a moment's thought. "You should be prepared to encounter reminders of the gods here. They could have left something that lingers as your Glascardy winters can, to turn a man into something else—something less."

Jenny nodded. The demented Mountain Men were the justification for generations of Overnmont suzerainty in Glascardy.

"I hadn't thought of that. The Quais would make ideal Mountain Men. They'd have no resistance at all to whatever it is that makes men beasts." She looked around at the trees and small meadows of the Hold. "We wouldn't have many places to run to, would we?"

"No," Rifkind agreed.

They moved at a steady pace, considering the ungainliness of their burdens, through the brightest hours of the afternoon. Frequent hills and outcroppings of rock cut their visibility and they had not sighted the ruins of the magician's home. The rock walls wormed their way over some of the gentler slopes without interruption, but fell into indistinct rubble where raw stone thrust up out of the soil.

Rifkind realized that the creation of the Felmargue swamp had done something to the land remaining in the Hold—else why had not the few surviving farmers taken up the fertile land of the plateau? And at least some of the forces that had hammered down the swamp had hit the Hold itself. The scars of the battle were obvious, once she had studied them: here a gentle warping still covered by soil and bounded by the old walls, there a brutal upheaval naked to the elements still. Only the twining walls remained to say to the visitor that mortals had once lived on the Hold.

The trees cast longer shadows across their path by the time they reached a broad expanse of sloping meadow

that had somehow escaped the encroaching forest.
Rifkind announced that it would be as good a place for
them to pass the night as any; and after a short search she
selected a site enclosed by vines and shrubs, concealed
from the direct sight of the meadow yet giving them a
clear view of the hill. She still sensed hidden observers,
but could not discern even the most minimal confirmation of her fears. The eyes of the invisible watchers had
always seemed to be in front of her, so she chanced placing the trees at her back to have the greatest visibility in
front. As in the swamp, as soon as the sunlight no longer
fell directly on the grass, the animals became bolder and
the grass-croppers emerged from hiding for their daily
feast.

Jenny broke out the small supply of sun-dried fish that
they had brought from the raft.

"It's a little ripe already," she commented, handing
Rifkind half of it. "Tomorrow we'll need fresh meat."

While they ate, a short-legged, sloe-eyed, brown and
furry animal crept boldly between them to nibble at the
oily leaves that had been wrapped around the fish. It was
alert to all their movements, but stood still to allow Jenny
to stroke its back. Rifkind watched in silence a moment,
then reached forward to rub the short fur under its jaw. It
extended its nose upward and closed its eyes, and a faint
rumbling purr could be felt in its throat.

"He doesn't seem to be afraid of us at all," Jenny said
after a moment.

"It must be a long time since men roamed the Hold,
then. It doesn't know what we are, much less to fear us."

Rifkind pulled her hand back. The animal opened its
eyes to stare at her, then settled on its haunches to preen.

"You won't kill it, will you?" Jenny asked. "It trusts us
now."

"We've eaten for today, but we'll need meat sooner or

later. I don't kill for pleasure, if that's what you're suggesting, but it will be harder for both of us if you look at every little animal that crosses our path as a pet. The animals that aren't cuddly are apt to be larger and harder to kill. And we would waste much of their meat."

"We don't need meat."

Rifkind pointed to the grass tips Jenny was offering to the curious animal. "I can't eat grass, and if I could there are far too many kinds for me to know what would be wholesome and what poisonous. Watch these animals— see how selective they are. If you want to eat grass or the first berries we find, you can. But I trust meat."

"But that's cruel," Jenny protested. "Why do we have to introduce fear to this place!"

"We're not going to set about slaughtering the forests. There are meat-eaters here already—and always have been or this little animal would have starved long ago. Even the ger-cat takes only the oldest and weakest from the herds. When he is not hunting he drinks at the same water-holes as his prey. Before winter in the Asheera we would cull our herds of those not likely to survive until spring. Does Turin act as if he fears me because I have eaten horsemeat?"

Rifkind had said her last word on the subject of objections to hunting, objections that only seemed to occur to persons who lived far from the herds and butchers who fed them.

Larger animals moved onto the meadow, many half the size of Turin and bearing horns like his, but built more like the gazelle on her gold hair-ornament. She saw at least one whose sides were gouged and scarred from encounters with the meat-eaters and others whose step was uncertain and stiff. If they did not find the ruins they could return to the meadow and find enough food to sustain them until they figured out a way back through the

Felmargue to more familiar lands.

"You will take the first watch, Jenny. Wake me when the Bright One rises and I'll watch until dawn."

"Do you really think we need a watch? The animals aren't afraid of us, why should we be afraid of them? We could both use a full night's sleep."

"We've been watched since we left the Quais," Rifkind answered sharply, her patience worn thin from lack of sleep.

"Followed!" Jenny went wild-eyed. "How? Who? Where are they? Why haven't you told me?"

"Watched, not followed."

"By what, by who?"

"I don't know. Turin's senses are better at these things than mine. I realize how much I'd come to rely on him when I travelled through strange country. All I can tell, if my vague feelings are true, is that we have been observed continuously since we left the cliff. You're right; the animals don't fear us, and I'm not convinced that whatever watches us means us harm, either. I just don't want to be rudely surprised. So we set a watch."

"What would I watch for? What sort of thing do you expect the magicians will set after us?"

"You have too many questions. Watch for something that doesn't fit in with the rest. It doesn't have to be magical, or a threat for that matter. I've seen the magician in the ruins—there's only one—and we do not have to fear him.

"I'm frightened."

"The animals are not afraid. I'm not afraid, just tired. And I hate surprises, so keep watch while I get some sleep."

Rifkind ignored Jenny's pinched, anxious face and stretched out, feet toward the meadow bottom. In her own mind she had eliminated the gold-aura'd master of the ruins as the source of the penetrating eyes that had followed them, but she had in no way eliminated the sense that the eyes were unfriendly. Her own watch would be far longer than Jenny's and more dangerous. She must rest in preparation, regardless of Jenny's fears.

CHAPTER 9

Rifkind sat up, wide-eyed and tense before she knew she was awake, and long before her consciousness could grapple with what had aroused her. The night was quiet and dark; the Bright One had not yet risen, though she soon would. Even the little brown animal lay beside her undisturbed.

"It's been very quiet," Jenny said, noticing Rifkind now sitting beside her. "Boring, but I have stayed awake."

Rifkind was centered enough to guess at what had awakened her, but still unable to find words to describe it. As the images of warning became clearer in her mind, she realized that the unseen eyes that had watched them were no longer present in the night.

Malice, she thought. Evil. The innocence of this place is completely gone now. The silence itself is ominous. We are stalked by some left-over nightmare. Did the staring block my sense of these things? Lull me into a blind security? Is it even possible that those staring eyes *were* the innocence of the land and now that they sleep malice walks?

The animal at her side stirred in its own sudden

wakefulness. It chittered once, the first sound it had made, and bolted into the darkness of the trees. Rifkind touched the still warm spot on her outer thigh where it had nestled.

False innocence, false security? But I can't tell what's real and what's false. Or, what form will this malice take?

"Rifkind, I see something," Jenny whispered.

So quickly? Now we find out. Bright One, be not late in Your arrival!

Rifkind rose to her knees, peering through the shrub branches that separated them from the rest of the meadow. Three . . . four . . . six torches held high and bobbing as if carried by walking men, emerged out of the darkness at the base of the meadow. Jenny started to stand; Rifkind caught her arm and held her behind the limited protection of the bushes.

"Keep quiet. Don't move or talk. They don't know exactly where we are,"

The torches fanned out, forming a wide line advancing up the slope. Straining her ears and eyes Rifkind lost a moment wishing for Turin's presence and his keener senses. Her ears picked up no sounds from the area around the torches and her eyes wished to deceive her with the notion that the figures advanced over the meadow grasses rather than through them. The torches glowed with an impossibly white and steady flame, yet somehow for all their brilliance cast little light; the bearers cast no shadows.

No matter how softly they moved, so many men should have made some sound. At least one would have stepped on a twig, or caught his cloak on a thorn. They moved slowly and cautiously up the meadow. Jenny and Rifkind remained as quiet as the torchbearers.

Moments lengthened until Rifkind truly feared that the Bright One was held fast below the horizon and would not reflect the light of truth onto the meadow. The torches were closer and still not flickering. Rifkind now could see that for every torch there were two or three trackers, barely visible in the darkness, peering and sniffing at the ground. She watched their legs, and though they walked like men she discovered they were not: the high grass was undisturbed by their passage. The sense of being watched returned, and was no longer benign. The crescent of the Bright Moon was visible through the trees at the opposite side of the meadow, and for the first time in her life, it brought Rifkind fear rather than reassurance.

The searchers continued forward in their wide pattern. If they held to it, the strange beings would pass them by. Rifkind steadied her grip on Jenny's arm and hoped.

The line drew abreast of them, the pattern undisturbed. The upturned crescent of the Bright One sent a sliver of moonlight across the meadow. Grimly Rifkind noted that though the light was distorted and discolored by those who bore the torches, it was not blocked. Only the clubs borne by the trackers passed like black lines in front of the silvery crescent. The Bright One rose further, clearing the trees to cast Her light undistorted into the bushes where Rifkind and Jenny hid.

Too cold, Rifkind thought as the ray struck her. Her light's too cold! Dear Goddess ... no! What have I done that You do this?

The figures turned swiftly, and formed a tighter pattern coming aimed directly at them. Their eyes were visible now, two cold pits in each face, blacker, even, than the surrounding night. The eyes could be Black Flames themselves.

"Run!"

Rifkind dropped Jenny's arm, thrusting her into a spin that would hopefully induce her to run into the trees behind them. They would have to separate. In their plight,

Rifkind could not forget that the Overnmonts professed no patron dieties, and that her own Goddess had betrayed her into this danger.

She decided that to run meant simply to be run down. She drew the long belt knife, then stood up and brandished its edge to the moonlight. The tremulous shriek of an Asheeran war cry was launched toward the eerie figures, who replied with a joint wailing more unworldly than her own had been.

Rifkind had known the stiffness of her hand would hinder her movements and had drawn the shorter, easier to maneuver knife rather than her sword, though she sacrificed precious hand-spans of reach to the club-bearers. Already her hands was becoming sticky from reopened wounds. She backed away from the bushes, easing toward the trees. Jenny's heavy panicked footfalls had ceased. Rifkind did not have time to consider the meaning of this before the wraiths were upon her.

The trees hindered her movements and evasions, but also limited the number of wraiths who could close with her at any one time. She cursed her hands more than the wraiths. There was no compensation against the grossness of her own movements, though she had inured herself to the pain. The very act of shutting off feeling produced a slowness in her reactions that further diminished her fighting ability because she was accustomed to better.

Branches bent and snapped now as the wraiths closed in. Their features had solidified as they neared her; she felt certain she could hurt them if she could hit them. They weren't particularly skilled fighters, but they had the inestimable advantages of number and freshness. Though she parried the first five of their strokes without mishap, she had not struck one of her own before a glancing blow bounced off her shoulder.

Not a serious blow, since their clubs could not cut. In another fight she might have blocked a fist or club in such a way deliberately. But somehow the shoulder was now numb and unresponsive. She shook the arm rapidly to restore feeling. The wraiths had backed away, seemingly expecting one blow to be the finish of her.

Feeling returned, and with it a bone-aching cold. She eyed the clubs with a new respect. She could not afford even a glancing touch from those unnaturally charged weapons.

Rifkind screamed again and charged her nearest opponent, laying open the arm that bore the club. The wraith dropped its weapon, which disappeared before it hit the ground, and though she could not be certain in the helter-skelter darkness, the wraith itself seemed to have stepped behind the others and then disappeared. Were that true, the battle might not be so hopeless; the wraiths were slower in their own defense than attack. She laid into another one, taking fullest advantage of their apparent surprise in the face of a weapon that could hurt them.

Battle lust warmed her veins, fighting the cold ache in her shoulder and surmounting the disadvantages of her cramped, damaged hands. Punctuating her movements with gutteral snarls, Rifkind disarmed two more of the wraiths before they seized an opportunity to counter her. Numbness, cold and pain were forgotten as she merged with a primitive battle-mentality that had nothing whatsoever to do with the exalted arts of ritual or healing. She dared face their cold eyes with hot-blooded violence. The wraiths fell back, muttering softly in a language she could not understand.

"Fight, demon-scum! Come near me—I'll show you true damnation!"

Her breathing was hard, but steady. A glow of sweat suffused her skin in the torchlight. She thought briefly of running back into the trees, but the Hold would offer no secure hiding place from the wraiths. She would not have chosen this time or place, but confronted by the inevitable —her own battle fury—Rifkind chose not to give ground.

Feinting, shifting her guard, she enticed their attack without success. She let a throwing knife drop into her hand from the harness in the small of her back that held three hiltless blades. The blade thunked home in the face of a torch-bearing wraith as she slashed forward to disarm yet another.

The odds had improved. The torchbearer had not disappeared with his torch, but he wailed an agony that echoed through the forest. She stepped aside quickly to cut, backhanded, a second wound in his side to end his misery. She was closer to them now. They had ceased muttering. Their eyes glowed inky-red as they rained down fierce blows, too many for her to dodge or parry. Scampering back to the trees she protected her sword-arm, legs and head, but the left shoulder and arm were useless, and would remain that way. Coldness inched out from bruises she could not feel, stiffening the muscles of her chest and making breathing a distracting agony.

Drawing ragged, painful breaths she confronted them with death-angered eyes. Had she been still capable of rational thought, she would have run then.

It came from behind. The impact alone was enough to drop her to her knees, but along with the nerve-rattling jolt came the first of uncountable waves of paralyzing cold. Rifkind twisted frantically to control her fall, succeeding only in landing hard and square on her back. Her legs flailed to avoid vengeful wraiths, but the clubs rained down until she was still.

Movement remained only in her head and neck; consciousness as well, for they had not struck her above the shoulders. She could crane her neck and see a wraith, far greater in size than the other, though still insubstantial. The giant raised a staff topped with a skull-carved chunk of Black Flame-stone and brought it down against the side of her head.

The crack against the bone brought blackness to her mind for more than a few moments, then, incredibly, consciousness and limited movement returned. She opened one eye, cautiously, and guessed from the ache that the staff had struck the gold-and-brass gazelle ornament she wore in her hair.

Luck? This time yesterday did Muroa call me lucky? Rifkind thought bitterly as the wraiths gathered around her and she closed her eyes. To be awake as they carry me off? That's luck? What offense *did* I commit to draw these things to me?

She slid into bleak despair as unseen cold hands grasped her arms and legs to drag her into the meadow. The wraiths murmured among themselves like deaf children babbling continually in low-pitched uncomprehending imitation of those around them. The giant dispatched two of the torchbearers into the trees and Rifkind realized, belatedly, both where her assailant had been and why she had not heard Jenny's footsteps as long as she should have.

Jenny's limp form was borne out and dumped in the grass beside her. They brought torches closer. Rifkind held her eyes closed as she was lifted up, examined and thrown over the shoulder of one of the most substantial wraiths. Opening her eyes once again she saw a matted clot of blood on Jenny's face marking where the skull-staff had struck her.

I must do something! she thought. I will *not* be carried off to some cave for sport or food! The Bright One's light is still colder than their clubs. I'll get no help from Her, but in Her service I've learned much.

There was no discomfort, except that the numbness was itself distressing. She took refuge in the meditative trances she had practiced even before the Goddess had revealed Herself to her as a novice healer. She searched and found the kernals of a plan in secrets the ruby had revealed to her back in An-Soren's tower a seeming lifetime ago.

Waiting until the giant, but now insubstantial, wraith had left the party again, she centered herself in her tal and dropped out of her body. The wild colors of the ethereal world whirled around her as she bounced to the ground and shrank to a conscious-mote as she had done (albeit with limited success) when she had spied on the dark sorcerer.

An-Soren had animated a chimera of himself once, and there were legends of other adepts who chose shapes other than man or woman to stalk on either the real or ethereal planes. She had felt the rage of the ger-cat herself when Krowlowja called Domhnall from her, and into that somewhat familiar frame of reference she strove to mold her tal, once the wraiths and their burdens were gone.

She was successful, though she passed moments of disorientation before she could realize this. The shape of the world was vaguely oval and far brighter than night had ever seemed before. Coiled suppleness and strength rested in each clawed limb, including the once-arms that now supported half her ethereal weight.

I'm a ger-cat! She purred to herself.

Rippling muscles stretched indolently under gold-tipped black fur. Forward-set eyes gave her a true hunter's view and demeanor. She glided effortlessly across the ethereal shadow of the meadow and snarled into the ether.

The tal-formed ger-cat moved silently and invisibly through the meadows and woods. No living creature needed to fear the ghostly cat, though many could sense its strange presence and fled.

She wandered until she found a mirror-smooth water pool in which she could observe the Goddess' face without directly confronting Her eyes. A shimmering nimbus, invisible except in the ethereal sphere, surrounded the silvery disk.

"Very well, I'm here," Rifkind snarled, annoyed that the Goddess had veiled Her image. The cat-eyes narrowed to slits and the gold-tipped tail lashed at her feet.

"You seek too much, my priestess. This land has been forbidden. You cannot pass through it." The Goddess did not lower her veils.

"I came this far at Your insistence. I might have been snug in Glascardy."

"I had thought to protect you from the fate of the others, but I have had to reveal your presence to the others. Punishment is to be carried out."

The Goddess' voice had softened slightly. When Rifkind refused to answer, the veils dropped to reveal a maternally beautiful face filled with concern. Rifkind would not lift her eyes from the water-reflection to face Her.

"I am to die here, then?" Rifkind let no tinge of emotion betray her, though the desire to scream with frustrated rage demanded expression.

"There are many lifetimes, Rifkind. You will return to me. I will keep your spirit safe. We use the creatures left here on the Hold for our own purposes; it is for the gods to decide when the Leveller shall come to the Felmargue —not you or the Quais. The Black Flame must never be returned to the hands of mortals. The Well and the Flame are ours. The ancient gods did not control them and so lost their dominion. We will not repeat their foolishness. I am sorry. I love you most of those who have served me."

Rifkind felt a low growl well up in her throat. The ger-cat's tail lashed like a whip. "Do you intend to say these same things to the Baleric seeress Krowlowja? Or are Humphry's plans more pleasing to you?" The throaty rumble of the predator underscored Rifkind's tightly spoken words.

The nimbus clouded, obscuring the Goddess' face completely for a moment. The air of the ethereal sphere sighed and the Goddess descended in an ethereal form behind Rifkind. The ger-cat stood, stretched and slowly turned to face the silver-draped woman whose head was crowned by a silver crescent of moonlight.

"You have seen these things?" the Goddess asked, no longer impervious or haughty.

Perhaps Muroa is right, Rifkind thought. I do seem to have unconscionable luck. My Goddess seems not to know of Krowlowja's designs upon the Well and Flames. The gods suffer from a critical lack of knowledge, but now is not the time to think of that. She hoped the diety could not penetrate her thoughts as she sought for a way to use her knowledge to save herself and Jenny. "The seeress has already cast enchantments into the ruins of the magicians' stronghold. I have felt their binding force."

The Goddess vanished, only to return heartbeats later. "Return to your body. You will be saved. I must go elsewhere for a time. You will not be hindered further as you approach."

CHAPTER 10

The ger-cat padded effortlessly along the easily followed trail the burdened wraiths had left from the meadow. Rifkind's only problem was to overcome the innate instincts of the form she had chosen to pursue the trail; the ger-cat was an ambusher, not a trailer. Her first thoughts after taking animal form had been to lie in wait at the bottom of the meadow where they had first seen the wraith and wait until the ethereal forms returned even though there was no reason to expect their immediate return to that locale.

The crescent of the Bright Moon hung at the midpoint of its night journey, but now she did not need the illumination—she was mainly aware that the crescent had an unnerving *vacancy* about it that suggested the Goddess was displaced from Her seat of power.

The Bright Moon is void, and the air is filled with all manner of unpleasant potential. To save Jenny and myself I seem to have set great forces into motion. Or at least tied our fates to them. I doubt I've saved us at all. I've heard it said that there are forces and fates more powerful than the gods; I'm certain we're being moved about by some grand and unseen fate, or doom.

She paused, sniffing at the air. The ger-cat's instincts could identify most of the animal scents; she used her own discrimination to find the ether-borne taint of the wraiths. They were close now. The aroma of musty death was potent in the air, old and permeating everything that still had life. She had found their lair.

Rifkind left the clear trail and circled up to high ground overlooking the concentration of wraith-scent. The long fur on her stomach dragged on the ground as she eased out to a point of barren rock overlooking the dark, lifeless encampment.

They live like swine—if they live at all. There are no lights anywhere, nor the smell of fires.

The wraiths, several more than she remembered from the attack, crouched in the ruins of what might have been a stone temple or manor house from the time before the Felmargue was separated from the Hold. Crude repairs seemed to have been made to parts of it, but the wraiths had settled down to sleep-like inactivity regardless of shelter or the lack of it.

Rifkind remained with the form of the ger-cat until she had approached the crude camp and located the ramshackle collection of stone and logs that accounted for the fishy scent that indicated the location of her body. The giant wraith leaned inert against what appeared to be the only door, his skull-staff lying at his feet. The cat's eyes saw shifting patterns swim across the surface of the Black Flame-stone. A low growl rose unbidden; Rifkind could not, in the form she had chosen, move closer.

The ger-cat contracted into the ethereally glowing point of pure tal-spirit, hovering as before. Though no more or less substantial or powerful than the cat-form had been, the nakedness of her tal made Rifkind feel more vulnerable. She probed the walls frantically, looking for the minutest opening. She found one and slipped into the magnetic well of her body.

"Rifkind? . . . Rifkind? . . . Are you awake now?"

The voice was urgent, desperate despite its whisper pitch. Rifkind centered herself quickly. Unlike the idealized form of the ger-cat, her own body was a crucible of aches, pain and cold. She had fallen, or been thrown, onto a pile of hard sharp objects that her first guess said were mouldering bones. The wraiths had not bothered to bind her arms or legs, but prolonged pressure on joints first paralyzed with cold, then cramped into unnatural positions, was almost as effective. She moaned.

"Rifkind? You're awake? Oh, please be awake!"

Familiar hands grasped her and accomplished the welcome relief of setting her upright. The objects that had supported her shifted, releasing a dusty stench.

"I'm coming around now, I think."

Rifkind had meant to sound reassuring, but she had already adapted to the ger-cat's vocal structure and her words emerged with hisses and growls. Jenny was not reassured.

"You're hurt. They've tried to turn you into one of them! Please say something else."

"Just a little slow. How long have I been out? I was afraid for you. When the wraiths started carrying us off you had a nasty head wound—I wanted to get some rest before I tried to heal you."

Jenny groaned. "I don't know. I've a headache, but that's all—except for the aches, pains and panic. I don't remember being brought here at all, or anything since that giant whatsit jumped out of the trees in front of me! I panicked, Rifkind, just froze. I didn't fight or run; he just hit me, as simple as that, and it was over. The next thing I knew I was in here and I thought you were dead."

Her tone was abject. In spite of the darkness Rifkind could visualize the ragged, tired woman, gripping her hands together, head lowered, apologetic and embarrassed at being bested by an unnatural creature, twice her size and armed with a staff of power. If Jenny hadn't been so sincere, and Rifkind's ribs so sore, she might have laughed.

"I fought them, and I'm here too. I remember them dragging us around like so many sacks of feed."

"Do you know where we are, then? In the ruins?"

"Ruins, yes, but not where we want to be. These creatures have carried us to their lair, not the magician's cloisters. If we get separated again, head toward sunset."

"Don't we have to get out of here before we can get separated?"

"I've been promised rescue." Rifkind paused, but was still able to answer Jenny's question before it was asked. "I wasn't really unconscious, in the truest sense; I was outside my body."

She heard Jenny stand, then pace a short distance that she had evidently marked off after regaining consciousness.

"Where ... no, don't tell me, I don't really want to know. You wouldn't leave me unless you had to, and if you say we'll be rescued—I'll believe you. But, Rifkind—I never expected this. I've seen wars; I was with the army when we regained Chatelgard and the Overnmont Pass. When you said 'danger' I really thought I could deal with it. I was terrified of the Ornaq—couldn't sleep for nights, but I got over it.

"But ... Rifkind, these are *bones*! You're sitting on a *skeleton*. These creatures, whatever they are, collect people like us and lock them in here until they *rot*! I don't want to die, I truly don't, especially in here, but if we're going to be rescued by something equally weird I'm going to die of *fright*!"

"Except that we aren't locked in here—the giant wraith

is leaning against what passes for a door to this place—you're right about our situation. I can't agree with you more."

"Thank you," Jenny snapped through the darkness.

"You're not going to be happy about this, but neither am I. I don't have any idea what form this rescue I've been promised is going to take. My Goddess simply said it would be arranged."

"You've been out talking with the *Gods* while I've been in here surrounded by dead people!"

"I think that you've been safer. She's left Her place of power, the Bright Moon—that's never happened before. But direct intervention is not their way. One of us could get lucky and find a back door to this prison, and She would still have kept her promise."

"I don't understand . . . and there's no other door out of here, I've already looked."

"It's getting more and more important that you don't try to understand these things—accept them. I never explained that properly to Linette, and so she made the mistake of expecting and demanding from the gods. You can't understand their ways. Just get used to them, and let's check over the walls again."

Jenny was mollified by the veiled indication that Rifkind would, in time, open up the world of ritual and magick to her. She shuffled through the heaps of shifting bones toward the furthest limit of their confinement, but before she could test the stone surfaces a series of loud booms rocked the camp, rousing the somnambulent wraiths and causing both women to clasp their hands over their ears.

A belch of foul, rotten air rose out of the ground itself, dwarfing the odor from the old bones. It was as if all the decayed and rotting matter encased within the scarred rocks of the Hold had found an outlet to open air. The demented sounds which served the wraiths as language came through the rough-hewn door. Rustling sounds indicated that the giant wraith who had held them prisoner had left to join his brethern.

Rifkind got to her feet, finding herself essentially uninjured despite the lingering cold and stiffness. The wraiths had kept her long belt knife but had failed to remove any of her other weapons, including her sword. The sword did not seem the most practical choice for the situation, so she drew a narrow-bladed knife from the inside of her boot. She tested the door as another series of booms rocked the camp.

"Our rescue, I think," she said, shoving the door gently until it opened just enough to offer them passage. "The wraiths are wandering around in circles out there. Whatever is happening seems to affect them more than us—so far."

As Rifkind spoke, rocks and chunks of soil that had lodged on the roof of the prison-tomb smashed through the ceiling.

"Is it permissible to wonder exactly what the gods are doing to rescue us? Were we in Glascardy I'd say a mountain-side was going to fall on us. Or should I expect a mountain-sized man to appear over the horizon and lift us out of here?"

"I hope not. It is well within normal coincidence for them to rattle the bones of the Land-Mother Herself and create this chaos. It doesn't seem to be their way to show their hands directly to ... the uninitiated. They thrive on faith, not revelation."

Rifkind stepped through the doorway and motioned for Jenny to follow her. The giant wraith had left his staff lying on the ground when he joined the others in a seemingly pointless frenzy of darting from rock to tree. The wraiths were passing through each other as they moved in some mystically incomprehensible dance. Hesitating for only a moment Rifkind hefted the staff. It was easily twice her height, top heavy, and not a reasonable substitute for the belt-knife, but it would deprive the wraiths of a weapon.

"The path I followed is back here. Follow me quietly." She levelled the staff in her grip and turned.

"You're not taking *that* with us?" Jenny whispered urgently.

"It nearly killed both of us. I think it deserves some study. I do not like facing weapons I don't understand."

Another series of booms and belches arose from the surrounding forests. The land beneath them shifted as if they had stood on a moving carpet, throwing them to their knees. The roof of the prison collapsed, billowing more dust into air that was already sufficiently murky. The wraiths' deep voices had ascended to high-pitched trills. They had joined hands and whirled about in a wild circle above the shifting ground, drawing dust and dead leaves toward them.

"She promised one rescue. I think we tempt fate by lingering."

The dervish shrieking intensified behind them. Rifkind and Jenny also linked hands to fight the cyclonic winds now pulling them toward the whirling wraiths. They reached the relative safety of the tall old trees that formed a wind break. The spiraling dust formed a black cloud that towered up toward the Bright Moon herself. Rifkind refrained from telling Jenny that she no longer had anything but the wildest guesses about the alliances of the gods and the natural forces at their commands. Her own notion of a benevolent diety overseeing Her healers had suffered repeated and possibly irremedial harm in this as yet uncompleted night.

The Moon's crescent still retained its vacant aspect

when she could see it through the clouds, and she dared not look back towards the howling wraiths. She wanted to detach the skull from the staff, but it was attached with heavy metal rings. Jenny donated one of her numerous underskirts as a wrapping around the empty-socketed face. They struggled forward, holding the staff upside-down.

"Rifkind, do you know where we're going?" Jenny asked after they had labored to the crest of yet another hill, and been twice thrown to their knees by the unstable ground.

"The magician's cloisters, if our luck holds. The source of the Well of Knowledge should be within it, and should be secure from these tremors. Our rescue seems to have gotten a bit out of hand. Everyone says the magician's cloisters survived the worst the gods could do. I'm hoping we can survive to get there, and that it's still strong enough to resist whatever's happening now. The gods might control the way to the Well, but not the Well itself. My Goddess said that we wouldn't be hindered further in our attempts to get there, but she was very concerned that someone else might be trying to get control over it."

Another ripple flowed through the ground around them. The forest echoed with tremors and the sounds of trees falling. The tall trees no longer seemed a secure shelter. Rifkind led them as fast as darkness and the gyrating landscape would allow towards the low land and meadows she remembered passing through in ger-cat form.

A fissure half again as wide as she was tall cracked open and gouted foul-smelling flames. Rifkind fell from the shock with Jenny on top of her.

"My god, what is that?" Jenny screamed.

"A sign that things are not going to go as easily as I had hoped. And either the sun is rising or the forest's on fire."

Rifkind's fall had turned her toward the roseate horizon behind them. They both sniffed the air for the odor of burning wood, but smelled nothing except the sulphurous air from the fissure. The flames had extinguished themselves and several trees had fallen, though none bridged the gap.

"I'll set the staff across it. It's long enough to span it and still strong enough to bear our weight. I'll go first, you can follow me."

"I don't think I can."

Rifkind did not reply, but simply braced the staff as best she could, knelt down and slung herself under the stout pole. She gripped it with her hands and knees, the way she'd hauled herself up the ropes not a day earlier. The air in the new chasm stank of brimstone and worse. Rifkind inched her way across as quickly as she could and scrambled out the other side. "Now you!" she shouted.

"Rifkind, I *can't!*"

"You have to!" Rifkind shouted back across the chasm as she scrambled to the surface.

"I'll climb down one side and up the other."

Jenny sat down, dangling her legs over the edge.

"No! Who knows how deep it is—or if it's really empty!"

"I can't do it!"

"You can! It'll hold you."

For emphasis, Rifkind kicked the wrapped skull at her feet. At once, sounds of violent collapse rumbled up from the depths of the chasm. Loose rock on both sides began to give way, and smoke rose from the cloth-wrapped skull.

"Get your legs out of there!" she screamed needlessly; I struck a magick object in anger, she thought to herself in horrified disbelief. Jenny had begun to move before Rifkind spoke.

The ground heaved upward. Somehow the staff remained in position as Rifkind was pitched screaming into the chasm. She grasped wildly; her hands closed around the wood of the staff. The cloth covering it had seared away. Rifkind stared into its glowing red eye-sockets as she dangled. She cursed loudly and profoundly.

"Rifkind are you all right?"

"Probably."

She moved as fast as overhand motion on her injured hands would allow away from those eyes, and toward Jenny. The chasm walls still popped and shifted. Gas belched up. Rifkind closed her eyes, almost losing her grip as she was caught in a fit of coughing.

"The walls are moving together!"

Rifkind forced control over her spasming lungs as Jenny's words confirmed her half-perceived fear that the space around her was contracting. Kicking out with her feet she struck against the moving walls and was able to scramble ungracefully over the top just as the walls slammed together.

"We'd both be across that thing if you hadn't balked," Rifkind snapped, venting her own panic on Jenny, who knelt trembling beside her.

"It's closed now, anyway. We could have waited and just stepped over it."

Jenny had hesitated before speaking, and Rifkind guessed that she wanted to say more, but she didn't. The ground was indeed sealed again with only a black line of rubble and fallen trees to mark the chasm's brief existence. The staff had slid along the moving walls and lay intact and inert on the ground, eyes no longer glowing. Rifkind picked it up carefully, nonetheless.

They stepped over the rubble line. The rosy horizon had paled into a faint pink-gold, revealing a sunrise rather than a holocaust. The wailing wraiths could still be heard, but the black funnel arising from their dance seemed to be fading, and the ground had become more stable. Rifkind led the way to the top of a nearby hill from which they were at last able to see the massive stone silhouette of the ruins they had sought with such disastrous results. A torch, flickering with real fire, burned like a beacon on one of the crenellated towers only half fallen to rubble.

"It's nowhere near the size of Chatelgard," Jenny said.

"It's not a farmhouse or a tomb, either. And we're expected. Let's go."

"What makes you think we're expected?"

Rifkind ignored her. Jenny demanded an answer, but Rifkind was already on her way down the hill headed straight for the torch and Jenny had either to follow or remain behind arguing with the fresh morning air.

CHAPTER II

Rifkind halted at some distance from a large gap in the crumbled stone wall. To judge from the arrangement of the buildings visible within, it might once have been the main door to the compound. The torch had disappeared from the parapet during their approach, and Rifkind had decided not to enter the walls until either the torchbearer appeared or the sun had risen high enough to cast full light on the interior. The ruins were more extensive than she had realized in her visions. Her memory-image had been of a few wizened men conjuring together and was supplanted by a real complex which, though smaller than the fortress of Chatelgard, was large enough to accomodate a hundred men plus the servants and livestock necessary to support them. The grey stone walls were overgrown with vines and no pathway led through the grass-choked breach.

She expected some indication of traffic in and out of the ruins. Perhaps they had found an unused entrance? Her visions had been wrong about the structure, but she still trusted them to provide her a living person with a golden ethereal aura. She placed the staff on the ground and sat. Jenny joined her.

"Well, here we are. It doesn't seem like much, does it, to have come all the way across Dro Daria in winter to visit a lot of tumble-down rocks," Rifkind said casually.

"What are we waiting for? Don't you want to go in? Let's find out what's in there. Maybe we can replace the stuff we lost last night, or at least climb one of those towers and get our bearings again."

"Umm, I forgot that. We lost everything, didn't we? Food, clothes, my boxes—the whole lot." Rifkind scanned along the horizon. "We'll go after them. The wraiths weren't interested in any of the things we carried. The animals might get to the food, but the rest should be safe. Maybe Domhnall can help us—at least tell us more about the wraiths and how to avoid them."

"Domhnall?"

"Ah, that's right, I never told you. After Drogan died I used my stones. I thought the Bright One might require some special sacrifice or ritual. She didn't seem to, but I did find someone named Domhnall living up here in the ruins. That same night I also discovered Lord Humphry and a seeress named Krowlowja ..."

"My father?" Jenny blinked with surprise, but quickly narrowed her eyes in thought. "With a seeress ...? My father has allied with another magicker? That does not bode well for Ejord. We should try to send word."

"They weren't poking around Glascardy—they were looking for the Black Flame, just like us."

Rifkind's voice took on an edge as it usually did when the subject of her one-time employer Lord Humphry came up. She and Jenny had tacitly avoided any mention of the Overnmont patriarch throughout the long journey. Rifkind was uncertain of Jenny's feelings toward the man she always called "father," though she had sided with Ejord in the civil war.

"I do not know their precise position. But they are ap-

proaching the Felmargue with a small army. Perhaps
they mean to bring the benefits of the reconstructed
Darian empire to the Quais—"

"That's unlikely."

"—or, if that's not the case, then they're looking for the
Black Flame."

"My father couldn't care less about a handful of ignorant fishers or trappers living on rafts in the middle of
the biggest swamp in the world. He's gotten wind that
you've been searching for the Black Flame; maybe Chandro or someone else we met along the way sent word to
him. Now he's come to find you."

"I'm sure his feelings for me are no more cordial than
mine for him, but I can't in any justice claim to have
drawn him here. I'm not that important to him.

"Bainbrose spent quite a bit of time as a prisoner with
Humphry. I never pressed him for details, but I never
completely believed he wanted me to come here for my
health and well-being. Evidently his fears were well
founded. Bainbrose has a good ear for rumors. I'd venture
that Krowlowja's led your father out here, and that she
wasn't expecting me to interfere with her plans.

"There's still an outside chance that your father doesn't
know who is responsible for crossing her."

Before Jenny could frame a reply they heard someone
approaching on the other side of the wall. Their visitor
was making no attempt to conceal his progress, scuffing
his feet along the unseen walkway and whistling merrily.
Rifkind was secure in the notion that Domhnall was the
only inhabitant of the ruins and that he was harmless.
Jenny, however, had not felt the golden aura and greeted
their prospective host, as he rounded the last corner and
appeared in their vision, with hostility and distrust.

"I've been waiting for you," the youth, dressed in

simple bleached homespun clothing, said as he stopped at the stone wall. "Please come in. I'm afraid it's impossible for me to come closer to you."

"Why?" Jenny demanded before realizing that Rifkind and the stranger were locked in an enrapt gaze of mutual longing and open admiration.

The sensations of liquid fire that Rifkind had first felt on the raft threatened to consume her now that she studied the physical being of the golden aura. Domhnall was tall, as fair of face and skin as she was dark. His hands were smooth and graceful without the knobs and scars that marked her own. His eyes were a deep sparkling blue, and once she had noticed them there was nothing else of equal excitement in the world.

"Why can't you come over here?" Jenny said, folding her arms resolutely in front of her.

"Don't pry, just get up and follow him," Rifkind said under her breath as she got to her feet.

"If he can't get out, how do I know I'll be able to get out?" Jenny retorted, not caring if the young man could hear her.

"If he had some grand trap laid in those walls he wouldn't announce the fact like that. If we're to get to the Black Flame we've got to go in. You were ready to go a few moments back. There's no point in arguing about it."

"I think he's enchanted you. I don't like this at all. You can go in, if you must. I'd rather that you didn't."

Rifkind shrugged, but did not deny Jenny's suspicions. She stood up and headed through the wall opening with the staff upright in her hand. The fair one she named Domhnall trembled and retreated several paces when he got a close look at the skull-staff.

He continued to back steadily away from her as she approached him. Rifkind stepped over the rubble of the wall to stand just inside the overgrown courtyard.

"You've got his staff," the youth exclaimed with quiet awe.

"You recognize this? I had considerable difficulty getting it. Aside from this staff and ourselves we have nothing to show for a journey across the breadth of Dro Daria itself." She stepped forward as she spoke, hoping to break the fixed distance he seemed determined to maintain; to no avail. Domhnall retreated away from the entrance apace with her.

"Rifkind, I can't see you any longer," Jenny called. "Back up!"

The comment annoyed Rifkind, but considering the circumstances of the young man's fear of the staff, Jenny's request could not reasonably be denied.

"Across Dro Daria?" The youth maintained the same distance between them as she retreated. "You've come all the way across Dro Daria. I've never left the Lyceum here."

"Then how do you survive—don't you at least go out to hunt?" Rifkind demanded. "Isn't it difficult finding food and water here?"

"No. Yes, at first it was, but I've learned a lot since then. Would you like to see?" He stepped to one side and gestured toward the main expanse of buildings, but was still careful to maintain a steady distance from the skull-staff.

"First tell me why you're afraid of this staff."

Since Jenny had mentioned the possibility, Rifkind had found herself wondering if exit from the ruins would be as easy as entrance had been. She settled back against the crumbling walls at the edge of the gap and awaited an explanation.

"It's very strange to see it here, though I'm certain that

it is Assim's staff. I'd seen that the head changed as he did, finally becoming a skull like that—though I haven't actually *seen* the staff with my own eyes in a long time. Perhaps if it can get in here—then maybe I could leave?"

He stepped forward toward the gap, but checked himself a few steps short of the rubble. He noticed Jenny for the first time.

"Don't you want to join us?" he asked.

"Enough has happened in the past day that I don't think I'll rush things. I'm not eager to make another one-way journey," Jenny said. But her voice contained far less hostility than before.

"It's only I who can't leave—I assure you of that. Not that anyone else has tried. When I warded the wraiths out, I inadvertantly set myself in."

"Then how did you get past the wraiths?" Rifkind interrupted to ask.

"I didn't, at least not in the way you mean. I've always been here."

"Since the . . ."

"The sack of the Felmargue? Yes. I had just come to the Lyceum. They admitted candidates once a year, and I'd been accepted only a few months before. Assim had finally harnessed the power of the Well which, of course, actually started the whole war. I never saw the Well until after . . . . I tended the pigs and chickens throughout the Hell-raising. All the years since then seem blurred somehow—they have been too much the same, I think. But I remember those days as clearly as if they were yesterday. The clouds and the noises. I heard them again last night, for the first time in at least four hundred years—but I never thought that the staff was going to return."

"So far as I know, the staff is an afterthought. It was lying there when we were getting away from the wraiths.

I rather think it requires some special knowledge to get reliable use from it. It's not really suited to my style of fighting."

He's telling the truth, she concluded to herself as she spoke. *I even believe that he tended the pigs. But that he's as old as the trees in the forest? Even An-Soren wasn't that old, and his age showed in his face. Dohmnall's eyes are younger than Ejord's.*

" . . . of course, after the war and Assim's betrayal," Domhnall continued, "I didn't even know where the Well was. Assim selected the candidates because they'd already shown some aptitude for the ritual arts, and eventually I found the Well by instinct. Now I know much more than Assim ever did, not that it's done me any good —I'd made most of my serious mistakes early on and the Well does not reverse itself.

"Please, won't you both come to the kitchen? It's more comfortable. I've got food, wine, fresh fruit . . . you must be hungry?"

Rifkind looked through the wall to Jenny.

"What's your name?" the red-haired woman asked.

"I call myself Domhnall. And you?"

Jenny stared briefly at the sky, then stepped through the rubble.

"Gwenifera Overnmont. Jenny."

"Rifkind."

"Where's he going to get fresh fruit at this time of year?" Jenny whispered as the women fell in step behind Domhnall.

"The same place he gets the wine, most likely."

Scars of a tremendous battle were visible on the fallen stones of the rambling cloistered buildings within the crumbling walls. Time had softened the ragged edges of the gaps, and early spring vines with delicate purple flowers covered almost all the exposed stone within the

outer walls. Domhnall led them through vacant corridors
and past rooms filled with the dusty remains of long-
abandoned furniture. Rifkind spotted two corridors that
were not as dusty as the ones they followed. She hesitated
at the second one, intrigued by a pair of iron-hinged doors
hung at the far end of it, but Domhnall affected not to
notice her and headed down a dog-leg corridor away
from the place.

He's been here so many years that he knows these corridors like the lines of his hands, she thought. He's leading
us in circles, too. He says he's learned more than the old
master, Assim, who seems to have been the one who
forced the alliance of the gods against him, yet my
Domhnall is nervous. I don't feel any of the latent power
that clung to An-Soren and his tower. I wonder just what
his "early mistakes" were? He is afraid of the staff and of
the outer walls. I suspect this whole maze-dance is a way
of protecting himself against us. Though I'll be in dire
straits if I'm wrong. I'm no such mistress of ritual and
magick as could tangle with the Black Flame successfully.

They had emerged into a series of inner cloisters, some
fallen into disuse, others showing the efforts of a persistent
if uninspired gardener. Also there were bird nests in the
eaves and vines, something Rifkind had never seen near
An-Soren's malignant residence. She found more signs of
a benign stability in the ruins and in Domhnall himself.
These interior cloisters ended in one that was both larger
and busier than the others. A small flock of chickens
scratched in the dirt, an immense sow wallowed in hock-
deep mud at the far wall, and a well-bred hunting bitch
led a litter of puppies through the haphazardly planted
gardens to greet them. It was not unlike the yard of a
prosperous inn or farm-house, or even the kitchen-keep at
Chatelgard.

Familiar surroundings after weeks of swamps and dan-

ger overcame Jenny's reservations about Domhnall and
his home. She called the dogs over to her and made a
happy fuss over the abundantly affectionate pups, but the
scene was too incongruous to set Rifkind completely at
ease. She followed Domhnall closely as he went into the
shadowed porch and from there into a high-ceilinged
kitchen.

"You were expecting us?" Rifkind asked, glancing
around at tables heaped with an awesome and un-
seasonable variety of food.

"I had hopes. I saw the wraiths rise at sunset, so I knew
someone had come up from the swamp. Whenever they
rise I set aside extra food. I don't mind being the Keeper
of the Well of Knowledge, but I get very lonely."

"The Quais said they leave their aged and injured atop
the Hold for you to tend."

Domhnall looked aside and grimaced. "Yes, and
those are the least able to fight or avoid the wraiths. I light
torches to guide them, but it is a long way from the cliffs.
I think they still remember when I could come to the edge
and guide them."

He looked directly into Rifkind's eyes. She received the
same sensations of appraisal that she was directing at
him.

"The Quais also say that none has ever returned from
the ruins."

"The lots fell hard after the Sack. Most of the masters
were dead. Assim and the Novitiates went out from here
to survey the damage; they never returned. Once they
were away from the Well, the gods struck—and with only
the staff, not the Well, Assim was unable to protect himself as he had done from here. He became the first wraith.
He's acquired companions over the years.

"I think all the Quais in the Felmargue are descended

from the few who survived the Sack by being in or near the Lyceum."

He shook his head, blond hair showing gold in the sunlight. Domhnall was as much attracted to gold as Rifkind herself was, though he had woven it into the natural white homespun of his clothes, while Rifkind wore her wealth attached to her black felt tunic and oiled leather sheaths. Domhnall did not appear armed at all.

The old-young man opened a clay pot, releasing a cloud of indifferently scented steam into the kitchen. With dexterity any palace-cook might envy he wrapped the ends of his sleeves over the handles and poured the contents into a decorative platter without spilling a drop. Never one to be impressed by domestic display, Rifkind nonetheless stood gazing transfixed at the gradually building form of a carefully dressed and roasted fowl much larger than any of the chickens.

"Ah ... Jenny?"

She turned and gestured to Jenny, who caught the sense of urgency in her voice and came at once, followed by the dogs.

Domhnall was fishing vegetables out of the pot with a deep ladle. Rifkind had been convinced that the ladle was filled solely with liquid until the various vegetables plopped onto the platter.

"He poured that bird out of that pot."

Jenny stared blankly. "You can cook meat in a pot, Rifkind. It doesn't have to be spitted. Looks and smells delectable!" She added the last in a louder voice for Domhnall's benefit as her eyes took in the array of fruits, cheeses and breads on the side tables.

The bitch looked up to her master and was rewarded with a meaty soupbone fished out of the same pot that had produced the fowl. She trotted to the hearth to gnaw

at it, followed by the pups, who demanded and received
their own feeding.

"Now he's gotten a meat-bone out of the same pot!"
Rifkind said weakly.

"It wouldn't hurt you to learn a little more about wom-
anly things. Bones add flavor to the stock."

"You don't understand—there's nothing solid in that
pot!"

"Of course not, it's empty except for the stock now. I
can see that—I'm taller than you."

"Let's eat!" Domhnall said as he carried the platter to
the table, cutting off any reply Rifkind wanted to make.

I'm not going mad. Rifkind thought as she selected a
knife and sliced away a hefty portion of the breast, following Domhnall's example. This is either an illusion, or he's
perfected a way of making any sort of food from the limited gardens here. It would get boring. I might be tempted
to create more appetizing foods myself. It's only a change
of form, not essence—that's not going to violate any of the
laws. The animals look healthy enough.

She bit into the meat. Just as the roast had been recognizable as nothing more specific than "bird" so the taste
was merely "fowl" and not any of the numerous domestic
or game birds eaten in the various parts of Dro Daria.

Maybe I've been eating fish and lizards too long. Maybe I've just forgotten what this is. Maybe cooking it in that
pot removed the flavor I expect. But she wasn't able to
convince herself. Still, she was hungry, and the roast, if
rather tasteless, was filling.

They demolished the remainder of the bird and began
on a regally appointed tray of cheeses of every shape and
description. Rifkind held her peace when every cheese
proved to taste the same. She was satisfied to observe that
Jenny was carefully tasting each variety, her face growing
more bewildered with each bite. Domhnall ate with

gusto, oblivious to any second thoughts his guests might be having.

Ritually induced form-change, she decided, applied to the very limited food varieties available within the confines of these walls. But for some reason his visual imagination outstrips his ability to impart proper taste. Possible, I guess.

"These cheeses all taste the same," Jenny whispered to her.

Rifkind nodded. "He makes everything up from those pots. Once I did something similar by wringing water from the air of the desert," she whispered in reply.

"Is it safe to eat?"

"Rather late to wonder about that, isn't it?" Rifkind arched one eyebrow. "I think it's safe, though. The dogs look healthy enough. There're flies in here. It's hard to fool vermin."

Jenny stared at the buzzing insects, trying to feel reassured by them.

"Is something wrong?" Domhnall rose to his feet, the look on his face and the tone of his voice suggesting that he thought there was something amiss, but had hoped it would not be noticed.

"I was thinking how very clever it is of you to be able to provide such a variety of food in this isolation." Rifkind spoke up quickly before Jenny could reveal her suspicions.

"Imitations, that's all they are—I know that," he explained with a bitter sigh. "It's been so long since I've eaten real food I don't remember what it tastes like. With every Black Flame-stone throughout Dro Daria serving as a mirror connected back here to the Well, I can watch the most glorious feasts in the land, but everything here tastes the same. Nothing can disguise that."

"Well, it's nourishing. Everyone here looks healthy. The

Quais live on lizards and fish—I'll take this any day. You've got chickens and such to provide real food now and again."

"They're no healthier than I am!" he said walking away from the table. "I was starving. Sometimes the wraiths would bring a kill into the courtyards and I would be able to steal the remains of it, but mostly I starved or caught rats. Finally I used the Well to provide food, a simulation of food. I wasn't hungry anymore and it was a long time before I realized I wasn't getting any older. I outlasted the wraiths, getting stronger until I could drive them out. But nothing which eats the food of the Well ever grows old. Sunshine there has nursed those puppies for over a hundred years. She's carried them since before the Sack."

Both women looked at the bitch lying on her side, the four eager puppies nuzzling and nursing.

"My god!" Jenny exclaimed softly. "You've made them practically immortal."

"In a way. She still catches an occasional rabbit, which is why she ages at all, I think. For me there's been no change, and I'm afraid to stop eating the Well-food. It's too late, one of my many mistakes I fear. I don't know if I'd start aging normally or not. What's normal for a five-hundred year old man?"

Rifkind looked at him intently. There was no reason to disbelieve him, yet his eyes refused to betray his age. He could not be as old as he claimed. Yet it was growing increasingly unarguable that he could not be other than the sole survivor of the Sack, one whom the fates and gods had conspired against to trap as the immortal yet un-godlike guardian of the Black Flame.

"You poor man!" Jenny exclaimed, suddenly leaving her chair and putting her arms around him.

Rifkind turned away. It was too much to watch. A

sorcerer capable of wrenching more than mere nourishment, of wrenching full and uncorrupt immortality from the glassy black stones, and he was burying his face in Jenny's apron-skirts crying like the child he had been when the Sack occurred.

She felt her hands and teeth clench against the sounds. She wanted to pull the two apart and have a raging tantrum of her own. She left the room, kicked her way through the chickens and skulked into one of the long-abandoned cloisters. The stone-pillared colonnades were sturdy enough to hold her weight, and she sat leaning her head against one of them.

The charm, she thought, Krowlowja's charm. I ought to have suspected. She meant to bind him to her to gain the power of the Well and the Black Flames. *That* is what I interfered with. I felt the affection in the ether. I should have guessed her charm was powerful enough to bind anyone it touched.

She stared at the high-noon sun and the active birds.

No. I should be honest with myself, if no one else. I felt this before Krowlowja appeared. I'm the one who fell in love, of my own will. I'm simply jealous that Jenny moved first.

She felt a measure of pride in her self-analysis and honesty, but it did nothing to lessen the feelings that raged inside her.

CHAPTER 12

"Your friend is very nice."

Rifkind looked up, startled by Domhnall's unheralded appearance in the cloister garden.

"Yes, she is."

"At first I did not recognize you. I thought she was the one who walked the ethereal winds that night and set me free from the one who wished to enchant me."

Rifkind stared at the vines by her feet.

"That one whom you fought—she caught me by surprise. I was so used to being the only one attuned to the Well of Knowledge that I never thought that I could be in danger."

"Krowlowja's the seeress of the Baleric Oracle. She can pull knowledge from the air around you if you don't ward against it. Personal warding is something even healers like myself learn—if only to keep from interfering with our sisters while they work. But, of course, if you learned by yourself, you would never have learned that."

"Perhaps you could teach me?" His eyes met hers with a question that did not seem wholly in reference to personal warding.

"The Goddess has enjoined us from teaching the arts to any man. The Dark Brethren were mostly men, and I think She came to believe that men were unfit."

"Do you believe that?"

Rifkind met his eyes for a moment, then returned to staring at her feet. The silence grew moribund between them. Having just discovered her own passion, Rifkind was ill-equipped to express her emotions to their object. She had spent too much of her life in the world of men without having learned to think of herself as a woman around them. Her femininity was bound to the Goddess and the healing arts, not to men.

Rifkind looked around for the dogs, or some other focus of conversation, but Domhnall saved her from further embarassment.

"Did you really come all the way across Dro Daria to find the Well?"

"Uh ... yes. It was complicated in a way ... no not really. I didn't feel wanted where I was, and an old man I knew suggested I come here. In a way I think he was trying to get me here before Krowlowja and Humphry arrived. Of course, neither of us realized that before I left Chatelgard. Lord Humphry's ..."

"I've heard of Chatelgard."

"Oh ... I hadn't—before I got there, that is. It's completely surrounded by high, barren mountains, and it has the longest, worst winters imaginable. Even if I'd felt wanted I might still have left. Every year you're completely trapped inside those mountains for at least four months."

Domhnall nodded sympathetically; he was used to being trapped behind walls.

I complain about four months in a big, living castle and he's been stranded inside here over four hundred years! she thought.

"Why do Lord Humphry and this seeress Krowlowja want the Well of Knowledge? In that one night I encountered two masters ... mistresses of the arts when in all this time there has been no one, and they were both looking for something. I can't help but feel that it is not a sudden interest in the Eternal Candidate, Domhnall, which draws them here."

"I think Lord Humphry wishes to use your Well to reform the world in his own image—though that's simply a guess."

The warmth and hesitancy of the conversation vanished in an instant. Domhnall jumped down from the wall to pace the length of the garden, ripping handfuls of leaves and flowers off the vines, riling the bees until Rifkind was forced to leave her own perch.

"They can't ... don't they know what will happen if the Well of Knowledge is used like that by men again? Haven't they heard of the Leveller?" he exclaimed when Rifkind stepped into his path.

"I doubt it. I'd never heard of the legend until I reached the Felmargue and the Quais. In most of the lands the Flame itself is left for children's stories. And, at that, the stories do not match with what you or the Quais tell me."

"The world of men should forget forever that the Well is here! Assim destroyed everything around him when he found the old temple and the Well of Knowledge beneath it. And he was a *good* man. The people loved him. He brought peace and learning to us. He established the Lyceum to train healers and scholars. Now he's a wraith, haunting the forests, killing anyone who comes near. Krowlowja and Humphry are *not* good people! They will create an even greater abomination, and the gods will destroy everything."

"It is perhaps tactless to mention this—but the Quais

who brought Jenny and me here believe that the Leveller will be their savior and will return their lands to them. They also believe that I'm the Leveller."

Rifkind lifted her hands as she spoke, expecting some outburst from Domhnall, but not knowing what form it would take. He grasped her arms above the elbow, made speechless by horror and sudden awareness. His grip was firm, but gentle.

"You! The staff ... the first outsider to reach the Lyceum after all these years ... the way you swelled through the ether and drove Krowlowja back to her source. Would that I were wrong, but yes, you are the Leveller. Pray your Goddess forgive you, and me!"

He pulled her closer, she moved without daring to resist. Releasing her arms he held her in a tight embrace.

Rifkind couldn't, didn't, relax in his arms. The feeling was too strange to be comfortable. She wanted to push him away and ask what he was talking about. She wanted to tell him the things the Goddess had said to her when she was in the ger-cat form. But an inner voice she had never heard before counselled her against such actions. He held her until it was a strain to remain stiff and unyielding against his arms. For the third or fourth time in her adult life, Rifkind found herself plagued by tears she could not control and emotions that had no place in the well-ordered life of a healer or warrior.

There are some things that cannot be understood—these must be accepted.

Her own voice, as an adolescent repeating a litany to Muroa at the start of her lessons, floated across the surface of her consciousness, then sank back into the depths of memory.

She has not forgotten Her priestess, Rifkind thought.

Rifkind relaxed. The tears flowed freely and came to a

natural end. Domhnall pushed her back slightly, looking with some dismay from her face of the moist spots on his shirt.

"It's been a very long day ..." Rifkind said absurdly, blotting her eyes on the coarse quilting of her sleeves, suddenly aware that they were filthy and frayed, as was the rest of her attire. She stepped back to a more comfortable distance beyond arm's reach. "We spend the bulk of the night unconscious in a once-occupied tomb guarded by one who was, I think, your master Assim. At least our guard was a giant and he carried the staff."

"It's so hard to believe you simply picked it up and carried it away. All my life I've believed I couldn't touch it, that it would turn me to dust."

"Its touch is cold—unpleasant, but not fatal."

"Very well. But I still do not intend to touch it. It is where you left it by the hearth in the kitchen, and will remain there, untouched until you claim it." Suddenly his manner changed.

"I've forgotten about manners and guests! All those years I watched noble families and priests lead their lives through their heirlooms of Black Flame on a mantle or shelf, all that time thinking of the perfect host I'd be if I ever had guests ... My feasts taste terrible and you're falling with exhaustion because I will not find a guest room for you!

"I've shown Jenny to a room. The Well can provide a semblance of anything you lost in the forests last night— clothing and the like. But you will probably want to return there for your healer's paraphernalia; semblance will not be adequate for your work, I think. But I forget myself again. Would you like to get some rest? May I take you to one of the guest rooms where a hot bath and soft linens await you?"

She nodded. "But first I'll struggle through a tour of

these buildings, and the normal way of getting from the outer walls to these gardens. You brought us here as if your Assim had built a maze."

Affection, exhaustion and emotion could obscure only so much of Rifkind's hard-learned habits. She would not rest until she knew her way out of the compound, or at least had confirmed her suspicions about the various corridors. Despite his tan, the young man blushed, admitted his subterfuge freely and offered a string of explanations as he led the way out of the cloister garden.

The Lyceum, as Domhnall called the ruins, was built in concentric squares, the outer ones having been built as the inner ones became too small for Assim's growing enclave. As Domhnall explained it, the entire complex had been completely constructed during the normal life-span of the master, Assim. The only exception to this was the central and incredibly ancient temple that Assim had explored alone in his youth and which had revealed in its hidden catacombs the chambers of the Well of Knowledge.

In its prime, when Domhnall had been accepted as a candidate, the Lyceum had housed as many as a hundred scholars and physicians and was the home base for as many more who roamed the farmlands and villages of the Fels. Domhnall himself had been the younger son of the local ducal family which had wholly embraced the wisdom and civilization emanating from the open cloisters.

The priests of the other religions, whose dieties had no place in Assim's enlightened vision of the world, had grumbled in their own temples, plotting with frequent success to acquire quantities of the potent substance skimmed off the Well. They called the glassy rocks Black Flames, the name by which the magically charged stones became known throughout the rest of Dro Daria.

Assim and his fellow masters—he had shared his authority as well as his knowledge—discounted the priestly discontent. In time they expected the priests would see the world and men in their way, and they were content to wait. The masters had been wrong about the priests, and they had been wrong about the Well. Domhnall himself, who had had much more time to learn the properties of the fountain in the temple basements, found that its knowledge impinged on the natural powers by which the gods maintained themselves. Left unrestrained the masters would have shortly succeeded in diminishing the gods themselves—a situation the Darian pantheon was not likely to permit.

Rifkind listened to his talk as they wove through the long colonnades and corridors. Unlike Chatelgard, which was first and foremost a fortress overlooking a series of crucial mountain passes, Assim's school had not been constructed with defense in mind. The crumbling outer bulwark was an afterthought of the war. The interior walls abounded with open porticoes, colonnades and lattice-walled classrooms. The climate of the Fels had always been mild. The scholars had opened their classrooms to the always warm breezes.

Those rooms which were well-enclosed had shelves filled with the crumbling dust of countless books. Though Rifkind had not yet learned to read anything more than her own name, she had heard Bainbrose extol the meager library at Chatelgard often enough to be awed by the Lyceum's academic detritus.

They passed rows of tiny rooms with doorless hinges, each of which had housed a novitiate or candidate. Domhnall's old room—they took a brief detour to walk past it—was no different from the others. Only Assim and the other masters seemed privileged enough to have had both sleeping quarters and antechamber. Yet the overall tone of the buildings was not ascetic.

Frescoes of the plain bountiful life of the old Fels still cast their faded colors into the corridors. Even the statues used in the anatomy lessons showed a grace and beauty that would have been cherished at any Darian court and unthinkable in the tents of the Asheeran nomads. Domhnall no longer used the huge open clerestory that had served as a common dining hall for the community. Cataclysm and time had taken all the glass out of its roof and brought the beginnings of a meadow garden to the largest single room of the Lyceum. The vast kitchen beneath it they had seen before, though now Domhnall showed her the fire fueled not by coal or wood but by chunks of glass from the Well.

When she boldly requested a visit to the Well itself he put her off, saying it would be best if she were rested before viewing it, and showed her to a suite of rooms considerably larger than Assim's quarters had been. The guest rooms had sheltered wealthy patrons of the school on their frequent visits to the center of culture and learning.

With a reminder that he could be found anytime in the gardens or the kitchen, Domhnall left her to the pursuit of sleep.

Her mind swam with questions. When she sat in a soft chair by the window her thought was not to draw a deep breath and relax, but to wonder if the chair had been preserved or if it, in its plush softness, was as much a product of the Black Flame's power as the food they had eaten. Her mind then naturally wandered to the power of the Black Flame, ranging from the mundane production of food to attributes that challenged the supremacy of the gods themselves. This led to thoughts about what would happen to her and Jenny now that they had eaten the same food as Domhnall.

When she could clear the Black Flame from her mind
its place was quickly taken by Domhnall himself, and a
gamut of far more perplexing questions about herself and
the man who disrupted the fabric of her emotions.
Rifkind knew, with a faint tinge of shame, that her feeling
for Ejord had never been comparable to the nascent passions she already felt for the white-garbed sorceror.

"Rifkind?"

There was a soft knock, then Jenny poked her head in.

"He's been very courteous. We have food, rest, clothing
—even hot bath water. But I can't sleep. I can't rest at all.
Half of me is as scared as when the Ornaq attacked, the
rest is more excited than a child waiting for Mid-sum-
mer."

"I'm not able to rest myself. It's too much activity and
excitement on too little sleep. I'm sure I'm doing things I'll
regret..." Rifkind thought of the conversation in the
garden and the new feelings within her.

"In a way you must be as excited to meet Domhnall as
he is to meet you. From what little you've told me, most
of the ritual masters and magicians are unpleasant. An-
Soren was evil, this Krowlowja seems at least as bad. The
priests of the Mountain Cults, or even the Mohandrists in
the valley, are so involved with dark and powerful things
that I don't believe they would ever notice if all their food
tasted the same. Whatever else he might be, Domhnall's a
personable sort."

"Which I'm not, I suppose?"

"He's much more relaxed than you are."

"He has had more time to learn how to relax. And,
make no mistake, in that time he's become far more powerful than I'll ever be. The secret of uncorrupted immortality has haunted healers, priests and sorcerers alike.
It has been the downfall of the most powerful who were
foolish enough to pursue it."

"That's just where you're wrong, Rifkind. Domhnall is more powerful than you are simply because he doesn't think in those terms at all. He only wanted to feed himself and survive; that's the source of his uncorrupted immortality! If others have sought after it and failed they were probably corrupt before they began their quest."

Rifkind nodded, unwilling to continue the discussion on its current path. It seemed to her that Jenny had struck at the essential substance of Domhnall's simple existence: he had never sought to become more than what he had to be to survive. He made no comparisons of his powers and so was unconsumed by them. It was an unambitious simplicity she did not think she could emulate were their situations reversed. But then, if Domhnall had been a young man in the Asheera he would not have had to cross forbidden barriers to become a warrior as she had had to do.

"I was really hoping," Jenny continued, "that you could say something to convince me not to be afraid; that side of me is gaining strength the longer I sit still. I feel an overwhelming sense of wrong and doom hanging over us as long as we're here. I trust Domhnall, but that doesn't make any difference. I don't know why. I've tried to sit back and accept it, like you said, but it's like a piece of bad meat—it won't stay down."

Rifkind sighed then got up from her chair to walk slowly around the room as she spoke.

"Domhnall has promised to show me the Well of Knowledge after I rest. For him it is benign Knowledge; for us it will be the very unpredictable Black Flames, and those flames are drawing Humphry and Krowlowja toward us." She pounded the fist of one hand into the palm of the other. "It is wrong! The gods are hiding something from us, using us mortals to do things in some way forbidden to them. I am afraid of this place."

Rifkind spoke her fears as she discovered them suddenly within her. She could not put any one cause to the source of them. Her hackles rose whenever Humphry injected himself into her life. The seeress Krowlowja had proven in one brief encounter to be an enemy of power and determination. Still, the picture refused to come clear in her mind. She was left with the vague impressions that all the mortals were insignificant detail on a vastly larger canvas woven about the Black Flame.

"The ewers contain wine, I've discovered." Jenny lifted a terra-cotta jug from the side-board. "The Black Flame produces a very acceptable vintage."

Jenny poured a goblet of the rich amber-colored liquid that was unlike any of the hearty red vintages to be found elsewhere in Dro Daria. It proved calming to a point where Rifkind suspected it was no ordinary wine, though she drank fully nonetheless.

The bathing pool that adjoined both Jenny's and Rifkind's suites was a deep terra cotta pool filled with naturally heated, mineral-laden waters. An arrangement of ducts and levers allowed water to be flushed out or added at the bather's convenience. The women allowed the pool to fill to overflowing. Rifkind had adapted to the Darian custom of immersion bathing as she had to no other. With the ewer of wine on the floor between them, she and Jenny eased into the warm water. A broad ledge beneath the surface allowed them to sit with the water above their shoulders.

The network of hard, pale scars on Rifkind's arms and legs puckered as she relaxed. She had forgotten the battles that had given her most of them. Even her breasts and stomach bore signs of the hard nomadic life. Only her face was free of blemishes and scars, and that only because of a young healer's powers and vanity. She stared at her reflection in the sunlit water. Her eyes, the proof of her pure-blooded Asheeran heritage, were, as Jenny cautiously remarked, different from any she'd seen these past three years. They were narrower, more upturned than the Darian norm, and so black that no pupil could be seen within them. Her cheek bones were high and shaped so that the silver crescent rode easily on the crest of the right one, a startling contrast to the dusky gold of her skin, and the raven hue of her hair, so black and straight that not even the Felmargue sun could lighten it.

Even the Asheerans had liked their women somewhat bigger and fuller than she was, and in Dro Daria she was simply a freak, exotically different at best, but the vision of no man's dreams. Rifkind swept her arms through the water to break the reflection into countless ripples. She concluded her bath without further thoughts of herself.

Rifkind left the bath wrapped in a sheet and collapsed into a sound sleep on the bed. Her last waking thoughts were that she had not been meant to fall in love, only to fight and serve the Goddess.

Domhnall entered the room without disturbing her. He studied the heap of worn, dirty clothes at the edge of the bathing pool, risked a glance at the half-covered woman, protected in modesty by her hip-length raven black hair, then left the room as silently as he had come.

CHAPTER 13

Assim's ancient temple was completely enclosed by the newer buildings of the Lyceum. More than any other part of the interior complex, however, it bore the scars of ferocious battle, and as they approached the center Domhnall cautioned both women frequently about weak spots in the floors. Great vines, their purple flowers closed for the night, spilled into the enclosure from gaps in the ceiling and walls. The trio's footsteps aroused the nesting birds, who dove down drom their perches to investigate the unusual noises. More than once they covered their faces with their arms and Domhnall shook the lit torch at the frantic creatures. All the activity was both unnerving and reassuring; song-birds and honey-bearing vines would not thrive in an area irredeemably damned by the Dro Darian pantheon.

The first chambers of the temple were inky dark despite the torches that Domhnall lit and placed in ornate wall-sconces. Intricate asymmetric designs ran riot over the walls in faded tones of black and red.

"Is this writing of some sort?" Jenny asked, examining the meandering lines more closely.

She carried a lute and planned to sit in one of the ante-
chambers of the Well. She had no desire to enter the
chamber, but had hesitated to remain alone in the other
portions of the complex, regardless of Domhnall's as-
surances.

"I think so—but no one knows for sure. Assim and the
others were never able to decipher it, if it is writing, and
even with the Well I've only been able to find a few repeating patterns—and no meanings."

Rifkind traced one section of the design with her fore-
finger. She could no more read its curves than she could
read common script, but the way the walls had been covered from floor to ceiling could not have been accidental,
and if there had been a ritual purpose to the activity she
hoped to feel it. It was no use; time had erased any of the
ritual content implied in the painting, and her fingers felt
only the rough surface of the sandy plaster.

They went down a dustless flight of stairs into a subter-
ranean part of the temple that was lit by an unseen source
of light. The walls were a translucent milky color, devoid
of all markings or signs, or even of the ravages of age that
showed so profoundly in the room above them.

The Lost Gods, Rifkind thought, shivering in the light
though the room was comfortably warm. The walls of
Hanju's palace in the mountains were like this.

She remembered her terror on awakening in the rep-
tillian god's quarters where he had explained the power
of her ruby to her. He had also convinced her that the last
surviving god from the old times was quite insane.

He taunted me with the walls. I remember breaking
through them with my mind to see the snow-barren
mountains outside. His palace is a type of illusion I don't
think the pantheon gods could maintain.

She wondered what would happen if she forced her
concentration and energies through these walls, and what

she would find if she did. She repressed the thought.

"You should stay here." Domhnall pointed to an alcove with an angular opalescent structure within it. Rifkind recognized the hard surfaces as seats for serpentine beings such as Hanju, but Jenny was clearly puzzled by them.

"The Font is just beyond this door. The masters were very adamant that the Well was dangerous to those who could not be attuned to it."

"Don't worry about me—I don't want my mind attuned to anything like that." Jenny settled herself in the alcove with her instrument.

Rifkind stared at a point on the floor while Domhnall released the wards on the inner chamber doors. Jenny was politely, and properly, concealing her deepest wishes as she sat picking out a melody on the lute, just as Rifkind longed to watch the sequence of the wards so that she might explore the Well on her own. But though Domhnall might reveal the structure of the wards if she asked, asking itself would be an admission of untrustworthiness on her own part.

Jenny was satisfied with the tone of the lute and began playing more intricate airs. Lady Anelda had insisted on high proficiency in all domestic arts from the ladies, fosterlings and unacknowledged children who passed through her care. Jenny had also learned the rollicking, bawdy songs sung in the out-of-the-way gaming rooms of the palace, but whether through her own mood or in deference to Domhnall, she chose stately court music.

Rifkind set her thoughts to drifting lest she pick up any inadvertent awareness of Domhnall's designs upon the Well-chamber door. As he had said earlier, he had never learned to shield his thoughts.

Hanju, what did he say? That the rubies were concentrations of power and attributes that enabled others of his kind to do things otherwise prohibited to them? He had none himself, I remember that. He cannot leave his mountains, which is just as well. The rubies and other talismans somehow weakened his fellows, I guess. He spoke as if our gods had once worshipped him and the other Lost Gods, and then somehow replaced them—and in the process the world of mortal men was created.

This is a temple to the Lost Gods, or maybe one where the Lost Gods came themselves. No wonder our pantheon moved with such determination against Assim. They made us to worship and serve them. It would be unthinkable that we should discover the gods of the gods.

The release of the final ward disrupted her reverie. The texture of the opalescent room changed. The walls were no longer serene but seethed with effervescent patterns that reacted to the notes that Jenny played, though any structure and purpose continued to elude Rifkind.

"Rifkind?"

Domhnall's voice created different movements on the walls of the room. Jenny didn't seem to notice the lavender and pink swirls created by her lute, or the blue burst that accompanied Domhnall's speech, but that was to be expected—she was not in any way attuned to the ethereal. Domhnall? Was he so accustomed to the shifting of the room that he no longer paid it any notice? Had he studied the painted meanderings in the above-ground part of the temple and not noticed their similarity to the patterns produced by his own voice?

Hanju, Rifkind remembered, did say I was the first of my race who could manipulate his walls.

"Rifkind, are you all right? Do you wish to leave?"

Domhnall reached out to take her hand, as she followed her thoughts to their conclusion. The Well of Knowledge is the source of the Lost Gods' power. My ruby, and An-Soren's, were nothing more or less than skimmings off the Well of Knowledge, no different in essence from Bainbrose's Black Flame trinkets!

She mumbled something to Domhnall about her distraction and followed him into the Font-chamber itself. Armed with her new-formed theory, she did not find the Well of Knowledge as surprising as it would otherwise have been. The walls, floor and ceiling of the chamber were of the same substance as the walls of the outer chamber, only even more alive with color and pattern. It was impossible to gauge the exact size of the room with the swirls moving on the walls, but she guessed that four or five strides would be enough to cross it from edge to edge. The Well of Knowledge rose inside a hexagonal font covered with small niches that collected and refracted the colors passing over them.

Scarcely noting that Domhnall still held her hand, Rifkind stepped closer to the font and glanced down into the thick black fluid. The rapid flow of pattern and intensity were too bewildering for her to make out any detail on the glassy surface itself. She shielded her eyes as if from a bright light, though there was nothing inherently brilliant within its depths.

"The first time I looked down I was blind for a week after." Domhnall led her back to the perimeter of the room, and helped her onto a ledge that she had not noticed, so complete was the dominance of the shifting colors and patterns across the walls.

"Not quite blinded." She rubbed her eyes gently and noticed as she did that the crescent implanted in her cheek was warmer than the rest of her skin.

"You've had much experience with the ethereal sphere."

Rifkind shook her head. Now that she had noticed it, the crescent seemed to be getting warmer still. Domhnall noticed her touching it.

"I'm sworn to the Goddess of the Bright Moon," she said in explanation. "She is with me always."

"Then perhaps She has forgiven those who used the Well in the past. The warding would not otherwise have released itself in the presence of one of those who sacked the Hold."

"As I say, She is with me always." Rifkind touched the warm silvery metal embedded in her cheek again.

"I see. I hadn't fully understood that before. If I had known ... but I'm certain if there were to be violence between She-within-you and the Well, it would have appeared before now. Before the wars a priest of Mohandru forced his way into this chamber. The novitiates spent three days scrubbing him off the walls."

"She promised me there would be no interference with my quest once we were past the wraiths. There is a certain mutuality of faith betwixt the Bright One and myself." She did not add that if the Well were not directly accessible to the gods, the Bright One would have no qualms about letting Her priestess be Her eyes.

"Can you see clearly enough yet for me to demonstrate the Well?"

She nodded but remained seated on the ledge while he went to the font. Poising his open hands over the surface, Domhnall caused it to bubble and build slow-moving prominences that almost touched his palms before arcing downward again. Activated by Domhnall's movements the Well stimulated the luminous walls to a colorful display that extended out to the ante-chamber and was visible even to Jenny, if that young woman's surprised yelp was any indication. Though Jenny had stopped playing, the notes of the lute continued, and expanded into a strange symphony echoing about the Font.

Domhnall turned his head toward her.

"Your presence, and Jenny's music, is charging the Well

in ways I've not seen before. I'll move slowly, for my own sake as well as yours. There is much more strength and will here. I will try to recreate my first lesson with the Well, when I first learned to ask it questions and to understand the answers."

He turned back to the Well. The activity on its surface intensified at once and in spite of the distance to the Well, Rifkind feared she would be drawn into its dazzling movements again. Wrenching herself free of the sensation, she missed the few words he spoke to phrase the question. Another series of changes passed over the Well. The superabundance of its patterns decreased in waves until only a few ripples and colors remained. These began at once to reinforce each other.

Rifkind watched expectantly, trying to make her mind receptive to the process unfolding before her, and at the same time trying to second-guess what his question had been. Bread?

An Asheeran, she had not eaten the yeast-lofted staple of the Dro Darian civilizations until long after her own hunger-images had been established—yet now her thoughts revolved around untold varieties of bread. She thought too of bread making, seed planting, fire laying and baking times and temperatures. She wrested herself away from the distraction.

".... of course, then I found out that there was no way I could bake bread, or grind flour or, especially, grow grain with what remained of the Lyceum larder, so I had to learn how to transform the substance of the Well itself, as I told you this morning."

"I see." Rifkind answered slowly, realizing that she had not been distracted but responding to the knowledge contained in the Well. "The transformation powers of the Well must be different in essence from the knowledge powers, then, though logically preceded by them?"

"Never thought of it that way, but I guess that they are."

He lifted a silver metal ladle from the edge of the font and dipped out a portion of the liquid as Rifkind gathered her courage to approach again. The Well itself responded to its loss with a violent display of colored prominences that darted across its surface. Domhnall eased the obviously solidifying substance into his hands and began molding it.

"For you." He handed her an inexpert but recognizable form of one of the purple-vine flowers. "Would you care to try it now?"

The glass flower was fairly solid, but when Rifkind held it the petals stretched and thinned, arching slightly until the black glass was an intricate duplicate of the flower she had observed so closely before. She looked up at Domhnall, and though she did not herself understand how she had completed the molding of the flower, she was unsurprised that he regarded her with undisguised awe.

"Is it best to begin with memory exercises like the bread?" she asked, without mentioning the stone flower still cradled in her hands.

"Yes, that is usually the safest." Domhnall spoke with his mind far from his words.

Rifkind stepped up to the font. Its height was awkward for her and she stepped carefully onto one of the lower ridges of carving, which darkened at once in response to her weight. She chose her thoughts carefully, lest the Well activate some random unpleasant thought and send her into shock or worse. Dramatic though Domhnall's demonstration had been, she wanted to test the powers herself and take her own measure of the Well of Knowledge. There had been another object, itself the spawn of this same font, whose powers had changed her forever and brought the downfall of the last of the Dark Brethren.

Despite her mental vow that she would not be lured into idle thoughts, she remembered the ruby and her encounter with the Lost God, Hanju.

The Well seized upon her thought, breaking away from her control and, she feared, controlling her. The dark surface of the seething liquid was discolored by a creeping crimson stain. Moments passed and the chamber in its entirety pulsed with the rich blood color of the lost stone. The Well-surface roiled again, prominences arose—a being not unlike Hanju did a miniatured serpentine dance across the surface. Rifkind recognized Leskayia, the one who had created the ruby.

She watched the surreal creature materialize a knife and plunge it into its own breast: from the gaping cavity the figure removed perfect miniatures of the two stones that had eventually found their way to An-Soren and herself.

The figure disolved back into the Well—only to be replaced by Hanju. He was no product of arcane memory. His inky blue-black iridescent scaled back was toward her. He turned and stared at her with tiny haunting gold eyes and a smile that revealed needlelike teeth within a delicate mouth.

"Rifkind! I see you again—but not in my own mountains? Ah, yes! I recognize this. Congratulations! But Leskayia's heart is stilled and you have returned to the Well to restore it?"

His voice was not distorted, despite his small size. Again Rifkind fought the twin feelings of revulsion and attraction toward the alien god. He spoke the Old Tongue, the language of ritual and trance that Muroa had taught Rifkind and which hissed so naturally through Hanju's fangs and across his hard-surfaced lips—the only language both men and the Lost Gods could speak.

"I am honored to see you well, within your mountains.

I had thought of you as I stepped up to the Well."

The Old Tongue came to her with difficulty. She seldom spoke it consciously and slipped into a conditioned attitude of humility.

"Yes, yes. I know all that. It has been long, so long, since I have been called to our ancient home. Yet *called* only! Not compelled. So ask no foolish questions of me, my love. But do visit me!" The tiny figure's voice echoed through the chamber flattening Domhnall to the wall. "Before I only *thought* you might be worthy of me, now I *know!* It has been too long!"

Hanju laughed, or sneered, Rifkind could not tell which, only that the sound loosened her shocked will. She wrested control of herself back from the Well and summoned a wave from the depth of the font to send it crashing over the animated figure. The wave splashed onto the font and drew her flower into itself and back to the now quiet depth.

"Never has such a creature come forth or spoken like that." Domhnall joined her at the font, rubbing his shoulders where they had been flattened against the wall.

"Did you recognize him at all, though?"

Domhnall hesitated.

"At first I neither recognized nor understood it. But I am attuned to the Well, for all that now I realize that our probings have explored only the most superficial of its secrets. I was able to understand, once I made myself receptive. It is the language which is written in such profusion on the upper chamber walls. And the demon was some creature who identified himself with life itself and said that it had been here often before, though not, of course, in the times of the Lyceum."

"We learn different things. I have long known the language of the Lost Gods. We call it the Old Tongue and use it to evoke the power of essences. I am surprised that you and your masters knew nothing of it. It is an unconscious hidden language revealed to a healer at her initiation and refined throughout her life. But it was while I lived in the mountains of Glascardy and saw the source of their Mountain Cults that I learned the Lost Gods were not entirely lost. At least one, Hanju, survives and claims some worship within his mountains. I've judged him mad, even by the standards of the pantheon. Isolation and the fact that he has lived past his time have done their worst. But he knows things our gods have forgotten or never knew."

"Hanju, so that's a name? I heard the word as 'life-itself.' " Domhnall paused, then smiled. "I have seen new things in the Well this night. Things I could not have begun to call forth from it, limited as I am by my own narrow experience and imagination. It has given me a key to many of the ancient mysteries which we have identified but never solved here at the Lyceum."

"I've lost your flower," Rifkind said, deliberately changing the subject and pointing to the already fading stain on the font where the Well had briefly overflowed.

"That is nothing; I can make you another, but I think we should wait until another time."

He reached forward for the ladle that still lay upon the lip.

"Wha ...?"

His shocked expression of warning was stifled as the Well erupted with sudden bursts of violence that seemed, in some undefinable way, not natural to it. Rifkind grabbed Domhnall's shirt, pulling both of them to safety on the wall-ledge as the Well-substance roared upward out of the font and into the shape of a green-eyed woman whom Rifkind recognized at once.

"Krowlowja!" she whispered.

They had trapped themselves at the wall furthest from

the entrance. The seeress chortled hideously and blocked their way to escape. Neither Rifkind nor Domhnall spoke. There was no great need for words. If either had been able to break the seeress' growing presence they would have done so, and Krowlowja's strengthening apparition indicated to each the other's helplessness as well as his own.

Alerted by the noise, Jenny appeared in the doorway. Horror showed in her face, but her screams did not penetrate the chamber.

"The Black Flame is Mine!" The shriek echoed through the minds of both of those pressed hard against the icy walls.

CHAPTER 14

This is the end, there can be nothing beyond this, Rifkind thought. Krowlowja is drawing the power of the Well to her and she will destroy us.

Already Rifkind felt consumed by lethargy as the rampant energies of the seeress surged through the chamber. The sinuous blending of patterns and color on the walls had frozen in place and showed brittle movements of fracture and decay moving across the stagnant colors as Krowlowja diverted and absorbed more of the essence of the Well. Gathering strength for a momumental effort Rifkind turned to face Domhnall. The fair youth's eyes were closed and his features contorted grotesquely by the insatiable hunger with which Krowlowja gutted the Well to which he was so exquisitely attuned.

The apparition, clothed in long fur-trimmed green robes over a heavy black undergown, was solid enough to block light from the opposite wall and to obscure the doorway behind it. Except for the oppressive psychic weight of its presence it had not, however, directed a physical assault against them. The lethargy had not affected Rifkind's mind and as she thought about it, no one in the Felmargue area would wear such heavy clothing. It could only be an ethereal manifestation of the seeress, however solid it seemed. Just as Rifkind in ger-cat form could assume only a limited physical reality, so too would Krowlowja be limited in her physical powers—should she need them. Rifkind doubted that the seeress would fight as a warrior.

I came so far from the Asheera to die like this at the hands of a vapor-sniffing seeress! she thought. I should have remained with some clan and been a quiet, undistinguished healer. But, that is all behind and lost. Krowlowja will end everything here. She doesn't know me, except through Humphry. I offer her no specific threat. I'm not under some geas to protect the Well, as Domnhall seems to be. Yet I shall die here.

When Jenny had awakened her earlier she had dressed in a light-weight blue gown Domhnall had sent to her. The gown had no slits for access to her thigh-knives, so, like an idiot moon-calf she hadn't worn them. The heavy oiled leather belt that held her sword and anchored the harness for her throwing knives was ill-suited to ladies' attire. She hadn't worn her boots, with their side-knives, preferring to walk barefoot over the smooth stones. She had one jewel-handled wrist-sheathed knife and the poisoned spike in her hair, neither of which seemed potent against she whose green eyes at last focused on the pair.

"It was generous for you to have opened the way for me, but not so generous that I will let you live. Even you whom I once thought to take as a lover to gain this place."

The apparition detached itself from the font and floated easily to the floor. It gestured once and with a groan of agony Domhnall slid from the ledge to his knees on the floor. He abased himself, then began a shuffling crawl to Krowlowja.

It is too far from the open air to hope that the Bright One's powers could reach; Rifkind thought. She had to summon all the healers to drive the Dark Brethren into Her light where She could affect them. *While Krowlowja waxes strong on the essence of godhood I cannot raise a hand or make a sound to offer even a mite of protest against her.*

The apparition had taken on a fleshly corporeality when Domhnall groveled to her feet. She offered lewd bargains of life to her helpless prisoner. But if Domhnall had lost dominion over his body, his mind and pride were intact and he would not yield, though she brought pressure that seemed to crush the breath from him.

The practices she described, though inverted, were not dissimilar from the orgies regularly held at the Asheeran Gathering feasts to initiate the auction of women captured from the caravans or borderlands, but Rifkind had never had to confront them in terms of a person she herself cared for. She struggled valiantly and finally managed to ease forth the wrist-knife. Its hilt was jeweled and ornate, uncomfortable to clutch for any length of time, but its blade was the same high quality steel as any of her other knives. Putting all her efforts into a gasp of a shout, Rifkind rose up from the ledge and threw the knife. It wobbled, moving slowly as if affected by the same lethargy that overwhelmed her. Though the blade touched home on the seeress's breast, it simply slid down the front of her robes, smearing the green and black illusion as it passed over it, but not damaging it in any significant way.

At least I got her attention, Rifkind thought wryly.

Krowlowja did not speak or toy with Rifkind. Rifkind watched the sorceress tense and draw back her hands, raising them above her shoulders.

"Steam-inhaling hag who lives in caves hidden from

true light! You'll have to fight to kill *me!* I'm a priestess of the Bright Goddess. I can encompass the essence of every living thing!"

Her challenge was probably an idle boast; she could commandeer the strength of any living thing near her, but just now the only living beings were Jenny and Domhnall. Still, her thoughts, as she hurled them through the resisting air, gave her focus. Krowlowja shot forth a brace of golden bolts from her palm. Like the knife, they were caught in the retarding air that now filled the chamber.

In the Asheera the women left behind to guard the camp when the warriors went raiding fought with spears. Asheeran warriors relished the ideal of catching such a woman-thrown spear in flight and reversing it. The slow moving light-bolts were small challenge to her even with the lethargy in her muscles.

The seeress elongated her image, easing between the returning bolts which smashed into the wall behind her. Her second series of gestures brought forth a glowing ball far smaller than the bolt, yet intensely brighter, which was unaffected by whatever lethargy infected the air. Rifkind threw herself under it, singed but otherwise uninjured. She sought for a counter-offensive as Krowlowja continued to refine her attack.

But I've never thought of ritual apart from healing— not even with the ruby. I've done what I had to do—but I've never thought it through beforehand.

She began to *push* back at the seeress until she could be driven from the Well. The walls crackled with sparks as Rifkind thrust her own taproot into the limitless essence of the Well. Air became a solid transparent wall surrounding and resisted by both of them as Krowlowja countered brute force with brute force and the battle sank to its most basic level of who was not so much strongest as best bal-

anced and most consistent in the application of that
strength.

Rifkind leaned into the pressures Krowlowja returned
until her body pointed at an unnatural angle over the
floor. She felt the force, however, as if it came straight
from the seeress and countered it with straight-seeming
thoughts of her own. Her thoughts were primitive im-
pulses focused only on the elimination of Krowlowja and
less centrally on preserving herself. There was not room
in her perceptions for any other being.

Domhnall wavered to his feet, but for the moment he
was oblivious to the conflict.

*Do not resist. There is no cause for us to fight—you
know that yourself. The Well is enough for us both, and
you may have the man, if you wish. Relax, there is no
reason to fight me, I will not hurt you,* Krowlowja
projected toward Rifkind, careful not to create a flaw in
her defenses as she did so.

Liar! Releasing any other reality than that of the iron-
hard presence of the seeress and her cold-steel opposition
to it, Rifkind linked every fiber of her physical existence to
the ethereal death struggle.

Domhnall shook his head yet again. His vision was returning. The seeress had had to release him to concentrate on Rifkind. Static arcs of lightning hung between
the two women. He knew better than to cross between
them, but they had concentrated their power so closely
that he could otherwise move freely about in the
chamber.

The silver ladle lay ignored behind Krowlowja, on the
lip of the font. Stealthily he went for it. But simultaneously
as he reached for it ... he pulled back. The seeress had
threatened him with a slavery as bad or worse than the
punishment laid upon Assim by the gods. Domnhall was

not a warrior, and he was afraid. But Domhnall knew he had to accept the risk of Krowlowja's further attentions or watch Rifkind be crushed. He took the handle in his hand.

The ladle raised a cloud of blue sparks as he dragged it out of the resistant sphere. The image of Krowlowja was built from the liquid of the Well of Knowledge and that fluid could be captured and changed by the ladle. In one motion he slashed it across her back and flung the matter thus ripped from her into the Well.

Krowlowja screamed. Random bolts of golden energy flailed away from her, but those few Rifkind could not counter were drawn in by the walls themselves. As suddenly as she had appeared the seeress was sucked back into the Well, was swallowed by whatever had allowed her into the chamber. The heavy air returned to normal; Rifkind crashed forward, breaking her fall with her face.

The breath had been knocked out of her, and for a blurred moment Rifkind could not determine what had happened. Had she won or lost? Had it all been a dream? Then she felt the aches of sprained muscles and her memory cleared. Warm salty fluid filled her mouth. A hard jagged object pressed against her tongue. Quickly she ran her tongue over the lines of her front teeth. Teeth could not be healed. The fragment had come from a wisdom tooth, but pain welled out of her lower jaw. Opening her mouth slightly increased the pain, but nothing was broken. Her nose was swelling with blood, making her breathing difficult. For all the brawls and battles she had been through, would she take her first disfiguring facial scar as the result of a fall?

Her limbs were too tired to obey her desire to stand or to roll to one side. Heedless, she spat the blood out of her mouth along with the useless tooth fragment and gave up breathing through her nose.

"She's spitting blood!" Domhnall knelt by Rifkind, tenderly wiping her torn lips. "Help me get her to her feet," he said to Jenny.

He put an arm under Rifkind's shoulders and began to lift her. Too soon, the blood drained from her face, leaving it a waxy yellow color. She opened her mouth again to protest but could only make bubbles with the blood.

"No! Put her back down. No, not like that, on her side so the blood will drain out her mouth, not down her throat."

"Are you a healer, too?" Domhnall asked her, wiping the blood off his hands and onto his already stained shirt.

"No, but I've been on hand when a rider took a fence that the horse wouldn't. There's not much difference. She's cut up and shaken, blood or no, she'll come around in a little. Move her too quickly, though, and she'll start to faint like that. With anyone else I'd worry about binding that cut, but I remember when I first saw Rifkind. She'd been cut through to the bone on her arm; it was gone in a week. The nose might need some help.

"Can you hear me?" Jenny turned her attention to Rifkind.

Rifkind tried to speak but found it difficult and Jenny motioned her to silence.

"One finger: yes. Two fingers: no."

Rifkind lifted one finger.

"Look from one side to the other." Rifkind did as requested though her own assessment of her injuries was complete; to have resisted would only have upset her friend.

"Nothing too serious. I can't see the size of her pupils, but if someone's had a bad knock on the head, one eye often won't move at all."

They waited moments longer, then Jenny allowed Domhnall to help Rifkind to a sitting position. Elevation was good for bleeding wounds, she explained, though with a head injury elevation had to be measured against the need to keep the patient conscious. It was still too soon for Rifkind to try moving about on her own. The nose-bleed had slowed to a trickle, mostly because her nose was swollen shut with the blood already within it. Jenny dabbed at Rifkind's chin to gauge the extent of the damage there. The chamber was pristinely clean and the wounds, though they cut clear through her lip and to the bone, were free of detritus.

"I can carry her up to her rooms now," Domhnall said.

"Are you strong enough? That witch got her fangs into you too."

"I can carry her."

The strains of exhaustion still lay heavily on Rifkind's arms and legs. Her face hurt, warning her of worse to come. She wanted to get somewhere where she could care for herself with as little interference and observation as possible. But Jenny would hear nothing of her moving unaided. To fend off argument, Rifkind let Domhnall lift her up and rested her throbbing head against his shoulder—until they started to leave the chamber.

"Put me down and set the wards ... no, we've got to ward the Well itself, not just the chamber. The bitch entered from beneath. Damned cave-dwelling vapor-sniffing bitch!" Rifkind spoke barely above a whisper but grimaced so that she loosened the blood clots on her chin.

"As soon as we've got you to your room I'll come back."

"We'll do it now!"

Domhnall set her back on her feet.

"I don't know how to ward the Well, just the chamber."

"We've got to ward the Well itself. There must be a way. If she can get into the chamber from below and start leeching the strength of the Well, no warding will hold. How did you learn to ward the chamber?"

"I looked into the Well," Domhnall admitted.

"Then look again."

Domhnall opened his mouth to protest, then looked again at Rifkind, pale and stained with blood. He returned to the font.

As he did so veils of multi-hued light spread up in a pyramid form rising to a point above the font, then cascaded to the floor, engulfing Domhnall for a moment. When he stepped out of it he was holding Rifkind's jeweled knife.

"The Well was waiting, as if it needed me to say the word but that it had already prepared the wards. This floated to the surface. I return it to you: the first object the Well has ever returned."

He handed the knife to Rifkind and began the less dramatic process of sealing the inner chamber. Jenny got her lute from the alcove where she had hurriedly left it.

The ante-chamber looked as it had when they had entered: milky translucent walls with just the faintest trace of a breeze in the air. The patterns in the upper chambers were no more comprehensible to Rifkind, but Domhnall saw new knowledge of the temple's history written there and would have shared it with them had Jenny not adamantly refused the honor.

Rifkind's temporary recovery was short-lived; the efforts of climbing the stairs herself had depleted her adrenalin-boosted stamina. While Domhnall spoke of the patterns on the walls, she stopped and wove blindly through the air groping for something solid enough to hold her. Before she could protest, and before Jenny could insist, Domhnall swept Rifkind up in his arms again.

"We've set the wards. The Well is safe, and grateful to you, but you were tired when you got here this morning."

It is pleasant to be cared for when you're hurt, she thought. The melting sensations she had felt when she had first seen him returned in full force, and she leaned more heavily on his shoulder.

They brought her to her room. Jenny went after a basin of warm water while Domhnall went after another gown. Jenny set the water beside Rifkind and ripped clean strips of cloth from the hem of the blood-stained gown.

Rifkind did not need to see the ravages of the fall to treat them: the Goddess gave a refined sense of personal injury to all Her healers. She nudged each flap of skin into position and held it until a ritually induced bond held it in place. Added to the strain of the battle, her self-healing left Rifkind prostrated.

"You've done a masterful job," Jenny appraised as Rifkind lay panting. "Just one tiny little line—one might think you'd got scratched by a kitten."

She tore thin strips of cloth and dipped them into a pool of candle wax, molding the cloth into short stumps as the wax began to harden.

"I don't feel very comfortable with this healing you do, but I don't deny its effectiveness. But don't you care what your nose looks like? I've packed a nose straight before —you can't breathe through it anyway so the cloth won't bother you. I'm told it hurts though. Do you want me to?"

Rifkind stared at her with glazed, unfocused eyes. She was too tired to do more—and anyway, the Goddess was concerned with health, not beauty. Muroa was ample proof that a healer's reputation did not rest on her appearance. And certainly a warrior was enhanced by his scars.

Then she thought of Domhnall, and of herself as something other than a warrior or healer, and nodded to Jenny. "Put them in," she whispered.

Jenny moved with sure gentleness, and it was soon done. Domhnall appeared with another blue gown, but Rifkind had played the obedient patient for as long as she could tolerate and ordered them both out of her room with a nasal voice she scarcely recognized as her own.

Then she removed the stained gown, pulled the other gown over her head, and lay down at last. The pain, the exhaustion and even the moonlight peeking into the open window were quickly forgotten.

CHAPTER 15

"The world has survived my broken nose," Rifkind sighed as she sat up in the rumpled bed. Sunlight streamed obliquely across the room. It was late afternoon. She had slept at least one day; since there was still a slight tingling of fatigue in her legs, she had probably slept no more than that. She probed the chin wound with her fingertips. The scabs loosened at the light pressure. Likewise when the waxed cloth was removed her nose felt normal-sized and straight—except for a palpable but invisible knob under the skin.

The side-board basin had been refilled while she slept. Her own clothing lay neatly folded, apparently cleaned and mended. She lifted up the linen undertunic, then set it down again. For once she would take the time to contemplate the future rather than just let it happen to her.

Krowlowja will lead Humphry and the Imperial forces to the Hold, she thought. How large a force? He wouldn't travel alone, even with a seeress like Krowlowja.

She knows where the Well is now, and that it's certainly no legend. She's tasted its power. I would not expect any natural object to resist that unholy pair for long. If there is a division within the pantheon, as my Goddess suggests, I would not be surprised if the seeress can find some divine assistance.

Rifkind's mind turned at once to the options and strategies available to them to protect the Well from the rapacious Humphry and his new ally. A dozen half-formed alternatives fluttered through her thoughts before she admitted, as she had admitted to Ejord during the Civil War, that she was no general. She was a superb fighter, but she could not conceive strategies.

The old question of why or how had she become involved in a situation plainly not suited to her abilities rose up. And with the question, the doubts about her loyalty to the Goddess to whom she was dedicated in peace and life and whom she served with war-cries and killings. Suddenly Rifkind realized that the questions and doubts no longer seemed relevant; her immersion in the Well of Knowledge had had an unexpected consequence.

I do what I do. It is as simple as that. The Goddess has always known what I am. My future and my past were known to her at my initiation. She would not have given me the crescent of Her honor without accepting me as I am. It is not for me to question why She would want, or need, a healer whose first instincts are to snarl and fight.

She fingered the crescent confidently. It was hers; a part of her life not likely to disappear. That knowledge alone made the struggle with the seeress worthwhile.

The Well itself had essence, but pieces of the Well, drawn out with the ladle or some other means, had a mutable essence which could be fixed by the Well-master. It would not be an abomination to create life from the Well of Knowledge. As this bit of Well-imparted knowledge passed through Rifkind's consciousness, she knew that the Well had been the means of creation by which the gods found their first worshippers. She shut that thought out of her mind—judging it unwise to consider the ways of the gods, even if it weren't an abomination.

So, she continued thinking to herself, each Black Flame removed from the Well of Knowledge is molded by the Master to one essence. There are the memory-stones of the Quais, the cooking-stones in the kitchen, the skull-staff that Assim wielded against the gods. Each Black Flame accomplishes the purpose which was intended for it ... and Bainbrose's stones do nothing—*magically!*

"And what will Humphry or Krowlowja do with the stones once they get here?"

She shook her head and threw her nightgown back on the bed. Thoughts of Humphry and the Well of Knowledge had awakened her completely. The Overnmont lord presented a problem, and the further from the Lyceum the problem was resolved, the better.

Her ruminations were interrupted as the ornate latch-handle on the outer door dropped a quarter turn. Rifkind froze by the bed.

"You're awake." Domhnall stepped into the room. "I felt you moving."

He'd exchanged his stained white and gold clothes for simpler and well-worn attire more like Ejord would have chosen: russet-dyed tunic and breeches, loosely fitted and radiating comfort. From across the room she would have guessed they were old familiars, but there was no sign of a laundry within the Lyceum and there was no reason the Well could not produce old clothes as easily as it produced new ones.

"Felt? You were able to 'feel' me moving around up here?"

"Yes, a short time ago there was a change—I can't explain it better than that, but there were more thoughts in the air."

Rifkind grunted and thought immediately of Krowlowja, who might be as sensitive to "thoughts in the air" as Domhnall was. She walked over to her clothes and began unselfconsciously to dress. Hadn't Ejord often stood in her tent conducting the business of the army while she dressed? Hadn't she sat in his tent for much the same reasons? But Domhnall wasn't Ejord, and she pulled the folds of cloth around her quickly and lightly. It was, she noted, a question of timing, rather than divine permission. She no longer felt need of the Goddess' blessing to do what she wanted, but neither would she be rushed.

"How long have I slept?" she asked, settling down in the window casement ledge.

"One day. We'll be eating soon. I told Jenny you were awake and she said you'd be hungry."

"Has everything been quiet? Did you check the wards, both on the Well and at the door? Has the Well been permanently affected by last night?"

"Yes, yes and no—in that order. I've been in the temple most of the day. The warding structure I set last night is very old, but I wasn't able to learn who had first constructed it, or why it was not apparent when Assim made his first investigations."

"A warding has to be renewed. A powerful ritualist might make a warding that would last far beyond his lifetime, but if the Well dates from the times of the Lost Gods, I do not think any warding would survive. I'm more curious about how you know the warding is of old design."

"When the surface of the Well is smooth I can see things in the past, in addition to what I can see of the present. The quality of the images changes the further back I look. I exerted myself as fully as I dared, using my new knowledge of the Lost Gods, but I could not clear the image of the first warding being set by an Old One." Domhnall seated himself on the side-board.

"Krowlowja materialized in the Well; she will have some of its essence about her, I think, at least for a few days. We should be able to trace her back to her body. Do you think that would be worthwhile?"

"I know she is with Humphry and that they are travelling with tents," Rifkind replied thoughtfully. "Humphrey will have a substantial number of his elite forces with him, and once he has determined that Jenny and I are here, I do not think it will be safe to go spying on them. I've always encouraged him to believe my powers are far greater than they actually are, but he will warn Krowlowja and I do not want a struggle on her territory."

Domhnall nodded.

"He's not in the Felmargue yet," Rifkind continued. "The vision I had of them that night showed them in open country, not the swamp. To move an army of any size through that interior swamp will take time, I should think. At the very least we'd have a month before he could bring an army to the Hold. It took the Quais almost that long."

"A month? That's not enough. A month won't make any difference. Either the Well is as safe now as it has always been, or we've lost it and the day of the Leveller is at hand."

He left the room before Rifkind thought to ask what he believed the role of the Leveller would be, in light of the changes he had seen. His fatalistic attitude surprised her, and she thought on it as she finished dressing.

The Hold and the Lyceum were a formidible position for any mortal army to take. The glass-smooth cliffs were bad enough. Clumsy siege-engines would have to be erected to scale them, and in the middle of the Felmargue such devices were all but unthinkable. The potential of the Well itself to aid in the defense was, as yet, unexplored, but if Assim had forced the gods to a standoff,

Humphry's forces would have their work cut out for
them.

Her clothes had been mended rather than replaced. She
was grateful for that; when she contemplated danger, the
clothes of a warrior gave security and comfort.

The bitch Sunshine and her pups greeted Rifkind as she
left the portico separating the living quarters from the
kitchen and garden. Rifkind stooped slightly to pat the
dog's head, then caught the scent of meat roasting. Real
meat. Ignoring the dogs she walked quickly to the kitchen
where Jenny stood cranking a heavy iron spit over a
hearth-fire which appeared to be made equally of wood
and black glass.

"You're here. We'll eat now. I know you're hungry."

Jenny hefted the heavy spit and laid it on an open platter. The unwieldy object perhaps required all her attention—but Rifkind sensed that Jenny was deliberately not
looking at her.

The array of food was as staggering as it had been the
first morning of their arrival, but the bland melded
aromas had been replaced by hearty, specific scents.
Rifkind shot a questioning glance to her friend, but Jenny
did not respond. There was an uneasy tension of polite
questions and responses. Jenny continued to avoid
Rifkind's glances and Domhnall eventually despaired of
starting a sustained conversation.

"Very well," Rifkind exclaimed, setting aside her filled,
but untouched plate. "What has happened? Jenny?"

"I've learned how to use the Black Flame."

Rifkind's attention was focused tightly on Jenny, but not
so tightly as to miss Domhnall creating a forced self-in-
terest in the dinner.

"Truly, I was able to guess that, just from the dinner,"
Rifkind said calmly.

"I was so tempted. You were asleep, Domhnall was in

the temple, it was simply sitting there, I was hungry. I tried, and it began to glow, almost at once. Then it all seemed so simple. I should have left it alone, I know. Now you'll never teach me anything."

Jenny had been at Chatelgard during the days when Rifkind had attempted, with disastrous results, to pass her ritual knowledge along to the peasant girl, Linette. Jenny assumed that those experiences were foremost in Rifkind's mind as the latter sat in reflective silence.

"Perhaps I never would have made a good healer, anyway. I've too much faith in hot wine laced with honey to do dazzling rituals with fire and strange languages. I don't have the lofty imagination that you do, Rifkind. Maybe just growing up at Chatelgard with Ejord, Bainbrose and Father burned all the godliness out of me."

"It's been a guarded secret, but Ejord's powers were more than a match for An-Soren, several times. If you can coax a fever out, or mend a wound with honeyed wine, you don't need my kind of ritual training."

Jenny was unconsoled, but Rifkind had no attention to spare as she herself grappled with the uncomfortable realization that Jenny did display uncanny talents, just as Ejord had done—and that they shared a common parent in her nemesis, Lord Humphry. Rifkind had been taught that ritual abilities were a gift bestowed by the Goddess at birth, in her own case through the curse of the lightstorm that had taken her mother's life. The idea that other gods disposed ritual talent in families, even families that did not offer them service or worship, was intriguing, but not comforting.

"But she's done no harm. I was at the Well-font when she raised the power of my 'oven.' The Flames separated from the Well are attuned to a purpose, not to an individual." Domhnall leaned forward to interrupt Rifkind's thoughts on Jenny's behalf.

"And perceived that purpose better than its creator did —the food has lost its vagueness. This is a meal fit for a king," Rifkind added in a far lighter tone.

"Then I've not disgraced myself? There's still a hope for me?"

"To become a healer? I meant what I said, you *are* a healer, after your own fashion, just as you are a conjuror of food of an order higher than Domhnall, or certainly myself. I'm not sure what more I could teach you—I do not understand the talents that run so easily in your family."

"Then I'd best accept the way things are, is that it?"

Rifkind nodded and Jenny seemed somewhat mollified, but the quiet tension was not completely broken. Determined to dispel the shadow of gloom and at the same time satisfy her truly ravenous hunger, Rifkind plunged into her meal. Jenny had probed the secrets of the dry, spicy way the Asheerans had cooked their meat during the long journey across Daria.

Rifkind had lived under the threat of annihilation most of her life and had never let it disturb her eating or digestion. Jenny and Domhnall had perceived a doom on the horizon and were both ready to go into mourning. It was an attitude she would not have the patience to deal with until her own stomach was full. Even if Humphry's army were at the Hold cliffs and Krowlowja raged in the temple sanctums, there was little sense in facing death on an empty stomach. Better to celebrate with feasting and songs of past glory.

"Now then," Rifkind said after carving off a third slab of meat and devouring it, "we do have some advantages." She set a heel of bread on end in front of her.

"This is the Hold. If Humphry's bringing an army he'll never get it up the cliffs. If he thinks to lay a siege he's badly misjudged the terrain. We can hold out up here longer than he can wait down there. We don't know exactly what Krowlowja can do, but if she's the seeress of the Baleric Oracle, she's not had much experience with sorcerous combat. And now that she's warded off from the Well, her innate strength should be a caution, but not a threat. She *is* a danger though, as a seeress who could learn our plans in her vile steam."

"Then we have a stalemate. They can't get to the Well and we can't get out," Domhnall grumbled.

"You haven't left these buildings for what, four hundred years? I retrieved our belongings; it's a long walk to where we were attacked, and longer still to the cliffs. We are trapped in a very large area," Jenny said softly.

"They've tried to kill all of us. Rifkind's fought with this Humphry before and he carries an enmity against her. I know I haven't left this place for four hundred years, but I've told you, that's all a blur to me. I know it passed, but already it's less real than the two of you being here. I've remembered things I don't think I could force myself to forget again."

"I don't think we'll have a lengthy stalemate. I'm not a general, I can't think about strategy or grand plans, but Humphry is. If he shows up here, he'll have a plan, a strategy that will be very well thought out, and one that's likely to work," Rifkind explained.

"Then you're giving up?" Jenny asked. "Ejord never gave up."

"Ejord was, is, more of a planner than I'll ever be, but I'm not giving up. If Humphry shows up, he'll have a good plan—I respect his abilities if nothing else. If we can learn that plan ... well, it doesn't take a general to spoil another general's plans. I can play the spoiler quite well."

"Can three people 'spoil' the attack of a man like this Humphry, with his allies and his army?"

"We have to believe so," Rifkind answered him.

"We could try to rally the Quais," Jenny suggested.

"They aren't fighters," Domhnall said.

"They would at least give us the semblence of an army. But I've no way of calling them here. We'll have to do it ourselves and not count on luck from the outside. We've got the help of the Black Flame. I would assume if it can make food and clothing, it can also make arrows and spears." Rifkind turned to Domhnall for confirmation.

"I don't know. Even during the Sack, Assim did not rely on the Well as a weapon. He was afraid to, but there's no reason why it can't be used as you suggest. Or why it can't teach us about strategy as it taught me about bread."

"I'll leave that to you; if you can also learn more than how to make us a lot of arrows, the more's the benefit. I think I'll do best using my moon-stones to locate their camp and learn their plans—I don't want to involve the Well in that. Even if it worked we might only draw Krowlowja back again."

"And I'll call the Quais," Jenny added.

"How will you do that?" Rifkind asked.

"I haven't quite decided yet. Jevan will come if I can reach him. There are memory-stones taken from the Well on every Quais raft. I've seen the Quais activate the stones to learn different things. Here, so close to the source, we could possibly send a message to each memory-stone. I don't know—but I'll do it."

Though Domhnall voiced doubts of Jenny's assumed talents, Rifkind had an uneasy certainty that the Quais could and would be rallied to defend the Hold. She was not normally prescient, but their presence at the defense fitted into half-formed images that had haunted the fringes of her understanding since Jevan had called her the Leveller.

The Quais had no great love or reverence for the Lyceum, whatever it might have done for them before the

Sack and the creation of the Great Swamp, but they believed that the Leveller was the cathartic savior of their punished land. That legendary figure would stride across the swamp and the chaos in his wake would be the beginning of a new Felmargue. With Krowlowja and Humphry looming on the horizon, Rifkind was certain she was not the Leveller, but merely some small part of the final, purging cataclysm to befall Assim's high-minded Lyceum.

"If we've only got a month, then there's no time to lose." Domhnall stood up from the table. "It took me many days to learn how to bake bread, and longer to realize I wouldn't be able to do it in the Lyceum here."

"We need the weapons first, then we can worry about counter-plans," Rifkind cautioned. "And the swamp is a month's journey across, at best. The rafts move constantly from the inner trading posts out beyond the Lyceum here to where they hunt and trap. There would never be more than a few rafts within easy distance of the cliffs."

Jenny nodded as if she had already considered that latter point and had taken it into account when she had made her promise.

"I've waited five hundred years to defend the Lyceum. I'm not going to waste any time now."

Domhnall half-ran to the cloistered path to the temple.

CHAPTER 16

Dohmnall was as good as his word, working from dusk to dawn in the temple. He emerged for a few words each morning before staggering off to his own chambers alongside the kitchen to sleep through the day. What little there was to his conversation was salted with obscure references to past events that meant nothing to either woman. He showed them prototypes of weapons the Well had revealed to him, and which Rifkind rejected saying that they lacked the time to learn competence with unfamiliar weaponry. Dohmnall's eyes would clear long enough for him to state firmly that Krowlowja had made no motions toward the Well.

Rifkind would have preferred to work more closely with him in planning the immediate defense of the Hold, but his researches had already surpassed her understanding of strategy and tactics. He had observed wars which had been fought long before men lived in Dro Daria and spoke of seeing things she did not wish to ever think on.

Jenny, though more in evidence, was equally elusive in behavior. The woman had no empathy for ritual preliminaries or paraphernalia, as Rifkind had suspected.

The night reminded the red-haired woman of wraiths and Ornaqs, so she would walk the parapets of the Lyceum during the afternoon thinking her summons toward the Quais rafts in each quarter beyond the Hold. There seemed no way such unceremonious ritual could achieve any results, but Rifkind did not want to be the one to say so. Jenny was steadfastly sure of her ability to call Jevan and the others.

"Today I'm sure that some of them have heard me," she explained, returning from her rounds and draping her cloak over the spit handle where it dripped rivulets to the stone floor.

Rifkind's cloak was dry and she kept it pulled around her against the chill of the rain which had begun in the middle of the night.

"I had thought they only used the memory-stones at night," she replied without turning to face Jenny, her attention having been absorbed by the skull-staff she had just removed from its hiding place for the first time since their arrival.

"That is true, but I imagine myself leaving a message for them in the stones until the next time they are used. Today I was certain that some of my earlier messages had been heard."

It is not for me to question what works or what will not, Rifkind thought as she propped the staff against the front of the hearth.

"I'm glad someone is getting results," she said.

"You have no idea, still, where my father is and what he is planning to do?" Jenny sat down, carefully moving the staff so that it did not occupy her field of vision.

"No more than I did before. I've cast the stones by sunlight, moonlight and firelight, and might just as well be casting them in the dark or behind my back. Every time I get a feeling that there's something terrifying hanging over *everything*. It's as if our entire way of life were threatened, that if we fail here the Leveller will take everything —and we, and our gods, will be as lost as Hanju and his kind are. I've tried everything I can think of and I can't get past that image."

"Wine, milady?" Jenny's years in service sometimes still surfaced when she was nervous or tired. The four days of failure and frustration on the parapets were affecting them all.

"I'm becoming convinced," Rifkind continued, "that my moon-stones are in some way related to the various Black Flame talismans except that they are clear crystal. The Lost God Hanju made them for me when I was his 'guest' in the mountains above Chatelgard . . . I wish I had the old clay ones Muroa gave me; I'd like to be able to compare them. Hanju said the new ones weren't inclined to any one god or goddess, but I've begun to suspect that they are aligned in some way to the Well. Today I risked casting them in Humphry's name and in Krowlowja's, and each time they were shadowed the same way ours had been."

"You think that there is some danger from the Well itself! It has seemed so benign and helpful. Do you think that it is being used against us?" Jenny stared into her nearly empty wine glass.

"It might have a purpose of its own. When Domhnall set the wards that first night it seemed to me that the Well was itself only one step away from life—but whether that step is higher or lower I don't know. Take a look at that skull-staff, will you?"

"Must I?"

But Jenny complied with Rifkind's request. When Rifkind had taken it from the wraith camp it had shown the likeness of a man's skull—hollow-eyed and -nosed, gape-mouthed and angular. Its contours had softened during the few days Rifkind had left it sitting in the dark corner by the hearth, but heat did not seem a likely source of the transformation. Still far from being attractive, it was, nonetheless, closer to being an image of a living being than it had been. Jenny looked at it, as Rifkind had been looking before, seeking a resemblance to one of them, Humphry or Krowlowja.

"It's changing," Jenny said, pointing its face toward the wall.

"It shouldn't. That is, it shouldn't if it is what I've thought it was—the personal talisman of Assim. The substance of the Well can only be fixed once. Assim made his staff to conform with his appearance; as he changed, it changed. Either Assim is no longer a wraith, or this staff is no longer attuned to him."

"Do you think it has something to do with this doom you've felt hanging over us?"

"I hadn't thought of that. I was so tired of seeing the same things over and over again in the moon-stones that I was thinking of taking a long walk outside in the rain to clear my thoughts. I was going to bring the staff. The ground will be slippery after all the rain, and I thought a sturdy staff would be useful—besides, I'm still looking for my belt-knife.

"Domhnall hasn't said anything more about the wraiths. I got the feeling that they were sucked up into that storm we saw forming there at the camp. You didn't have any trouble with them when you brought our baskets back when I was recovering. It must have been an awful job."

Jenny poured Rifkind a second goblet of wine.

"Ah . . . I didn't have any trouble, because I didn't bring the stuff back," Jenny said slowly. "I never expected you to believe that, but I wanted to convince Domhnall to agree with you. I didn't want to say anything about our baskets getting back here. Now with what you're telling me, and looking at the staff changing like that, I guess I'd better confess what happened.

"It wasn't you—you rested comfortably all that night, I checked often enough. I didn't see Domhnall, but I don't think he left the Lyceum during the night, and even if he had, he didn't know where to look. I don't think he would have had enough time, anyway.

"I got up before dawn. I heard noises outside my room. I thought I was you, but I glanced in your door and you were sound asleep. It had gotten very quiet again; I thought of locking myself in my room, but that seemed a very ladylike and cowardly thing to do, so I got a torch from the wall, lit it from my lamp and went down to the kitchen. All our baskets were there on the floor. They'd been knocked about and our things were strewn all over —but that was probably the dogs; they had that guilty look about them. I tucked everything back inside and hauled them upstairs before Domhnall got up. Later I said I couldn't sleep and had gone out to get them. He acted surprised that I would have gone out again at night, seeing as I'd said I was afraid to stay in the kitchen alone while you were in the temple, but he didn't argue with me."

"Perhaps Domhnall doesn't want to admit that he had ventured outside the walls. He's very sensitive on that subject."

Jenny shooked her head, biting her lower lip as she did.

"It couldn't have been Domhnall. Your belt-knife lay across the table here, and the skull-staff on top of it. Domhnall won't go near that staff and who but the wraiths would have known where your knife was?"

"Assim could have been passing the staff to me? That's intriguing. Perhaps he wanted to be rid of it. When someone else held it perhaps he was freed from whatever geas the gods had laid upon him," Rifkind mused.

"You're taking all this very lightly, milady. I think that they've laid a curse upon us. Your casting-stones were in those baskets. They probably did something to them. The wraiths haven't been destroyed. They plan to kill us all, then maybe they'll wait for Krowlowja and my father as well! I keep thinking of those bones."

Rifkind nodded. "I've just about lost any ability to trust anything, but I don't really believe that the wraiths are our problem. If they could enter the kitchen, they could have covered the little extra distance to our rooms. To put the staff across the knife like that is a challenge: to regain the knife I would have to take up the staff. Of course, they did not know about you."

"And now, now that I've lifted both the knife and the staff? Have I done something to myself?" Jenny had become sincerely frightened.

"Bound yourself still more closely with my fate, perhaps, that's all. Let's talk of other things. In your calling after the Quais, have you encountered Jevan and the others?"

Jenny smiled, a trace of color coming to her cheeks. Her touch was not so precise, she explained, as to distinguish one raft-group from another, but her thoughts for Jevan were special and she was certain that when Chakri unwrapped his memory-stone, Jevan would bring their raft back to the Hold. She was counting on that, for without Jevan to interpret her actions to the Quais, and to inform her of their traditions, Jenny doubted that it would be possible to explain the situation to them. The first speeches would have to be handled delicately or the Quais would likely head to the dankest parts of the interior swamp before they'd try to counter Humphry.

The wind and rain gathered strength. The two women sought refuge in the warmest part of the kitchen. Spring in the Felmargue was not so cool or rainy as it was in Glascardy, but when the weather did turn bad, the open construction of the place left everyone at its mercy.

Jenny refilled their goblets from a hanging wine-skin, as they had emptied the jug. "When this is all over, if it's all over, I shall ask Jevan to return with me to the mountains."

"And if he asks you to stay here instead?" Rifkind inquired.

Jenny stared into her wine. "I don't know. I couldn't spend the rest of my life on a raft like that. Maybe if we were up here at the Lyceum? No, maybe not even then. I do not want to eat this food for long. I keep looking at Sunshine and those pups. Uncorrupted immortality in the middle of a swamp might be all right for you ..."

The last part of Jenny's musings was lost as Rifkind thought about the eventuality that Jenny seemed to take for granted. She had been long past the marriageable age when she had first left the Asheera. Even with her reputation as a headstrong, willful woman always ready to end an argument with a knife, she had had several suitors. Or, rather, brawny men from clans near and distant who had made their way to her blind and crippled father's tent where they offered riches and status for the privilege of breaking the woman who was notorious at clan gatherings for ten days' journey.

If old Tahrman had accepted, would she have submitted? Or would she have left the clan to lead a furtive life in the rocky caves where Muroa had taught her the ritual arts? Married women in the clans wore heavy black veils trimmed in gold that displayed the wealth and power of their masters. It did not matter if their teeth had been beaten loose, or their noses broken under the veil, so long as they could bear sons.

The sons of slaves could become warriors, but only the

sons of pure-blooded Asheeran women could compete for the clan or gathering leadership. The number of blooded women was low; even a narrow-hipped woman, were she a hetman's daughter, might still be worth an armed raid.

Rifkind studied her reflection in the half-empty goblet.

"Well, where else would you go? I could bring Jevan home to Chatelgard. After the experience he will have had here he would be accepted as a man-at-arms. As a dowry, Ejord could provide him a sword and horse. But *you*, Rifkind—your station is too high to go bringing in an outsider. You'd have to marry a man who was already well-propertied within Glascardy, or leave. You can't marry beneath yourself! And if you brought a man like Domhnall home with you ..."

"Chatelgard is not my home," Rifkind interrupted harshly. "My home is a tent turned to ashes and a cave big enough only for myself. I do not marry of my own free will. I may decide to take Domhnall as a lover, but I have not found another place to call home, nor the man to take away my will."

Jenny shook her head. "You'll grow old alone, then."

"Warriors do not grow old." And her memory was of her father lying within his tents, disgraced and blinded, and unwilling to use what little strength remained to him to make an honorable ending.

Rifkind left Jenny sitting by the hearth. The wine was not enough to warm her against the fine cold rain that still fell. The cloister garden where she had talked with Domhnall on their first day within the ruins was a wet, dismal place. The dark green vines clung wearily to the walls; sodden masses of purple lay in heaps at the base of each column. Shallow puddles reflected back the steel-grey of the skies and the dew-grizzled nap of her cloak. She crouched under a wide arch, protected from the worst of the rain, and cast her five crystals onto the rain-slick paving stones.

The gods mock my questions, Rifkind thought sullenly, and perhaps stupidly as well. I seek to know what I should look for in my life, and they reply with the pattern of warmth as I sit here wet and shivering. Such simple wants I can deduce for myself! I could return to the kitchen and drape my cloak over the hearth until it steams—but such warmth does nothing for my spirit. I remain here because there is no way out—and there is no way out because I let the Quais leave us here and I sent Turin to find his own company.

She snatched the stones up in one sweep of her hand. The skull-staff still rested against the hearth-wall, but she no longer wished to carry it. The belt-knife had been returned. Following passages that she and Jenny had marked with chalk, Rifkind set out for the crumbling walls and the soggy grass meadow, sharing the mood of the rain-storm.

One color dominated the forests and meadows: deep green, in hundreds of shades and textures set against the dark tree trunks, the meandering stone wall and the heavy sky. There were no shadows, and any one direction looked much the same as any other. She knew she would get lost, but despite that knowledge did not mark a trail behind her. Moisture seeped through the seams of her boots, her feet grew cold, cramped and chafed. The return would be painful, but she did not turn back.

Fallen trees and mudslides marked the path they had taken from the wraith camp. Rifkind slipped on one such exposed piece of ground, smearing her breeches with the dark brown mud. She crossed the place where the fissure had opened before them and then closed, and finally reached the camp itself. The molded smell of death was enhanced by the soaking rain. The prison that had held

them was a muddy ruin in a shallow stream. Rifkind
pulled the door away from the sagging walls.

Bones, all right; but not Quais, from the colors of the
cloths still around them. The wraiths must take their victims from the adventurers who come in search of the
Flame. If the Quais had died, it was because they were
already sick and lost.

A branch gave way, crackling and falling to the
ground. Rifkind spun around expecting to see the shad-
owy forms of the wraiths, but there was no sign of movement in the camp. The rain and wind alone had brought
down the branch. Waiting, still and silent, for a second
sound she reached behind her back for one of the throwing knives and set her other hand on the still solid door
jamb, certain she could wrench it from the wall if the
need arose. When no sound but the rain greeted her, she
scrambled up the slick embankment where the ger-cat
had surveyed the camp. She continued into the forest.

Voices! They were too far away to have caused the falling branch back at the camp, and too far ahead for her to
make out their number or sense—but they were not
wraiths. The sounds were normal in pitch. With the black
cloak pulled tight around her, she was almost invisible in
the moisture-deadened scenery and was able to approach
the sound with little danger to herself. They were men.
She swung down-wind of them and caught the scent of a
wet fire.

Quais. About ten of them, and none familiar! Jenny's
done it!

Drenched, shivering and faintly blue from the un-
seasonable cold, they huddled in reed-fiber capes around
a fire that seemed to produce nothing but smoke. They
wore necklaces of coins and shells and short pants made
of leather. There were no women among them. Each had

a steel knife slung at his waist in clear defiance of the taboo against metals.

Rifkind chose her words carefully as she stepped into their sight.

"You have come in answer to the call?" she asked, the throwing knife invisible against her forearm.

They looked cautiously at her, exchanging glances before one with greying hair stepped forward to speak for all of them.

"Yes, but it was not you who called. We saw a different one. How is that? The stones have not misled us before."

"Nor do they now. There are several of us at the ruins seeking to . . ."

The very situation she had wished to avoid was upon her. Jenny, with her gentle ways and firm words was the one to explain the danger to the Hold and to rally the Quais who answered her call.

". . . seeking to call the Quais to a council that will change the fate of the Felmargue."

"She speaks of the meeting that is said to come before the Leveller is summoned! That is one with what the memory-stones showed, and with my dreams!" A younger, more impulsive man said loudly enough for Rifkind to hear.

"We saw no other rafts tied at the base of the cliffs."

"You are the first to arrive. The call went out but a few days ago. Within all the vastness of the Felmargue, you were the closest who heard and chose to come."

They conferred and agreed that they had been within sight of the Hold when the memory-stone had been consulted to aid in a difficult birthing on the raft. The healer within Rifkind rose to the fore, but the chief spoke before she could.

"None will hear the call and not come. For many generations we have kept the stones hidden and waiting, but it is time for the curse laid upon our fathers to be lifted. The Quais will come from every part of the Felmargue. We will place our memory-stones together and take council with them and the Leveller for the fate of our land."

Jenny has a task in front of her to convince these fatalistic men to listen to us and not to their stones or legends, she thought. I do not trust the stones and legends to come down on our side of the line. These events were not foreseen by the gods and have not been woven into their myths. Unless Jenny can continue to manipulate the stones, we will have trouble.

"Did the mother and child survive?" she asked, instead of venting her fears or frustrations. "I see no women among you."

"They remain on the raft; all the women and children. This is not a matter for them. But the woman died. Her son is to be suckled by another who bore a daughter a few weeks back."

Rifkind's eyes hardened. "I am a healer. I will attend to the child and any others who need aid, then I will lead them to the ruins. This is a matter for all the Quais, not merely the men. Food and dry clothes await you at the ruins. You and others are expected."

The men grumbled behind their leader, and if any of them nursed an injury he did not step forward to be healed of it. Rifkind gave them general instructions about the path to the ruins. They marched away from her.

Rifkind continued on her way toward the rafts, stamping through the wet grass.

CHAPTER 17

The rain could not slow Rifkind as much as the baskets had slowed her and Jenny when they first left the Quais. And the Quais men had left a trail easy enough to follow in a storm far worse than the steady rain that continued to drench the Hold. The tree-filled horizon cleared to a blank grey before the quick dusk brought darkness to the cliff-edge. She should have warned the men about the wraiths. It was far too late now.

"Hail the raft!"

She stood a few steps back from the lip of the cliff. These Quais seemed more bellicose than those she had travelled with. They might have lied about the raft bearing only women, or the women themselves might be able to loft a spear into a moon-outlined intruder. There were squeals and shouts from the darkness below as the women considered her hail.

"Our men will be back very soon. What do you want with us?" One clear voice rose above the others.

Rifkind dropped the stored coils of reed-fiber rope over the precipice; the men had made certain their women didn't follow them.

"I ask permission to board your raft" she shouted. "I've met with your men-folk and told them that the decisions facing the Quais are for all the Quais to make, not just the men."

This generated more noise from the raft, but hands reached up to steady the rope when she finally descended. The craft itself was larger than either Jevan's or Chandro's. A greater wealth of material things lay visible in the flickering torchlight, and the women lacked the soft carefree features of Elyssa and the other Quais women Rifkind had met. This was undeniably a sturdier and more efficient lot.

"Is the infant well? Your men said a woman recently died in childbirth."

The women glanced at each other, unwilling to speak to a stranger, even a woman like themselves. Rifkind counted five adults plus a handful of children peering out from behind soggy capes. Rifkind studied each face, unable to guess who had shouted up to her.

Crude hoods had been fastened over the torches, allowing some light despite the rain, but the oil sputtered and sent deceptive shadows across the women's faces. Rifkind felt awkward with water starting to seep through the matted fiber of her cloak and loose tendrils of hair escaping from her braids to plaster against her wet face. The Quais women looked cold, but far more at ease. They were suspicious of her, and concealing things from her. She wondered what the men had not told her, and how many others were cramped down under the lean-to's half-visible in the torchlight.

"I am a healer. I have come to rid you of the fever. My name is Rifkind. Please take me to those who are sick."

She guessed that there was a fever on board, and her guess was confirmed by the sudden break in tension. The women and children offered her their names. Rifkind heard and remembered only one, Hylyn, the one with the gold earring who had spoken while the rest were silent. It was Hylyn then who stepped back to let Rifkind into another part of the raft where the mewling of infants and the groans of sickness could be heard over the rain.

A wide-eyed woman, herself hardly more than a child, reclined against a pile of cloth and reeds with two babies, one smaller than the other, pressed against her uncovered breasts. The woman's eyes were glassy and she made no sign of recognition when Hylyn brought the torch closer.

"Fever. It devours them as it devoured Selam, the one who died."

Rifkind stepped forward to feel the woman's forehead. All her healer's equipment was in the room over the kitchen at the Lyceum; she had not even brought a small pouch of herbs tied to her belt for her own protection, much less the brazier and oils essential to the more complex healing rituals such as this one promised to be.

"Fetch me boiled water," she said, turning to Hylyn and the others.

"Our fire went out with the storm. We have only rainwater until it clears and we can dry our tinder again."

"Rainwater will be pure enough. Be sure there's no swamp brine in it. Someone take the infants. I'll take care of the woman first, she most likely carries the infection to the children. If I heal her, the milk may be enough for them. What is her name?"

"Drusina."

Rifkind knelt by the young woman, arranging her in a relaxed position on the crude bedding. Her skin was warm and dry despite the damp. Her breath was like rotting fruit. Milk, yellowish and thin, oozed from her breasts.

"Drusina? Do you hear me? Nod, or close your eyes if you can hear me."

There was no movement. Rifkind brushed a hand against the woman's cheek. It felt like old parchment, in no way like the face of a youthful woman. A basin made from a hollowed nut-pod was set down beside her.

"We have tried cooling her with water and giving her herb-tea, but since sundown she has been like this, and the infants also."

Rifkind could have asked more questions, but this was the Felmargue, not the Asheera and she would not have recognized the symptoms of specific fevers even if they were given precisely. She washed her hands in the basin. Closing her eyes she thought about healing, sinking deep into the meditative state and centering within the unconscious, generational memories of her tal. It was harder to find the key to the Old Tongue without the scent of sweet-oils rising from the brazier, but in time she found it and the knife blade pressed between her palms grew warm.

Something was wrong, she knew it the instant her eyes opened and she gazed on the near comatose woman. The life-forces were unfocused, yet in violent movement throughout Drusina's sphere of being. The fever and sickness had won in battle, but the woman had not died.

Rifkind hesitated, a rare event in her healing once she had attained communication with the generational memories within the tal and the Old Tongue. There was no point of origin, no vortex of strength or weakness susceptible to her powers. With the blade point against one palm and the hilt against the other, Rifkind held the knife a hand-span above Drusina's face then swept it along her body.

Sparks that only Rifkind could see shot up to the knife and seized it. The blade became searing hot, impossible to hold. The sparks spread to her skin, a plague of tiny insects attacking until she felt swollen and numb from their venom. Desparate now, because the disease sought to jump the thin border between her life and Drusina's, and knowing that she lacked the knowledge to combat it, Rifkind dropped the knife and thrust her hands back into the water.

The other women in the lean-to backed away as rancid, foul steam rose from what had been sweet rainwater. Rifkind drew her breath in short, painful gasps. Tears streamed from her eyes. She wiped them off on her tunic sleeve. Coughing, she lurched out of the enclosure and spat thick bile into the rain-pocked channels.

"Poison!" She exclaimed, still gasping. "It runs rampant within her, and into the infants. The venom rules her!"

"Were-blood!" one of the other women exclaimed, sucking in her breath.

"That fish? Hanchon caught it two days ago!" another added.

"What fish? What is were-blood?" Rifkind asked from her knees. Her voice rasped in her throat and a vile and bitter taste filled her mouth, but the venom had been purged. She hacked and spoke again. "What are these things you speak of? Tell me! With more knowledge I may yet be able to save her!"

The women had dragged Drusina and the children from the lean-to and were binding their arms and legs together. Rifkind needed to see no more to guess what was intended.

"No! Wait!" She got to her feet and wrestled with the women tying the ropes. These stepped back, waiting for Hylyn to set things right.

"Two days ago we hunted in the marsh beyond the Hold." Hylyn gestured toward the distant ocean. "The men had layed a trapline through the tussocks. We came by each morning to check them. In one of Hanchon's there was a fish unlike any we'd seen in these parts before, even more unusual because it was alive, yet out of the water. We had set traps for oryx and myrts—we were after fur, not fish.

"Hanchon jumped from the raft, not realizing that the fish was alive, to heave it back into the water and reset the trap. It snapped at him and he called for the women to beat it with the poles. When it was still we dragged it to the raft. Hanchon said that for so much trouble we might as well get a meal out of it.

"It looked dead in the reeds, but it started thrashing about again when we brought it to the raft. Drusina and Selam were nearest to its head. It had no teeth, but a sucker-mouth and bumps covered with slime. They wouldn't take their knives to it, and kicked it overboard. Hanchon was furious."

The venom seemed too strong to come from an ordinary creature. Rifkind thought of the Ornaq.

"You say you had never seen such a fish before in these parts, but you are ready to kill Drusina now. Do you remember things like this in the memory-stones?"

The women were confused. They were clearly not about to mention the prophecies and revelations of the sacred lumps of glass, even though Rifkind, it seemed, already knew about the stones.

"It's were-blood," an unrecognized woman who held the leather thongs binding Drusina's wrists said at last. "We've got the proof now. I thought it was from the first. Selam had it too, the way she groaned like that all through her labor. Were-blood, all of them. Throw them off before we're all killed."

As if aroused by the threatened fate, Drusina's body arched and snapped violently to one side, knocking her captor over. The damp hair at the back of Rifkind's neck rose when she heard the poisoned woman shriek and howl. She grapped a nearby torch and told a frightened woman to keep a light on them, or else, then grappled with the writhing, but still bound, Drusina.

Drusina's face was almost purple with the venom. Her eyes dilated and bulged as she struggled with Rifkind, who once again had taken up her long boot knife. Drusina's head arched back and Rifkind plunged the knife through the soft skin of her under-jaw, then into the brain-pan itself. She grabbed the pod-basin of rainwater and poured it into the gaping wound. She withdrew the knife; the blood flow slowed to a stop.

"She's either dead or cured," Rifkind announced.

The rigidly curved back relaxed. Drusina eased onto the deck of the raft with a sigh, then, her hands and feet still bound, she curled up and began to sleep peacefully. The other women dampened cloths in the rainwater and sponged the foul blood from the girl's face and chest.

The two children whose infection was due entirely to the envenomed milk began mewling before the last of the blood had been wiped from Drusina's breasts. An infant was settled in each of the sleeping woman's arms. The trio rested comfortably. Hylyn had the lean-to moved to shelter them, though the rain had almost stopped.

Hylyn handed strips of salted, dried fish to Rifkind, who ate them gratefully. They produced a cold green tea to share with her that was soothing and mildly narcotic, and unknown to the Quais of Chandro's party.

"Tomorrow morning we will scale the cliff. All of us will head for the ruins. Others will have arrived by now and perhaps we can start preparing the defense," Rifkind said to them, not remembering that she had intended to leave all detailed instructions to Jenny.

"Defense?" Hylyn picked up the cue almost at once. "Are we under some sort of attack?" She paused, then nodded to herself. "Yes, the message in the memory-

stones. There would not be such a summons for a simple
council. Our Fathers have never done such a thing before,
and it was not our Fathers who spoke to us. The Hold is
under attack once more—but why should we defend it?
Let the Leveller come and restore the Felmargue after his
own fashion. We Quais have had enough of gods."

"When have you seen were-blood so close to the Hold,
or so far oceanward? The Felmargue itself, not just the
Hold, is under attack. We must return to the Hold and
take our places there." A quiet, dark skinned woman
whose beauty had not quite faded with her youth stepped
forward. She reached into her tunic to retrieve a small
object, indistinct in the torchlight. "The new Felmargue
will not be like the old; we will sit in council," the woman, whose name was Pasca, said soberly.

Pasca held the memory stone at arm's length for the
others to see. The last vestiges of doubts or opposition
faded.

One stone, thought Rifkind, to each man who survived
the attack, handed down from father to son, or daughter,
until the families were divided out over all the rafts. The
strongest, or wisest, man leads the raft-people but the line
of the stone-bearers is not broken.

Rifkind tried again to make sense of the Quais social
structure, staying out of the way of the other women who
were suddenly busy cleaning the raft under the orders,
and watchful eyes, of Pasca and Hylyn.

"You did not speak your case clearly or well, healer."
Pasca stepped over to Rifkind.

"It is not a pleasant subject. An army prepares to
march through the Felmargue to sieze the Well of Knowledge that lies atop the Hold. And with the army is an evil
seeress of power who might be able to do what the army
cannot. The gods are involved, but I do not see their ways
or motives. Before the arrival of your menfolk there were

only three of us up in the ruins. I've heard the stories of the Leveller, and though I don't know if he is the cause of our problems, if ever there were a time for him, it is now."

"Or her?" Pasca asked, cocking her head. "The men will not be pleased to see us. They are very jealous of their rights and their stones."

Pasca led Rifkind further away from the bustle. Rifkind was uncomfortable in close proximity to a woman who stood head and shoulders above her, though she sensed that in this case her discomfort came more from similarities in their characters than differences in their heights.

"I've moved from raft to raft since the Ornaqs took the rest of my family many years ago. But, until tonight I'd told no one that I preserved a part of the memory-stone of my Father. I feel that you and the others with you will bring change to the Quais."

"That may be, though our purpose is more tied to the Well of Knowledge and the stones like your memory-stones. It is true that without all the memory-stones in the Felmargue the Quais will be unable to make council?" Rifkind asked, less concerned for Pasca's glassy sliver than for those rafts which might be unable to reach the Hold in time.

Pasca shook her head. "Who knows? Without me, a part of my Father's memory will not be there, but I do not know *who* my Father was or if his memory is important. The stone is small, it was split long ago. Some distant brother carries a greater part. I've seen the stones of a dozen or more rafts, and each is different in some way from the others. They don't all have the same knowledge. Our Fathers were not equal, and none of them did anything more astounding than survive the Sack. I am not sure anyone of wisdom would want to make council with them, or with their living sons."

Rifkind nodded. Pasca's accounts tallied with

Domhnall's assumptions that all the Quais were descended from those few peasants and townsfolk who had
found refuge in the environs of Assim's school.

"The stones contain all our past, but only, I think, su-
perstitions about our future. I believe in the legend of the
Leveller, but only as a tale that conceals as much truth as
it reveals. The gods are not going to send us a hero who
can raise the swamp and settle the Hold. The Quais who
live now believe that the next storm is a portent of their
redemption. It will not be that way.

"The Leveller is a threat left with our Fathers to keep
them, and us, from trying to throw off our fate. The Quais
do nothing unless it has been done before. Hanchon
trades for metal and cloth. When we pass other rafts in
the ports they cover their eyes and shout insults at us because we are different. When they pass us in open water,
they would try to board our raft—but the trading had giv-
en us knives, and they know the risks of attacking us. Even
Hanchon, though, dares only so much. He will not bring
the traders to the Hold, or the other aventurers, like yourself, who approach us with offers of gold. He tells them
silly stories about strange beasts and walking dead to
scare them away."

Rifkind deemed it pointless to mention that there were
wraiths walking the forests of the Hold. If Pasca could see
the effects of were-blood or lose her family to the Ornaqs
and still believe that there were no strange beasts in the
Felmargue, she wasn't apt to be alarmed by grey shadows carrying clubs.

She learned little more from Pasca, though they sat until the rain had stopped revealing bits of their personal
exploits to each other. Rifkind knew how much she concealed and disguised in her own tales, and thus distrusted
much of what Pasca told her.

Her feet ached and were swollen by morning, but she

helped the other women raise each other to the Hold, then stayed with Pasca and Hylyn until the raft was covered with a tangle of rushes and looked no different from any other straw-and-reed tussock at the base of the cliffs. They wrenched the rusted climbing spikes out of the cliff-face and pulled all the ropes up after them.

The youngest children were carried in slings, the oldest puffed and panted to keep the pace. Pasca was long-legged, Rifkind was fast-paced. They strove to maintain an equal cadence and constantly increased the speed of the party until Drusina would plead with them to stop or slow down.

Drusina herself could remember nothing of her illness. She grieved for Selam more than the others, and held both infants tightly.

CHAPTER 18

"Who's guarding our raft? That's what I'd like to know —with them up here where they don't belong!"

The men Rifkind had met the night before reacted with something less than enthusiasm as they saw Hylyn, Pasca and the others walking through the colonnade at the Lyceum. They had a large campfire going in the middle of the unkempt cloister garden adjoining the kitchen cloister. They had pursuaded Jenny or Domhnall to provide them with wine as well as food to ward off what chill the fire could not.

"That high speakin' female's set herself above my orders!"

One man left the fire, the others followed him. They marched toward her across the rows of plants Domhnall had tended, and with the sounds of the snapping stems, Rifkind's sense of fellowship vanished.

"Hanchon's coming. We never should have left the raft!" Hylyn whispered from behind Rifkind.

"What are we going to do?"

"He'll beat us for sure!"

The men blocked the cobbled pathway to the kitchen-cloister, standing with folded arms and scowling faces. Rifkind walked forward until she had to look up to meet Hanchon's stare.

"I am going to the kitchen-cloister. These women are my guests. They are going with me. Step aside."

She kept her tone soft and her eyes unblinking. Oh Goddess, she silently appealed, make them move, they're more than a match for me when my sword-belt's tucked away where I can't get to it. We need the Quais to defend the Well, but this Hanchon is worse than Humphry. Where is Jevan?

Hanchon's hand twitched toward his waist-slung knife. It was one movement too many for Rifkind, who opened her arms and dropped the wrist-knives into her hands. Even thus armed she was in a poor position, but at least she was not out-gestured.

"Some kind of mean woman, with knives like that," a broad-faced man behind Hanchon exclaimed, with a glint in his eyes for more than Rifkind's knives.

With a sub-vocal growl, Rifkind tensed her entire body. "Don't even think about it if you wish to see another day!" she snarled.

Hanchon was stalled by her slight tensing movements. The Quais brawled but never with the cold gleam such as had come into Rifkind's eyes. They were men of passions, and proud of them. It seemed an icy-faced healer sprouting knives from both hands was not Hanchon's idea of fun. The others grumbled but followed suit.

"Rifkind!"

Jenny's bright voice broke the spell of tension. The men looked to her with a nod of acceptance. Jenny's face and voice had first come to them in the memory-stones. She was no more a real woman to them than a goddess would be. Jenny's greeting to the black-garbed Rifkind calmed many of their fears and quashed any notions of challenge that might be building in their minds. As the two women embraced, the men went back to their fire and wine.

"Rifkind! If you had not returned by sundown I would have fallen into despair. I didn't sleep at all last night. I'm sorry for all the things I said yesterday in the rain.

"The Quais have arrived—they said they saw you. Oh, what brutes they are! Hanchon's are the worst. Another four rafts-full arrived this morning. I've scarcely met them. They've camped on the far side of the kitchen. They won't come near this Hanchon. But all that was this morning. The wraiths came last night. They were right outside the walls, and they howled until sunrise!

"Domhnall says they stay away only when you're here with the staff. I don't want to know why he thinks that, but I'll be glad if it's true now that you're back. I wish Jevan were here. I don't know what to do with this Hanchon."

Jenny spoke non-stop the entire length of the walk into the kitchen. The carving tables showed how Jenny had struggled to prepare the increased volume of food for the hungry and demanding Quais. Even with the Black Flame it had been difficult work. Jenny had been taught to manage a kitchen and enough cookery to insure the honesty of servants, but she had never been a drudge. Strain and a hint of disillusion had begun to show on her face.

Hylyn led the women on a quick exploration of the tables and side-boards, sampling freely as they moved. Jenny blanched beneath her tan.

"And when *all* the Quais are here?" She sighed.

"Enough are here already. It is enough that you called them; you don't have to care for them." Rifkind strode into the kitchen proper and used one of the pot-lids as a gong to get everyone's attention. "This hearth is large enough to cook for a hundred or more at a meal—and we'll be doing that within a few days. It will be hard work, and no one can do it alone. Jenny and I will show you how to prepare meat and vegetables—there are no fish or lizards available on the Hold. There will be ample food—but only with cooperation!"

The women were more disturbed by the notion of diet without fish and lizard than by the idea that they were expected to run the kitchen. When this initial doubt was conquered, they accepted the food the Black Fame produced as one more indication of how severely the gods had punished their ancestors. While the women peered into simmering pots and the children played messy games with the fruit piled on the side-boards, Jenny and Rifkind melted back to the shadowed alcove stairway that led up to their chambers.

"I feel very much as if we've loosed a herd of animals into our home. When the army returned to Chatelgard it was not half so raucous." Jenny eyed the whirlpools of chaos.

"Let's hope we haven't. Perhaps Domhnall will think of some way to adapt the Well of Knowledge . . ."

Jenny shook her head and laid a hand on Rifkind's arm. "Domhnall is most unhappy with all this. I think it is too many people too soon for him. He sulks in the temple or the abandoned rooms. As soon as the second group arrived he moved his belongings away from this part of the Lyceum."

Rifkind nodded.

"I'll find him and talk to him. It must be this way. The Quais have to come home, but it is a delicate process. You think of the army returned from the war. I remember the Gathering feasts of my childhood when a guest, instead of the roast, was apt to be carved before dinner."

"Will it get that bad?" Jenny whispered.

Pasca left the others to join them, somehow moved by
Jenny's words though it seemed unlikely she could have
heard them. Rifkind shrugged inwardly. Of all the wom-
en it was least surprising that Pasca had not been caught
up in the domestic activity of the kitchen. Jenny was uneasy at once, casting furtive glances to Rifkind for an explanation of the tall woman's presence.

"It has been a long time since these buildings have
housed so many people. It will be difficult to bed and
board them all. If we have been too successful in our calling of the Quais, things will be uncomfortable for
everyone." Rifkind spoke quickly and by her evasions
hoped to alert Jenny to the importance of the intruder's
suspicions and good-will.

"If you have called, then you will have enough room
and food. I'll trust the legends for that much. Hanchon
blusters and bullies, but if you fear fights between the
rafters instead of a shortage of food, it is good that he is
here first. Show him your trick with the knives and he will
jump to your orders—and see that everyone else does
also."

A young boy with dimpled face and knees broke free of
a knot of children and puppies. Tears streamed down his
face and his wails soared above the surrounding noise.
Pasca glanced at him, then turned back to Rifkind. The
toddler squalled hysterically and ran toward the alcove,
only to stop abruptly half-way there. He plopped down on
the floor and wailed all the louder.

"He knows if he runs farther he'll fall off the raft. What
he knows is more powerful than what he sees." Pasca
smiled weakly and went to console the little boy who was
obviously her son.

"Who is she?" Jenny asked, her eyes fixed on Pasca's
broad back.

"Pasca, an uncommon woman, especially for a Quais.

I expect there is much more to her story than what she has told me—I did not suspect she had a brat among them. She's right, though. Hanchon is one we want on our side to help keep the others in line. He's a natural bully."

"If there must be a first among the Quais, it will be Jevan. He *will* be here. Since Hanchon and his men have arrived other rafts have come. Jevan won't be long now."

"But Hanchon sits at his fire in the cloister next to the kitchen. No one will get closer to us, so long as we keep these rooms and use the kitchen to prepare our food. He guards us, in effect, and controls the path to our presence. We will lose more good will than it is worth to displace him."

Jenny smiled, she had already thought of that. "I placed him in the *second* cloister because Jevan and the Quais we know will be in here!"

"With the pig and the chickens? That is unlikely, and unwise. This cloister will be for the women and children who tend the kitchen-fires—Hanchon's women from the look of it. Jevan would dwell here as your captive among women, maybe your lover. He'd lose his position among the men; that is their way. Jevan would have to fight Hanchon to take his place, and if Hanchon sensed that the love of the memory-stone speaker was involved it would be an honor-fight to death."

Jenny's smile faded. "No, there's only Jevan. There's no one else I would trust, much less love."

"I don't say you should trust Hanchon, much less love him. Brel's tits, you'd wind up with Pasca jealous, judging from the family resemblance in that little boy. But he has chosen his position well and I believe Pasca is right. He wants honor and status. It is far more likely that Jevan will understand Hanchon than that Hanchon will understand your love for Jevan."

The fabric of her sleeve wrinkled as Jenny picked at it.

"You won't leave again, will you? The wraiths howl, and I don't know what to do with the Quais. I was so certain that Jevan would be here first. I felt it in my heart . . ."

"Jevan will be here. These others have heard your call, he has too. But they could be five days from here. Neither Jevan nor Chandro would normally range near the Hold. They would have headed as fast as they could back to their usual waters. I will stay at least until they get here."

Rifkind gave her word grudgingly. She had still had no luck with her search for the army, Humphry or Krowlow-ja. The thought had crossed her mind that it would be more difficult to find the quiet necessary for the ethereal search now that the Lyceum was filling with Quais.

"Where is Domhnall?" she asked.

"I think he's in the temple. If he's not there, I don't know where he is."

Rifkind looked again at Jenny; dark circles under her eyes attested to her night without sleep and the conversation about Jevan had broken the false strength that had sustained her through the long day. Her hands trembled as she twisted her sleeves and belt.

"Go upstairs and rest. Domhnall will find me."

Jenny smiled and fled up the stairs. The slide bolt of her door could be heard clicking shut. It would not keep out a determined child, but it would give Jenny the peace of mind she required to get her needed rest.

Rifkind moved from one alcove passage to another one separating Hanchon and his men from the kitchen. The cloister gardens were not large but the Quais had not spread out within them, preferring a tight knot of activity. Rifkind stood quietly until Hanchon noticed her.

Following Pasca's advice, she demonstrated the wrist-snap motions that dropped the knives into her hands from their sheaths. She worked mostly with her left hand; if Hanchon took a nation to challenge her, then would be soon enough for him to discover that her right was the stronger and faster.

Though the Quais men were proud of their knives, they had little skill in handling them. And these were the men who might have to face Humphry's army in one short month. She found a stout twig and began demonstrating the dexterity games she had played as a child in the Asheera. Disdaining such child's play, Hanchon insisted on using his knife. In short order he boffed the exercises and opened cuts on both hands.

Rifkind watched in silence as he sucked the red stream from the worst of his mistakes. He grinned sheepishly, picked up the twig and went back to his men and despite obvious discomfort, taught them the game. From a quick glance at the cut, Rifkind guessed it went clean to the knuckle-bone. She could have applied an ointment to hasten the healing, but the wounds of careless learning must be left to scar, or the lesson would not be learned.

As she returned to the kitchen she caught a glimpse of Domhnall, who seemed to be headed toward her chamber. The kitchen itself had settled to an even furor and Hanchon was amusing his men, so without another word Rifkind broke into a run, arriving on the landing outside her door just as Domhnall turned away from it.

"I thought you would come to the temple once you'd set the women up in the kitchen," he said, with mild reproach.

She remembered that he could use any piece of glass from the Well as a window to the world. He had been spying through the cooking fire, but she didn't blame him.

"Jenny was exhausted. I believe that she didn't sleep

last night because of the wraiths, and the Quais are proving to be quite a challenge for her," Rifkind replied evenly.

Her rooms had a more complicated lock than Jenny's simple slide bolt, as befitted the sword and ritual objects contained within it. The key was old and rusted, but the chain Domhnall had given her to keep on her belt was of fine new gold. She handled it carefully and they entered the spacious rooms overlooking the bustle of the kitchen.

"I have lived too long without having lived at all." Domhnall sighed as he leaned against the window. "I remember them. I still see their faces as they finally left the Lyceum after Assim became a wraith and they knew that there was no more hope."

"Why didn't you go with them?" Rifkind inquired gently while attaching the belt-knife sheath to her belt.

"Jenny was distraught when you didn't come back yesterday. She thought she had upset you and came to the temple to tell me what had happened. I don't know how she found her way. Just when I had her reassured that you needed to be with your Goddess, the wraiths started up."

Rifkind took note that he had not answered the question, but did not press the issue. The man she would take as a lover, and the immortal, mysterious master of the Well of Knowledge might well have been two separate people in her thoughts. In the confines of her bedroom, after a day without seeing him, she dealt only with the man, not the magician.

"So she said. Also that you think the wraiths moved so close because I was absent?"

"They sensed the loss of your presence—as I did."

He moved closer to her, giving Rifkind the faintly unpleasant idea that he had observed more than feasts through the Black Flame windows. It was one thing to say to herself that she would sate the longing and curiosity of her passions with this man, and quite another to feel his breath on her face and his arm around her shoulder. Too strange, too unfamiliar, and too much like a threat for safety. She backed away from him.

"I've told Jenny I will remain here at least until the Quais are settled in and Jevan, the one who guided us here, arrives."

"I would rather that you didn't leave again, especially so abruptly. I've learned much from the Well. I'm confident now that we can win our fight with this outland emperor, regardless of his ally."

There was a fluttering spasm in her breast, as if something vital had been wounded. The words to promise Domhnall that she would remain at the Lyceum regardless of everything else caught in her throat.

"I will have to drill them," she said slowly and after a few moments of thought. "It will be worse than when Ejord rallied his army. The peasants and farmers at least understood picks and hoes; it was only necessary to teach them to fight. The Quais are hardly used to walking on solid land, much less to battle.

"Have you made spears and arrows for us? There is wood in the forests for bows. I think it would be best to make the bows from natural wood. I don't know if I can train archers, anyway..." Her voice trailed off to nothing as Domhnall's eyes bore relentlessly into her own. "You *have* made the arrows and spears?" she asked, her voice barely audible.

"They won't be necessary. All that we need will be provided. The Well has overseen battles since time's beginning, and I have learned to work with it. It will be our defense, we will need nothing more. If Assim had known what I know, the gods would have failed to create the Felmargue and be themselves like that ridiculous little fig-

ure you summoned up. The Well itself will be the Leveller
—it will raise the lands again. You and the Quais will be
safe here, and you will not have to train them, nor fight
yourself."

He moved suddenly, arms locking around her shoulders, pulling her tight against him. Rifkind opened her
mouth to protest, not thinking that it would provide the
opportunity and semblance of consent that he wanted.
Neither warrior's nor healer's instinct was potent against
the rush of sexuality as it broke the dam of her frustration
and repression. Eyes closed, back arched, her fingers
pressed against the back of his neck, not to choke or resist,
but to hold him more firmly against her.

They stepped back from each other, equally dazed and
embarrassed. Domhnall mumbled something, farewell
or apology, Rifkind could not tell which, and disappeared
out the door leaving it open behind him. She crossed her
arms over her breast in a tight self-embrace, her unblinking eyes never leaving the empty doorway.

I am now my own enemy, she thought. There is little I
will not do for him, or give him if he asks. My mind is not
turned toward Humphry, the Quais or the Well, but to
him. I must master myself again, or I will be consumed
in my own passions.

CHAPTER 19

The sounds of renewed excitement set against the chirping of the innumerable birds housed under the eaves lifted Rifkind from the timeless moment of Domhnall's kiss. She lowered her arms to her sides; the moment passed into memory. There were men's voices in the cacophony rising from the kitchen cloister. She went to the window to watch, secure in the knowledge that the Quais would not think to look up and see her.

Dinner was being served. The women poured steaming roasts of red meat from the terra-cotta pots Jenny had set over the glistening Black Flames, but the ascendant note of the aroma was salted fish—the Black Flame was highly susceptible to the imaginations of those who worked with it. Rifkind's stomach growled protest at the combined sight and smell. She resolved to wait and eat later.

The men, and a few other women she did not recognize at all, made their noisy way to the cloister for the feast. Rifkind watched them maneuver through the gauntlet of Hanchon's bullying, and their expressions of mild displeasure when Jenny was not there to serve the miraculous dinner. Many poked at the food in curiosity or

distaste. Rifkind was not the only one who found the sight
of red meat attached to the smell of fish unsettling.

Hanchon's cloister was, in large part, obscured from
her view by the colonnade that separated it from the kitch-
en. She heard, rather than saw, the insults and bullying
and thought nothing strange when the steady trickle of
men through the archway ceased and shouts from behind
the grey stone columns grew louder than the conversa-
tions of those already eating.

"Chakri?"

The head and shoulders of a man who resembled the
shy Quais appeared in that corner of the outer cloister
visible to her, then darted back into the obscured portion.
She had not been certain of the identity, but could not let
it go unchecked. Kneeling on the window-ledge added
only a few degrees of visibility, and the commotion had
attracted the attention of those already eating to block her
vision even more.

The confrontation she had warned Jenny about was
taking place of its own initiative. She did not want to go
running through the cloisters adding her own presence to
the square-off. It would be better if the Quais settled their
own questions of honor and status, but it would be utterly
disastrous if she let something happen to Jevan while
Jenny slept.

A window opening out from the corridor behind her
room let her climb onto the tiled roof without being observed. Her footing was precarious on the steeply sloped
and half-rounded tiles. She despaired of her brilliant idea
for observing the fracas at a distance, but eased along
until she could peek over the top and observe the fight.

"Brel's tits!"

It was impossible to guess how the fight had begun, but
Jevan, Chakri and Drocour were sporting livid bruises on

their faces and bodies from the effects of fighting Hanchon and his greater number of men. To Rifkind's surprise, her friends were holding their own and had vocal partisans among those who had already been subjected to Hanchon's bullying. Jevan and the rest were, however, unarmed and as yet the knives Hanchon and his men carried were tucked into their waist-bands. The brave display would end the moment that situation changed.

Moving with care, but hastily, Rifkind clambered back to her room. Sliding on her stomach over the edge of the roof, she grabbed for the rim of the drain tiles, caught herself and swung into the corridor without dislodging anything. Assim had built his Lyceum well. She rapped on Jenny's door until it opened.

"You've got to come down to the courtyard!" she exclaimed while pushing the disheveled woman back into her room.

"Is something wrong? With the Quais?" Jenny dabbed at her sleepy eyes with a moistened cloth. "I will be so happy when Jevan gets here and I can rest."

"He's here."

Rifkind's flat tone clashed with Jenny's exuberant reaction and for a moment Rifkind regretted the necessity of dampening her enthusiasm.

"It is not as you think. He led his men into Hanchon's court and before I knew he was here, they were fighting. They fight with fists now, but Hanchon's men carry knives. You know that Jevan and the rest do not."

"Well, stop them!" Jenny protested as Rifkind rummaged through a basket and produced an ornately embroidered belt of gold and silver threads that was Jenny's chief claim to membership in the Darian aristocracy.

"There's no time for me to do it—you must," Rifkind

said, wrapping the belt about Jenny's waist and hips. "Be lordly to them. Act like your father. Stop their fighting and lead them."

She grasped Jenny's wrist tightly and led her down the corridor and stairway.

"Rifkind!" Jenny protested. "I can't do this. Take your sword and separate them yourself!"

"You are the one who called them. They will follow you if they will follow anyone. I am not to be their leader. It is not my fate to lead, only to go my own way, helping where I can. *Do not tempt me!*"

The kitchen was empty of people; the dogs stole food from the abandoned plates and even the sow had left her wallow to explore the tidbits left behind. Sounds of conflict grown more desperate came through the colonnade. With Jenny's wrist still locked in her grip, Rifkind forced a path through the anxious Quais. She stopped just at the edge of the crowd.

Hanchon had drawn his knife. Jevan circled him, his left forearm wrapped with his belt so his breeches hung loose, threatening to trip him. The dark band of leather showed deep scores where Jevan had deflected the knife blade. Blood dripped into Hanchon's eye from a livid contusion on his brow. That punch had probably brought out the knives. Drocour had disarmed one of his opponents and now held his own against knife fighters no more competent than he.

To one side lay Chakri, unmoving, on the ground. His fingers were spread over a gaping, bleeding hole in his groin.

Jenny stepped forward, finally intent on doing what she had been told to do, only to be stopped again by Rifkind's strong grip.

"Move carefully. Distract Hanchon first. He will not die

if Jevan adds one more bruise to him. It would not be so the other way."

Though Jenny was not one brought up to think of herself as regal, the belt Rifkind had wrapped around her served its purpose in lending her that appearance; she moved perforce in the erect, flowing walk necessary to keep the tassels and fringe from tangling. The attention of the onlookers moved at once from the fighters to her. Following Rifkind's advice, Jenny approached the fighters from behind Jevan.

"No fighting within these walls!"

Her voice was louder than Rifkind had dared hope it would be. The late afternoon sunlight caught in her red hair, crowning her with gold. Hanchon froze in the gaze of her displeasure. Jevan, who heard but did not recognize the voice, started a round-house punch from a point far behind his waist and sent Hanchon sprawling backwards. His opponent incapacitated, he turned, ready to face the voice.

"Jenny!"

He was as astounded as Hanchon struggling to get up from the ground and trying to get his bearings on the swirling world.

"Let that be the end of it, then! There will be no more fighting!" Jenny's tone was less firm now that the fight was ending, but still adequate for the task.

Rifkind went to Chakri, who had yet to move or groan. Kneeling at his side, she felt for a pulse at his neck, only half listening to Jenny's pleading, yet emotionally effective, speech.

"I have not called you here to have you fight like children among yourselves. There is an army approaching. The man who leads it seeks the power of the Well of Knowledge, but he will not be content with that. He will

take your young men into his army, and the ones that
remain will be taxed harshly to support them. If you slip
into the dark Felmargue, he will send envoys to wait at
the trading towns, knowing that if you cannot trade, you
will soon be less than men out here. I know this man—his
plans, his cruelties and his lies: he is my father.

"If you will not fight to protect the Hold, fight for each
other and yourselves. If you fight with one another instead
of for each other, you will have no chance. Those who
escape to the Felmargue will be lost to the world of men
forever, those whom he can find and enslave will wish
that they were."

Jenny stopped. Rifkind's attention focused entirely on
Chakri while storms of protest and division flashed across
the crowd. The shy young man was beyond her help. His
pulse was too weak, too much of his blood lay in the
damp soil. He had taken a deep and mortal wound. His
breath was shallow, and liquid could be heard moving in
his chest. The healers could not save a man whose time
was past.

Chakri was unconscious. There was no need to give
him draughts to east the final pain, he would not notice.
It was fitting and proper, though, that she stay by him for
the last moments of his life to ease his spirit into the
beyond.

Rifkind listened to the voices of the crowd as she
crouched by the youth. Affa and Elyssa had joined her,
but following her example made no sound. The petty ri-
valries Pasca had alluded to were rampant. Each voice
called to have its own grievances settled by the council of
the Fathers before common cause could be made. The
voices spoke to each other, Jenny had lost the initiative.
Fearful that more fights would break out, Rifkind resolved
that she must leave Chakri to die in his own time to help
Jenny. A hand fell on her shoulder before she could rise.

"They will not listen to you either," Domhnall whispered to her, squatting down himself. "There is no way they can be anything but a hindrance to us, though we must protect them with the Well."

Their eyes met tacitly, acknowledging that their passions must find fuller expression but ... not just now.

"It feels right that they be here, but very wrong that they fight among themselves. Jenny must succeed," Rifkind replied.

"Jenny is an outstanding woman, but she has no grasp of strategy or tactics." Domhnall's voice carried open disdain; he stood up, as did Rifkind. "She cannot take them against an army or anything else. That is for you or me to do, if it is necessary."

"As I have said to her, it is not for me to lead, and it should not be for you, either. I chose my path long ago when I began my ritual training. I serve the Goddess and those who need me—people do not serve me. I risk my immortal spirit with corruption if I betray these things."

A rumbling belch came from deep within Chakri. His eyes opened, showing widened pupils fixed in an agonized stare. His mouth worked in frantic silence, bringing forth dark trickles of blood. Rifkind dropped to her knees again to attend him. Domhnall walked away from her. Other scuffles broke out and Jenny's voice rose, both shrill and impotent, to stop them. Rifkind judged Chakri conscious of his dying and could not leave him.

"Stop this!" A man's voice rose above the others. The din ebbed, but Rifkind listened to Chakri's labored whispers rather than to Domhnall's speech.

"The stone ... I have no sons ... the stone must go back! Tell ..." His whispers were lost in wracking coughs that brought up more dark blood and left his forehead pasty and glistening with cold sweat. His hands grasped her. He did not react to the wrenching pain the movement should have caused when he ripped the soft clots of the wound beneath his fingers.

"Tell ... Jevan ... that it must go back!"

Chakri's eyes closed, he seemed to relax as if having disposed of the memory-stone he had no fear of dying. Yet he held her tightly and she would not untwine his bloody fingers from her hand until his breathing ceased.

"The Well was our Father's downfall—we want nothing of it! If Jenny called us to defend the Hold from the armies of her Father we shall do so, because it is as evil for the Well to fall into one man's hands as into another's." An angry voice Rifkind recognized as Jevan's was echoed by men far less eloquent.

"You are swamp rats ... squabbling, killing yourselves. For five hundred years you have lived on squalid little rafts drifting further away from your heritage. I have seen them within those stones you prize so highly; I knew those men you revere as the Fathers. They left here with the stones, determined that their children would not suffer as they had. But they would laugh and scorn your cowardliness. They fought against the gods themselves. They would use the Well against an army, they would have used it against the gods if they had known how."

Rifkind heard the half-truths in Domhnall's rhetoric. A chill passed through her as Chakri's spirit passed out of his body, but it was not from the presence of death. Domhnall's words had brought a palpable hostility to the crowded cloister. She loosened Chakri's fingers from her hands and stood up, still marked with red.

"Our Fathers lost their lands because of your gods and your Wells. We keep them in the memory-stones because we have nothing else. Maybe you're right and we're swamp-rats beneath your feet. We lived for the dream of the Leveller so long that we won't know what to do when we do get our lands back. But we fight only for the

Felmargue, our land, and for the Lady, not for you or your Well." Hanchon spoke with the low growl of a man prepared to fight for his words.

He clapped his hand hard on Jevan's shoulder, an image of solidarity beyond misinterpretation. Rifkind flashed a smile at Domhnall. He had allowed them to vent their hostility against him so that they could see themselves as a unit. The smile froze and faded from her face. Domhnall's brooding features showed a man who had not cleverly executed a flanking gambit, but one filled with the bitterness and anger of the betrayed.

"Fools! You cannot fight an army. You cannot even imagine an army." He pointed to the sky above them: the Bright Moon shone, as She often did in the afternoons of her full phase. "Before the Moon comes full again, you'll come and beg me to destroy the army for you!"

He turned and marched through the crowd. The Quais divided wide before him, blocking Rifkind from his glance.

It is my fault, she berated herself. I sent him to the Well to see the armies of the past. He is wrong, but he knows too much to believe that. Even if I go to him and tell him he is making terrible mistakes, he will dazzle my ears with the Well's secrets. I love him still, but he's wrong.

The Bright Moon was still empty of Her presence. There was no one by whom Rifkind could swear an oath for her intuition, but she no longer needed reassurance from the Goddess for her judgments. The same Well that was so misguiding Domhnall had strengthened her faith and cleansed her of doubt.

"O, Chakri!" Jenny came over to gaze at the dead man, followed by several of the others. She covered her mouth and nose with her fingers. "Could you not save him?"

"Wounds are not like diseases. They do not grow from within the body, they come from the outside and in vio-

lence. This wound was too deep, and I was too late."
Rifkind saw the disappointment in Jenny's face. "I am not
the Goddess, Jenny. I cannot make miracles happen. All
too often I fail. I'm sorry."

"He is dead?" Hanchon asked, pushing the women
aside to look down at the dead man.

His hand still rested on Jevan's shoulder. Their cam-
araderie did not seem forced or insincere to Rifkind, and
her judgment was apparently shared by the other Quais,
who filed back into the other cloister where their dinners
were cooling.

"Yes, he lost much blood and did not linger. He wishes
Jevan to take the memory-stone 'back,' those were his
final wishes. I trust you can do this? I do not fully understand the significance of the return of the stone."

"A stone-bearer! Blood of the Fathers!" Hanchon's arm
dropped, he turned to glare at his men and shout in a
voice that boomed back from the walls. "Who has taken
this man's blood!"

While Jevan bent down to retrieve the stone from
Chakri's belt-pouch, Hanchon appraised his silent men.
At last one stepped forward, trembling for reasons
Rifkind, who had been born to blood-justice, could understand. To preserve his newly-made friendship, Hanchon
would exact the blood-price, from his own men. He
would, of course, prefer the accused to perform the act
himself, but the man did not seem so inclined.

Jevan fondled Chakri's stone nervously. The Quais
brought their dinner plates with them as they returned to
the death-quiet cloister.

"Give me the knife that killed this man," Hanchon demanded.

Hanchon held out his hand for the rust-colored weapon
that was offered unwillingly. The chieftain did not bother
to wipe the blade, but stepped forward for the coup-de-

grace. His victim's nerve failed. Though there was no possibility of escape he broke into a run toward the outer colonnade. The others of Hanchon's company pursued him, grappling and shouting, and dragged him back to the waiting executioner.

"Hold him!" Hanchon snarled.

His order was obeyed by men only slightly less fearful than the terrified man they pinned between them. Hanchon's arm rose. The others, Jevan included, averted their eyes. Rifkind watched calmly. This was justice, necessary and quick, designed to preserve the order and well-being of the survivors, not to produce mercy.

"No! Stop! There will be no more killing, no more blood. Killing this man will not bring Chakri back." Jenny rushed forward, placing herself between Hanchon and the prisoner.

"Lady?" Hanchon pulled his arm back at once. He stared at her with a profound confusion. "Lady, this is the way. Not until the blood is returned can there be peace and unity among us." He spoke slowly, as if to a child, but he was the one who did not understand.

"A man who sheds the blood of the Quais cannot be of the Quais. *This* shall be the way from now on. This man killed Chakri, he would not have if he had understood the law. There are no rafts within these walls. The days of the rafts are over forever. It is the time of the Quais of the land, and of new laws."

Jenny's magic returned to her as the passions of her beliefs gripped her.

"Take back your knife."

Hanchon offered the blade to the one who was no longer to be killed. Salvation had not yet brought calm to the reprieved man's eyes. He refused his chief's offer and the men who had restrained him had to put the knife in its sheath for him. The trio walked slowly away. Hanchon glanced helplessly at Jevan. Blood had not been returned. He had tried to do things the honored way, but he could not set aside the Lady's commands.

Jevan had not been over-eager for blood. He did not carry a knife and was content with the older justice of shaming rather than the newer one of blood. He was visibly relieved by the solution Jenny had created. His eyes did not move from the one they now called simply "Lady." Her face was flushed with her own passions, delicate and unconquerable at the same time.

Jevan threw his arm around Hanchon, but his smile and words were for Jenny.

"What of this army that dares to face us?" he asked with a quiet laugh.

The spell of Hanchon's confusion was broken. He was the brawler and chief once more. His smile deepened into triumph.

"The Quais!"

He thrust a saluting fist into the air. Jevan joined him, the crowd put aside their food and raised their fists to join in the rippling salute. A people had been born again, aided by the magic within the cloisters and the legendary Overnmont charisma. Rifkind felt its first pulse.

Her pleasure and pride for them was tempered by the question mark in her mind. Domhnall, the man she loved, had suddenly become a force apart from them, disappearing back into the Lyceum while she and Jenny showed arms-raised solidarity with the Quais. Without his support, they might face two enemies—one physical, and the other ethereal.

CHAPTER 20

It was late, well past the point where darkness ceases to be night and becomes early morning. Rifkind had sat alone in her large room, thinking and waiting for the grounds to become quiet. The Bright Moon had long since ascended past her windows and the coppery disk of the Dark Moon cast its eerie shadows onto the carpets. Vitivar, her Goddess's dark counterpart, was absent from his seat of power also. The two deities were opposites, yet caught so tightly in each other's grip that one was not truly complete without the other. The absence of them both could not be coincidental, and it did not bode well for the affairs of those mortals upon the Hold of Felmargue.

At last the Lyceum was still. The last fires smelled of dying embers and no voices could be heard arising from the cloisters or dormitories where the Quais now lived. Three more rafts of Quais had arrived since dinner. If the blanket-count was an accurate measure, some one hundred and twenty adults now resided within the battered walls. But now even the latest arrivals had quieted down, and there would not likely be new ones until after dawn.

Rifkind eased silently from the window ledge onto the roof. The half-round tiles and steep slopes were interspaced with flat platforms as if Assim had recognized the need for his colleagues to sit alone and unsurrounded by walls.

She set one of her crystals at each corner of the square platform and held the fifth one in her hands. Sitting cross-legged she sought meditative trance.

Humphry Overmont—where are you? What do you do, what are your plans and dreams as you lie asleep this night? Show yourself to me! Her thoughts poured into the god-empty ether, drifting slowly over the Lyceum roof. Her tal manifested itself, rising until it halo'd her in red light intensified by the rusty reflections of the Dark Moon. The halo was absorbed into the crystal and she was free to move through the ether as a mote of consciousness while her body was protected and preserved by the crystal-set wards.

Disorientation startled her for a moment. Memories of the ethereal were held in a physically real mind and could never prepare her for the shock of its differentness. It was, she knew, subtly different each time she ascended into it, because each time she herself was different and seeking new answers. Her purpose rose with her and she found herself moving with incomprehensible speed across the Felmargue following an instinctive stalking pattern that was not fully conscious until she knew she had found Humphry.

The army, she saw, was very small—in fact not an army at all, closer to a rather large and heavily armed escort. He is not so foolish, she thought, as to bring a large force into such a place. Strange. They are well into the interior swamp, and yet are not huddled together on rafts.

The mote whirled closer to the concentration of life.

Ah, Krowlowja has allies. The ground itself is pushed

up as in a causeway ... yes, like a road, running straight
back to Lowenrat. Who aids her? No sniffing seeress
could do these things alone.

Her consciousness settled into the newly lifted soil
which fairly reeked of arcane activity. It was not
Krowlowja's personal mark, nor any other she could recognize; whatever had lifted the causeway had changed
physical reality with its activity—not merely bound va-
grant spirits with rituals.

She is far more the Leveller than I would dare be,
Rifkind thought. She's trying to raise the ground up to the
Hold! Perhaps if Domhnall and I were to weave a binding
through the muck that surrounds our stronghold she
would call demons from farther away and make them
work all the harder. Then it might be I could learn to
whom she herself is bound. We might be able to ward her
off completely.

Rifkind had learned all that she required. The camp's
location and numbers were fixed in her mind and the
upheaval of the causeway would make it easy to locate
again. Probing Krowlowja's alliances would best be done
by changing the wards beside her body and though she
had called Humphry's name to find the encampment, she
did not truly need to find the man himself. And as long as
she stayed she was in horrible danger.

But Humphry was her obsession, a man who had betrayed her and haunted her dreams. Hanging motionless
in the drifting ether the mote whispered his name and
was drawn to a tent she should have guessed by its size
and position was the Emperor's. Its canvas roof was no
match for her ethereality and she placed the mote of her
presence with the smoke rising from a lantern slung on
the massive centerpole.

Humphry Overnmont left lanterns blazing in his
pavilion while he slept. Too many demons have crossed

his path, Rifkind thought, and he thinks to avoid their curse by banishing the darkness. How little you know, Lord, of the ways of ritual magick. No ... wait. He does not sleep alone. Who travels with him through the Felmargue?

The Emperor of all Dro Daria lay on his back, arms outstretched and silken comforters heaved to one side. His face was flushed, with a bluish-red mottling under the skin of his nose and cheeks wherever the bristling red beard did not conceal it. At least a part of Rifkind's dislike of the man had grown from his continued and obscene robustness in the midst of decadence and decay. He was essentially healthy despite years of dissipation in mind and body. His sleep was untroubled for all its energy and movement. Humphry conquered worlds while he slept.

His companion was kitten-curled among the pillows and silks as far from the man as the sleeping platform would allow. It was not Krowlowja. Rifkind knew that at once, but it was some moments before she recognized the peasant girl she had pulled, injured and feverish, from the muddy road of Glascardy so long ago. Linette, now a lady and consort, did not appear at all secure or happy in the future she had so eagerly envisioned for herself. Three years before the blonde girl had seemed possessed of a sensuality and passion that had overwhelmed and daunted her supposed teacher. Now rings, with gold chains connecting them to her bracelets, adorned her hands, and glistening gems confined her hair even while she slept. But Linette clutched the silken coverlet as she made whimpering noises, small and frightened, in her sleep.

Rifkind's thoughts turned to the woman-child whom she had once saved from death. It is for you, then, that the pavilion is lit? Humphry shows such concern for his child-consort? The lantern flame flickered as Rifkind remembered. But your nightmares are not afraid of oil-wicks. I failed you and have shared some of those night-mares. I wrenched you away from what you were and set you down in a world I myself did not understand. I was suspicious of all things; you were trusting.

Rifkind wandered into thoughts made more vivid by her ethereal imagination. Winds gathered around her to carry her back to the past times of memory. No! I will not relive those things! From the first you were enthralled by the world Humphry dangled before you. If I failed you, I failed myself more for not understanding your ambitions and greed. You cling to the silks in your own nightmares, not mine!

With a shudder Rifkind was aloft through the vent-hole. She had roiled the delicate balance of the ether with her emotions. It whirled and eddied, alerting any who could comprehend its movement to the presence of a careless adept. The mote shrank still further, losing itself in the movements, hoping to be mistaken for a nightmare or a pocket of extinguished magick suddenly vented through the soft soil of the causeway. Ethereal disturbances could have many causes.

Rifkind let unseen winds carry her along, unresisting until she might be cast aside. Passively she listened to the dream-thoughts of the soldiers, unanimous in their dislike of the swamp and their desire to be anywhere else. The nervousness of the pack-horses spiked upward as the tang of unfamiliar dangers reached their nostrils. She was still a passenger of the winds when the questing beacon of Krowlowja's ethereal presence loomed upward, far from the dreams of the mortal soldiers.

The seeress had her own guard of acolytes from the Oracle surrounding her. The dangers the seeress faced required defenses inimical to those of the mortals. Her acolytes burned incense whose smoke curled through the

night air and into the ether itself where it hung like a
screen, sifting through a constant stream of thought and
dream for dangerous omens.

Rifkind considered her situation while she moved
against the currents before they carried her into the incense screen: If they have such fixed defenses, they may
have nothing more aggressive hidden nearby. Though
the sealed sphere itself is ample evidence that they have
cause to distrust something. If they fear me, or Domhnall,
it is an unnecessary drain on their strength—only a god
could challenge that screen. Do they guard against a god?

There was still some time before dawn, and a moss-
hung brooding tree was nearby, trapping lost dreams in
its veiled branches. She let herself be caught in its web,
becoming just another wisp of consciousness. Only one of
her names carried on the ether wind could draw her out
of its safety.

The small encampment around Krowlowja was not
asleep: closer observation of the screen revealed that it
was a trap, as filled with consciousness as her own mote,
straining at every quarter, though it was not looking for
her. She felt the pressure of trained minds pass over the
tree in routine boredom. Did Krowlowja fear her enemies,
or distrust her allies? Was the screen a general precaution, or thrown up for a specific purpose? Krowlowja
would not have been the Baleric Oracle's chief seeress if
she had trouble judging the true proportions of danger.

Dawn approached and Rifkind grew tired. Waiting
ethereally in the crook of a tree was, if anything, more
boring than such a task would have been in her own
body. She had eased back along the branches and was
prepared to dart back to the Lyceum when pungent antic-
ipation wafted past and the screen set up an alarm.

The god who crushed the causeway with his advancing
presence was worthy of the defenses arrayed before him.

Rifkind lifted each name she knew, holding each like a template in front of the ominous cloud, but none would confine the image. Even Vitivar, the most capricious of those deities whose name she knew, was not nearly so malignant as the one before her. Krowlowja was foolhardy, desperate, or both to have gathered the attention of such a god. His mighty aura trailed behind him, tugging real leaves off the trees.

The most stomach-bound would know that they were not alone in such a wind, Rifkind thought. Yet I think he would not notice any one consciousness—there is some safety in insignificance.

The incense screen flared with unholy iridescence and was gone. A wind, real this time, roared along the causeway, billowing unnaturally from the ground up, collapsing the tents of Krowlowja's party as it passed over them. The deity gave evidence of being displeased with her distrust. Rifkind's tree groaned as the wind tore at it. Its roots went deep into the muck, the ground itself flowed with the wind and the tree with it, but its deep tap-roots held while smaller trees toppled with great splashes into the swamp water. Humphry's camp could be heard shouting as the blasts of wind reached them. Rifkind wondered briefly what effect the god's presence would have on the two sleeping in the large pavilion, before her attention was drawn back to the tree.

To her credit, Krowlowja rose to the monstrous challenge, sheltering the weaker acolytes behind her, weaving their strength to her own. She appeared as she had at the Well, clad in green and black and rising to unnatural dimensions. Her words were directed to, and absorbed by, the enormity confronting her. Rifkind saw only their effect.

The seeress had learned a highly compelling name for her divine ally, for though he hissed and shot lightning toward her, he also shrank and took on mortal, though massive, semblance. His aura had not been deceiving; he assumed the form of a man, well-proportioned, naked and rampant. Krowlowja embraced him, and he, in turn, enveloped them both with a discreet darkness.

That is a way I had not considered for affixing a god's power within me. It is most effective, though I should think the risks are considerable, almost as great as the discomfort. Despite herself, Rifkind laughed.

Rifkind knew how the seeress acquired her awesome power. The Well of Knowledge could supply the names Rifkind would need if she dared to interfere. She had no great desire to witness the climax of their union. Moving with haste she tried to guide the mote back toward the Lyceum.

Horror gripped her as the god froze the ether around her and slowly drew her back toward his vortex. Rifkind swerved violently from side to side, attempting to throw off the contact. He had yet to call her name to stop her struggles, but she was no less ensnared for that. With the same tactics the wily fish demonstrated she banked into material outcroppings, writhing and cursing until she broke free into the shelter of the brooding-tree.

O Bright Mother, I've done it for sure this time! There's no escaping and Krowlowja will tell him my name, for jealousy's sake if for no other reason.

But the god broke away from Krowlowja to pursue Rifkind without first calling her name. Rifkind moved quickly and wisely, the god close behind her. She could not find a maneuver that would both keep her in front of him and let her head back to the school—not that she was entirely certain that she wanted to return to the Lyceum with such a force bearing down behind her.

The mote was as close to nothing as something could be, yet it still required energy to move it, and she had extended herself beyond all limit. Unending water stretched beneath her, and still the god pursued. She could not retrieve the mote any longer, even if the god were to vanish suddenly.

The crystals! I have one tal, one spirit, and it is here! And *here* is both over the water and between my hands at the Lyceum. Thoughts moved too quickly within her to be called plans. The water had changed to grey dimensionless fog that rose to envelop her. She turned within herself and dove for the crystal held between her hands.

Tumbling through a kaleidoscope of activity too frantic to remember, Rifkind clung to herself with a stubborn sanity. I have done what I intended. I have escaped the god. He cannot follow me. Reality will return once I am centered again. I will find myself back at the Lyceum. I know what I am doing.

The universe steadied. Rifkind felt familiar senses again, but was still surprised when she opened her eyes not to the rooftops of the Lyceum but to the translucent walls of the Well-Chamber. A woman who seemed familiar, though unrecognizable and certainly not one of the Quais-women, leaned against the Well-Font.

"You have caused us no end of consternation, Rifkind. We would thank you for revealing Colomandiz' treachery, but not for luring him to our very gates. There was much discussion when I wished you to be released from that demon-spawned crystal in which you had tried to escape him."

Rifkind was too tired to think, or to keep her composure. "Who are you?" she demanded, unwilling to endure new mysteries.

The woman's face changed in a thousand little ways, each almost imperceptible, though the effect was to reveal the painful perfection of the Goddess' beauty. Rifkind covered her eyes and fell to her knees, though the latter was

more from shock than adoration. The radiance ebbed until the Goddess was as She had been beside the reflecting
pool—substantially mortal yet crowned with the moon's
crescent.

"I had thought you would recognize me without my
diadem. We do not wish to frighten our loyal worshippers
by revealing our true radiance to them. The least of our
images is normally the most acceptable for mortal eyes."

"I am always honored to be of service to you, Lady, I
should have known you, but the danger seemed so great
I plunged unthinking into the crystals rather than face the
god, and seem to be slow in recovering myself."

"You would have been trapped for an eternity in the
crystal's structure. You can see the problems we had in
releasing you."

Rifkind rolled the small fracture-ridden stone in her
palm; it shattered into several pieces from the movement.
It had been through tremendous stresses, but unbidden
instinct said she had never been captured by it. The pantheon, or perhaps the Bright One alone, had acted to destroy the gift she had received from the Lost God Hanju in
his mountain fortress. Rifkind stifled her imprudent
thoughts and faced the Goddess again.

"Colomandiz pursued me, but did not call my name. I
did not know him, either. He chased me beyond the limits
of my power without knowing who or what I was. I was
not luring him anywhere." Rifkind remained respectful,
yet demanded an explanation.

"Colomandiz was judged deficient long ago. By luring
him into our grasp you earned the favor of many besides
myself, and we were able to free you."

"And Krowlowja? How does anyone, even a seeress,
summon a god who is not a part of the pantheon?"
Rifkind had been raised at the side of crafty men who
disposed of lives and destinies in casual campfire con-

versations. She knew how to read discomfort, even within a Goddess, and how to press her advantage.

"She did not summon him, but opened herself to his power. She is the one who sundered the spheres around the Felmargue and the Hold. We have once again expelled Colomandiz; he will not return. But the rupture they made lingers. The danger continues." The Goddess' manner was no longer casual.

"There is a doom hanging over all of us within these old walls, Lady. Your moon-stones do not help me penetrate. When I seek the answers for myself, I find a seeress consorting with an unknown god. I fear for my world and all those living and dead within it!"

"You are of the created! If you were not to be a pawn you would not have been born! I have done all I can for you. You know too much already. You cannot be controlled, and you find things that have been hidden even from Us! You are my favorite, and my delight, but I will not answer your questions as though I were a common oracle! Things will be as they must be. Colomandiz has been expelled. That has not ended Our danger. It does not end yours. You will be safest if you play your part as it is given to you."

The Goddess disappeared in a flash of unbearable silver light. Rifkind rubbed her sore, bedazzled eyes for a moment, then leaned against the font herself.

How powerful this Well must be that my Lady, the Bright One, shows such strain and fear in its presence, Rifkind thought. It is easy to appreciate the temptations of such powers as the gods possess. I begin now to see the danger the Knowledge contained in this glassy fluid is to a mortal such as myself. The menace of power is more than mere corruption.

Her face was drawn, Her eyes ringed beneath the illusion, as if in Her divine form She is so truly tired that She

cannot attain perfection in Her mortal guise. So must it
have been in the time of Assim, five hundred years ago—
and five hundred years must be like a day in the times of
the gods. They are constantly threatened by those they
have created or favored. Their authority is challenged and
their responsibilities endless. Assim was a fool to wish to
replace the gods!

They have their friendships and alliances. And they
make a clan war-gathering seem like a quiet friendly dinner at Chatelgard. They are immortal, but otherwise, not
unlike us.

She shook her head and stared at the fissured crystal.
Hanju had pointed out the flaws and biases in the old
ones; what might his comment be toward this one now?
The Wall bubbled in immediate response to her idle
thought. She could call, and possibly compel, the Lost
God. He would certainly be able to add interesting pieces
to the information the Bright One had given her.

But Rifkind shook off the temptation.

The static wards Domhnall had placed over the
doorway sputtered to activity when she neared them.
Rifkind suspected she could walk through the wards, just
as she had passed through her crystal without aid. But
Domhnall would come in time, and she was tired of
tempting the fates.

CHAPTER 21

Full spring arrived while Rifkind conducted open-air demonstrations of hand-to-hand fighting and weaponry. A riot of wildflowers had appeared on the meadows outside the Lyceum walls, and amid their pastel colors, Rifkind forged a militia out of the eager Quais. Domhnall, in continuing pique against the raft-people, refused to supply her with the spears, arrows and knives she wanted, so she taught them the rudiments of staff-work and forced sharpened stones through leather-wrapped stakes and called them maces. As well, perhaps: the crude bashing style of the mace was better suited to the amateur Quais than any more refined technique.

While Domhnall toiled with powerful incantations in the bowels of the ancient temple, Rifkind sketched giant slings and cooking pots that could discharge a hail of stones or a stream of heated oil. No matter how good Humphry's strategy, Rifkind reasoned he'd be under the Quais once at the bottom of the cliffs, and a second time when he moved into the Lyceum itself. Furthermore, there were many more Quais than Humphry had elite guardsmen; her militia could lose life after life and still emerge victorious. Jenny had seen this ruthless mathematics in Rifkind's plans and privately grieved over it. She stayed quiet, though, in the meetings Rifkind held every day outside the broken walls.

There was always an aura of tension at such meetings when men and women grappled with problems each was convinced was beyond the group's abilities. Jenny and the four Quais, Hanchon, Jevan and two others from the later arrivals, Vaincas and Moigal, were already waiting beneath the usual tree sipping amber wine from a wineskin Jenny had brought along from the kitchen. Rifkind was still working with the men as she had been since early morning.

Her hair was tightly braided and wound about her head. She had shed all but the short linen tunic, her boots and the quilted upper-body armor. Her arms and legs glistened with sweat in the late afternoon sunlight. At times Rifkind could seem adequately feminine, occasionally demure, but while shouting hoarse commands and encouragements to the trio surrounding her with stripped saplings, she resembled nothing so much as an otherworldly demon.

"Higher! Quicker! Think *attack!* I could take your arm off, there!"

She flashed the sword, letting the bright sunlight reflect off it and into her leftmost opponent's eyes, illustrating his danger. She was good enough with her sword to pull her attacks and parries, but by late afternoon she was tired and apt to make mistakes. The live steel was necessary. The Quais would not fight men armed as they were, with sticks and rocks, but an elite guard armed with sword, spear and armor.

Ducking low beneath a viciously aimed swing, Rifkind's long-curbed skills exploded outward. One knee took the man in the stomach, and the hardened edge of her forearm shot out to knock a second staff away from its target.

"Hold!" she bellowed.

The sword dangled from one hand, she bent over at the waist to catch her breath quickly. Brushing aside a rivulet of sweat from beside her eye, leaving a dark smear on her already filthy face, Rifkind stood to face her attackers.

"That one ... was good. You'd have had me ... Humphry's men know nothing of circle-fighting ... but some may carry shields with sharpened bosses ... guard yourself carefully if you must attack over an enemy."

She walked over to the man who still crouched on the ground clutching his stomach. Offering a hand she helped him to his feet.

"It hurts to kill a man," she explained, looking back to the other two. "When it stops hurting, you've lost a part of yourself you can never get back. You two were afraid of being hurt. When you fight to the death you must expect to feel pain."

They wouldn't likely doubt her. Bruises and scrapes showed on her where she had failed to deflect a strike. In two weeks she had fought them a thousand times; singly, in pairs, and in threes. She healed quickly; a healer's blessing, though her scars were visible beneath the sweat-streaked dirt. The flacidness she had felt after the long raft trips was gone. She was ready for battle and a drink of cool water poured over tart spices.

"Three times around the walls. Full pace. Chandro, count the pace!"

The seventy-odd men practicing on the meadow groaned in unison. The middle-aged man who had once thought to slay this woman and her companion picked up his sapling and his mace, beginning the final exercise of the day. They ran like young Asheerans chasing the herds, striving for endurance rather than sprinting speed, with a rolling gait that spared the heart and legs. If the Quais couldn't fight, they would at least know how to retreat.

"I can't hear you!"

Rifkind's voice seemed to rise from somewhere beneath her feet, drowning out the men's chanted cadence. She watched with satisfaction as their gait evened when the louder cadence forced them into a regular breathing rhythm. She sheathed her sword, picked up a discarded sapling and mounted the slope to where the others waited. She tossed the sapling to Jevan, who caught it one-handed.

"Your turn!" she announced, drawing the sword.

"Rifkind," Jevan grumbled, setting aside the sapling, but Rifkind came on guard the instant her sword was free and jumped toward Jevan.

The others scrambled away, and Jevan hurriedly grabbed back the sapling and bounded to his feet. He had bathed and changed his clothes, expecting to eat with Jenny in secluded privacy beyond the walls when the meeting was over. Rifkind had seen this, but had not singled him out on account of jealousy or her own frustrations. Jevan, like the others who waited, would command a group of Quais. He was a quick and agile fighter of great promise in leadership—if he ever learned to conquer his emotions.

He was angry and careless as he fought her. The sapling chipped as it bounced along her sword, sliding ineffectively past her quilt-armored shoulder. He raised the staff again, ignoring her movements toward him. With a blood-curdling shriek she snap-kicked a heavy-soled boot against his thigh. He toppled backwards, only barely able to roll under a downward slice of her sword. She had moved with deliberate care, but the on-lookers began to shout their concern that she was out for blood.

He swung wild again, aiming for the small of her back and catching only her outer thigh. Jenny and the others shouted louder. Rifkind shut their protesting noises out of her mind. She kicked again, taking Jevan's legs out from under him. He rebounded more slowly this time, grass and blood staining the legs of his breeches. Snarling with rage he kept at his large, wild swings and at being toppled or frustrated, until the narrow glint in his eye showed *he*, at least for the blood-red moment, meant to slay this tormentor.

Rifkind met his blood-lust charge, lowering her sword once he was committed to his attack. She ducked under him, raising her head to butt into his belly as he charged, uncontrolled, over her. Carried upward by his own momentum, Jevan flew head-first over her shoulder and landed in a heap, the staff more than an arm's length away.

Rifkind raised her sword again. His chest heaved—she had no doubt cracked several ribs. Her own head rang. The hot fire was out of his eyes, replaced with a look of cold determination that filled Rifkind with pride and satisfaction. Ignoring his pain, Jevan rolled to the staff and came to a half-crouch with it poised in front of him, waiting...

"Hold!" she shouted, stepping back, lowering but not abandoning her guard. They stared at each other a moment. Jevan smiled and dropped his staff. Rifkind sheathed the sword and offered him her hand.

"Be damned if you weren't right, woman," Jevan exclaimed, clutching at his ribs while Rifkind braced her feet against his weight, hauling him to his feet. "You'd have killed me ten times over in my anger, but this last time, this last time you'd have had a fight!" He laughed painfully, clutching at his ribs.

"Why else would I have stopped it? I can fight an angry man without hurting him—but not a determined man."

"Not hurt? Be damned again, woman!"

He pointed to the creeping stains on his breeches and, in turn, she lifted the quilting aside to show him a brilliant contusion on her thigh. He nodded, mumbled apologies and they joined the group nervously awaiting them.

"Rifkind!" Jenny scolded, her arm going around Jevan's waist at once. "That was unnecessary!"

"For you, yes. Your brother made sure you always fought with your head, but until he learned otherwise, Jevan thought it was best to barrel in, thrashing about the moment he got riled. Don't worry though, everyone will get his turn."

She found the jug of spiced water and drank deeply of it before offering some to Jevan. She threw the quilting into the dirt and sat down, the damp, dirty material of her tunic rising high on her legs. If the others were discomforted by her battlefield manners, or need of a long bath, they wisely refrained from mentioning it. Rifkind began the meeting.

"How goes the war?"

"We have fifteen skins of oil. Some will be light enough to burn, but most will just scald the men badly. I think I've got the knack now for churning the stuff out of the kitchen hearth, but we're going to be short of food if I try to get us back up to our schedule." Jenny spoke of her conversion of the kitchen-cloister to a munitions factory.

"We need more stones!" Vaincas explained, referring of course to the glassy black stones skimmed from the Well. "If Domhnall won't give them to us, we'll just have to go down there and take them ourselves! It's our Well too! I've tried and tried every combination I can think of, and we

just don't have enough memory-stones to bring the
Fathers forward to council."

It was a sore subject and one Rifkind would have preferred to drop from their meetings altogether, though the
Quais refused to give up their beliefs in the memory-
stones. Whispers and rumors were rampant, many claim-
ing that the Fathers had abandoned their children for the
crime of consorting with Domhnall. Rifkind herself was
deeply concerned with Domhnall's growing refusal to aid
her in arming the Quais or planning a coordinated defense of the Lyceum, though only Jenny could guess the
full extent of her distress.

The immortal youth spent all his time in the temple
catacombs. Even by daylight strange glows could be seen
hovering over that portion of the tiled roof. The Quais
feared and distrusted this supposed ally and there was
little Rifkind could do to reconcile the two. The Quais insisted on holding their strategy meetings beyond the
walls, where Domnhall still refused to go.

But Rifkind still yearned for him. She waited until he
left the temple for a few hours' sleep, and no longer attempted to interest him in her plans, only to maintain the
friendship, respect and hope of love that had come to be
very important to her in a short time.

"I shall speak to him about our need, but you know
what the answer will likely be. The Well without
Domhnall is useless to us. His purposes are not opposed
to ours, only his methods. Meanwhile I will detail men for
hunting parties. The woods are well filled with animals
and can withstand our hunting for a short time."

"How do we know that Domhnall won't betray us in
the end?" Hanchon asked, and the group became silent to
hear her answer. "We've all the Quais in the Felmargue
here, each with their stones, and yet the Fathers are
mute."

"Domhnall seeks to protect the Well, just as we do. He has made it quiet to throw Krowlowja off our trail," Jenny interjected quickly.

The issue was oft argued, and no afternoon was complete without its reiteration. Domhnall had his interests—keeping all outsiders away from the Well, especially outsiders who had already, and personally, attacked him. Jenny and Rifkind had their interest—keeping Jenny's father from harnessing the incalculable energies to his own purposes. The Quais had theirs—a faith in the whole enterprise as the birth-pangs of a new era in which they would be farmers and tradesmen again instead of swamp rats and trappers. Each group had its own notion of the Leveller legend and used it to support its cause.

Rifkind and Jenny knew the whole alliance was one of means, not ends, but aside from Humphry they were the most politically sophisticated inhabitants of the Felmargue. As the discussion under the lengthening shadows of the trees grew more heated, they were also the quietest.

Rifkind would not re-exert her authority until everyone had had his say. She disliked the role of planner and arbiter that had been thrust upon her, disliked even more that she resorted to the same aloof tactics that had so enraged her with Humphry and later Ejord. But she was too much of a pragmatist to deny effectiveness. They talked out each subject in turn, and she guided them to the conclusions she had reached before the discussion began.

"The hunting parties will go out starting tomorrow. Now, what of the constructions?"

She looked to Jevan, who in turn signed to Moigal.

"We've got carts made now, following your advice on the wheels, Lady Rifkind, but they'll not do for carrying the towers and slings from one part of the cliffs to another.

Those we shall have to put up in place. One of the men's had an idea for building the towers and such here, marking each joint, then taking them down again to load them on the carts and move them. We would halve our time building them, but it'd still take a day at the cliffs, maybe more. I say that we'll have to know where this Humphry'll climb well afore he can climb up so as we can be there an' waiting."

"There will be time. Marking the joints of collapsed towers sounds clever. The wood can be left in the carts and sledges at the most likely landing points and only moved if necessary."

"Yes, Lady Rifkind."

"The men are now in as good shape and condition as they're likely to see. They'll stay at this peak maybe a month, by which time the fighting should be over. I'll start splitting them into teams tomorrow. It's time they got used to working with the siege equipment. We'll drill first thing in the morning and before supper. During the rest of the day I'll start working with the women. Once the teams are made up, I don't intend to adjust them. In another week or so you'll build your commands from these teams."

"What of the women?" Jenny asked.

"If the defense falls back to these walls they'll have as much as they can do. The men will be exhausted and decimated. The women will conduct the defense of the Lyceum itself."

There was muttering as the men and Jenny reacted to Rifkind's implicit pessimism. The sun had sunk far enough that the shadows were cool and the old gong which had once summoned Assim's brotherhood was announcing another dinner. Jevan still wanted time with Jenny, and the other men wanted to eat and speak with friends and women. Rifkind smiled to herself as they agreed to her plan despite their misgivings.

She hesitated a moment after dismissing them to gather her discarded clothes and to speak with Jevan.

"If your ribs still hurt before you bed down, send some-one up to me and I'll attend to them. I'm more tired and sore than I expected; I may have hit you harder than I thought."

Jevan waved her off and she headed back to the school. The bruises throbbed with dull aches, her thighs and stomach hurt from the beating she had taken, and her own senses, accustomed as they were to the water-poor Asheera, agreed she stank of sweat and exertion.

Musing that she had never been intended to be a leader or trainer, she was still dissatisfied with her own perfor-mance, watching the men limp through the cloisters nursing battered ribs and legs from those moments when she *had* felt attacked and had struck back determined to save herself. She felt a wistful admiration for the grizzled, scarred warriors of the clans who sparred with a never-ending group of youngsters without ever seeming to lose their tempers. Of course, they had twelve years or more to make a warrior, not a month.

There is a temperament to teaching which escapes me, and would escape me even if I had all the time in the world to teach these men to fight and protect themselves, she thought. Even with Jevan my interest lasts for only a few moments and I would just as soon be elsewhere. I would be maddened long before I could teach each of these men his own proper style. The smallest is bigger than me, and all have some resentment of being taught manly arts by a woman; even as my father warned me long ago that the clan would never accept me as their chief, no matter how many successful raids I led.

Dear gods, I ache!

She wandered along little-used corridors to reach her

rooms without attracting the notice of the Quais. She ripped the laces from her tunic and let it drop to the floor rather than ease it over her head. The glass-like surface of the bathing-pool reflected far more of the ravages of her existence than she cared to consider. She did not ease into the water, but splashed, creating whirls and eddies to destroy the water's memory. She gasped slightly as the mineral-laden water cleansed still open sores.

These Quais pursue my instructions with unnecessarily great enthusiasm. Each wants to be one of those who can boast "I set *her* on her backside!" But it will be worth it if they set Humphry and his men back a few moments. With the burning oil and their vigor, we just might make it.

Throwing the thongs that bound her braids to one side, Rifkind ducked under the water to drench her sweat-matted hair and scalp. When she sat back on the bathing seat to wring the water from the arm-long plaits she was astounded to find she had a visitor bearing a tray of food and scented oils.

"Pasca?"

Her eyesight would not deceive her, yet Rifkind resisted the thought that any of the Quais would enter her chambers unannounced.

"I have seen that you do not eat the food our hearth produces, and Hanchon made great tales of the hurts you received in fights with him and the others. I've brought you a meal I prepared myself, and oils for your bruises, for though you are a healer, there are places you cannot reach.

"It is not fitting that the men be lavished with our attentions while you suffer alone."

Pasca moved swiftly to the edge of the pool, moistening her hands first with the water, then with the oils.

But I am not a man, Rifkind thought while she edged

out of the pool and reached for a length of drying cloth to wrap about her. And that is why I choose to suffer alone. I want no one's ministrations but my own. Or didn't you notice that I have a lock on my door?

The oil had a heavy dark appearance, as if it might have been distilled from fish oil, and the meat looked like lizard. Rifkind wanted nothing to do with the oils or the meal, and suffered the uncomfortable notion that Pasca curried her favor as she would have done with a similarly powerful man. With the cloth tucked about her, Rifkind escaped into her own room.

"Share the meal here with me," Rifkind said, clearing a place on the side-board, "and we shall discuss whatever troubles you."

Pasca seemed unsettled by Rifkind's suggestions, just as Rifkind had been disturbed by Pasca's sudden appearance. The Quais woman followed, quiet and suddenly discreet.

"Lady, the men say tomorrow you will take the women and show them the defense of the walls here. They say you have said they will be exhausted and unable to help should the time come. They are upset by this and feel you have misjudged them."

"Defense of the homestead is the woman's usual lot. They *will* be beyond exhaustion, trust me."

But Rifkind did not think that Pasca had come to her to press the men's complaints and insecurities.

"Ay, but all the Felmargue is our home—is it not? The men say they will be strong enough to defend all of it, and wish us to cower down to sing victory songs of them. You came to our raft with healing and promises. I gave you my memory-stone because you said things would be different, but it is no different. *You* fight, yet you are not convinced that *we* can fight!"

That was more along the lines of what Rifkind had

been expecting, and she was wary before five words were out of Pasca's mouth. Instincts said Pasca might deem it necessary to attack to prove her ability to fight or brawl.

"There is much to be done. Everyone must do what he or she can do best."

"I am more than a head taller than you, and stronger than most of the men. Yet you have not looked at me to do what I can do best. You look at the women and see bait-fish, nothing more."

"It would not, I suppose, do any good to tell you that I do not think anyone, man or woman, who has spent his life on a tiny raft is going to be able to adapt very well to the battle conditions I envision here within the next month?"

Pasca did not react. Rifkind could not remember the promises that the Quais woman remembered her making, but did not doubt that she could have at least implied them. Ejord had had trouble with the aftereffects of many of his recruitment speeches, also. She was grateful she had not had any of the oil rubbed on her skin nor eaten any of the food. Her sword lay a step beyond her reach, almost within her grasp if she needed it, but before such extremes she still had another tactic to defuse the situation.

"As I have said, there are many things to be done. I do not know what all of them may be. Much of the decision-making and work will not begin until I am more certain of Humphry's final approach to the Hold. We will be digging pit-falls between here and the cliffs they climb. Guards, of course, will be set where they can oversee the swamp when the army does approach. Someone will have to be near the edge during the battles to call back to those who will load and fire the slings, which must, themselves, be crewed and co-ordinated.

"Within a few days I shall have more than I can do,

even with those I have already chosen to help me. You are very eager to show ambition and aggression; how do you feel about responsibility? If I give you a task, will you perform it? If I ask you to guide other men or women, will you lead them knowing their lives depend on your judgment?"

Pasca smiled, her hostility melted. Rifkind relaxed, but was not surprised. How many times had she bridled in irritation and wished for an opportunity to prove herself? Pasca left as quietly as she had arrived.

The blue gowns Domhnall provided were not adequate for Rifkind's dreams and desires. After bathing, she rubbed her own sweet oils and perfumes into her skin until long after the Bright Moon had arisen and she stood in a circle of moonlight. She spun about, arms extended until the silvery radiance clung to her body. The smells of the Glascardy mountains in the spring when the lush fields of wildflowers bloomed crowded around her and the sounds of the breezes rippling through the Asheeran grasslands followed her as she moved. Her freshly washed and scented hair fell to just above her hips, picking up the glints of the moonlight surrounding her.

She was ready. Domhnall had not told her where his room was located, or even that he would be there instead of working in the temple. Rifkind's confidence in her own timing was, however, total. She moved, a vision of moonlight and gentle spring breezes, through the back corridors and cloisters, providing for herself all the light she needed. The narrow room Domhnall had once pointed out as his had a new stout-hinged door. She lifted the latch to let it swing open.

"I had hoped you would come."

Domhnall wore the white and gold attire she had seen the first time they met. He had a bowl of scented oil with

a wick in it burning beside a silk- and pillow-covered bed.
Moonlight flowed through the unshuttered window to
add to Rifkind's radiance. He lifted a ewer of wine to pour
two crystal goblets of the richly colored fluid. They drank
deeply, their eyes never leaving each other, but in silence,
sensing that words would reveal their awkwardness and
destroy the mood that was so vital to them both.

The gown of moonlight slipped from her shoulders as
he touched her. She drew the laces from his shirt and cast
it to one side. They stood entwined in each other within
the moonlight around their feet until passions rose and
hesitancy departed. The light of the oil lamp was especially kind to Rifkind, resting gently on her golden skin, hiding all traces of the warrior and healer behind the
emergent woman. She pulled him to the bed beside her,
caressing him with heavy-lidded eyes and soft lips.

There was no pain as Domhnall brought her across the
last threshold to womanhood. The healer within her attended to that as Rifkind had attended to other new brides
or terrified young captive slaves. But for Rifkind, the
woman herself, there was no terror, pain or panic. A far-
reaching satisfaction filled her, and though she had not
waited as long as Domhnall had, it had been long
enough.

She slept cradled in his arms until the first glow of
dawn pervaded the room. The oil lamp had extinguished
itself. The gown of moonlight had departed with the
Goddess. Rifkind shifted Domhnall's arms and legs until
she could ease out of the silken bed without disturbing
him. Shaking the sleep-tangles from her hair she draped
the white and gold shirt around her shoulders and
slipped out the door.

She would return to him as often as she could, and if
the time ever came that she no longer sought his company she would find another to share the greatest ecstasy

of mortal life. This first experience would never be repeated; she knew that, but didn't grieve for it. Domhnall's life had joined with hers. It was the privilege of a healer to know the exact moment of conception.

The gold threads in the borrowed shirt glittered in the dawn as she ran across the cloisters and kitchens to the privacy of her own rooms.

CHAPTER 22

It was some days later when Rifkind leaned against the open colonnade of a still-abandoned cloister. A mist lay over the red tile roofs and the new dawn sunlight had not been yet able to lift it or the night chill from the air. She pulled the heavy black cloak more tightly around her shoulders, though it was not the damp morning air which caused her shivering, but a cold knowledge within her. The others would arrive soon.

The children she had awakened and sent on her errands reported that save for Jevan everyone she wished to summon had been roused from sleep. Rifkind left the shelter of the colonnade to prod a small fire with a stick. The water had finally boiled. She reached into the folds of her cloak for a packet of herbs, throwing them into the pottery jug and inhaling the scented steam as it rose to join the greater mist.

Chandro was the first of her council to arrive. The Quais were too sparse of leadership for her to reject an able man on the trivial ground that he had tried to incite his own band against her. Indeed, his very qualification was his near-success in that endeavor. He had reacted well when they handed him his son's slice of memory-stone and let him speak the eulogy before the pyre Rifkind had insisted be built for him.

The older Quais worked hard; the men both liked and trusted him, and because he had witnessed the battle with the Ornaq he was willing to believe things many of the others would not. He did not know, of course, that he would be one of the two Quais Rifkind would choose to have with her when she left the Hold to venture after the new powers Krowlowja had ensorceled to her aid.

Others arrived and helped themselves to the fresh brewed tea, finding it invigorating and perhaps a bit more "real" than their usual fare prepared over the black-glass hearth. Domhnall headed for his rooms on his way from a night's activity in the temple, wandered by the council and lingered in the still deep shadows of the colonnade, his curiosity aroused, as Rifkind had known it would be when she chose this location for her meeting.

He was not lured farther into the group by the steaming tea. Pasca ignored him as she entered, carrying her own cup. She stood apart from him and the others. Lastly Jenny and Jevan arrived together and surrounded by an aura plainly declaring that while the matter which brought them to the foggy cloister was important, it was not nearly as important as what they had left behind.

"I listened to the winds last night, as is my custom," Rifkind began. "Our reprieve is over. We have gained an extra two weeks while Humphry and his men foundered without direction in the muck of the inner Felmargue. But he has again found his way and moves with greater speed than before."

They all looked concerned at her words, but only Jenny and Domhnall mirrored the full impact of Rifkind's short speech. Only they knew how Humphry's cohort had moved before or why it had been slowed. Domhnall slipped around the colonnade and into full view. Several of those who had not noticed him muttered in discontent, not wanting the strange young man to know of their problems or their plans, yet aware that Rifkind had included him.

"Do you mean to go out and see this new source of movement for yourself?" Domhnall asked, leaning against the pillar and not facing anyone as he spoke.

"I think so. If they have acquired some unknown assistance we'd best know about it in advance."

"When do we leave?" Jenny asked, though gripping Jevan's wrist tightly.

Rifkind hesitated. None of them could have guessed how little she wanted to leave the Lyceum, but her moonstones had lost one-fifth their potency. And the child growing under her heart required her presence and guidance. It would not survive were she to separate her body from her tal to explore the Felmargue as a mote of consciousness.

If Krowlowja's magicks had been any less tumultuous she might not have suspected that she had new allies. As it was, the very violence with which the ether was assaulted frightened Rifkind. The causeway was being thrown up again. Krowlowja's new ally moved with a reckless power that showed no regard at all for the fragile interconnected spheres of reality and ether. Rifkind had to learn about this new invader for more reasons and imperatives than she could count, and she would have to learn in her own physical body unless she wished to abort her child.

She had thought about casting lots to choose those who would travel with her across the swamp. She knew she could not travel alone. She would have preferred simply to travel with Jenny and Jevan, both for their compatibility and their knowledge. But once, when she had complained after yet another detached flanking position far from the day's activity in the civil war, Ejord had explained that a commander could put his most trusted officers anywhere and know that they would do their job; the dubious, less competent ones belonged where he could see them.

"Pasca and Chandro will leave with me as soon after this meeting as possible. I expect we shall be gone for three days, if everything goes well. While I'm gone Jenny and Jevan will oversee our own preparations at the Hold with the understanding that everything must move quickly. If for some reason we're delayed, or don't come back, no one must follow us. Assume then that the attack will come much sooner than we had anticipated, perhaps in as little time as one week, certainly no more than two. Assume the worst."

Rifkind stared into Jenny's eyes as she spoke, regretting the twinge of betrayal she saw there. Jenny understood the dangers that remained and the responsibilities Rifkind left to her, but could not shake the idea that she was being left behind.

Domhnall's fists were clenched in silent fury. Though he still hated the Quais' presence within the Lyceum, he and Rifkind no longer argued. She knew he believed their peace to be a sign that she had acquiesed to his notions of defense. His opinions of her wandering, physical or ethereal, were equally well known to them both.

"We're all from the Felmargue, Lady." Hanchon stood up, the strong yet sorrowful look on his face reminding Rifkind of nothing so much as her father in the days of the clan's glory. "For every one of us who answered the call to be here, how many were swallowed up? We know the dangers of our poor land and would not come out looking for you, however much we would grieve for you and our friends with you. But what dangers do you, yourself, see that cause you to show such anxiety? I do not believe that you fear being lost in our soil without honorable rites." He sat down.

Rifkind brushed the palms of her hands against her breeches and wondered at the fast-flowing rivulets of perspiration coursing down her sides.

They know me far better than I thought, Rifkind realized, and they care more than I can claim to care for them. How long have they known we will face something not of the world of men? Is it because I did not argue loudly enough against the enchantment Domhnall practices? Or do they see the fear in my own face?

"Humphry must have aid to travel as steadily and as fast as he does. It would seem that he travels with a seeress who can summon and bargain with the gods."

Her words had a shattering effect on the assemblage, even though from their faces she guessed that many were not so much surprised as stripped of cherished hope by her relevations. She would not tell them any more. There would be time enough for that when they returned.

"Pasca, Chandro, we meet at the practice meadow as soon as you can be ready."

She pulled the cloak around her and stood up, hoping to leave the cloister before the silence broke. But they called her back, each with a problem, blessing, or both, which let them hold on to her for one moment. Domhnall slipped back into the shadows and Jenny stared silently at her skirts. Rifkind accepted the responsibility of her own role and sat down again to listen to them and to speak calmly of the future. When she did leave the cloister it was with Jenny tight at her side.

"How? Three weeks ago you said Krowlowja had lost her ally and that we would fight my father's men only. Was that only to bolster our courage?"

"Jenny, that's not fair . . ." Rifkind felt the reproach as

steel between her ribs. "I would not have asked you to join with me in keeping Krowlowja's existence a secret from the Quais unless I truly believed that she no longer was a threat to us. I believed that when Colomandiz was removed she would lose her ability to summon allies."

"And now?" The reproach remained unchecked in Jenny's voice.

"I find no contradictions, simply a misjudgment. I thought she could not find new allies, having lost her first one in that way. I was wrong. The immortal gods conduct their affairs much more nakedly than we do. The Bright One warned me that there would be others, I simply did not think they would flock to Krowlowja. Whatever Krowlowja has 'summoned' this time is both more powerful and less controlled than Colomandiz.

"If our more successful tactics are mirrors of the divine ones, then Colomandiz was the weakest god who could come to Krowlowja and think to do what was necessary to move the cohort closer to the Hold and the Well. As I believe that there are many gods outside the pantheon, I think that now they've found another of their number to go to Krowlowja's steamy incantations. If they gain the Well through their mortal servants, I believe that the powers of my Goddess, of the whole pantheon, will be much diminished."

"Do you know of other gods who watch us or interfere with us? Other gods who might hear our pleas?"

The reproach had left Jenny's voice, but not the need for a few more questions, a few more answers, a little more time before Rifkind left them. The women entered Jenny's rooms. The great bed was rumpled far more than one slender woman could have made it. A wide leather belt had been left dangling off the side-board. Jenny threw the heavy comforter over the chaotic linens, inviting Rifkind to sit down and talk longer with her.

"Vitivar, for one, might help us," she answered.

"The Dark One?"

Rifkind shook her head. "Since I confronted An-Soren I have known that Vitivar and my Lady are two aspects of the same power. Perhaps as all river gods are much the same, our two moon gods are alike."

"That's heresy!"

Rifkind shrugged. "You've never made protestations of belief in my Goddess before, or even the stone gods of your mountains. What is called heresy is often truth which must be denied. I still fear Vitivar and make signs against Him if I must travel under his light or influence. But His seat of power is as vacant as my Lady's own, and that cannot be coincidence."

"You think then that such gods as Mohandru of the Darian Plains, or even Belaria, might be welded into an alliance to defend the Hold?"

Rifkind shook her head. "That I can't begin to guess. Not all gods have worshippers within our reality, but those that do are bound to their priests and temples. They lose a measure of their strength as they travel—this was true even when the Lost Gods dominated this world. Only Vitivar and my Lady do not draw their power from this sphere, though they have some small number of adherents.

"I think most of our enemies are displaced or free-ranging spirits who quest after more solid powers among mortals and are opposed by the known pantheon, who were once usurpers themselves. If we fail, but still survive, we will see new cults starting up all over Dro Daria by winter. Mortals will be god-bound a generation or more while the new ones settle their hierarchy and remold man to their own image."

Jenny gave an involuntary shudder. "How long have you thought this? It makes things much more ominous. I should think that my father would be opposed to an up-surge in godly activity. He is a god-hating rather than god-fearing man."

Rifkind nodded. "I cannot however imagine myself walking into his camp and announcing that he must give up his plans of using the Well because it is more powerful than he suspects and that if he is successful he will become a slave of new and greedy gods."

"Would you even try?"

"I might ... I really don't know. Our mortal race is certainly more important than my obsession with your father."

Jenny bit the fingernail off one finger while she thought. "Take this with you," she said suddenly, opening a basket to remove the ornate belt she had worn when the Quais arrived. "If you see my father and talk to him, show him this and say that *I* believe you and that this is the token of my belief."

Rifkind folded it carefully, but without much enthusiasm. "I'll carry it with me, though I'd rather not have such a valuable work as this with me. I've never suspected that Humphry was susceptible to oaths or tokens."

"He's not, generally. But for that he might be. It's been in the Overnmont family since they took the oaths for Glascardy generations ago. He gave it to me as proof of my name; no matter what, he knows I wouldn't give it away lightly. Regardless of the stories about who wore it when, or the other legends, if you carry that belt, in a way you carry the name. It might make him pause long enough to listen to you."

"I'll try, if I can."

They exchanged farewells, Jenny holding back tears while Rifkind bemoaned the manifest concerns she was causing everyone. She had half-decided to call off the expedition, to wait for the inevitable with her friends; but

Jenny had filled her mind with a need to find and talk with Humphry.

Her own door was still locked. She fumbled with her necklaces to find the key, only to have the latch swing down before she touched it. She was to have at least one more stormy, upsetting conversation before leaving the Lyceum.

"Domhnall?" she called, pushing open the unlatched door.

He sat in the large throne-like chair, drumming his fingers and staring out the window at the fog. He looked posed, and with a smile he could not see, Rifkind wondered which Darian aristocrat had once sat before his hearth mulling over some lordly decision while Domhnall watched from within a smoky crystal on the mantle.

"You gave me your word," he said, spinning about in the chair to face her. "You know what's out there. You don't need to take three days to find out. You know who, or at least what, she's called to get them moving again. Do you even begin to understand the dangers you throw yourself into with such disregard? The Well can handle anything they throw at us, tomorrow, next month, next year. There's no good need for you to do this."

"There is," she explained simply, thrusting the belt into a pouch that could then be thonged onto her sword belt.

"What need other than your own insufferable pride? Why else than because I can take care of you the way your Father and Ejord couldn't?"

The pouch thumped against her leg as Rifkind jerked up to look at him, startled and angry beyond her limits of expression.

"Yes, I've seen your dreams when we sleep together," he replied to her unspoken accusations.

"There is no justice for that! I will not be spied upon.

Get out! Get out of my rooms! Stay away from me! I'll
have nothing more to do with you!"

She felt weak, nauseous and overcome with emotion.
She sought within herself for the energies to laugh at him
and to say his stolen glimpses of her secrets did not matter. This was not a pain from a cleanly fought fight. It had
come from some place sacred and hammered deep on
the keystones of her being. Domhnall stared dumbly back
at her, unaware until he felt her reaction that he had committed so heinous a crime. She was reminded that he was
socially regressed and had not deliberately hurt her, but
that was not enough. She pointed to the door. He rose
stiffly from the chair.

"Rifkind!" he protested, walking nearer to her. "I love
you. Five hundred years. Everyone I knew was gone. We
weren't a religious order—scholars, yes, but not monks. I
made myself forget all that, but now ... Please don't go
out there. I couldn't lose all that again."

He stood a half-step in front of her, still short of the
door, exuding raw emotion that assaulted her even within
her anger and rage. The life-mote within her vibrated in
sympathy with its father. With a tremor she lowered her
arm to her side and let the door close.

"It is not that my father or Ejord could not protect me.
You should realize that. My dreams are only my way of
seeing what was real, but they are not themselves real.
My father offered me in marriage warriors from clans far
from our own, any one of whom could have protected
me, and a few who might have learned to love me in time.
Ejord offered me half of Glascardy once—and would still
have me consider Chatelgard my home and haven. But *I*
will not be protected. Any walls, no matter how soft or
transparent, are a cage, and once inside a cage I will myself to die.

"There in the basements of the temple you toy with

power that makes the gods hesitate—but though it may destroy you, I will not try to stop you. In time perhaps you could lose interest in such things, as I might lose my head to wander and experience my own dangers."

Domhnall nodded, then removed a gold chain from his neck on which hung a black flower like the one he'd made for her that first night in the temple. Smiling, she let him drape it around her neck, knowing what would follow. She no longer thought of resisting when he kissed her, indeed was tempted once again to cancel the expedition—this time until her passions were fully explored and sated.

Voices rose up from the kitchen. Pasca and Chandro were shouting at each other. Rifkind stepped out of her lover's embrace.

"I must go."

She snapped the sword chain into its clasps on her belt, drew the laces tight on the wrist sheaths, then snapped the knives into place. Domhnall had not moved, nor seemed about to. She kissed him lightly and left him standing in her room.

"What is the problem here?" she demanded, stepping between the two yelling Quais and forgetting completely about the desperate and beloved man she had just left. "With noise like this Humphry'd hear us a day from the camp."

They both explained their cases, interjecting continual rounds of insults at each other as they fought for Rifkind's attention and sympathy.

"Enough! Pasca, what happened?"

"He walked up to me with *that* bag and said *I* was to carry it because it was unseemly for a man to carry woman's things. Then that slime-covered egg-hatched belly-crawling *man* said he thought it was necessary that I be *told* to carry it because I would not have remembered of my own accord!"

Rifkind turned to Chandro. "What is in the bag?"

Chandro fiddled with his fingers, looking awkward, then defiant. "Woman's things, Lady. Fish toggles, and line, stones for splitting reed fiber and the like."

"Are these things important?" Rifkind asked Pasca.

"Of course, they're ..."

"Did you have them in your own gear?"

"No, but ..."

"Could someone survive long in the Felmargue without them?"

"No ..."

"Then find two more bags like that, and we'll each have one, in case we should get separated during the journey."

Other Quais moved quickly to assemble and offer similar paraphernalia to Rifkind and Chandro. Rifkind lashed hers to the outside of her already prepared knapsack; the others gathered everything into less orderly bundles and announced they were ready. They set out as a group for the meadow rather than meet there. Rifkind shot a passing glance at the wraith-staff still face-in by the hearth chimney, but decided against taking it.

Most of the men followed with them as Hanchon and Jevan led them for the morning drill. Rifkind had already relinquished many of her daily tasks, such as that one, so it would not be until she was well gone that her absence would be felt. She saluted the exercising men from the top of the meadow, then led the other two into the forest.

"It wasn't necessary. I had the fish-toggles; Pruchon had been playing with them and I sent someone to fetch another set," Pasca complained to Chandro as they walked along.

"Just like the stones?" he replied. "No! You're so wrapped up in being treated like a man you've forgotten you've got woman's things to attend to first!"

"I tend to my own responsibilities first, which no longer happen to be in the kitchen."

"Eh? Then who's to do the women's work now? You want to stop the Lady and send back for someone from the kitchen—but it'll probably be a woman. Or do you think that the Lady should be hauling and cleaning our fish?"

Rifkind walked a few paces ahead of the arguing pair, listening to them with a smile. She had been surprised it had taken them so long to resume their argument. They bickered over questions she had long since stopped seeking answers to. Unless they came to blows or failed to find some way of distributing the chores she would leave them alone. The "Lady" had hauled and cleaned her own fish before, and would do it again, if necessary, but she had long since become expert at finding situations in which it was simply not necessary.

CHAPTER 23

Chandro went down the reed-fiber rope first and maneuvered through the reeds on a small raft until he located one of the concealed rafts the Quais had left after their ascent. Rifkind was silently astounded by the decay and corrosion the salt water had inflicted in such a relatively short time. They lost much of the morning making the pods water-worthy again, winding up with a four-unit raft less than a quarter of the size Chandro had first uncovered. By the time the Quais were ready to leave the Hold they would have to completely rebuild their rafts.

"Never thought I'd do that again!" Chandro complained as he yanked a reed rope taut and the pods began to drift away from the cliffs.

"You get used to it again, it would seem, very quickly," Rifkind answered, not wanting to admit that she had never gotten used to it. She had thought her hands had been toughened by all the sword work she had been doing, but the reed-fibers had sliced through her calluses again. A month or so of inactivity had not appreciably softened the horn-like surfaces the Quais referred to as their palms. To be sure, many of them had difficulty doing delicate or precise operations, but they could grab tufts of the saw-grass, wrenching them by the roots from the muck.

"Used to it, maybe. But like it, never. That's what finally got us here, you know. I didn't want anything to do with this place, the legends or you, for that matter. Then I thought—if only we could be rid of this thrice-damned swamp and have our Father's lands back again!" Chandro explained.

"So much for what you say, and what it is worth."

Pasca's humor had not improved during their exertions and though she had done her share without complaining, that was all she had done. She had once or twice vented her caustic tongue on Rifkind's failings as a crew member. It was not likely to be a pleasant journey unless something happened to mold them into a group, a circumstance Rifkind judged unlikely and, from her own experiences with the obstacles the swamp could throw up, not desirable.

The current was swifter beyond the Hold than she remembered. The water seemed muddier, but that could be simply because Rifkind disliked the whole swamp and had allowed her memory to cleanse the overall experience. She watched for tangles of roots and branches along part of the front and one side of the raft while Pasca did the same on the other side and Chandro worked a pole at the back that attempted to steer them through the channels.

"Look! Wild horses!" Pasca called not long after the Hold plateau had dropped out of sight.

Rifkind would have turned around to see the herd, but a snarl of weeds and stalks jutted into the raft's right-of-way and she had to side-step her way along the raft, holding the mess clear. To break concentration would invite tripping, entanglement and disparaging remarks. Even though she felt a questing presence at the back of her mind that could only be Turin, she tended her duties. The weed-mat swept clear and she was free to turn around.

Turin stood ready to splash onto the raft to get closer to her. The scarred grey stallion was nowhere to be seen, but the dozen or so mares stood nervously and obediently behind their leader.

"Will you look at that!" Chandro exclaimed, recognizing Turin.

"Don't go near him! Those horns could kill you!" Pasca warned, extending her arm to stop Rifkind's approach and causing snorts of displeasure from Turin.

"She's got no worries from that one. I was wondering what you did with him, since I didn't see him on the Hold. Afraid to ask, you know; the Felmargue's not a hospitable place for most animals—though the horses seem to survive. He's done all right by himself, it appears."

Chandro restrained Pasca verbally while he thrust the steering pole deep into the swamp-bottom to stop the raft's movement with the current. In the brack channels the water was only calf-deep and the bottom, beneath a finger's depth of ooze, was solid enough to support even Turin's weight. Rifkind jumped from the raft to the reeds, circling his neck with her arms.

He snorted and nibbled at the back of her neck. She scratched his forehead, then quickly ran her hands down each leg and lifted his hooves. He butted her gently, prancing and vocal in his enthusiasm to see her again. Images of long runs over grassy turf Rifkind had not guessed existed in the Felmargue flooded into her mind, as well as a profoundly animal pride in the mares that followed him.

No Turin, not yet! Rifkind thought to him, gently restraining the chestnut from leaping onto the raft. He whuffled and pawed impatiently at the matted reeds beneath their feet. You're a colt again—full of untamed fire

and spirit. I'm happy to see you like this—and sounder
than I feared. I was certain that salt would damage your
hooves, but you don't spend too much time in the water,
do you?

She returned to scratching his forehead. His enthusiasm and boundless faith in her restored what the
long weeks on the Hold had taken away. The leap from
the reeds to his back could be a short one. She could run
with him, using his knowledge of the higher grounds of
the swamp. The saddles and halter were for comfort only.
The bond could be renewed and there would be no need
of raft or reins. Turin caught the flavor of her thoughts.

Not yet, not yet, she thought reluctantly, calming him.
But not long either.

Giving him a final pat on the shoulder she backed
away from him and jumped onto the raft. Turin tried to
follow, but met the iron resistance of her command to
remain where he was. The raft began moving again, taking Rifkind, and her commands, further away. He
churned through the channels and tussocks, the mares
still obedient to his sharp whinnies, refusing to be abandoned by his Rider again.

"It's not natural, a horse following a raft that way. The
herds are descended from horses whose riders fell victims
to the Felmargue. The beasts have no sense of loyalty—but
that one?" Pasca grumbled, her hands sliding nervously
up and down the smooth raft-pole.

Rifkind recognized the classic symptoms of a non-
rider's fear of horses, but was powerless, under the circumstances, to do anything about it. When she had released the bond between Turin and herself, she had relinquished much of her authority, and except when they
were in close physical contact she could no longer compel the war-horse. The habits of loyalty Pasca so quickly
dismissed kept Turin continually pressing to join them.

In time, though, the mares were reluctant to continue the senseless, and for them frightening, pursuit. They required more urgings from the stallion and the raft drew farther ahead. Rifkind continued to attend her duties as side-runner on the raft, but she watched Turin's horned head until the tall reeds of the swamp hid him.

By then she was convinced that the Felmargue had changed markedly since she had last been in it. The interior swamp should be many days away; by her own guess Humphry and his men had cleared the interior and should be into the tidal zone. She did not expect their journey to take them into the more dangerous Ornaq infested waters. But the water they moved through was marked with long streamers of moss and vines. The air itself had the heavy, fetid quality she had been glad to leave behind once they encountered the crisper salt breezes of the tidal marsh.

"Chandro," she asked, squatting down and speaking softly, "what's wrong with the Felmargue?"

"Lady, I don't rightly know. Sometimes the spring washoff from the uplands around the Felmargue'll trick the currents and carry whole trees out into the tidal flats, but ... don't know. We'll be poling by nightfall from the feel of it."

Pasca shouted and jumped away from the edge of the raft. A globular, glistening lump plopped onto the raft as she retreated. It propelled itself toward her on slimy pseudopods. Rifkind watched it more with amusement than concern though Pasca was plainly terrified of the creature that was no larger than a man's two fists. Then it folded back on itself, lifting a handful of waving appendages, each a finger-length long and ringed with feathery teeth.

Young Ornaqs? Rifkind's thought was impetus enough for a lunge to her nearby sword, while Chandro leaped

forward with the dripping pole. The pole was more suited
to the work at hand than her sword. He battered it to a
smeared pulp. They stepped back from the stain to collect
their wits.

"It stung me!"

Pasca held out her wrist where a large red weal was
already forming. Rifkind took one look at the mottled skin
and began rummaging through her knapsack for herbs.
She made a thick paste of rain-water and chopped leaves
and pressed the hastily prepared poultice on the weal.

Ornaq young, what they called were-blood, it's all the
same, and deadlier than rocksnake venom, though it
doesn't kill cleanly. Gods, whatever power protects
horses, she prayed, keep Turin back, don't let him and his
mares follow us into this!

Bitter steam rose out of the poultice. Rifkind ordered
Pasca to hold her arm downwind of them all and swallowed her fear of what terror she might be unleashing
into the breezes that would break against the Hold in due
time. The venom, or were-blood, could be lifted out of a
living body, but she was unsure if it could be destroyed
completely. Tears ran down Pasca's cheeks. She braced
her trembling injured arm with the other. But she had
seen Rifkind heal Drusina and did not complain.

"Behind you."

Chandro's voice was low, calculated and his grip on the
steering pole changed as he spoke. Rifkind flexed her fingers around the sword hilt, turning slowly to confront
whatever menace had produced his battle-alert.

The battered creature, little more than a smear on the
reeds, was congealing back upon itself, leaving seared
marks on the reed mats as it retreated. Rifkind made a
quick assessment of its movements and size. It was going
to be larger when, if, it waxed back to its former lumpy
condition. Pasca shrieked and threw the poultice at it.

Impulsive, but not ill-considered. Unfortunately, not effective, Rifkind thought.

The poultice disappeared in a belch of steam. Rifkind felt rather than heard the creature's pipping rage. She did not laugh at the hollow sounds. A quickly and abstractly prepared poultice would not be the solution to their problem. She lacked leaves enough to consume the beast, nor would she heave it over the side as Chandro wanted to do. She drew her thin-bladed boot knife, sinking quickly, deeply, into a trance.

"Can you kill it?" Chandro asked, filled with worry and fear.

She answered, but her mind was already given over to the trance and her words were phrased in the harsh, yet sibilant, Old Tongue. The unborn life within her shrank back on her command until no master could have seen its faint pulsing beneath her own violently throbbing tal. The two sides of her nature came together with unprecedented harmony. To destroy the death-bearing thing was healing and fighting art at their mutual highest. The point of her knife slid up and down both palms leaving a crimson gash. Her hands, thus protected with her living blood, grabbed the skull-sized lump. It became a seething mass of tentacles flashing at her, recoiling in shrill rage when the blood shield repelled its attacks.

Pressing harder, confining more of the squishy substance in her still bleeding hands, Rifkind brought her tal to bear upon it, subjecting it to the weight of her own anger. It fought back with a mental whine that could shatter a being who lacked the tal-training of a priestess. Rifkind envisioned the sound that pierced her mind as a ringing sword, then imagined herself as a forge hammer pounding the sword into an arc, driving the point back into the mindless malignancy writhing in her grasp. It jumped as its own weapons were turned against it. She held it fast until it had compelled its own annihilation. Streams of lumpy matter oozed out from between her fingers. Rifkind snapped back to reality with a shudder, staggering to the edge of the raft to wash her hands and retch.

The swamp had changed during her trance. Yellow mats of dead reeds replaced the waving green carpet of the tidal marshes. A faintly putrid odor wafted through the air.

"That ... that was your true power?" Chandro asked, afraid to come too close to her. "Are you not a goddess yourself then?"

Rifkind looked up, astounded to see Chandro and Pasca with their arms protectively around each other.

"How long did it take to destroy it?" she asked, feeling waves of exhaustion crest over her. She would have to sleep soon.

"Long, very long," Chandro answered. "We had begun to fear for you—for ourselves. Is it dead now?"

"It is gone, but there are more of them. I felt it calling to the others. If we're careful, though, we'll be all right. I'll have to examine everything we eat or drink. Don't lean out over the edge of the raft, or dangle your feet in the water."

"What was it?" Chandro asked softly.

"Ornaq," she answered.

"Ornaqs? They can't leave their lairs. If they could move about no place in the Felmargue would be safe. Anyway, it was too small. Maybe it was a myrt swollen with were-blood?"

Rifkind shrugged. "If it was a myrt once, it's become an Ornaq. And they're no longer tied to their lairs, even the huge ones. I felt them move when the spawnling called. The Felmargue is under siege. Whatever force contained the Ornaqs is weakening. Their curse is free to spread across the waters. It is the end. I don't know how that can be, or what it means. I've got to rest ... think. Keep moving on the course I've set. Stop when you feel it necessary. The water we've got is good, so is the food we brought from the Hold. Try to let me sleep, if you can."

The continued effort of talking was too much for Rifkind. She felt the hard new scars on her hands from a healing so desperate, so violent, she could not herself emerge unmarked. With her last waking energies she shoved the knife back into its sheath and threw her arms around the hard leather knapsack. They muttered about her in faint, concerned, voices, but that wasn't enough to forestall the sleep she craved.

Nightmares stalked her. Visions of ill-formed creatures erupting from the mud challenged her peace of mind. The conscious mote of her intelligence probed the perverted scenes for meaning, cause or explanation of the growing manifestations of non-life.

She searched her own trove of ritually inherited knowledge: a cache not unlike the Quais memory-stones, but vastly larger. She sought among the hard lessons of all those who had ever served the Bright One. There were no experiences with these abominations in the cult memory which were not already in her own mind. Even the proscribed secrets of An-Soren's Dark Brethren which she searched in her frantic and desperate abandon could offer no explanation.

The Dark Brethren had sought to animate life, but even their excesses fell far short of the exploration of death. The questing mote let go of its searches and curled up next to the growing life within her. The power of gestation banished the nightmares. Rifkind slept.

Pasca and Chandro were obedient to her wishes, letting her sleep until she awoke in the afternoon sunlight. They should have needed her for something, she thought; a direction check, fresh water? But they had let her sleep. As always, she wondered how she must have seemed to them while caught in the throes of a difficult ritual. The raft moved steadily through the water. The two Quais alternated verses and chorus of ribald songs to keep the rhythm of their poling even. She took advantage of the calm to awaken completely before opening her eyes.

"Morning to you," Chandro greeted her.

She returned the greeting, and they pointed to the front of the raft. Along the horizon a pall of clouds too black to be thunderstorms hung. There was no doubt now, they had let her sleep because they knew what she would do when she saw the pall. It was as ominous as the glob-beast had been, and Chandro kept the raft steadfastly pointed toward it. Smells of smoke and ooze were heavy in the air. The water was stained a frothy rust color, and most unusual of all, the swamp was utterly quiet.

"We could use some water, Lady, if you can oblige, but I don't think we'll find any fish in these waters. We've eaten carefully. Your pack is still full." Pasca looked up from her poling as she spoke.

Rifkind nodded and filled up one of the bowls with water. The new scars on her hands tingled and quaked her fingers with painful spasms as she swirled them through the swamp water, but it was fit to drink, if over-thick with scum and particles. They let it settle in the sun, then sipped carefully from it.

Pasca was right, there was no living thing apparent in the water of the reeds. Bloated corpses, however, abounded. Mire-dragons and every type of smaller beast had fallen victim to whatever stalked the dying Felmargue. Some bodies crawled with maggots, isolated pockets of life, but most showed gouging holes through them and even the insects refused to swarm after the meat.

"We've been following it since you fell asleep. It was more or less in front of us then. We could see it all night. I figured you would have followed it yourself. It's not far off the course you said we'd follow to find them." Chandro looked to Rifkind for approval of his initiative.

"No, stay on this heading, that's undoubtedly what we want to look at. Could it be that there's some sort of fire burning up there?"

"Could be, who's to say?"

Rifkind knew from Chandro's tone that he did not believe the pall to be the smoke from any natural fire. She herself had had no visions of such natural catastrophe surrounding Humphry's camp on the ethereal winds two nights before. Yet there was no point in discussing the matter further. She didn't know what the pall was, and was not about to wander away from the raft and her companions to find out more about it. There was always the chance it was some sudden storm, unsuspected on the ether and unassociated with Krowlowja.

They passed a mire-dragon floating belly-up in the channel, a gaping hole gouged up through the yellowish scales. They pushed its bloated and stinking body far from the raft. Again, even the flies and maggot shunned the blasted feast.

The black clouds hung in front of them; their progress was slow and measureless against the unchanging horizon, but they moved steadily into more death-ridden areas. Rifkind saw a long-necked bird struggle to lift itself on tattered wings, a bloody hole in its breast. The bird watched her with a red and predatory eye, but the creature it had been had fought too sincerely against the death-beast it had become; it could not pursue them.

What manner of ensorcelment is this, Rifkind wondered, if that cloud is the apparition of the ower Krowlowja has summoned this time? Nothing mortal could survive within that. What of Humphry? Has he repressed his aversion to ritual so far in pursuit of the Well? I don't know. Should we turn back? Run? Sooner or later this will spread, even to the Asheera, unless it is stopped. It might be better to die now, before it reaches its full strength. And if we cannot defeat it? It won't kill us; we won't find true death within it.

Rifkind thought of the exhaustion that had followed her confrontation with the small Ornaq, and her own pitiful reserve of strength if she were set against a pernicious horde such as that black pall might contain. Her two companions could surely see the same, and they had no choice but to rely on her. They could not fight alone. They would suspect how truly weak she was. Yet, they did not suggest turning back, and neither would she.

The fear oppressed them, and as each in his own way was inclined to fight such oppression they began to tell grizzly jokes and begged pardon of those blasted hulks they had to push out of the way to give the raft passage. They sang and refused to think about nightfall. The pall drew closer, until it seemed to cover the whole forward horizon, and still they laughed.

Then the screams started.

CHAPTER 24

At first they told each other it was the wind. When the wind could no longer be held responsible for the sounds they heard, they said it must be animals dying. They pushed forward, the sun already obscured by the pall.

"It's men, isn't it," Pasca asked.

The tall Quais-woman let the pole hang limply in her hands while she stared into the wind and the pall. Chandro passed her a dark look as if he already knew but forebore to mention the subject.

"Mind the pole," he grumbled.

They stopped singing, stopped joking, finally stopped talking. Rifkind listened carefully to the wind-borne screams. There had not been enough men in Humphry's cohort to produce the constant wailing they heard. Demons, most likely, perhaps the winds of the grey-black pall itself. She pondered which would upset them more, mortals screaming in the wind, or the wind itself carrying the tormented hunger of the spirits and demons attendant on the god whom Krowlowja had brought to the swamp. They would know the truth soon enough. She continued the silence.

The pall was like a thick fog once they entered it. Chandro affixed torches to the corners of the raft, but Rifkind would not let him light them. Flames would not increase their own vision half so much as they would alert anything else of their presence. There were other sounds on the wind now, gnawings and croakings, an occasional splash, but nothing had yet to approach them. The raft was slowed enough by the dark fog that they could not risk extra danger.

Rifkind drew in her pole and sat at the center of the raft to take their bearings within her tal. The ethereal was as polluted as the real, but things shone of their own existence in the ethereal rather than requiring the light of the sun or a fire. Her tal centered among them and watched their course, doing a balancing act between the two spheres of existence. The orange smears she had come to equate with the mobile death of the Felmargue roamed freely around them. Seemingly disinterested, they were mindless and unaware of her spying on them. She dared not probe too deeply into their activities lest their relatively benign status be changed and the unconquerable mass of orange converge upon them.

We're mad to think we could slip unnoticed through this, observe Krowlowja, and escape. Even if we can take the measure of this new god, if I must know the full degree of our futility, only a miracle will see us out of here again. But I will not go back to the Hold unless I know what we face. We are mortals and insignificant, we are safer approaching this way than using the Well to probe the ethereal sphere.

Humphry's camp was ringed by great torches that cast dim reddish light into the immediate area. The Quais and Rifkind abandoned their raft, marking its location in their minds and with bundles of weeds. Soft, rich soil had been brought up from deep within the Felmargue. If the omnipresent taint of death and worse could be purged from it, Rifkind suspected it would be a very productive land for the Quais to inherit. If it could be purged, and if they survived. Pasca and Chandro breathed soft words about the Leveller as they stepped onto the new dry land.

"Our land, returned to us!" Chandro picked up a handful of the dark dirt.

"Pah! It reeks of death. *This* Leveller brings doom," Pasca exclaimed drawing away from the odiferous matter. "For the Quais to receive the land, it will have to come from the Hold."

"Hold your voices, both of you! There're men within those torches!"

Rifkind led the trio in a stalking half-crouch. The screaming had intensified to where she doubted Pasca and Chandro could hear each other. She wanted their cooperation more than safety in silence. She was now convinced that they heard the language and laughter of demons rather than the torment of men, but would not say anything until they scouted the torch-ringed camp.

"Fathers-in-stone, what is that?" Pasca exclaimed, ducking down behind an uprooted bush, manifestly refusing to move again until an explanation was provided.

The men, if they were still men, moved with slow precision within the camp. Pasca had come within an arm's reach of a sentry patrolling the torch-lit perimeter. The guard's movements were rigid, his eyes dilated and unblinking. He saw only what was minimally necessary to keep him from tripping on the uneven ground. He did not acknowledge Pasca's blunder, though despite the fog, she had been clearly visible to him. When he reached the end of his patrol, he properly executed a military about-face and began the return.

She has brought such things to bear in this accursed place that mortal minds no longer attempt to comprehend their horror, Rifkind thought. That one patrols with the others, but they guard nothing, they see nothing. The focus of their being has been swept away by fear. Rifkind felt no satisfaction in the degradation of the once-proud elite imperial cohort.

"Wait here, I must look into the large pavilion, but I would prefer to be alone. I don't know what might lurk within the camp."

"You're not going in there?" Chandro asked in evident disbelief.

"I must know the fate of Humphry and ... others. I won't be long."

The soldiers could see her. They stopped their mindless tasks as she hurried through the encampment to find Humphry's pavilion. Eyes, devoid of both fear and curiosity, followed her, but as soon as she had passed them, they went back to routines of polishing weapons or leather—any task that could be done without thought or notice. A young man, possibly Humphry's orderly, carried an untouched dinner tray out of the pavilion while Rifkind crouched amid the guy-lines. A sudden and particularly demonic eruption of screams swirled through the pall. Rifkind pressed close against the tent canvas, but the orderly moved on oblivious to the noise.

She slipped through the unguarded entrance. Sleeping silks and pillows lay strewn across much of the tent. A small fire had started where an oil lamp had fallen, but it had been put out before much damage was done. The smell of burnt silk was almost pleasant compared to the aroma of the pall. The pavilion was deserted. Rifkind prodded the silks with her sword to be certain, but there were no signs of Humphry or Linette. She was about to leave when the shifting wind revealed a tear in the canvas. On the impulse of instinct Rifkind squeezed through the opening.

A knife lay discarded on the ground, bits of canvas thread caught on its jewelled hilt. It had been dropped some time before, but Rifkind had only to pick it up and feel its balance to know that it was Linette's personal property—the girl had learned much about knives.

Linette got away, or at least tried to. She could not use any ritual to save herself or Humphry, but she might have had more warning than the others.

Bushes, carried in the upheaved soil from some other place, but still upright and affording some semblance of cover, lay a short distance away. It was unlikely that the young woman would still be there, but a trail might start from there. There was a lone guard stoically and obliviously patrolling the camp perimeter in the area; aside from that there seemed to be nothing but the screaming pall beyond the bushes. Despite certain knowledge that he would not respond to her, Rifkind waited until the sentry walked by before darting into the bushes.

Linette crouched in the dirt, her expression only slightly less abstracted than the soldiers' were. When Rifkind stepped in front of her there was a flicker of recognition replaced by fear far more profound than anything produced by the pall or the demon-song.

"Linette?" Rifkind whispered, kneeling down beside her.

The huddled figure whimpered and hunched far away from her.

"Linette, I'm going to take you away from this. Come with me."

Rifkind spoke slowly, though with sufficient intensity to pierce the wailing around them. She had captured Linette's attention and would not have been worthy of being called a healer if she had not been able to soothe with her voice and touch alone. She held her hand steady as if there were no limit to time in the screaming

darkness. She made her face and eyes the image of sereni-
ty. Linette crawled forward to take her hand.

The golden-blond hair was matted and flying around
her face. Her hands were cold and shook even in Rifkind's
firm grasp. When Rifkind tried to get Linette to her feet,
the girl went limp and flopped back to the ground.
Rifkind remained patient although uncanny senses told
her that time was limited and the great forces that dominated the place were becoming aware of her intrusion.

"Come with me. I'll take you where it's safe. I've friends
waiting not far from here."

She hoped she did; she could not be certain of the impact of the wailing on a mortal mind that did not have
recourse to ritual understanding of the situation. The soldiers and the pathetic figure of Linette as she rose to un-
steady feet, clinging to Rifkind with tense, clawed fingers,
boded ill for mere mortals.

With constant coaxing, Rifkind got Linette out of the
blind and moving across the camp. Bird-like choked
sounds rose out of the imperial consort's throat each time
a soldier came into their vision. Rifkind would not let her
turn towards the pavilion, fearing a total breakdown in
Linette's control if she did. But she had to look at the sentries to recognize the one who had startled Pasca. The
Quais woman's reaction could hardly be classed as fear
compared with Linette's state.

"Rifkind?" Chandro called into the dark wind.

"Who's she got with her?" Pasca asked loudly enough
for Rifkind to hear.

"A friend, an old friend."

No amount of chaos could obscure the suspicious
glances the two Quais exchanged as Rifkind maneuvered
Linette into a squatting position.

"How do you come to know someone here? Is that why
you wished to explore the camp alone?" Chandro asked.

"I was looking for Humphry, and I'll probably go back to continue the search. This is Linette. She was once my pupil."

"Another healer?" Pasca questioned.

"She tried, but lacked the aptitude. Later she caught Humphry's eye. She's been subjected to terrible shocks; I couldn't leave her there."

"What will you do with her?" Pasca asked again.

The sight and sound of more or less normally animated faces brought Linette far enough back towards reality that her horror was no longer mute and trembling. She cried and made a desperate lunge out of the group, but not quickly enough to escape Rifkind's fast movements.

"No!" The healer said sharply. "You're safe here. You belong here. Don't try to run away. We cannot help you if you run. Linette? Do you understand me? I'm Rifkind, you remember me, don't you? I'm here to help you."

Tears glistened in the faint torchlight. "Rifkind? Rifkind? Oh, no! You can't be here!"

Linette fell forward into Rifkind's arms, sobbing and trying to speak. Rifkind accepted the hysteria for a few moments then braced the woman's shoulders, shaking her slightly.

"It's over, do you hear me? Whatever happened back there, it's over now. It won't happen again."

"Huh ... Humphry! Humphry, they've taken Humphry! They've taken Humphry!"

The girl's hysteria rose and showed no sign of abating. Rifkind tried speaking to her, but the horror that had originated her despair was fixed in Linette's mind's eye and would not be moved. Even the guard turned and stared in their direction for a moment. Rifkind grabbed Linette by the neck and pressed inward until the girl collapsed. The guard shook his head vaguely and moved on.

"Chandro, take her with you. Head back to the raft and then back to the Lyceum. Jenny will take care of Linette. She'll recover in time, with sunshine and fresh air. Tell them what you've seen, but don't let them cut back on the defenses."

"But Lady, what about you?" he asked.

"We can't leave you here! Let's all get back to the Hold, prepare the rafts and move as far from here as possible," Pasca enjoined.

"There is no place far enough away. Go back to the Hold with Linette and wait. It may be that only Domhnall can help, but you're not beaten yet. I've got to go back. I've got to find the name and purpose of the power that has done all this—and I've got an old debt to settle."

"We won't go without you, Lady. We're not so afraid that we can't wait." Chandro stood defiant, palms resting atop his hips.

Rifkind drew her sword and pointed it at him. The time for subtlety had passed. Already the demon-song contained syllables of her names.

"It is not a question of fear. I know you are brave. I do not plan to stay here! I will return to the Hold in my own time and after my own fashion. In this I am not like you; that is why you must follow my orders and leave now. You have seen my powers, now understand that I can take care of myself, but no more than myself. Go back to the raft. Set the poles with the current and depart from this place."

"But food, water?" Pasca asked, weakly.

"Do not tell me that you have not endured worse. The longer you delay the leaving the longer until you eat. There is still food in my pack; be welcome to it."

Brandishing the sword once, Rifkind thrust it back into the scabbard and stepped away from them. They backed into the darkness.

*   *   *

First she must cease to be Rifkind, now that she was alone, and remove from her knowledge all those names which were Rifkind's through her initiation and the other rituals she had passed through. Removing the stag-comb ornament from her braids, she held it to her lips and exhaled her names into its surface. She had but one identity left, not truly a name but a description given to her by her sword-teacher for her swift strikes with a knife—ger-cat. Such syllables, even if they were carried on the ethereal winds, could not compel her.

When she had left the Hold, Rifkind had seen no alternative but to approach the seeress Krowlowja in her own mortal form lest the growing life within her be damaged or destroyed. The ordeal with the ornaq-spawn had brought at least one unexpected benefit. The secret knowledges of the Dark Brethren, normally closed to consecrated healers, had revealed the rituals of bodily transformation. Such physical changes would not harm the life within her. The ger-cat, whose form she chose, had a predatory power more suited to the increasing alert pall, and would be less likely to betray Rifkind's identity now that she had removed all knowledge of her names from her mind.

Glancing behind once, to be certain the others were well on their way, Rifkind knelt down on all fours and performed the transformation. Her clothes and weapons vanished as she worked the solemn spell. The ritual incantation she had found in the ancient memories did not speak of such accoutrements, only of transformation and reaffirmation of self at a later time.

The cat shook itself and padded away. She found the acolytes standing in a circle, arms extended, palms touching. Their mouths were open, their eyes closed. The ger-cat slitted its eyes to decide that all the daemonic noise and much of the pall itself emanated from the small circle. They were possessed and transfixed. A single wild song seemed to emerge from their lips. "Rifkind ..." it began and after a time repeated. The ger-cat stole by them. It had no name, only several purposes and directions.

Krowlowja stood in front of a bonfire. The black cat had a purpose: to see this woman and record her image in its mind. She was tall, pale, strong-featured. The flames of the bonfire danced to her commands, took on shapes and rose into the pall above them. The gold-tufted ears flicked forward to hear and remember the syllables it heard. She might have been beautiful, with dark hair, flashing eyes and graceful movements, but the power had distorted her. She was not transfixed by what she had summoned, though she was possessed by it. The cat padded on.

A smaller pavilion, its door flaps tightly laced, drew the attention of the ger-cat. It still had purposes to explore. It leaped against the taut fabric of the pavilion walls. Long claws caught in the weave and ripped through material long weakened by contact with the roaring ethereal. The cat gathered itself and leapt through the hole it had made. The tent was darker than it had been outside. The cat's eyes grew wide as it studied refinements and intensities of shadow.

Humphry. The purpose was to find Humphry. A middle-aged man was bound at the high point of the pavilion, his arms outstretched along a timber, as he dangled by ropes from a truss. Without knowing why, the ger-cat growled and began to pace beneath the dangling man. Rifkind had foreseen, as she stripped out of her identity to leave only purposes, that finding Humphry would not give her purposeful self all the information it would need for revenge. Now the beast sat back, its tail

curling around to its front paws, as memory and consciousness trickled into its mind.

"Humphry Overnmont!" The ger-cat's thoughts were
clear and directed to the dangling man's mind, if any
mind was left.

His head jerked up, disturbing the balance of the ropes
that suspended him. The movement sent him spinning,
the cat waited.

"Do you remember me? The ger-cat? The Asheeran
witch you used to start all this?"

"Rifkind?"

The voice was hoarse; neither cat nor consciousness
could tell if the man had been tortured or if hanging was
torture enough. Stripped down to a breech-clout he
looked like any humbled mortal awaiting the pleasure of
a hungry god.

"Rifkind? Do I hear your voice? Have you come to
watch the ruin of my dreams? Take your revenge—and
give me mine. She builds a fire to her new god and will
throw me on it to give Him life and form. Slay me so that
no god may move in my stead!"

Muscles knotted in the cat's legs; it leapt upward, front
claws digging through his shoulders to find purchase on
wood and bone. The hind legs and claws gouged for balance against his groin as the man swung and the cat's
fangs aimed deep into Humphry's neck. The sudden additional weight swayed the truss-supports and the tent
listed to one side, then began a slow collapse. The cat
braced itself, landing on its feet and worming through the
timbers and canvas.

Krowlowja ran to her pavilion carrying a flaming
branch from the bonfire. Its light fell on the cat as it licked
the blood and gore off its paws.

"Rifkind! Humphry! You've taken the sacrifice!"

The seeress chanted the litany of Rifkind's names, but the ger-cat had only its own identity as an Asheeran predator with several irritating imperatives in its mind. It was not compelled by the names. One female with a torch was no fright to the black and gold cat. Its paws were finally clean. It yawned, long pink tongue curling over its lips to cleanse them of the blood. The woman thrust her torch at it, and stepped back when it growled and lashed out with a fore-paw.

Then the woman began chanting another set of names that the cat recognized as those it had heard by the bonfire. Those were more menacing sounds, a greater cause for concern. It bounded off the pile of rubble, sprinting into the darkness as a vortex grew at its back.

The thwarted god joined in the chant of Rifkind's names, but unused to the ways of the pantheon's mortals, it did not suspect their craftiness. The ger-cat was obviously a ritually-formed beast. Moreover they knew that the ger-cat could only be Rifkind. Neither Krowlowja nor her god could imagine that a magician or sorcerer powerful enough to change her physical form could risk everything by abandoning all her names.

The ger-cat was an ambush hunter: well-toned muscles delivered short bursts of speed and power, but they were not designed to travel great distances, and certainly not at a run. Consciousness pushed the ger-cat long after it would have stopped to rest. It itself was able to avoid the menace of the were-blood creatures, an advantage consciousness did not wish to abandon. But the self that was pure cat became balky at this constant irritation, and in the manner of cats, lay down to wait until the irritation passed. Reluctantly consciousness asserted itself to its last purpose, a mental recitation of meaningless phrases which, as they were sub-vocalized, had the effect of reaffirming Rifkind's natural form, if not her identity.

A woman's stomach churned with the knowledge of its contents. She shuddered and got control of herself. Her clothes were intact; the knives, she felt for each; the sword, she shifted it in its scabbard; the stag-comb in her hair, her fingers touched the gold and bronze ornament. As they did a tingling sensation consumed her and she knew, again, who and what she was.

It was not the best of times for the revival of her identity. Krowlowja and her master might still be searching and calling names that could now bind her if she heard them. More importantly, she had inherited the cat's sense of fatigue and would not be able to flee or change her form until she was rested.

Her bold assertion that she would arrive at the Hold in her own way and time seemed hollow, as did the knowledge that Humphry was dead. She would not want to tell Jenny, Linette or Ejord the facts about their father or consort's death, nor consider its impact on Daria. Better political chaos, she concluded, than a god in mortal trappings. She assayed her chances of telling the story to anyone as poor at best when a familiar shape appeared on a reed tussock just behind her.

"Turin?"

The war-horse reared. The cat-smell enraged him. Rifkind feared she might not be able to approach him, but the taint did not follow her and she mounted him with no difficulty. He was rested and raced easily ahead of the dark breezes that carried just the faintest trace of her name.

CHAPTER 25

Turin avoided the pockets of living malignancy with the same agility as the ger-cat had done. He found his way to the grassy plains where the ancient and implacable Landmother Goddess had begun Her redesign of the Felmargue. He chose his own route and set his own pace at a ground-covering lope. His coat was unmarked; he had left the mares behind of his own choosing. Other small herds could be seen from time to time, but whatever interest they had held for the war-horse had been replaced by his loyalty to his Rider. And he carried her for his own satisfaction, as she had fallen asleep before she had been able to renew the bonds of their affection.

As Rifkind slept the pall retreated behind her. The whisper of her name on the wind did not disturb her thoughts any longer. At times her mind was blissfully empty, but mostly she thought of Humphry.

Vengeance . . . justice. I have seen my enemy laid in an unhonorable grave of canvas and wood. He asked me to take my vengeance and grant his. I wonder if his spirit feels the same emptiness that mine does. He was a good enemy. Perhaps if I had slain him in battle while he fought me with all his strength there would be some satisfaction, but I gain no honor for slaying him as he hung there, especially in the manner in which the ger-cat took him.

I would rather he were still alive, a rattling enemy I could respect. I cannot tell Jenny or Linette. It would be better if they thought he died in a mighty battle, having seen the error and danger of allying with rampant sorcery.

It was not likely to matter if the truth were never known. Not even Krowlowja, should she and her master triumph, would be apt to speak of things as they had occurred. Humphry's death had died with him. Rifkind vowed softly to the absent Bright One to never again assume the form of an animal that killed with the casual cruelty of the ger-cat.

She rode through the night and into the next day. The pall was barely visible as a dark grey plume on the horizon behind them when the flat expanse of the Hold plateau rose in the distance. Still it was nearly nightfall by the time they reached the green cliffs. Turin's mane was matted with sweat that also stained his chestnut coat a muddy brown. His head hung and he cropped listlessly at the tender green shoots emerging from the bracken water. Rifkind guided him to the very base of the cliffs where the rusted spikes could be seen marking a difficult path up the wall. She was about to grab a hold of one and swing off Turin's back when a fiber rope bounced off her head and trailed into the water.

"Wait another moment 'til it's knotted, Lady, and we'll lift you up!"

Either I no longer pay any attention to where I'm going or by the Bright One, they've learned their lessons! she thought, looking up to a broadly smiling face she did not at once recognize. He spoke with an authority befitting a raft-leader. She made immediate mental note to single

him for congratulations and to be certain that he manned
the lookouts when the pall drew nearer. The rope had a
loop woven into its end, they obviously did intend to haul
their commander up the cliff face. Rifkind showered Turin with gratitude and love as she stepped into the loop. He
nuzzled her until her foot rose above his reach. The Quais
obviously meant to show Rifkind honor and respect, but
being hauled up the cliff-face like a basket was no great
improvement over climbing the ropes herself. She used
one foot and arm to fend off the worst bumps against the
green rocks and dared not look down to Turin when he
whinnied a farewell to her. By the time she had cleared
the cliff-edge and gotten to her feet, he had ambled to one
of the dry tussocks and was resting before returning to the
grasslands.

"Chandro told all of us what happened when he and
the others got here earlier. He said to watch and pray for
your safe return. We Quais have no gods, so I told my
men to pray to the Bright Moon. Your Goddess is a powerful one."

Rifkind smiled. Experienced horsewoman that she
was, she had never before understood the true value of a
saddle. The journey had rubbed her skin raw. She had
little enthusiasm for the long walk back to the Lyceum in
the gathering darkness, and was glad enough to stand still
a moment talking to friendly and eager faces.

"Were there three of them, a blonde woman also?"

"That there was. Chandro didn't say much about her
except that you found her at that place he spoke about.
She didn't speak at all, just stared and stumbled along. We
wondered what had happened to her, but they wouldn't
say. Pasca had her well in tow, just took her hand like a
child's and led her towards the Lyceum. Pretty lass, if she
weren't so pale and off in her head."

"And you, how go the preparations?"

"Strange, once you left, that sorcerer-fellow Domhnall come up and spoke to all of us. Says we've got to set guards out here at the cliffs. Every sun-up a new group leaves the Lyceum and stays out here at one of three lookouts 'til the next day's arrive. Myself, I'd be for walkin' back to the Lyceum—there's sure to be a pretty feast with everyone back safe—but I'm not one to tangle with that sorcerer-fellow. We'll stay here until we're relieved proper."

Rifkind was glad to hear Domhnall took greater interest in the Quais, but as with most blessings, it would be a mixed one if he had supplanted the authority she had entrusted to Jenny and Jevan.

"Is he setting the pace now?" she asked cautiously.

Not many of the Quais knew of her liaison with Domhnall. They were unsurprised by her show of suspicion, as they were most often suspicious of him themselves.

"Not at all. He spoke to us that once, and again this morning to say that the grey smoke was on the horizon and that it was the sign of the army coming toward us. Other than that he stays pretty much to himself—as he should, consorting with who knows what through the Well."

Rifkind spoke with them a few minutes longer, learning their names and personalities, then set off for the Lyceum. The journey started quickly but slowed once she was out of sight of the guard post. Her herbs and oils were in the pack Pasca and Chandro had brought back on the raft and movement had become very painful. She stopped by a free-running stream to bathe in its cold waters until darkness had fallen and the worst of her indignities had been numbed.

It proved easy to forget everything in the quiet and peaceful forests of the Hold. Krowlowja's new god and his demons, even the murder of Humphry, faded in the cold water. She was hungry and eager for the feast, without thought to the distance she still had to travel, or the people she would have to talk to once she got to the Lyceum.

There were reminders to constantly bring back the sore subjects as she walked carefully through the darkened forests. At several points where they had determined a mortal enemy would be likely to pass, large pits had been dug and covered with matted ropes and soil. They would have taken only a few men to their death on the concealed, sharpened stakes at the bottom, but only a few days before Rifkind had thought that any reductions in Humphry's mortal forces could be decisive for the Quais. That was before, and she doubted the glaze-faced soldiers she had seen patrolling in the pall would be capable of any assault. The daemonic forces they were apt to face instead would not be stopped by snares or pits.

She chose high-ground paths over rocks and through tightly planted groves of trees to avoid any more of the pits, and despite her aches and tiredness entered the practice meadow before midnight. Again she was hailed by sentries and Jenny was waiting for her when she entered the first cloister.

"Once again I started worrying about you when they came back earlier; when will I learn to trust that you will be all right?" the red-haired woman asked in the midst of a heartfelt embrace.

"Just before the last time I disappear, no doubt."

Rifkind was cheerful but more interested in the meal she could smell throughout the corridors. As soon as they entered the kitchen cloister she broke off large chunks of cheese and bread, eating voraciously before they could bring her a plate of meat.

"I must admit I'm at a loss as to why you brought *her* back here. She's trouble for you no matter what happens.

She talks only of Father and things even Chandro says cannot be true, though gods know, the stories he and Pasca brought back were frightening enough. I tried giving her a room of her own, but she wouldn't stay in it. Fortunately she was so exhausted that after a few sips of wine it didn't make any difference."

"I'll have to see her when she wakes up, but now I want to talk with you—alone," Rifkind said, standing up and carrying her plate to the stairway.

Jenny sank back into her familiar role as quiet follower.

"Something's very wrong, isn't it? Worse than what Chandro had to say?"

Rifkind closed the door to Jenny's room, set her place on the sideboard and removed the embroidered belt from the pouch at her waist, handing it gently to her friend.

"I don't know what Linette said, but if she spoke of Humphry being carried out of their pavilion on unseen hands or the like, it is most likely true. Krowlowja deals with a new god who has no cult or worshippers except for her. She has opened the gates to some other world to let these things into ours. Colomandiz was a child compared to the one who surrounds her now. It seems that this new abomination schemed to take a mortal shape, the shape of your father. This Humphry said to me, though he had been through severe trials by the time I found him. He had fought long and hard against their plots and was determined to die before he could be so used. He was successful."

"Father is dead?"

Rifkind nodded.

"We must send word . . . no, that would be impossible, we cannot spare anyone. There will be chaos in the land. No one will rule. Ejord must know, for Glascardy's sake, and Daria's."

Jenny's mind jumped from one thought to the next,

blotting out the painful reality of what Rifkind had told her. She had loved her half-brother more than her father and stayed with Ejord during the civil war, though she had little choice as Humphry did not try to bring his Chatelgard household to the Imperial palace. Rifkind was silent while Jenny grappled with the sudden and distressing knowledge, expecting the staccato rhythm of broken sentences to give way to tears. But after a few more moments, Jenny picked up the belt, folded it again and replaced it in its basket.

"You said he was successful; then Krowlowja and her servants failed. In some small way he vindicated himself. But for us, now, how has our danger changed? The grey clouds Domhnall told us to watch for have appeared since his death. What do they mean?"

"The soldiers are reduced to mindless beasts. I do not see how they can fight. Neither Krowlowja nor her god would know anything about leading an assault on our cliffs, so they will fight with the demons. Maybe they will surround us with screaming and laughter as they did the soldiers until we no longer have the minds to resist them. Perhaps they will do something different.

"If Linette is still asleep, I'll go and speak with Domhnall. The time has come to do things his way."

Jenny sighed but offered no argument.

Circles marked some of the faded inscriptions in the upper temple chambers, and several had been written over with charcoal. The wards had been moved to the upper doors, presumably to deter any curious Quais from unwelcome explorations. Rifkind lifted the black flower from her neck and held it before the sparkling wards, hoping it might in some way attract Domhnall's attention. She had only to wait a few moments before he appeared on the other side and with a single gesture made the wards vanish.

"I did not expect you to visit me until tomorrow," he apologized, hastily clearing away the remnants of several meals from the side ledges so they could sit.

"I would have thought you'd be waiting for me," she chided gently, still standing. "We have much to do, now that you are proven correct."

"It is a pretty flower, but I could not bring myself to look through it, knowing how you would feel."

She smiled and despite the many things of greater importance, nothing had greater urgency than the long embrace they now shared. They sat, hands together on the side ledge. She told him of the events of the previous days, telling the story of Humphry's death in the same abstracted way she had told it to Jenny. Even if Domhnall had spied on her, the black flower had been displaced to some unthinkable void during those hours while she roamed the swamp as a ger-cat. There was nothing in Domhnall's reactions to let her feel that he had been anything but truthful.

He listened while she repeated the names Krowlowja had chanted before the bonfire, but none of them were familiar to him, despite the time he had spent probing the secrets of the advancing pall with the Well. Still holding her hand he led the way to the lower chamber, where the Well itself could hear the names.

The clutter and intensity of his researches was more evident in the inner chamber. Prototypes whose purposes Rifkind could not, would not, begin to guess were scattered everywhere. The walls were darkened in places as if by a fire that had flared momentarily out of hand before it was mastered. A half-sphere of black glass sat on the edge of the font, leaping back into the Well of its own accord once they passed through the last set of wards.

"Do you experiment with life itself?" she asked cautiously, eyeing the vacant font-edge.

"Not yet, though the Well has the power to create or recall any living thing. But I doubt I could control it. Such things as we just saw are more frequent. They aren't alive and I perceive no harm in them; they disturb me as they disturb you. I've learned much I would rather not know in these past weeks. Yet I'm certain the Well is our only reliable source of answers.

"I'll prepare it to listen to you. It will take less time than if I taught you, and time, I suspect, is increasingly valuable."

She nodded and left him to the incantations. Such high and deliberate rituals were not to her tastes. She was still most uncomfortable with the itinerant, spontaneous way of healing, though she had long since recognized that her own uses of the healing arts had long exceeded the simple purposes she had been taught. Had the Goddess not favored her growth, she would have been crushed long before. She no longer worried about her instincts or judgments. Idly she cocked a lever on one of the devices lying about. It released a small cloud of burning, irritating gas.

"I thought that one to be highly effective, until I realized that the way the winds work around here, our own men and women would suffer most in its use. The Well is ready. Just speak the names, and we'll watch the surface."

They were unpleasant sounding syllables. Rifkind wished to do no more than whisper them, but the Well would only respond when the words were shouted aloud. A streak of gold flame rose up above their heads, releasing a shower of like-colored sparks that burned when they touched the skin. When the sparks died away, and Rifkind dared to open her eyes again, the surface of the black liquid had become a concave whirlpool.

"Does it always do this?" she asked incredulously, stepping down from the edge. "I don't find this very informa..."

Her voice trailed off as a familiar grey-black smoke billowed out of the vortex.

"Bright One! We've summoned him!" She grabbed one of the prototypes to throw into the well, hoping to disrupt the forces she had set into motion. Domhnall reached up to restrain her. The whirling screaming of demons filled the air and Rifkind grew frantic.

"No, don't," Domhnall shouted at her. "This *is* the way it works. That's all the Well knows of the words you chanted. Only that they are the same as that grey stuff on the horizon. Now wait, and we'll see if it shows anything more."

The smoke and shrieking had indeed begun to dissipate. The living designs on the walls were perturbed by the foreign substances, but within a few moments even that was gone, leaving only the hushed swirling of the black vortex. A second eruption of golden sparks ended the display. The vortex was gone.

"Not terribly impressive for a Well of Knowledge," Rifkind complained.

"The sheer magnitude of our ignorance explains a great deal. The golden sparks are associated with most of the gods' names I've given to the Well, Colomandiz, your Bright One, even Brel and the Landmother all give off that shower. So we are dealing with something whose abilities are god-like."

"And whose motives are therefore incomprehensible."

"Not necessarily. The Well did not set the walls moving with tableaux of the god's interventions. Colomandiz had a few such scenes, mostly erotic, I might add, but this new one—nothing. He is direct from the void. Until lately he did not even have a name, either in mortal tongue or in the Old Tongue. 'Hyta-Ysha,' if that collection of noises actually is his name, isn't too much aware of who or what he is, and knows even less about us."

"I don't think that that will be enough," Rifkind sighed. "I don't think that we can beat him. The days of our gods and world would seem to be waning. The Bright One was tired when She brought me to this room; She has yet to return to her seat of power."

"Perhaps we know nothing about Hyta-Ysha, but I have learned about the grey fog that accompanies him. If I set the black glass here to burning, the Black Flame of the out-land legends, I can make the pall retreat for a time."

"It will only linger."

"It's a tactic we can't give up."

There was an appreciable irony in having Domhnall chide her for lack of faith in their abilities, but one that was not wholly capable of reversing the situation. She had come to the temple filled with the unconscious belief that the names the ger-cat had heard would be the key to some simple and devastating assault on Krowlowja and her ally. The explosion of that idea had left Rifkind tired, drained and without even the desire for optimism.

She described their encounter with the small were-blooded creature, hoping to convince him they faced enemies beyond their mortal ability to destroy, but Domhnall demonstrated another of his prototypes; it hurled the same substance as the Well, causing a white-hot ball of flame that left another indelible scorch on the walls. She was impressed, but not cheered.

Domhnall led her through dark maze-like passages she had not guessed existed, wandering between the walls of building additions and only at the end emptying onto familiar walkways. They walked to his room, where he poured her a cool goblet of the amber wine. She drank without protest.

"You should rest before we continue this discussion, beloved. Those things you have seen have blinded you to the possible. Sleep now."

Rifkind nodded, loosening the sword belt, then her braids. She kicked her boots to one side, then lay down on the bed where he lay waiting.

CHAPTER 26

Rifkind dreamt of all those things that had ever been comfort or security to her; warm layers of fur and felt blocking out the winds of a winter storm, the gigantic feather bed at Chatelgard with the scented pomander balls hung on the bed-posts, even the tapestry-hung walls of the stone castle, which surprised the consciousness within the dream, for she had never found those dark thick walls anywhere before but in her nightmares. She dreamt of the Lyceum, covered with a profusion of vines, their purple flowers a more intense, luminous color than could ever be found in nature. She dreamt of Domhnall being with her in each of those idylls. It was a warm, pleasant sensation and she instinctively resented whatever intrusion wrenched her free and threw her, startled and disoriented, into an unfamiliar night-dark room.

She was naked and alone in a room whose hidden dimensions were wrong. Light should come through the window on her left; it came instead from an opening beyond her feet. All her senses assaulted her consciousness. Where was the room? Why had she fallen asleep here? What had awakened her? All answers, save the last, came to her in a rush.

"Domhnall?" she whispered into the darkness; except for her eyes she had not moved. "Where are you?"

She reached quietly for her clothes and all-protective knives. Her eyes had adjusted to the dark; she was alone in the room.

I would not have awakened unless something had happened out here to alarm me, she thought. Yet everything is quiet and the bed is cold where Domhnall would have slept.

The linen undertunic was still bunched over her hips when she walked to the open window. Domhnall had chosen his quarters for their view; no Quais could be seen from his window, only the forests doubly lit by the two moons.

The Goddess is back in Her place of power! But I would not have awakened just for that. Her light has cast through this window a fair time now. Her presence would have awakened me before this, and not with such a hollow feeling.

The Goddess was impassive; staring at the silvery crescent brought no inspiration, only a vague comfort that She had returned. Leaving the window Rifkind dressed quickly and walked softly down the darkened corridors. Her night vision had lost the acuteness it had had when she had lived in the day-fearing Asheera, but she could forget more than the average Wet-lander knew about moving in the dark and still never have to light a candle.

Arriving at Jenny's door she hesitated, listening. She could have jarred the latch loose, but would not intrude on the lovers' privacy unless the danger became clearer or more imminent. There were voices and movements on the other side of the door. Rifkind had barely enough time to enter her own room before there was a gentle tapping on the door.

"Rifkind, are you awake?" Jenny inquired.

"Yes." There was no point to sounding tired, completely dressed as she was.

"I'm not sure what I should say to them."

It was clearly a request for help, and a confirmation that something had roused the Lyceum. Rifkind glanced out the window to the Bright Moon, imploring guidance, before she opened the door.

"What do you think you should tell them?" Rifkind asked gently, not wanting to compromise her status as the source of wisdom by admitting that she did not know what had awakened her.

"I should say something encouraging—'We'll triumph!' or the like. I can't go out there and tell everyone that the red lightning has me terrified too!"

Rifkind bit her lip as she lit a lamp. Jenny was accustomed to entering Rifkind's quarters and finding her companion fully dressed and contemplating something in the dark, and did not comment on Rifkind's dressed and armed appearance.

"If you're terrified, you should tell them so, and tell them that we'll win anyway. They don't want to think that they are afraid of nothing. Though I myself haven't seen this lightning to say for sure."

"Oh, you should be able to see it from here."

Rifkind had to stand on the tips of her toes to see the phenomenon Jenny pointed out. The sky from Domhnall's window had been moon-lit and starry, but from her own window a low-lying black cloud obscured much of the sky. Rifkind inhaled deeply, catching the scent of acrid death on the air. A bolt of crimson lightning flashed through the cloud and came to rest beyond the

Lyceum. She began making fists, a finger at a time; she had folded her eighth finger by the time they heard the faint rumble of thunder.

"They are still below the Hold," she said at last.

Voices in the cloisters called their names, imploring them for guidance and reassurance.

"What shall I tell them?" Jenny repeated.

"Tell them that the battle will be joined as soon as we've spoken with the guard outposts. Set the women to preparing food—if Pasca objects, send her up here to me. Tell them it will be a terrible battle against an awesome foe, but stress that you have faith in them."

"Do you?"

"Of course."

Jenny sighed with relief, then took off down the stairs at a run. Rifkind glared out the window at the clouds.

They've followed one or another of us, and probably left the men behind, what was left of them, to die. So we will send fresh mortal men to face a hungry, jealous god. They haven't got a chance, and I can see no other course but to send them anyway. Our gods have returned to their places of power to join the battle from there, perhaps, but if they fight while we are still on the field, we become expendable. If we wait here for them to fight for us, they may well judge us wanting in devotion. The cause is great enough to warrant our sacrifice, but it all seems very futile.

There was a hard knocking at her door and Pasca burst in.

"Cooking! You've got us cooking!" She drew her dagger.

"Pasca, put that away and follow your orders. This is no time for men to be bumbling through the kitchen. The women have prepared the meals while the men have prepared the weapons. You've accepted this for weeks now, or would you just as soon go into battle hungry? I can arrange that also!"

Pasca stepped back and sheathed her dagger. Casting aside her own doubts and fears, Rifkind had become the battle leader. A tight and familiar knot bound her stomach. She would not eat before the coming battle, and neither would she tolerate disobedience. Through force of habit her hand rested lightly on the hilt of her sword. Pasca read the gesture as a dire warning and backed noiselessly out of the room, never having guessed that the true danger was the throwing knife concealed in Rifkind's other hand.

One victory. Be the others half so easy, we will dine victorious by sunset.

She braided the four heavy plaits that Domhnall had undone earlier. Her sword should have been sharpened, if she was to lead her army toward any mortal enemy. But it might not be used at all in the coming fray. Her stones had been useless since the fifth one shattered, and at any rate were too small to serve as a rallying talisman for the Quais. They won't know the sword is dull...

But she would, and a battle talisman must work for her also. She came down the stairs to the kitchen in deep thought, then her eyes took in Assim's staff resting in the hearth corner. It had been more attractive as a skull, she concluded, removing it into the light, undisturbed if not unobserved by the women and children. The black stone's transformation appeared complete. It bore a gnarled, hideous mockery of a female face, a face so grotesque that it could only inspire revulsion in the beholder.

faced away from the Quais.

The men flocked around her when she entered the second cloister where Hanchon already had a bonfire burning. Jenny might be the one who had summoned them to the Hold and the one whom they regarded with devotion akin to godhood, but Rifkind had taught them to fight. They could all see the black cloud with its intermittent lacing of red and hear the low roll of thunder. None but their battle-leader could give them the soul-deep re-assurance that they craved.

"Lady, what will that do to us?"

"They wish to break your confidence with displays of color," she answered a faceless question.

"How will we fight it?"

"We do not fight air."

"When will we leave?"

"Shortly after dawn. Eat well, but lightly. Put some food in your packs, fill the skins with water. You carry your own supplies, remember that."

She moved past the first group of men eating in the colonnade. When she had thought they would face an army of men, Rifkind had believed her words as a mortal ritualist could summon such a storm to frighten the ene-my or inspire her own men. She did not have the courage to tell them that the cloud was the god Hyta-Ysha himself.

Her council, except for the chastened Pasca, sat around a bonfire. They lacked experience, but so had many of the officers and soldiers in Ejord's army, and she had trained most of them. She was not wrong to feel proud of them. They sat in deep discussion, unaware of her approach, Jevan drawing maps in the ashes when she stepped into the light.

"That's a horrible thing you've got there." Chandro glanced nervously away from her staff.

"It's to be our battle-standard; let's hope our enemy reacts the same way you did."

"Aye, Rifkind, I've told them what we saw. Those men in Humphry's camp, they'd never have made the pace. They had no rafts or horses. There's no men down there waitin' for us." Chandro poked at the fire without looking at her while he spoke.

"Is that true, what he says?" Hanchon asked.

"It is."

"We can't fight that!" Vaincas exclaimed, his face going white in horror.

"But we can't all wait here for it to roll over us. Is there word from any of the outposts? They should have sent someone back."

"Maybe it's taken them like Chandro says it took Humphry's men," Vaincas continued.

"We'll wait a while longer. Jevan, there are several who might not manage a forced march to the cliffs: anyone who's injured or lame, or just not strong enough. Gather them in the empty cloister just beyond the temple where we met before. I will have special orders for them, and you, before I address everyone on the meadow."

"Done, Rifkind."

Jevan led the others away from the fire. They quickly split up to search out the disabled men and women she wanted to speak with, though if any of them guessed what her orders would be, they did not speak of it.

Many of the men and women, young and old, sat staring at their trencher plates, unable to eat. Rifkind walked among them a few moments more, assuaging their fears with kind, confidently spoken half-truths and evasions. She had many things to do, however, and could not talk for as long as they wanted. Slipping into the shadows she moved swiftly toward the temple.

The wards dropped as she approached them, and she ran down the flight of stairs calling his name.

"How're they taking it?" Domhnall asked, stepping out of the inner chamber. For the first time since she'd met him, he was not immaculately clean. Dark smudges stained his skin and clothes; a patch of blood showed on his knuckles where he had scraped them raw.

"What's happened to you—are they attacking the Well?"

"No, no, the Well is safe. I'm just not accustomed to doing things the hard way. When I realized the clouds were closing, I knew you were going to need help, in your own way, so I've been down here making more of those exploding stones I showed you. At least you'll have a chance with them."

She peeked into the inner chamber, which seemed piled everywhere with round or oval stones. The pyramid warding over the well-font shimmered brightly as if it were already fending off an attack.

"Did you have trouble setting the wards?" She looked at him again.

"No, I had trouble piling up all those stones! The Quais can come down and carry them up themselves! Use them sparingly. I still do not dare to leave this place, and I'll have no way of getting more to you after you leave."

"How do you know I plan to leave?"

"This time I did watch. I saw you pick up the staff. You intend to lead the Quais right down Hyta-Ysha's gullet and give him divine indigestion."

His tone was light and meant as grim humor, but Rifkind could not make light of her fears.

"You're frightened?" he asked when she remained silent.

"Of course," she snapped, irritated at having to admit it.

"I had thought you would be excited and eager for fighting—to prove yourself or die trying."

"I stopped feeling that way the first time I knew that I had to kill, or be killed. I've no desire to die, and since I've left the Asheera I've only fought to survive. Time was I'd go out raiding for sheer battle-joy, but those days are long past."

"You are . . . worried about surviving?" He seemed surprised.

"More so than ever. I bear your child—I do not want to die. I do not want the life within me battered by sword parries or the workings of rituals too potent to be truly safe for mortals."

"Child?" he asked incredulously.

"I'm a healer; I know myself in special ways or I could not do my work. I've known from the moment our child was conceived."

His puzzlement could not overshadow pride and excitement. Rifkind had seen the exuberance of other new or prospective fathers, but she had never associated it with Domhnall or herself. He lifted her off her feet, sword and all, to embrace and kiss her until she struggled and demanded to set back on the floor, flustered and embarrassed. She had never intended to tell him of their child, knowing that if she survived the battle she would want to leave the Felmargue and have the child where she herself had been born, in the open steppes of the Asheera. She guessed that Domhnall would not choose to join her.

"You must be careful now," he chided her.

"I always am."

He did not suggest she remain in the Lyceum with him. She read a profound sense of relief under all his enthusiasm.

It is as if knowing I am to bear his child he can relax from many of those things that have tormented him, she thought. Peace and completeness radiate from him; for all I know he is concealing something as I have concealed the child from him. And this time, I should not ask him about what he does not say.

"Rifkind, leave me something of yours—the ornament you wear in your hair, perhaps?"

She hesitated, then removed the spike. "Be careful with it. If you scratch along the edges you'll release the venom under the resin. That venom is deadly beyond any remedy. It is what we call in the Asheera a last weapon."

He nodded, accepting the palm-sized antelope and its spike comb with care. "The Quais can enter the temple to remove the stones. I will say good-bye to you now."

They kissed with a passion that brought tears to Rifkind's eyes and unspoken curses to her mind. Curses directed to the gods and fates who would let her love, then force her along such narrow paths. She watched him go up the stairs in silence and without looking back. Tears fell, but the implacable knot in her stomach would not tolerate prolonged despair. She left the temple knowing he would have disappeared into unused parts of the Lyceum. Her council and a half dozen men who for various reasons would not march with them waited in the cloister.

"Domhnall has made us weapons from the Well of Knowledge that will not be ignored by our enemy," she explained with a smile. "Have the guards returned yet?"

"Two of the three posts. They say a blast of fire was hurled at the other post when they tried to load the sling with stones to fire at the cloud. They did not approach more closely, but they swear none could have survived. They left half their men, but did not start moving the slings.

"They . . . they doubt it would make any difference after what happened to the other guards," Jevan reported.

"They are most likely right, I fear. I will instruct the men to come to the temple to pick up the stones Domhnall has made for them. Each must carry as many as he or she can."

"The women are coming too?" Pasca asked with both satisfaction and disbelief.

"Everyone who can march the distance will leave the Lyceum with us at dawn. Only the disabled and the children will stay here." Rifkind looked at the six men who stood uncomfortably apart. "Your tasks will be unpleasant, but absolutely necessary. There will be no one but yourselves to see that they are performed, but I believe that if the need arises you will understand and obey me. . . . If we are defeated and cannot return here you will slay *all* the children and yourselves. No living mortal must fall into the hands of our enemy. His spirit is not of our world. He has destroyed Humphry and his army in ways too horrible to speak of, and though he lusts after the power of the Well, his victory will not be complete without worshippers."

They all, disabled and council alike, stared at her in horror. The red lightning lit up the sky in back of them, and none dared argue.

"Have everyone file through here for the stones and be in the meadow at the full rising of the sun. I will speak to them and we will begin our journey."

"What of the woman we brought back?" Chandro asked.

"She will accompany us. I will see to her. If she is able, she will fight with us, if not . . . if not I will slay her myself."

There were no more questions as she left the cloister. She found a flight of stairs to the roof and walked along the tiles and platforms. Too much needed to be done, but in the larger sense it was all unimportant and too late. . . . At least they could launch a few volleys of flaming stones, enough to tell Hyta-Ysha that the mortals of this world preferred death to his divinity—it might be all they could do.

Both moons were full and would remain in the sky until dawn overpowered them. They were close enough together that she could not meditate on the Bright One without having the Dark One entering her thoughts. She included them both in her final entreaties for the lives and spirits of those who would follow her to certain destruction after the sun rose.

Rifkind sat utterly still until the first brightness of dawn removed the faintest stars from the heavens. The gods had promised nothing, revealed no omens or secrets, yet she felt a sense of justice and peace as she stretched her legs and stood up. Below, in all the cloisters surrounding her platform, the adult Quais sat cross-legged emulating her. A cold chill ran down Rifkind's spine; she could think of no words or inspirations to give them, only to lift Assim's staff and brandish the face at the dark red-laced clouds. Her ragtag army stood up in silence and raised their fists into the air. But where she had challenged the god, they saluted her.

The knot tightened until she could scarcely breathe and the red of the lightning lost its color. She swayed, caught herself, and jumped down to a corridor beneath her platform.

CHAPTER 27

There was nothing Rifkind could say when she stood before the three hundred Quais waiting for her in the meadow. What little emotional reserve she had left after their silent salute had been devoured by Linette when she told the young woman both what had happened to Humphry and what would be expected of her if she stayed at the Lyceum or marched with them.

Linette remembered too much of the terror of Humphry's abduction to be bought off with anything less than the full truth. She accepted and understood it, and so forgave Rifkind. She swung a stone-tipped mace over her head. The perfumed courtesan had become a brawny woman of peasant stock whose life had meaning only in revenge. Still clad in the remnants of her silken sleeping clothes Linette marched in Moigel's column, her eyes seeing nothing but the thunderclouds in front of them.

The weeks of conditioning paid off in a steady forced-march pace Rifkind set and the Quais maintained. The nine columns fanned out, moving relentlessly through the woods and clearings. They would arrive at the cliffs before noon with enough strength for one sortie against whatever they found there.

From time to time Rifkind thought she saw dark shadows moving through the trees in front of her: an impossibility since she led the force, unless the wraiths had been drawn to the staff again. Since the rainy night she'd spent on Pasca's raft, their howling had not been heard nor had any of the hunting parties reported their disturbances. Rifkind had not had time to investigate or to consider how the wraiths might align themselves if they still existed.

Thunder shook the Hold with greater frequency and force the closer they drew to the cliffs. Rifkind guessed they had covered over half the distance when a devastating peal deafened them and the ground beneath their feet shuddered and began to shift like so much pudding sliding off a plate. The lucky ones dropped to their knees of their own accord; the less fortunate found themselves thrown into rocks, trees or head-first onto the ground. Rifkind was among those who found themselves over-balanced and then flat on their backs. The staff lay beside her, the mismatched eyes glowing as they had the night she and Jenny escaped from the wraiths.

Ignoring the pain that hinted to her that her back had been snapped like a string of beads, Rifkind got to her knees, raised the staff upright and brought the ebony end in contact with the soil.

"Be still!" she exhorted the groaning plateau.

The eyes of the staff glowed beyond red to golden amber and finally to brilliant yellow. The men and women around her saw the staff and the sudden stability of all that was around Rifkind, who, in turn, felt she had become one with the Landmother and that all the plateau's pains and tremors were within her.

Heal me! a voice that spoke within her insisted.

Horrified, Rifkind looked up to discover the brilliant points of light focused on her and the grotesque face mind-linked to hers with its demand. The spasms were very nearly shaking her apart and would spread soon to her heart or head, when she would be helpless. Rifkind had little choice and less time. She exhorted her quaking limbs as she had the land, but with more dedication. As her arms and legs returned slowly to her control, the land quieted, the eyes of the grotesque face dimmed and the Quais nearest her began to whisper that they, too, had a powerful ally. None would speak to her or approach her as she held tightly to the staff and waited for strength to flow back to her legs.

There were more peals of thunder from the red-laced cloud, but the ground held steady. The columns moved forward again.

So Assim used the Well to raise the Landmother Herself and placed Her names and summonings imperfectly within her staff. A powerful ally indeed, Rifkind thought, one whom not even the pantheon could defeat. But the Landmother is so many things, no name, no number of names, could bind her completely. Assim must have forgotten that. Even the Well of Knowledge could not be older than the Landmother. It could not know *all* Her names.

Together they had weathered the first trial. There were scrapes and bruises on everyone, but nothing worse than a sprain among their injuries. The columns moved more slowly. Many of the trees had loose dangling branches, and potholes had opened, but they proceeded in safety.

Hyta-Ysha had broken the warding they had set at the base of the cliffs. His thunderous hammerings had attacked the very essence of the stone itself. The Landmother, having been healed, repelled his assaults more readily—but it could only be a matter of time. The peals of thunder continued.

"Lady, how shall we approach the cliffs?"

Even Jevan had been awed enough to drop the familiarity of her given name and used the title she shared with Jenny. They had reached the line where the constant breezes swept the trees back at a steep angle, where scrub and grass would be their only cover. Green-glass shards and boulders were thrown up at the lips of the plateau; there was no sign of the remaining guards. The thunderhead loomed monstrously in front of them, pelting incessantly at the cliffs. Rifkind waited for a lull in the oppressive noise, then shouted loudly enough to reach her own deafened ears.

"Send scouts around in an arc; let them approach the cliffs there, and there." She pointed to the farthest limits of the god's upheaval. "We will wait and hope for them."

"Should they be volunteers?"

"If you think the best men for the job will volunteer, then ask—otherwise give orders."

Jevan sent a pair of men to each point while Rifkind retreated back into the forest. As surely as she was the most powerful among them, she was also the most visible and vulnerable. With each reddening flash she expected doom to open at her feet. The ground jarred with each concussion, but held solid. The demon wailing seemed more tired than the renewed Landmother.

Two scouts returned and were brought to her.

"There is no army," the first reported, "only one woman."

Rifkind nodded, unsurprised. "No others surround her?"

"The land itself rises and falls as if it were alive. She stands on a mound half the height of the Hold and behind her, when the cloud moves, there is only black ground where nothing grows," the second man explained.

"Does she speak?"

"Who is to say? It is quiet here compared to up there. Her arms wave in the air and a red glow appears on the rock. She staggers back and the noise is unleashed." The first spoke again.

"When she staggers back, she almost disappears into the cloud itself," his companion added.

"The glow fades and a few chunks fall off the cliff. She staggers forward and it starts again."

"Did you sense that you were watched?"

"No, Lady!" they chorused together.

"But you returned before the other party—or did they have troubles? Did they approach more closely than you?" Rifkind tried to sound curious rather than condemning, though her voice had little subtlety at that volume. The scouts were visibly frightened.

"We could not see them to know how closely they approached. We were told to watch from the piles of rock, we did not think to approach closer ... What would we have gained? There was nothing else to see."

Rifkind sent them back to their companions. The ground rocked with an explosion different from all the others that had preceded it, louder, perhaps, but less forceful. A fine spray of dirt, pebbles and moisture filtered down on the rocks where Rifkind waited out of direct view of the cloud. She heard screams through the echoes of thunder and moved out into the open.

"My Gods! Lady!"

An anguished face, incoherent with shock, raced to her, stumbling and grovelling before her feet.

"What is it?" She squatted down, laying a hand on his trembling shoulder.

"They came apart in the air!"

His voice became a howl. Through physical closeness Rifkind received a forced image of the other two scouts doing as described. Had she seen it herself the scene would simply have been a gruesome tableau of war, but through empathy she felt two long-time friends die in an unthinkably terrible way.

"Get up," she said gently, her voice lost to the next percussive blast, but the sympathy and tone was carried in her hands. "Go back to the others and be comforted, comfort them." She let him rise and walk away. It is only the first of many, she thought, and by sundown you will neither feel nor care.

Would the god know the two he had blasted out of their lives were only the first of many who would swarm at him like gnats? Did it matter? A power that hurled men like dust and sundered them in mid-air was not likely to notice three hundred any more than it had noticed two. Still, the thunder was not continuous. Krowlowja reeled back from each expenditure. Even if she was renewed by Hyta-Ysha, how many times could mortal fiber hurl that force? How many times could Rifkind send the Quais forward to distract her? To what purpose? If she could think of no great plan or strategy, would it not be better to simply run at them at once? Or wiser to let the Quais return to the Felmargue beyond the Lyceum and simply abandon all to fate?

Rifkind pondered while the Landmother repelled indignities from the out-world god who had no home within her. She pondered until her deafened mind dared realize it was no longer assaulted and that she need not think at so loud a pitch.

"Send scouts again! What changed? Why has everything turned quiet?"

Her council selected men according to her wishes. Two

pair went out again from the forest. They waited in silence, no one dared to talk, to hear the sound of another
voice. Before the scouts could return the blasting began
once more. But Hanchon reported the four had all escaped from the rocks and could at least report on the
silence.

"She lay on the ground as if dead. Arms of lightning
from the cloud tried to touch her, they hissed and spat like
terrible living things, but they could not touch her . . ."

"She crawled first, on her hands and knees. She was
screaming, no, growling like an animal and walking in
circles until the lightning did touch her. Then she was still
and with her arms caused a glow to emerge from the
cliffs . . ."

"We were frightened and ran back . . ."

Rifkind smiled.

Krowlowja was still mortal. She tired, and the God
could not revive her until she had recovered enough on
her own to accept his aid. She was still the weak point in
his attack. They must destroy the cliff because Krowlowja
could not climb it herself and was warded away from the
Well. Likewise Hyta-Ysha was confined by her movement
and perceptions since they had been unable to affect
transfer to Humphry's body, and he could not enter the
woman unless there was a third party available to chant
the ritual.

She unslung her bow from over her shoulders and
began tightening the string. A dishonorable weapon because it allowed wanton slaying without retaliation. If one
came close enough to an archer to slay him with a sword,
honorably, then he was not nearly the threat he had
been. But death was death and to threaten an archer with
death Rifkind had learned to use the bow as a weapon of
battle. With a single arrow she could change the outcome

of the day, and perhaps the world.

With the bow now fully curved and taut, she approached her council.

"Our only hope is to destroy Krowlowja, the woman who stands before the god. She remains mortal and can be killed the same as any of us, if we can get past her defenses. Again, choose pairs, have one set to leave cover when the first are half-way to one pile of rocks—send the second pair to the other rocks, alternating and spacing in that way. Have them hurl their fire-stones toward her, then return."

"They haven't a chance. Our slings lie buried under all that rubble," Chandro exclaimed.

"They'll throw with their mortal arms and hands, and pray to the gods of the mortals for accuracy."

"We shall all be killed," Jenny breathed slowly.

Rifkind continued as if she had not heard. "I myself will descend the cliffs some distance back and work my way along the walls until I can get a clear arrow shot at her. If, of course, one of you has not already solved the problem for us."

If they were doubtful of their own abilities they would not admit to doubting hers, not with the staff held upright in her left hand and the Glascardy bow in the other.

"Someone watch me. Start sending out men when you see me go over the side." She started to walk away.

"Rifkind! Good luck!" Jenny called after her.

Rifkind turned, waving the staff at them. The thing would be an absolute horror to get down the cliff, but she could not leave it with anyone else. The ropes at each landing site were carefully maintained and in excellent condition, coiled about their upper rings. The concussions still had the solid thumping quality she associated with Krowlowja's attacks on the Hold itself rather than the crackling counter moves that had sent the two scouts to oblivion earlier. With a sigh as she threw the coil over the edge, Rifkind admitted to herself that she did not know what, if anything, her council would do on its own under this pressure.

Shinnying down the rope was more awkward than she'd imagined. The long staff was slung through her belt, constantly threatening to slip free, and the delicate bow seemed invariably to be struck by it every time she released one hand to adjust the staff. Her sense of precariousness was further enhanced by the constant tremors that were carried, and intensified, by the rope. Had she not feared damage to her bow above all else she would have dangled and dropped from a point only a few lengths below the edge. The hard knot in her stomach had finally loosened to nausea by the time she attained the upchurned soil.

The odor arising from the newly-revealed swamp floor was still tangy and fresh. It had yet to develop the rancidness sunlight was sure to bring. Rifkind had no notion of where all the water had gone, though if Hyta-Ysha was storm-like it was not inconceivable that he was at fault for the sudden drying out of the Felmargue. Deprived of a buoyant surrounding, the reeds had fallen against each other, lying flat on the mulch. The more adaptable of the Felmargue's denizens went about their daily business, but the fish had already been doomed.

She had walked halfway to her hoped-for vantage point before any changes became apparent. The thunder finally changed. It crackled in a more broken rhythm as if the Quais were succeeding in throwing Krowlowja and her master off stride, and threatening her enough that none of the ground-destroying forces could be hurled back at the cliffs. Rifkind hurried, fully aware of the toll in lives the distraction was causing.

The second change took her more by surprise, for in

the noise and supposed isolation she had not been watching closely behind her. Turin's nudge at her back was greeted with a swing from the heavy staff. The stallion recoiled, lowering his head to bring the deadly horns on target.

"You frightened me," she explained, making the thoughts both imagistic and empathic. His horns could parry steel and he could strike as quickly as a snake if he wanted to, and their empatic bond had not been fully renewed. Her images were acceptable. His head rose and he extended his muzzle for a conciliatory scratch.

"Yes," she agreed with the images he passed to her, "I could do this much better from your back."

Mounted, she still strove to keep the staff in contact with the ground. They moved carefully through the increasing rubble. Turin chose his footing while Rifkind watched the black and red cloud. It radiated a noise and discord that her most intensive meditative techniques could not dull. Turin flattened his ears against his head, normally a sign of his anger or fear, now merely a futile attempt to shut out the noise.

Krowlowja was too far away for her expression to be read, but she must be tiring and frantic. Domhnall's gifts were effective: blinding bright points of light until they struck in a sheet of flame. The Quais, by accident or design, did not coordinate their attack. The seeress had to be constantly ready to ward off as many as a half-dozen of the missiles thrown in a continuous volley. She was holding her own, but seemed unable to formulate a counter-strategy. A distant corner of Rifkind's mind sneered at the sheltered seeress striving against the tactics of a lifelong fighter.

Neither god nor seeress had taken note of a single mounted figure, with an absurdly long staff resting against her thigh, an arrow held in her teeth and another one nocked and aimed in the bow. The first arrow must strike home, for although Rifkind held a second ready, she was not so good an archer as to get off two in time. The winds were surprisingly calm and steady. It was not, by most standards, a particularly difficult shot. She gauged her distance and wind a last time, held her breath and let fly.

Long agonizing heartbeats passed before the envenomed arrow struck Krowlowja below her left shoulder. The green-clad woman stood motionless in shock as Rifkind drew the second arrow and let fly, though she was certain the first shot would have been fatal even without the venom.

The rumblings within Hyta-Ysha's cloud-column faded to an ominous disquiet, but Rifkind could not force herself to run until she'd seen the second arrow strike or miss. The seeress' right hand clutched at her wound, the left swung in a wide arc, pointing directly at Rifkind when it came to rest as the second arrow slipped into her face.

The seeress' final scream was as loud as the thunder as she released a bolt of lightning that went wide of Rifkind only because she had already begun to collapse backwards. Crimson fury focused on the mound where she and Turin stood. Rifkind had a bare moment to snatch the staff before Turin took matters into his own head and bolted from the god's wrath. The bow fell unnoticed, unmourned, into the mud.

CHAPTER 28

The next few moments would never come completely untangled in Rifkind's mind, but then a god, even one who had no rightful place in her world, might not be subject to mortal limitations of time and place. Turin retraced his careful steps through the rubble, moving this time at a dangerous speed and setting loose clods of dirt to rolling and shifting.

Hyta-Ysha loomed in front of the rope, certain death in his flashing anger. Turin lurched to a halt, puzzled by this flagrant violation of the proper order, and Rifkind was thrown forward against his neck, the momentum of the heavy staff carrying her arm forward and upward into a defiant gesture of its own.

Her grip held and Turin turned tail to gallop back toward the rubble and Krowlowja. The menace could not be there also, but it was. Translucent red streamers surrounded the fallen woman. Turin squealed. Too much strangeness, too much violation, more than he could, or would, accept. He would no longer run but stand and fight this thing. Rifkind exerted her control, though her mind reeled as badly as his. Her notion of proper action was to make a desperate full-tilt run up the rubble and by some miracle gain the plateau.

The grotesque bust of the Landmother bounced beside them as Rifkind slammed it downward into the rubble, hoping in some primitive way to help Turin's footing. Turin resented her will, but could not resist it. He skittered up shifting rocks and dirt, mindful only of the compulsion within him.

The path hammered down by the staff held firm. At their speed and desperation it was not important that the earth crumbled or caved in behind them: stopping would be death. Then, unbelievably, his hooves churned over grass, not dirt. He slowed, without need of Rifkind's urgings, and came to a stop. The crimson lightning flashed around them, but it had no power on the plateau.

Rifkind slid to the ground and with the staff still in her hand approached the remains of the cliff edge. A deathly stillness hung over the plateau as she moved forward. No one cheered, the birds did not start singing, the breezes themselves seemed reluctant to blow again. Mangled bodies lay scattered in the glass-strewn grass. The Quais had paid a price for the victory. Hyta-Ysha still radiated a faint turbulence, but the red fire glowed only around the prone figure of Krowlowja, her skin darkened to black by the effects of the poison and the light. As Rifkind watched, the base of the column enveloped the red-glowing figure, then began to rise from the ground. Turin reared and challenged, but Rifkind sent her thoughts to him, ordering him back to cover and silence while she continued to crouch amid the rocks and bodies.

The cloud grew smaller and rose until it was one grey blotch among the white ones carried along by the ocean breezes. Krowlowja had been absorbed completely by the god; only the two arrows remained on the ground below the cliffs to show where she had stood. Rifkind thrust the staff out over the edge to be certain the Landmother had seen, then she walked back to the wind-swept groves where her people awaited her.

The men of her council considered it their privilege to retrieve the arrows that had destroyed their enemy while those who had known the ones who threw exploding stones over the edge came forward to claim their fellows' bodies. Some, incredibly, had survived the suicide run and were accorded the honor of heroes of lesser rank, but most had not survived. There were no injured for Rifkind to attend to. She sat apart from the others, watching the now-peaceful sky.

They had won, yet Rifkind felt no exultation. The danger was over, the ground quiet beneath their feet, yet the knot in her stomach held fast. She would not join in any victory celebration tonight, and did not know why.

The Felmargue is gone, she thought. Its waters were drawn somehow into Hyta-Ysha's cloud-being. Snakes of upturned ground run across it, yet I had expected something different from the Leveller. Krowlowja, with her god, was the Leveller, not I. It is as if this was but an interruption in the plans My Goddess had made long ago. The waters will return, the Quais will rebuild their rafts and all will be as it was, except for the memories a few of us will carry away.

"We should like to keep these arrows, to set atop the stones we have back at the cloisters. They are the tokens of our deliverance and forgiving."

Hanchon spoke. He was the only one of the council with grey hair and in her absence seemed to speak as leader of the Quais. He would not look into Rifkind's face as he spoke, leaving her isolated and alone before them.

"They are yours, though the tips should be scrubbed with both oil and hot water. The poison lingers and is dangerous even in very small amounts."

"Should we return to the Lyceum now? Everyone is hungry, and the danger is past."

But it's not past. Or am I just the victim of my own anxiety and exhaustion? she thought, but said instead, "Yes, but we must leave a guard, as we did before."

"Lady, there's no food here, the danger's past and no one wants to stay in a place of death like this. Let's all return to the Lyceum, have a feast and celebration. Singing and dancing.

"There must be a guard here! I will stay myself if you can find no one else who will remain."

Her voice had taken a low threatening tone, more intense than she had intended. The men stepped back from her. Belatedly she realized she had emphasized her statements by shaking the staff at them.

"We will find men to do as you say."

The council left, their pace too fast to be called a dignified walk. Even Jevan and Jenny were cowed; those who knew her best and had called her by her given name glanced fearfully over their shoulders. Ten men were swiftly chosen and set to watch the battleground. All the while Rifkind stood impervious and alone, leaning on the staff. None would walk with her except Linette, who patted Turin and was not afraid of the staff.

"You called the Landmother with this staff. I remember Her. It was She who set right my summoning and made me mute to the gods," Linette explained as they walked under bird-filled trees.

The blonde girl seemed older and tired, but she offered companionship and conversation while the rest shunned their savior. Rifkind nodded.

"Can you still feel Her presence? She is not yet secure. I feel Her moving. She had been greatly outraged."

It was possible that Rifkind's sense of despair came from without. She mulled that over in silence, still not

wishing to speak with anyone. Since Linette had left
Rifkind she had learned the art of silence. Perhaps her
inability to call upon the gods had produced a physical
muteness as well, or perhaps Humphry had wished only
to see her, not to hear her. She walked beside Rifkind
neither offering more conversation nor offended that there
was none offered. The rooftops of the Lyceum were in
sight before Rifkind's thoughts rose to an urgency that
required speech.

"She must be dead. Her skin was dark as only rocksnake venom leaves it victims. Both arrows struck her. I
do not understand. A god must take mortal form in ritual
before he can attain lasting power in our world. He could
not approach the Well directly. Krowlowja is dead. Yet
she lingers in my mind. I cannot erase her face or the
feeling that she has a part yet to play in my own life."

"It is possible that that cloud-thing would subvert our
pantheon and be worshipped as he is," Linette suggested.

"We have many covetous gods, yet all have had to become part of what already is. This god is not of us, not *for*
us."

"Maybe he will create his worshippers after his own
image?"

"He is a cloud of power in this reality and in the
ethereal also. Little clouds would not be likely worshippers."

Linette shrugged. "He must have another image?"

Rifkind did not answer. They stopped outside the walls.

"It is a good land. Generations of plants have rotted into
the soil. Farming will be easier here than in the tired
fields outside the capital. The Felmargue has a future as
farmlands ... these people will need someone to teach
them," Linette said with a shrug that suggested she had
thought of at least one potential teacher.

"They have stones from the Well of Knowledge that

contain the wisdom of the times before the Felmargue was a swamp."

"Fah! You don't 'tell' farming with words and lectures. You feel the soil with your hands, know what it can produce and when. It's too soon to plant grain, the days are light enough, warm enough, but the nights are still cool and we've yet to pass both new moons—what stone's going to be able to tell them that?"

"If you plant ... you yourself said the Landmother is not still," Rifkind retorted sharply.

"It *will* be farmland." Linette's voice had a certainty even Rifkind had to respect.

Rifkind left Turin to graze on the grasses and wild-flowers of the meadows while she walked apart from the Quais until she reached the temple where she knew Domhnall would be waiting for her.

"You're both victorious and safe! Your Goddess cares well for you. Those arrows could not have flown truer if Her hand had guided them!"

He was at the top of the steps waiting for her. There was no need to ask if he had spied upon her, and she would have been uncomfortable telling him of the day's exploits, anyway.

"They did not expect it, so it worked."

"For one who has saved so much, you're more than a little dispirited—maybe it's finally time to rest?"

"I have a nagging feeling that I haven't saved anything, merely postponed."

"Postponed what? Hyta-Ysha is departed. I lifted the wards from the Well to call his name and there was only emptiness. He is gone back to limbo, or wherever he belongs."

"Put them back. Don't leave the Well unprotected."

"Beloved," Domhnall put his arms around her. "You need rest, you're tired. I kept you awake last night, and you were tired enough then. Go up to your rooms, I won't let anyone disturb you."

Rifkind shook free. "I'm not a child to be comforted from some fear in the night. Things are not yet settled. The Landmother lurks and frets below us. The Well is *not* safe!"

"Rest. I'll see to the Well."

"I'll come with you."

"You don't trust me?"

"I do ... but—"

"You've got to see for yourself? Then will you rest? I can hear them cheering now, and your rooms are right over them. Mine will be quieter. You have my word—nothing, not even I, will disturb you."

"All right, but I want the staff nearby, outside the door if you can't have it too near you, but it must be within easy reach."

He grimaced, but agreed. The wards were set to her specifications. The inner chamber shone from the crystaline pyramid-warding, though the structure was quiescent and without the brilliance it had displayed while under attack.

"I told you we were safe."

"Call it a whim, or a nightmare. I won't rest so long as it's not protected. But I should give praise and thanks to everyone, especially those who died. It is only just. I'll get my rest later."

The first items produced by the hearth were large tuns of wine. Goblets had already been passed among the Quais more than once. The celebration had begun on empty stomachs and would continue until all but the wisest and heartiest had collapsed. Rifkind had difficulty getting their attention and their quiet. Spontaneous cheers drowned out her words. Not until Linette appeared with the staff could Rifkind get their undivided attention.

"We have accomplished much today. The seeress is dead, the god drawn back."

"It went running like a scared myrt!" A voice rose from the crowd.

"Gods know better than to meddle with the Felmarquais!" Another chorused.

Rifkind held her next words until the uproar had died down again. Each man and woman of them is flush with the pride of a newly made warrior, she thought while they cheered. They've won the world, or so they think, and they think that they can do it again and again. Am I jealous of their victory because I feel old and cautious?

"Gods leave no corpses," she began aloud again. "Nothing remains to bury or burn. There is no steaming belly for me to open and read the fate of the victors."

The image chilled the Quais, whose traditions held no equivalent of the gory customs of the Asheera. Several of them fled the cloister where she stood and spoke. Rifkind herself would have hesitated to perform the ritual on Krowlowja's body if they had brought it back. Muroa had insisted she learn the powerful art, but the hair had to be singed away, and Rifkind had never overcome her aversion to the sight or smell of a burning body.

"A god has no body. A god has no death. This god should have had no power, yet he threatened our survival. We know only that he withdrew from the field in defeat. We don't know where he licks his wounds!"

She had meant to cheer them and praise them, not frighten them with the suspicions she herself did not want to believe. The staff in her hand was alive with apprehension. She could not let them discard their vigilance, half-drunk as they mostly were. But how long could the suspicions endure? The Landmother was old beyond comprehension. How did *she* perceive the threat? To her it could be the cultivation of crops instead of her divine chaos. Perhaps the fear had always been in the staff and that had driven Assim to wraithdom.

The mood was quieter, but resentful rather than contemplative. They quaffed their wine in long hard gulps without conversation as she stood before them. With the staff in her hand, Rifkind had nothing but exhortations for them. When she released it to lean against the wall of the cloisters, the overwhelming tiredness claimed her and she had nothing to say.

"She killed 'im, didn't she?"

"We don't need gods, or doomsayers, either."

Later the whispered voices lingered in her ears. These were the Quais who had listened to Chandro's fierce speech and wished to set them adrift in the swamp. For generations they had distrusted gods and those who trafficked with them as much as they had distrusted metal. Hanchon had convinced the rest of the Quais of the need for weapons, but they would never accept an authoritative god until they both needed and could appease it.

Rifkind swung the heavy wooden shutters over the windows and locked the door. Enough light seeped into the chamber that she could undress without lighting a lamp. She thought of the warm water in the next room, but had crawled into the bed before being aware that she had decided against a bath. Raucousness returned to the celebration. She pulled the heavy pillow over her head, though it seemed only to concentrate the noise.

She could not sleep, nor did she want to get up. The anxious knot in her stomach would give her no release. The staff rested invisible in the far corner, but its presence dominated her room. Grey twilight had come to the Hold, but the moons would not rise for some time. Frustrated and exhausted she poured a goblet of stale and dusty wine from the side-board ewer, draining it in a few swallows, and two more like it before the jug was empty. She would not go the short distance to the kitchen for more.

"Ejord was like this, Humphry too. There's no joy in commanding. The battle's over and you look behind your shoulder. Once you win, you know you will only have to fight again."

She pulled the pillow over her head, then fistfuls of the linens until a small mountain formed over her. The grotesque face and the now brawling, drunken Quais would not be gone from her thoughts, but they were a second to her struggle for breath beneath the mound of cloth and feathers.

"Rifkind?"

Domhnall. She heard, but would not move. His hands massaged the taut strained muscles of her shoulders and arms. He left the mountain of pillow and linen over her head and did not chide her for retreating to her own rooms instead of his. She made no protests as his hands moved over her back and thighs. She began to relax; small shudders shaking the muscles he caressed both gently and firmly. The knot released itself. Its great dam of emotion and passion demanding release or threatening to overwhelm her.

He had always been gentle, and she had responded in the same way, delighting in the newness of the sensations. She believed herself the stronger, by virtue of the scars which coarsened her skin and mind. Predatory and demanding she threw off the mountain that concealed her and pulled him towards her, forgetting for the moment that all other things being equal, size and weight are the ultimate advantage, and not caring when she finally remembered.

CHAPTER 29

"Rifkind, beloved, wake up!"

Domhnall's voice was soft in her ear, but his hand was insistently shaking her shoulder. She grabbed his wrist and held it close to her.

"No, you've got to wake up."

There was an urgency to his voice she was awake enough to hear and therefore too awake to ignore.

"What is it? Morning already?" She rubbed her eyes and stretched in the darkness.

"Look."

Her hand brushed along his arm until she found the direction he meant. The far corner of the room was filled with a pale, ruddy light. The terror and oppression fell back around her shoulders.

"He returns!" she said, inhaling as she spoke. "Through what perversion of our world I cannot guess, but Hyta-Ysha returns to the Hold."

The staff flared into brilliance the moment her fingers closed around it, dimming quickly once she began moving it towards the Well. Regardless of all the risks, she was determined to learn what dangers lurked in the shadows of her knowledge. The room rocked to one side with a groan that was echoed and amplified by every other cloister and colonnade.

"Bright One help us! He's attacking the Well directly!"

With Domhnall beside her, Rifkind wrenched open the heavy wooden shutters. They grated and squealed on their hinges now that the walls were thrown out of alignment. There was chaos below: crying and whimpering as the celebration-weary Quais staggered to their feet and tried to comprehend this new assault.

"Leave the Lyceum!" Rifkind shouted in the battle-ground voice that rose out of the pit of her stomach. "Run! Get out to the meadows! Lie flat!"

Voices chorused up to her, expecting her to calm the Landmother again, but she had felt the staff and knew it would be different this time.

"Fools! Don't argue—run! Get away from the walls before they kill you!"

Another jolt, not so bad as the first, but enough to bring roof tiles clattering to the ground, added conviction to her words. They started running. Other more distant cloisters wailed in the night, frightened and unable to hear her voice. There might not be time to save them. The complex ground was struck by an invisible hammer for yet a third time. Jenny and Jevan appeared in the next doorway.

"Go tell the others, as many as you can. Get them out of this place. Get yourselves out!" Rifkind's voice cracked as it rose above the growing noise. If she survived she would never lose the memory of such mind-numbing noise.

"Where are you going?" Jenny demanded.

"To the Well, to find out what attacks us and if we're truly doomed!"

"No!" Domhnall interrupted her. "I'll see to that, you leave with the Quais and your friends. Our child . . ."

Rifkind saw the surprise on Jenny's face, but there was no time for congratulations or discreet questions.

"I must see what attacks us!"

She grabbed the staff again; it flared crimson, the face more grotesque and powerful now, outlined in the deep fiery shades. While the others were still speechless, Rifkind made her way down the stairs. Sunshine and her pups howled and jumped against her legs. The shocks had disoriented them and deprived them of their sense. Rifkind threatened them with the staff. They fell back slightly but pursued her from a greater distance.

Another blast threw her against a still-solid wall while the far colonnade crumbled. Cries of panic and fear were augmented by those of pain. She should go to them, to the ones lying broken under the stones. That was the duty of a healer—mindless, unbiased service to the suffering. The leaders and warriors could turn blind eyes to the maimed and worry about the whole, knowing that the clan's healers would do their jobs. It was dark in the corridors and only her ears bore witness to those she denied as she pressed on into the Lyceum with Domhnall close behind her.

"Lady! Help me!"

Pasca pushed Domhnall aside, her strong fingers grasping the loose tunic around Rifkind's shoulders.

"Run, get to the meadows. The shocks will get worse, don't follow me!" Rifkind twisted, but the other woman would not release her.

"Pruchan, my little boy! A stone fell across his back. He lives, but cannot move. Help me!"

The darkness masked Rifkind's agony. A child lay broken in the rubble. Children were nothing until they proved themselves, replaceable, expendable—like the one now within her? The ground snapped again. They were all thrown to the ground, each imploring silently for

mercy from the demons assaulting them. Pasca held
Rifkind tightly with both hands.

"My little boy is going to die! Help him!"

No one life, not hers or her child's, was more important
than the hopes of them all. She was prepared to break
Pasca's hold with force to subdue her if necessary when
the woman crumpled to the floor.

"Let's go!"

Domhnall touched her arm and they went on down the
corridors. Rifkind did not ask what her lover had done to
Pasca, lest he tell her and the knowledge be more than
she could bear. The reddish light of the Dark Moon
seeped through the new cracks in the walls. They
emerged into a damaged cloister only to look up and see
that both moons were copper red.

"The Bright One stained with blood! We're doomed,
every mortal one of us and our gods with us!"

The temple itself was noise. Vibrations battered at them
until Rifkind wanted to be ill or faint or writhe on the
floor like a demented animal. Domhnall suffered also.
The wards would not yield to his shaking hands, nor,
more importantly, could they be certain they could be
properly replaced once they were dropped.

"I can use the Well itself without releasing the wards.
We won't be conjuring, only questioning and watching.
The power should be purely reflexive—if we can see
through the wards of the Well. What should I name?
Hyta-Ysha?" Domhnall bellowed into her ear.

"No, speak Krowlowja's names."

Domhnall looked puzzled, but had the sense to avoid
foolish questions. The Well chamber did not quiver as the
ground and Lyceum did. The Well was the focus of the
assault and, had the chamber yielded at all, it would have
collapsed. Domhnall stepped away from her to begin the
invocations. She watched his lips move, but the words

were lost. When he was still, she stepped forward to watch the image that formed on the black surface through the flashing and shimmering wards.

The seeress had followed their path to the Lyceum. Behind her showed death, destruction and the terror-twisted faces of the men she had insisted watch the cliff.

"It can't be! Bright Mother, the seeress is dead! She was the seeress of Baleria. She was born mortal; her flesh will stiffen and rot!"

Her voice was a desperate denial of what she knew was true. The image zoomed closer until only Krowlowja's face showed on the surface, a great bloody hole where her left eye had been. The flesh was torn and swollen with the poison, though the blue color was gone. And the other eye . . .

"The eyes go first," she whispered to herself, staring at the mobile corpse. "She *is* dead. The god moves her body from place to place, but he cannot preserve her. She rots while she moves. He has only a limited amount of time. He could kill all the Quais and use them the same way, but only Domhnall or I could give him what he needs."

Rifkind would kill herself first. Alive she was a ritually trained priestess intimate with the powers of the real and the ethereal; dead she was only another piece of meat. She was lost in her own thoughts, barely noticing the unfocused black surface until the image sharpened again.

The seeress' body moved stiffly, the result of its own decline and the god's unfamiliarity with mortal forms. Its spasms and jerks were almost comic, but if they felt the need to smile, they had only to look at the moving wall that crept, jumped and oozed along behind her.

"What is that?" Domhnall exclaimed.

"Were-bloods," Rifkind answered softly, not caring if he heard.

They were all sizes and propelled themselves behind

the stiffly advancing mortal form. The great Ornaqs, deprived of buoyant water and mud, were further behind, but they extended their poisonous tentacles and heaved their bulks forward. The were-blooded had no intelligence, just hunger. Rifkind refused to open her thoughts to the consideration of the manner of god who would choose such as its allies.

"Even the Well cannot say if they're dead or alive." Domhnall stepped back from the font.

"Our world, I think, is doomed. Hyta-Ysha's powers are beyond our ability to defeat him."

"*That* will not take possession of Assim's Well so long as I live to stop it."

The incessant noise slowed Rifkind's thoughts. She gazed at the glistening wards several long moments before remembering that their goal was simply to keep the Well out of the god's clutches at any cost, even the destruction of the Well itself. They could trust the deep warding Domhnall had set.

"The Well can take care of itself. Let's just get us out of here and stay out of that plague's way!" she shouted.

"I can't leave the Well," he protested. The almost forgotten anxiety any mention of leaving brought had returned.

"The wards are enough. You said anything strong enough to void the wards would destroy the Well. Mortals have thrived without the Well. We will not be the poorer for its destruction and it will insure that Hyta-Ysha never gains power in our reality."

She reached out to take his hand, but he would not extend his arm back to her.

"No, the Well is my life, I must stay with it. You go, find safety, but I will stay with the Well. We will fight, and maybe the Well will be left for mortals."

"Domhnall, it is death to stay here. Please . . ."

"I can't, Rifkind. It was death long ago to leave, so I stayed." He took her hand and pulled her close to him, his lips touching her ear as he spoke. "Long ago I made a choice. The Gods sent a madness across the Hold, the madness that made Assim and the others into wraiths. I should have gone with them. I was only a Candidate, but I was marked for punishment like the others. Assim accepted their judgment; he'd fought for years, seen the destruction of all his dreams. He was ready.

"But I wasn't. I was young, I hadn't fought. I had ideas and I took them secretly to the Well and hid here while Assim searched for me with the staff. He believed I'd run away, that the judgment would reach me since it was in the air itself. He thought there was no other way, but I'd merged myself with the Well.

"Later, when it was safe, and I separated my essence from the Well, I was Assim's enemy even more than the gods had been. I didn't save him, only myself."

"The wraiths are gone now, impotent. The staff was their power and it no longer bears their image. You've no fear of vengeance. Come with us," Rifkind implored.

"Still no. The Well itself exacted a price for my salvation. I am a part of it still. If it is destroyed, so am I. If I leave it, I do not know how it would punish my betrayal. I might become a wraith as I was once supposed to; it might be worse. It is a chance I will not take. The vengeance of the Well of Knowledge scares me more than Hyta-Ysha."

Domhnall would not leave the Lyceum, even for her. He stepped away from her. The chamber went dark suddenly and only the wards glowed with pastel colors. When the light returned the pyramid warding touched the ceiling at a different point than before.

"Go, beloved, there's not much time left."

"I'll stay with you. I love you." Her heart spoke, but

there was no other thought within her to deny or change the sentiment; the world had been reduced to an isolated room.

"Go! Take the child away from here. The child is the only true immortality. He is my revenge on the gods, on Assim, on the Well itself. GO!"

Rifkind gave him one last glance, fixing his tense anxious face forever in her mind and ran from the chamber. The stairway was blocked with rubble from the upper rooms. She had gone through one set of wards; Domhnall was sealed behind her. It would all be futile if she could not get out of the complex. The eyes of the staff glowed again, filling her with the idea of using its power to guide her out of the prison.

Using the power of the staff she pushed aside huge blocks of stone and mortar, but she would clear a short path only to have it collapse again when the god's anger and lust shook the Lyceum. Ironic certainty grew within her that by the time she reached them the false, dead Krowlowja would be standing at the upper landings.

The sky was dark and empty when she finally got out of the ancient ruined buildings. The rumbling had been replaced by a fierce wind fueled with the mad voices of demons. The air carried the odor of death and were-blood in the triply-red light of the moons and the staff. Rifkind was certain the worst visions of the afterlife could not be more obscene or terrifying than that which surrounded her at the outer bulwarks of the fallen temple.

"Mother, find me a path."

She fought the drive to crawl away and hide under the rubble, uncaring and conceding any moments of life that might be left to her. But she had been born in a lightstorm when the fabric of reality was torn into a myriad of colors and sounds. She had not died then, and could not die now. Her entreaties had been to the once-gentle Goddess now stained with blood, though it was the staff-face that cast a beam of eerie light across the disaster showing her the safest of the undesirable paths.

Rifkind lost count of the bodies in the cloisters and corridors. Except for her war-horse, the meadow, when she finally escaped to it, was deserted. Turin was lathered with sweat, but sound. Though the ground no longer heaved, she was too fearful to ride him. He walked at her side, following the path the staff unveiled for them.

"Everything's gone, Turin. Everything! I won't see him again. There's not a roof still covering a room, or a wall without a crack to its base—and the final battle hasn't started yet. This is just the warning: the sounds of the approaching army."

The red line moved slowly through the ruined forests. The old twining walls were little more than scattered piles of rock. The light easily crossed chasms and climbed raw new escarpments the passage of which was torture to a woman and a war-horse. She longed for the dawn and light to reveal both the extent of the damage and the branches that snared her ankles.

She shivered and remembered the warm black cloak she had had since Turin was foaled and she'd won her sword. The sword had broken during the war, an honorable, life-saving break; it hung in the armorial hall at Chatelgard. The cloak lay beside the rumpled bed, wherever that was, and with it all her other ties to her past. The pouches of herbs, vials of oil, braziers and bowls, many of her knives, Turin's tack, all were lost to her. But there was still Turin beside her, his living presence more valuable than anything, almost anything, else.

What had happened to the mares?

The forests were deserted, if far from quiet. The Quais had, to a man, woman and child, found other places to hide, if they had found their way out of the Lyceum at all.

If it had not been for the eerie light of the staff she would have chosen a less precipitous path, and when the light dimmed to two faintly luminous dots deep within the stone, Rifkind stopped.

She had wandered to a hilltop. The two moons were near setting, she was too tired to guess which was which now that there was no color difference between them. A dark jangle of shadows seeming darker than the others might be the Lyceum and the golden line along the horizon might be the dawn. In the depths of her spirit, Rifkind no longer cared.

Turin tried to shelter her from the wind, but it swirled maniacally and nothing could block its insistent coldness. She found rocks and branches and dragged them into a crude fortress-shape, crouching within it and drawing her arms up the sleeves of her tunic. Clasping the black-flower pendant in her hands she swayed back and forth in the wind.

I've done what you asked. I'm far from the Lyceum. I won't go back. I won't forget you.

CHAPTER 30

The clean golden light of dawn was quickly replaced by a high grey haze as if the sun itself had drawn a veil over the Hold and refused to look down upon the advancing doom. The mindless wave—it could not be called an army or even a horde—fanned out behind a single point where marched the corpse of Krowlowja and the possessed Quais guards. They cut a swath of death in their passage across the fertile land of the Hold. From the arrow straightness of the course it was certain they had no other objective than the Lyceum and its treasure. Surely any Quais who had fled toward the battleground rather than away from it had been crushed, but the others would be safe, for a little while.

Turin quivered as the valley breezes brought the carrion odor of the enemy to them. Rifkind calmed him with her mind and hands. It was too soon; they could escape only in the way Turin had arrived, which would mean riding across the advancing plague's rear and hoping the cliff had been levelled enough to create a decent passage for his hooves. They were safely wide of the death-path and would in all probability be safe until the battle was over. Anyway, Rifkind could not leave yet: she must witness the destruction and offer prayers for the passage of Domhnall's spirit.

When they were roughly in front of her the fan-shape widened to become an arc ringing the Lyceum. Rifkind squinted and could barely make out a flash of green in the darkness. They had stopped a good distance from the walls. Too far for a swift charge, mud- and water-dwellers that they were, and poorly suited to dry land. The Well would not fall until there was some sort of direct attack.

Rifkind clutched the flower tightly in one hand, unwilling to turn her back to the scene, afraid to watch.

Domhnall made the first move. A radiant dome appeared within the ruins, rising until it was a room-sized sphere moving against the morning breezes. A keening arose from the black assemblage and a thin shaft of light shot forward to pierce the globe. It exploded harmlessly. More of the slow-moving projectiles rose from the temple area, each deflected and destroyed. The plague grew bolder with its victories and advanced. A flock of smaller spheres release at great speeds were launched, searing anything they touched. Rifkind marked the locations of the ashes. Domhnall had a limited effective radius and he had lured his enemy within it, at least for a moment.

The green-clad figure was alive, after its fashion, despite the closeness of the ashen smears. The line withdrew, unlikely to be tempted to repeat the same mistake. The duel had barely begun. They traded gambits and tricks to lure out the other's strengths and weaknesses while revealing none of their own. Domhnall was the master of the air. His spheres and bolts of corrosive light probed Hyta-Ysha's reflexes and defenses. But from time to time a snaking ripple along the ground would topple a tower or release a cloud of steam into the air.

Moments passed and the effort of complete tension

gradually gave way to a more relaxed terror and morbid curiosity. Rifkind watched the feintings as if she were an impartial referee observing the clever ruses—until she spotted the cleverest ruse of all: Hyta-Ysha's minions were multiplying. The malignant arc extended itself without losing depth. She knew to expect surprises, but was unprepared for the swiftness of the attack as the ends of the arc swept in like pincers, assaulting the walls. The more agile were-bloods seemed to bound over the walls, but the Ornaqs surged forward to melt the stones with their slime.

Domhnall parried. Gouts of corrosive flame belched along the ground, melting rocks themselves and singing the liquid Ornaqs to the accompaniment of an odor reminiscent of burning eggs. Huge tentacles writhing, the beasts retreated, but did not surrender all their advance. The point was clearly against Domhnall as the misshapen plague continued to multiply.

Domhnall had either been waiting, or was inspired by the god's techniques. His spheres no longer exploded, but settled on the ground or foe to spout Ornaq-like fingers. The battle widened. Glowing things grappled with writhing death, neither one victorious, so that the conflict spread like a virulent disease. Their mindless forces thus stalemated, the god and the blond youth dueled directly with each other.

Poxes and curses floundered malignantly at the edges of the battlefield where they'd been tossed after a magical counter-punch. Deprived of their rightful, intended victims these equally mindless amalgams vented their cargoes upon each other, producing yet a third form of contentious non-life.

Rifkind shook her head in nauseated disbelief.

Beloved, it were better to die than give birth to these

things that crawl and limp away from your control. While you battle the god, all mortal life around you is being destroyed so completely not all our generations could renew it . . .

And I am priestess of life, beloved. I cannot watch this happen. I am too tightly bound to the Goddess. I love you, but Her hold on me is strong enough to rip me in two. I dare not wait longer . . . Please understand.

"I have no other choice!"

She screamed this last in her personal agony, her eyes closed and her face knotted with strain. Turin pranced beside her. Half-rearing he charged forward, the sounds of his hooves on the grass and weeds coming to a sudden halt. Rifkind opened her eyes.

A tall woman walked toward her. She wore a gown of silver light, a disk drawn slightly back from a full circle hovered over her head. The woman, neither old nor young, gazed at her in compassion.

"You chose this a long time ago," the Goddess said softly.

It was true enough. No Goddess compelled her to raise the staff, then strike the ground with all her strength. She did it with love, despite love, and without knowing the result of her actions except that the Landmother alone had the reservoir of slow strength to vanquish the two opponents.

The staff took root, stabilizing, thickening, growing with a rapidity that astounded Rifkind and Turin, as the Bright Goddess spread her arms protectively in front of Her priestess. With the silver glow to protect them, the trio backed away from the still-growing staff.

A groove appeared, then a full cleft down the base of the gnarled umber column became tree-like legs. Arms sprouted and the staff-form was replaced by bulges and lumps not found in any mortal anatomy. Other colors: red, greens, golds mottled what was obviously the back of the figure.

"It's the Landmother," Rifkind repeated to herself, steeling for that moment when the fetish-face would turn towards them. Its face she knew would be hideous beyond imagination. When the Landmother rose, she was not the gentle, fertile mother but the archetype of witches, the mother of magic and death. She knew, but knowing could not prepare her for the reality.

Her eyes had not lids, her mouth no lips. Worm-like roots protruded everywhere, becoming a nightmare nest above her eyes, a parody of hair. Clods of dirt clung to her, falling as she moved and grew. She made no sound, but still growing began to stalk toward the battlefield.

The Landmother sank back into the material of the Hold as a bather wading in a lake. With half her size hidden, She was vast enough to lift an Ornaq in one root-gnarled hand, crush it and fling it beyond the horizon. The buildings of the Lyceum disappeared in one cyclonic sweep of her arms. The green-clad figure was swallowed up. The Landmother's anger was slow building, but her vengeance was complete.

Whole sections of the forest fell as She pressed her shoulders against the surface of the Hold, crumpling the plateau. The Leveller had come. The Landmother erased the marks of all her errant children. The chatelaine of mortal reality set her house aright. When She had erased all signs of the battle, She turned to Rifkind, Turin and the Bright One.

"How do we confine her again?" Rifkind whispered.

"When She is satisfied, She will sleep again."

"And us?"

"You have My protection."

It was no additional reassurance, though, to have the

Bright One evaporate as She spoke Her final words. Turin had again seen more strangeness than his mind could comprehend. He did not challenge the advancing ogress or the vanished Goddess but rubbed his muzzle along Rifkind's arms like a foal returned to its dam.

"I'm not sure we can outrun Her, but we'll be planted for sure if we don't try."

The Landmother had gouged out the hillside in front on them. The upper layers of soil and grass had begun to slide forward, threatening to carry the pair to certain oblivion. Rifkind knotted her fingers in Turin's mane. He half-carried, half-dragged her along the slipping carpet of the Hold. Trees fell in front of them, creating a living maze in which one false step would cost them the precious moments and little distance that separated them from the methodical, life-blind Landmother.

It was inevitable; Turin stumbled and to avoid his thrashing hooves, Rifkind released her hold on his mane and could not regain it. A cold shadow fell over them; a silent breezeless sweep of Her arm carried Rifkind away from Turin. She grabbed onto a tree trunk embedded in the Landmother's surface and crawled frantically along it, unable to cease fighting for survival. The Landmother went about Her tasks of restoration, heaving masses of stone, dirt and trees about as a child might rearrange fine sand. She was unmindful of the clinging healer working her way up the gnarled and tuberous arm.

Rifkind had seen insects crawl about a moving body without ever marveling at the talent which enabled them to hold fast regardless of their orientation. Mortal hands and feet were ill-adapted to the challenge, but the insects lacked Rifkind's intelligence and few mobile creatures offered the crannies and hand-holds of the Landmother's skin.

She crept upward, when upward was toward the

Landmother's shoulder, and dug in with hands and feet when upward was anywhere else. So intense was her determination to reach the shoulders that it was not until she wedged herself into a relatively stable cavelike pockmark that she remembered what had, so recently, existed on the newly cleared land stretching beneath her perch.

The Lyceum, the were-death horde, the Hold itself and everything that had once been on it were gone, erased completely from the land's memory. Rifkind's memory recited the names and faces of those she had known who were now lost. Tears clouded her eyes, but determination to survive would not allow the wracking sobs to loosen her from the precarious life-hold she had found.

Terror and exhaustion overtook her as the Landmother strode across the remains of the swamp to complete her housekeeping with an awesome thoroughness. Even those coves which had remained untouched by the horrors released by Krowlowja's alliances were swept away. Rifkind clung to her perch, her mind now numb to the vastness of what went on around her. Only gradually did the thought stir within her that the Landmother would return to her deep-hidden home to sleep again. It wasn't until the ground moved suddenly closer that Rifkind realized the Landmother was, at last, subsiding and taking the clinging healer with Her into the ground.

The freshly turned soil was still dangerously far away when the disintegration of the Landmother's form made Rifkind's cave a shuddering travesty of stability. Without thinking, driven by her desire to live, Rifkind thrust herself outward as the Landmother's shoulders sagged downward. She curled into a ball to take the impact with the ground while rolling rather than as a flat object. Still, she hit too hard and consciousness was snuffed out like a candle-flame.

*   *   *

I'm alive, she thought when consciousness finally returned. Alive because the dead did not have cramps in every muscle that could be tensed, or hopefully relaxed.

The sun had burned through the haze. A few birds flew over her, their quest for food resumed after the extraordinary interruption. The ground smelled fresh and peaceful. Rifkind stood up and stretched slowly. Except for the hovering birds she was alone, completely alone as she had never been before. Her thoughts enumerated all she had lost, but could focus only on the isolation and desolation. She had no food, no way to hunt or provide for herself. Her unsolved problems were also uncountable. But before she could starve or go mad she had to sleep.

"Rifkind! Gods be thanked, we've found her!"

Rifkind rolled over, afraid to believe her ears. Jevan was bounding over the loose, uneven ground and not far behind him, red hair flying, was Jenny.

"She's alive! She's moving!" Jevan shouted behind him, nearly tripping himself in the process.

She had not slept long enough. Her body rebelled at the thought of movement, but its protests were ignored. Jevan caught her by the waist, lifting her above his head and releasing her only when Jenny caught up with them.

"I just couldn't believe we'd all be alive and not you. It wouldn't be right," Jenny exclaimed while Jevan embraced both women.

"All!" Rifkind asked as soon as she was able.

"Everybody who got to the forests survived the Levelling. All of the council, except Pasca, maybe a hundred in all, including your friend Linette," Jevan said.

"How did you survive? The Landmother does not think of a few lives."

"We clung to each other, to trees, to anything. It was

like being on a raft in the mother-of-all-storms."

The stepped back to look fully at each other, satisfying themselves that they were not deceived. Then thoughts turned to those who were missing.

"Domhnall?" Jenny asked softly.

"He stayed with his Well," Rifkind answered in a still softer tone. "There's no way." She fingered the black flower, half expecting it to crumble.

"He fought to the end," Jevan acknowledged. "We were wrong about him."

They stood in silence.

"Turin?" Rifkind asked.

"With the others. He's got a few scrapes, like the rest of us. Nothing that won't mend. He stayed behind; I thought that meant you were lost, but Jenny said it must mean you were alive and close by or he would be wild."

"He would avoid people altogether."

The Quais were gathered in a hollow. They'd dug out enough wood to start a fire and sent out scavengers who rounded up a surprising variety of foodstuffs. The fire would draw any stragglers to the hollow. Fate could not provide them more bounty; it was time to mourn.

They stayed in the little hollow for three days of slow realization. The Quais had lost two out of every three who had celebrated the now unreal victory over Krowlowja. With few exceptions they were strangers clinging to each other. Everything was a reminder, every laugh a cause for new grief. No one mentioned the Leveller. The fulfillment of their dream had brought the surviving Quais to a crucible of unmentionable pain.

Jenny and Jevan were set apart by their happiness. Of the rest, Linette made the first recovery, perhaps because she had experienced desolation before and knew the way back better than the rest. She collected seeds and told stories of the farms she had been raised on. On the morning of the fourth day it was Linette who pointed out that they would have to move. The hollow could not provision even their shrunken numbers for long. They would have to travel to the old trading posts to exchange legends and stories for the stuffs with which to start a new life.

They expected to find traces of the Felmargue as they moved farther from what had been the Hold, but the Landmother had been thorough. Where Assim had battled the gods there was only the same level, rough-plowed soil that they'd seen on the Hold. But it was rebirth rather than death: a green fuzz covered the land before they had reached the old limits of the swamp. The Landmother wanted her children to have another chance. Her children could be difficult, but they were still her children.

Rifkind watched the others. Her grief was different. She made her peace with the Bright One slowly, accepting her role as the instigator of the cataclysm that had created this land, if not the Leveller itself. She cherished herself, and the life within her, resisting the strong temptation to find Domhnall and join him in oblivion. She shunned company and the well-meaning attempts of the others to cheer her, though Jenny refused to admit defeat.

"It seems hopeless," Jenny began, not noticing that Rifkind turned further away from her on the old wooden pier that now stood in fresh dirt rather than in mud. "We have nothing to trade for horses and the people here are going to need stock more than Jevan and I will. We've decided to start walking tomorrow."

"Jevan's agreed to go with you to Chatelgard?" It was the first indication Rifkind had given in days that she had heard another's words.

"Yes. Perhaps I've made it sound better than it is, but we want to be together, and I'm not a farm-wife. I've got to get to Glascardy; no one else knows what has happened. We're hoping you will join us."

"I'm going home, myself, I think."

"Good!"

"To the Asheera. My child will be born as far from walls, swamps and destinies as possible."

"Rifkind, you know you're welcome at Chatelgard. You yourself have said your clan is gone and the other clans will be hostile at best."

"I'll find my teacher's cave. The Bright One will show me the way back. I think She wants me to go home and be a healer again."

Jenny was speechless. Rifkind stood up and embraced her.

"Much as I would like to, I don't see myself living forever in a cave. I've been gone from the clans too long. I know in my heart I will not feel any more comfortable in the Asheera than I would at Chatelgard, but . . . I will miss you most of all. The Asheera is dull, but I must go there for a time at least."

Jenny nodded. "Jevan will be disappointed. He counted on having you with us."

"It's a sensible idea. I'm not going to march across the Death Wastes again. I need a less direct route to my Gathering; it may as well be the road to Glascardy.

Turin looked up the grass he cropped and trotted to their sides. Jenny smiled.

"It's not good-bye?"

"Not yet certainly, and when it is . . . well, have faith. You will always be able to call me through the Bright One." Rifkind's voice held both friendship and regret.

EPILOGUE

The woman sat awkwardly upon her horse. The high front pommel pressed against her bulging abdomen. She travelled alone and had ridden through the night to be at the desolate rocks by dawn. Many times in her journey she had been forced to approach occupied wells and beg for food and water. She told them stories of the adventure that had befallen a healer wandering through the Wetlands and listened as the elders and chiefs told her of the violent storms and strange behavior of the wells in the past spring. She took their word that the worst of the storms came from the Death-Wastes, until she passed through that desolate anvil of heat and light. Then she saw that the storms were rising in the brown rock hills where she had grown up.

She avoided her own Gathering as she had avoided none of the others. They would remember her and would not be enthralled by her fireside tales. The wells of her clan, or rather, the single foul-smelling cistern of their final days, was still deserted. Tent poles had bleached like bones and only a few remnants of cloth hung limply in the midnight air.

She had started travelling by night again, the stars proving better navigation aids than any landmark. The night air was cooler, now that summer had come to the Asheera, and provided safety from the dread and maddening lightstorms. She herself had been born in such a storm, and her mother dead before she drew her second breath. Her own child, now growing and turning within her, would not be so endangered.

Turin was dismayed at the barren caves where Rifkind chose to stop. They both saw the bleached skeleton of a war-horse not far from what Rifkind remembered as a little cache where Muroa had kept her grain. The old healer was dead, Rifkind had known that, but she was not prepared to find the wind-dried corpse resting on the platform inside the cave. Wisps of grey hair covered Muroa's face. Her hands lay palms flat under her head. The woman had died peacefully in her sleep.

There was no mourning left within Rifkind. Domhnall's disappearance had created an emptiness within her that could not be filled and which dwarfed all others. Though she had replaced her knives and sword during the long journey, she had foresworn healing until she believed in life again. She wrapped Muroa's body in the uppermost layers of her bed and carried the light burden out into the morning light. Turin shied away until she had settled it in a rocky crevice and piled a cairn of stones over it. Then they rested until sundown.

Her own private cave had remained undiscovered in her long absence. Her second-best cloak was intact and warm against the chill summer night. Her jewels and trinkets and a plainer, older, set of ritual vessels were also as she had left them. She slung them over the saddle and walked back to Muroa's cave that would now be her home.

Before the second dawn she set Turin free. The rocks

could not supply food and water for both of them, and if she had need of him he would return as he always had. She arranged her possessions in Muroa's cave and examined the old healer's treasure, surprised by its richness and variety, until her fire burned itself out and she curled up on the platform for sleep.

"There's no sign of anyone here."

A voice, a young woman's, awoke her. The slant of sunlight showed late afternoon. Rifkind had been more tired than she had thought.

"The fire-reader said she would be here by the Earmoon, we will wait. Look, the ashes are warm."

The second voice, also female, perhaps slightly older, more patient and observant, spoke.

"Perhaps she's inside." The second voice, again.

"Idi!"

The first voice warned caution, but the second had already blocked the light across the entrance to the cave.

"She's sleeping."

"Not anymore."

Rifkind got up slowly, knife lightly in one hand. The child grew strong and she had not been plagued with the illnesses of other women in such times, but her movements were difficult and rising from sleep was momentarily unpleasant. She stepped out of the cave.

The women, both barely more than girls, were veiled with a transparent, gauzy material instead of the heavy opaque cloth traditional in most parts of the Asheera. They stood together in the concealing robes, distinguished only by height and stance. A little boy lay on the ground beside them. His feet and legs were twisted. He rolled rather than crawled through the dust of her camp.

"Healer?"

Rifkind recognized the voice as belonging to the taller woman, the one who had blocked the entrance to her cave. There was a note of uncertainty in the question; after all, Rifkind was still dressed as a warrior and bulging with advanced pregnancy herself. Reluctantly, Rifkind nodded.

"We are new to this land—cousins-by-marriage to Kerdal, of Brown Hills Gathering, who took our sister to wed."

"Is Kerdal still Gathering-head?" Rifkind asked, her mind at once filled with images of the man who had ordered the massacre of her clan.

"Yes, and much feared for days' journeying. He came to our Gathering to demand tribute—Roshan, our sister. Tribute could not be refused, but Hamarach, as a favor to our father, came to protect her interests." The other woman, Idi, spoke.

"How then fares Mardou, who bore his first sons?" Rifkind could remember the name of her half-sister, but the face was lost to her.

"I know no one called Mardou, though there are many who claim Kerdal's blood-parentage."

Rifkind could not remember enough of Mardou to know whether to rejoice or mourn her evident fall from favor and probable death. Certainly none of her own clan would have tried to protect her "interests." "Why do you seek a healer?" Rifkind asked finally, though the boy's legs were answer enough.

"Our fire-reader said one would come," Idi responded.

"Fire-reader?" Rifkind asked, the term unfamiliar to her.

"An old man, once our chief, who sees images in the camp-fire flames. He told of a great battle among the gods, and that the Bright One was returning a healer to us. This boy is our son; he needs your help."

The women, then, were not merely sisters, but sisters who had both been married to the same man, undoubtedly a wealthy one as their beauty was ill-concealed by the veils. They shared responsibility for the man's children, especially his deformed son. Rifkind presumed they had both been beaten for the child's deformity, though their faces were unscarred and their bearing did not suggest broken or cowed spirits.

The boy reached for a pebble, rising to a crouch to grab it in his well-formed hands. It was apparent he could neither stand nor walk. Rifkind knew the time had come to take up the healer's tools again for the arduous task of straightening the boy's legs. She could not face more suffering.

"We are not poor," the tall quiet one said. "We, too, have gold from our father."

The robes billowed, a hand emerged holding a spiked comb surmounted with a stag. Combined with the fire-reader's vision, the comb was too great an omen to be ignored.

"The child should have seen a healer in his first hours —the damage was apparent, I'm sure."

"There was none. The old woman no longer came to the clans!" Idi spoke with a particular desperation that revealed her to be the child's natural mother.

"The bones have hardened now. He will have to stay with me a long time."

The two veiled faces stared at each other, anxiety evident despite the sheer cloth. "We can bring him back, perhaps, but dare not leave him. Hamarach will not be long separated from his son. We meant to bring you with us," the taller woman said.

"Which are your wells?"

They listed four, all once belonging to Rifkind's clan, but not including the well of the massacre, which was only a short ride from the caves.

"If his son means so much to him, tell Hamarach to

move your clan to Nine-black-stones-cairn."

"It is cursed! Kerdal forbids any of the Gathering to abide there. The water is poisoned!" Idi exclaimed, making a warding sign against the evil of the place.

"Kerdal," Rifkind said with an unhealer-like smile, "will know I have returned soon enough. As for the poison, I shall remove the curse he laid on it. The child will flourish in its waters."

Caught between their distant husband and the quietly powerful Rifkind, the women hastily agreed to her conditions. They waited while Rifkind made salves and ointments for the boy's legs, as proof that the sisters had indeed visited a healer. They mounted two well-matched mares and promised to be with Hamarach at the cursed well the next dawn.

Word and rumor travelled fast. Kerdal rode into the camp while the Bright One was still in the sky, but Rifkind had arrived afoot long before. She wore the tunic and split skirt traditional to a healer and the clan totems of her vanished family that had rested in her cave with her other possessions. The looks that passed between the healer and the Gathering-head were not pleasant, but Kerdal hesitated to order the ten warriors who had accompanied him to slay her outright.

"The well is cursed," he said without dismounting. "You, of all people, should know this."

Only changed, husband-of-my-sister, Rifkind thought as she stared at the black-garbed man. A little boy with a crooked leg will live here. His father, I think, will not let you frighten him away. Her thoughts were filled with the hope that the child might somehow avenge her clan as she had not, but that would be in the future, and for now she would be polite to the mounted, heavily armed men. "Let the past be forgotten, husband-of-my-sister. Today I will cleanse the well of all that has gone before. Nine-black-stones-cairn will bubble clear and sweet."

Kerdal muttered under his breath. He would have preferred her insolence as an excust to kill her, but faced her calm demeanor with an equally grim politeness. He and his men dismounted to wait in oppressive silence until Hamarach, his wives, warriors and swaddled son arrived.

The out-clanner veiled his women less closely than any other Rifkind had seen. He let them ride astride the mares. The women had plainly feared him, yet it was he who carried the child securely in his arms. Two curved swords in cross-harness poked over his shoulders. His skin was darker than most in the Brown Hills Gathering. Rifkind was pleased with the clan which was to live at the purified well.

"I have brought my son to be healed." His voice was deeper than Kerdal's.

"I explained to your wives that I cannot heal him at once. The bones must first be softened, then straightened. Then, he must learn to walk. If you will not let him live with me, then you must abide here. I will clear the well that you may have faith in my powers."

He left the boy with his mothers. His warriors joined with Kerdal's and the men formed a circle around Rifkind as she knelt by the well. As her knees rested on the ground, she gave her first thoughts to the ritual she had so confidently spoken of: The Goddess will provide.

She drew aside the warped wooden cover of the well, momentarily overcome by the stench arising from the ground, and by the memories it evoked of times not so very long past. Kerdal smiled hopefully. He could execute a healer who lied and overstepped herself. Rifkind closed her eyes, abandoning herself to meditation and thoughts of the Bright One and life itself.

Her hands plunged into the fetid well-shaft. The waters rushed up to meet her fingers. The liquid was stained and cloudy as she lifted it into the light. It cleared as it dripped from her fingers. She lowered her hands again.

A woman in white lawn robes lay in a sunlight-filled room. She had a gentle face, large friendly eyes; she was not beautiful but very pleasant. A tiny bundle lay in her arms; a child. Ejord sat on the edge of the bed, though Rifkind could not see his face. Tiny hands caught his fingers as he waved them in front of the child. The woman smiled and laughed.

The scene broke up as the water again ran through Rifkind's fingers. Its noxious smell had all but disappeared. The healer thrust her hands into the water another time. Her skin tingled, imparting life and vitality to the water. Her child moved within her. She felt its mind for the first time.

Flowers wound around a white canopy. Two silver bracelets hung from the arched center catching the swirls of smoke from a brazier of incense. The mountains of Glascardy towered behind it. Two priests stepped forward, man and woman. They joined arms over the altar holding the incense and called the others forward. Jenny wore the embroidered belt her father had given her. Jevan wore a russet tunic and breeches Ejord had worn in the past. They knelt together and the priests placed the bracelets on their outstretched arms.

Water as clear and cold as the mountain streams ran off Rifkind's fingers and onto the rocks of the cairn. Kerdal, as befitted a leader, accepted the first mouthful of sweet water from the purged well. Rifkind held up her hands for him, cold water running back down her sleeves. Kerdal stepped back and the others partook of the miracle in turn, the women and child also. Rifkind plunged her hands in one last time for herself.

A room dimly lit, without candles or lanterns. Iridescent, ever-changing walls now solemn shades of blue, their movements all but stilled. A doorway still protected by shimmering wards held out rocks and dirt. A second warding covered a broken well-font and a dry well. Domhnall lay on the side-ledge, his hands folded over his open shirt. A running stag, worked in Asheeran gold, protruded through his laced fingers. A smile still rested on his unmoving lips.

Tears formed in Rifkind's eyes; she buried her face in the healing water before they could be shed. The cool, fresh liquid reached to the core of her despair, soothing the raw sores of her grief. Her unborn child turned within her.

Go in peace, beloved. You will not be forgotten.

She removed the chain and black flower from her neck and dropped it into the water.

FRITZ LEIBER

FAFHRD AND THE GRAY MOUSER SAGA